**"You do yourself a disservice, Christa.
There may be some women more beautiful,
but few are more alluring."**

She said curiously, "I have always wondered why I am singled out, but when one has just kicked a man in the ankles, it is not a good time to ask why he tried his luck. I would swear I do nothing to provoke attack—what is it that men find desirable in a woman?"

Alex looked down at her, his face becoming very still. Thoughtfully he said, "It is not one feature alone, but rather a quality of . . . perhaps 'womanliness' is the best word, or perhaps 'sensuality' is better."

The left side of Christa's body was limned by firelight, emphasizing the richness of form. He continued, "For example, you have one of the smallest waists I have ever seen, almost as if you wore a corset. But you don't."

Alex reached out with his left hand and placed it on her waist, feeling the warmth of her skin through the thin fabric. "And though you are slim, there is a roundness, a fullness to your figure, that cries out to be touched and explored."

LADY OF FORTUNE

MARY JO PUTNEY

ZEBRA BOOKS
KENSINGTON PUBLISHING CORP.
www.kensingtonbooks.com

ZEBRA BOOKS are published by

Kensington Publishing Corp.
119 West 40th Street
New York, NY 10018

All Kensington titles, imprints, and distributed lines are available at special quantity discounts for bulk purchases for sales promotion, premiums, fund-raising, and educational or institutional use.

Special book excerpts or customized printings can also be created to fit specific needs. For details, write or phone the office of the Kensington Sales Manager: Kensington Publishing Corp., 119 West 40th Street, New York, NY 10018. Attn. Sales Department. Phone: 1-800-221-2647.

First Zebra Books printing: March 2023
ISBN-13: 978-1-4201-5505-1
ISBN-13: 978-1-4201-5506-8 (eBook)

10 9 8 7 6 5 4 3 2 1

Printed in the United States of America

Prologue

Normandy, France

March 15, 1794

The moon's cool, bright fullness made the escape attempt more hazardous, but scudding clouds and fitful wind drew a dark veil of safety over the fugitives. The stealthy figures following the cliff side path kept silent even though the crashing waves far below them would have obscured their voices. They moved by touch and instinct as the damp, bitterly cold wind numbed hands and feet.

They were only a headland from their goal when the leader slipped on an unexpectedly icy patch of rock. Cat quick, the smaller figure, anchored to a convenient branch, reached out to secure the other. Pulled back from the brink, the leader wrapped an arm around his companion, gasping his thanks in a voice that still retained a thread of laughter.

"One more for you, Christa. I make it three times you have saved my life tonight, while I have rescued you but once."

The clouds broke for a moment, silvering the pair with moonlight. Even in the unreliable shadows, the smaller figure was clearly female, though she wore breeches for her dangerous trek. She answered in English as fluent as her companion's, but her low chuckling voice had a definite French accent.

"Women are always more surefooted than men, Charles. Even when we were children I could out climb you." She took advantage of the moment's pause to rest her aching body against her half brother's lean strength. This nightmare flight across France seemed endless; she had trouble believing safety was within grasp. Concentrating on the hazardous footing blocked her worry about her mother, who was following another path to the rendezvous point. Their party of five had split up to reduce the chance of attracting attention, with her and Charles taking the more dangerous coast path while their longtime servants Jean-Claude and Anne Bohnet accompanied her mother, Marie-Claire.

While Christa knew it was safer to separate, she felt irrational fear at letting her mother out of her sight. During the long months of nursing Marie-Claire after her husband's death, Christa had come to feel more like the parent herself. Her mother's fragile strength had been tested to the limit in these last days.

For the thousandth time, Christa blessed the kindly providence that had taken her father's life before the Committee of Public Safety could send him to the guillotine. His well-known liberal sympathies and friendship with Lafayette had protected them all through the early years of the revolution, but the spiraling madness of the Reign of Terror left no one safe. Friends and relatives she had known all her life had fled or died. Her father's failing health kept them in France, and his wife and daughter refused to abandon him.

Her father had been Philippe, Comte d'Estelle, with properties across the breadth of France. Under the French rules of succession, Christa was a countess in her own right as well as her father's sole heir, and she had been one of the most sought-after young ladies in Paris during her one brief social season before the ancien régime collapsed around their ears. Afterward, the d'Estelles lived quietly in Paris while the count worked for the social reforms he had urged for the previous two decades.

Christa privately thought her father's illness was caused by a broken heart over the tragedy that revolution was bringing to his beloved France. Her half brother, Charles Radleigh, the Earl of Radcliffe, had repeatedly urged them to come to England, but her father refused, determined to use his influence to moderate the explosive political situation. After his death and her mother's subsequent collapse, Christa waited in an agony of anxiety until Marie-Claire had regained some of her strength.

As soon as her mother was able, Christa hired a shabby cart and started them north from Paris toward Normandy and the small estate where they had often summered. The d'Estelles had been well liked in the area, and she thought a fisherman would take them across the Channel. The noblewomen and their two servants had dressed in the drab clothes of peasants to prevent unwelcome attention from suspicious Guards or hostile sansculottes.

Alarmed by the lack of news, Charles had crossed the Channel to find them. For all his blond English looks, his long visits in France with his mother and her second family enabled him to pass as a Frenchman. He and his young half sister were closer than most full siblings, and he used that bond to deduce what she had done. After weeks of searching, he found them resting in a village fifty miles south of their goal.

Christa had never been so glad to see anyone in her life; she hadn't really acknowledged her fear and exhaustion until she had someone to share the responsibility. With Charles's help they made much better speed. He had crossed the Channel with a helpful English fisherman cum smuggler who promised to return once a month for three consecutive months to a remote cove on the night of the full moon. The deserted site chosen was accessible only on the high, twice-monthly spring tides. March was the third month; if they missed this meeting, they would have to find other transport, running the risk of being seized as traitors.

Christa released her brother and put as much raillery into her tone as she could. "And you, great oaf, must move those clumsy feet or we shall be late for our appointment. On with you!"

He squeezed her hand encouragingly. "Almost there, little one. We shall be there in plenty of time."

Christa's world narrowed to the rhythm of her footsteps. Place the foot carefully, don't shift full weight until you're sure it will be supported. Ignore the twisted ankle and bruises from earlier falls, the hunger from a day and a half's fasting, the fear of being discovered by Guardsmen or bandits. Left, right. Left, right.

The path slanted down to the shore, and she collided with Charles when he reached the beach level and stopped. He put one arm out warningly, his eyes scanning the shadowed beach for the smugglers' skiff. They both jumped when a voice sounded from no more than two arms' lengths away.

"Are ye looking for us, yer lordship?"

Charles's soft laughter was shaky with relief. "Alan, you blackguard! Are you trying to scare me into an early grave?"

"I 'spect it would take more than me. Would this be her ladyship?" The voice was uneducated but immensely comforting to Christa—the sailor sounded so very English. In these past months she had come to fear the voices of her own countrymen, always worried that someone would choose to denounce the d'Estelles for some imagined crime.

She stepped forward, one hand outstretched. "Is this the so-brave English captain? You have my gratitude, monsieur."

"Eh, I'm no monsewer, little lady. Just plain Alan Brown the fisherman. And happy the lads and me are able to save some folk from the chopping block."

A thinning of the clouds showed her his burly shape, with the shadows of two more sailors behind him. She grasped the captain's hard hand. In the moment of silence that followed, the explosive sound of bullets shattered the night air. All three of them whirled. The shots were close, perhaps no farther than the other side of the sea cliff. A woman screamed, her voice cutting off abruptly as another shot sounded.

"*Maman*!" Christa cried out and tried to bolt toward the cliff.

Before she could take three steps, Charles seized her and pulled her back. His voice razor sharp with tension, he said tersely, "Alan, take care of Christa! I will see what has happened."

"Charles! I am going with you!"

"You can do nothing but cause me worry. I am armed. If anything can be done, I will do it. Alan, hold her! Bind her if you must, but don't let her follow. Promise me you will get her to safety . . . no matter what happens to the rest of us." He grabbed her in a quick savage hug. "If *Maman* and I don't make it back—remember that you must do enough living for all of us."

Christa hugged him in fierce response but released him quickly. Though her heart cried to follow, she knew he was right—her presence might only make things worse. One of the silent sailors from the darkness beyond Alan slipped up the path after Charles as a fusillade of new gunshots sounded. Her body shaking uncontrollably, Christa saw the two men dimly silhouetted against the night sky as they silently moved over the bluff. She was possessed by an icy conviction that she would never see her brother and mother again.

Alan grasped her upper arm and said with rough kindness, "Come on, lass, I'll row you out to the ship. Whether they return or not, we'll have to leave soon or we'll lose the tide."

Her shivering worsened on the short ride to the vessel, and she almost fell from the rope ladder as she pulled her exhausted body up. Alan Brown sent the skiff back to the beach as a stiffening wind broke up the clouds, revealing the shore with dangerous clarity. The boat had hardly touched ground before a dark figure ran over the bluff, skidded down the sandy incline, and raced across the beach to hurl himself into the waiting vessel as wild shots pursued him. The skiff flew across the choppy water to the mother ship; as soon as it was secured, the three sailors inside scrambled up over the railing, their leader calling hoarsely, "Away, now!"

Christa watched it all, numb to her very core. As desperately as she hoped the fugitive was Charles, she had known immediately that it must be Alan's crewman—the height and build were wrong for her brother. As sails were raised and the anchor lifted, Alan conferred with the man who had escaped. Her teeth chattered and she gripped the railing with blue-white fingers as the captain turned and came reluctantly toward her. She was paralyzed by the fear of learning irrevocably what she had lost.

"I'm sorry, lass. Apparently, Guardsmen set on your

mother's party. Bob here saw your brother take a bullet in the head." He stopped, unnerved by the implacability of the words, then added quietly, "No survivors." He took her arm again and said, "Come below now, miss. Have some soup to warm you. We'll see you make it home to England."

She stared at the black shore falling away behind them, orange flashes and dark echoes rolling across the water as futile shots followed the rapidly departing ship. In a voice as stark as death she said, "I have no home."

She watched until nothing more could be seen, the creak of rigging and forlorn cries of gulls making a mournful accompaniment to her desolation. When she finally slid into a faint, only Alan's watchfulness saved her from falling over the railing. As he carried her below, he glanced at the still white face and thought it a mercy that for the moment she could feel no more.

Radcliffe Hall
Berkshire, England

March 16, 1795

Marie-Christine Madeline Louise d'Estelle, Comtesse d'Estelle, usually known as Christa, sat in the velvet-cushioned window seat and traced patterns on the fogged window. When she looked at what she had drawn and saw that it was the d'Estelle coat of arms, she smiled with faint sadness. The time had come to let go of her old life and to begin again.

She rose and crossed the richly furnished room to the fireplace, where a lively blaze worked against the damp chill of the gray March morning. On her way she picked up three pastel sketches from the satinwood Sheraton table. Kneeling before the flames, she lifted the first drawing and studied it. She was not a great artist but had a knack for portraits and had made many drawings in the last year. From her portfolio she had chosen three pictures as the most characteristic.

This first one was of her father, and it caught him well. Philippe and her mother had been cousins and they shared the dark hair and slight stature she had inherited. Her father's merry, irreverent face was much like her own, not strikingly handsome, but with a brimming charm and vitality. He had given Christa his own curiosity and passion for learning and the ability to find laughter in the midst of blackest tragedy. Laying the sketch carefully on the fire, she watched it char and curl around the edges before bursting into flames. "*Adieu*, Papa," she said softly.

When the paper was completely reduced to ash, she lifted the next sketch, studying the classically lovely face that radiated peace and serenity. Her mother was the most remarkable woman Christa had ever known, wise in the ways of the heart, knowledgeable about many things ladies seldom understood, and showing unshakable bravery during the horrifying months of the Terror.

Most of all, Marie-Claire knew how to love with courage and generosity, never counting the cost though she had lost two husbands and an infant son to premature death. Her daughter knew that if Marie-Claire were still alive, she would go forth and love again after she had done with mourning. Christa had never known her mother's equal for womanly warmth and strength; while she herself was incurably frivolous and too impatient to achieve such heights, she dreamed that someday she would be at least half the woman her mother was.

She looked one last time at the portrait, at Marie-Claire's wondrously clear and expressive gray eyes, which she had bequeathed to her children. "I know you are taking care of Papa and your children, *Maman*, wherever you may be.

Do not fear for me; you taught me well. I shall strive to be worthy of you." She watched as the flames consumed the picture, then looked at the last portrait.

"You are the one who gave me the idea for this, Charles," she said thoughtfully as she studied the handsome laughing face. "Remember the song you taught me, called the 'The Unquiet Grave'? You have forgotten? So careless, Charles! It was about a maiden who sat and wept on her true love's grave for twelve months and a day. Then his spirit rose and complained that her grief disturbed his peace, and she must cease to mourn. You told me I must live for both you and *Maman*, and I promise you I shall."

The portrait was overlaid with a vivid mental image of her brother, and her voice was a whisper as she added, "But I would not be denied my year of grieving."

Christa laid the picture on the flames and continued unsteadily, "No one has ever been more fortunate in her father or mother or brother. I thank you all for the love and joy you brought into my life. And now I release you."

She stood and watched as the last scrap of paper was devoured, Charles's smile lingering in her memory. "*Va avec le bon Dieu, ma chere famille*," she said quietly. There were no tears; she had shed enough in the past twelve-month.

Now that she had performed this private ritual to honor her lost family, she felt a sudden rush of freedom and lightness. Throwing her head back and spreading her arms outward, she reached inside to the central core of exuberance she had voluntarily abandoned in the last year. "I have honored my dead with grieving, Now it is time to honor them with *life!*"

Chapter 1

British Crown Colony of Gibraltar

March 1795

Peter Harrington braced himself before knocking on the door. His noble patient, Captain Lord Alexander Kingsley, Viscount Kingsley and officer of His Majesty's Royal Navy, had been raising merry Hades with the household ever since he had recovered consciousness. His good-natured mischief made him a handful under normal conditions. How would he react to Harrington's unwelcome news?

He knocked and entered the high-ceilinged bedroom without waiting, only to be walloped full face with a feather pillow. "Alex Kingsley! What the devil . . .?" Further comment was cut off by a new barrage of pillows. Abandoning his Hippocratic oath and doctorly dignity, Peter scooped up one of the pillows and fired it back at the tanned face grinning from the bed. The ensuing five minutes bore considerably more resemblance to a nursery riot than a meeting between two gentlemen of mature years and superior station.

The battle ended when Peter collapsed laughing into a chair by the bed. "What the devil was *that* all about?" he demanded. Alex brushed a few feathers out of his collar-length blond hair and chuckled, amber-brown eyes twinkling from his long, high-cheek boned face.

"I wanted to prove that my throwing arm has recovered from its wounds. *Now* will you let me out of this cell?"

Peter scanned the whitewashed walls, comfortable furniture, and bright fabrics, then snorted. He was a solid man of middle height, the premature streaks of gray in his dark hair making him look older than his thirty-one years. "If you think this is a cell, I should have left you in the military hospital. This is a palace by comparison."

His gaze was affectionate as it rested on his childhood friend. They had grown up on adjoining estates, running wild together whenever they could escape their keepers. Both had cherished inappropriate ambitions—Peter to become a doctor, Alex to go to sea. It had been hard for Peter to convince his father to let him study such a middle-class profession as medicine, but he was the youngest of three sons in a family of no extraordinary fortune, and his father was an understanding man. The Honorable Alexander had a much harder struggle; his father had been reluctant to let his heir embark on the dangers of a military career and had given permission only after a younger son was born and giving every evidence of lusty good health.

Alex looked repentant. "You must know how much I appreciate your taking me in, Peter. If you hadn't stopped them, they would have cut off my left arm. Cursed nuisance, since I'm left-handed." He gave a half smile and added, "Considering the shape I was in at the time, they could have taken anything they wanted, and welcome to it. I'm still surprised Sarah would let you in when you brought my battered carcass home."

"She was a doctor's daughter. She knew what she was getting into when she married me," Peter replied dryly. "Besides, Sarah had heard me speak of you often and was

anxious to meet you. Though not, perhaps, in this particular
way. It's a miracle I recognized you under all the blood
and bandages. After all, it had been . . . what—a dozen
years?—since we had seen each other."

As soon as he had recognized his old friend, Peter
whisked him away to his own Spanish-style villa, where
the captain would have the best possible nursing. Had the
winds of fate not brought the Harringtons to Gibraltar, Alex
might have died, and would certainly have been crippled
had he survived. Instead, he exhibited remarkable powers
of recuperation—within a month he was beating Peter at
cards and teaching bawdy sailor songs to the three-year-old
son of the house. From the cook to the spaniel, everyone in
the house adored him.

Alex swung his long legs off the bed and reached for the
cane he still needed. The whole left side of his body had
been ripped by metal fragments when a cannonball shattered on the quarterdeck where he was directing the fight
against a French ship of the line. He had stayed in command until the battle was won, the French ship secured,
and his own frigate, *Antagonist*, on course to nearby
Gibraltar with her prize. Only then did he collapse.

Even during the years of peace after the American
Revolution, Alex had always found employment shipboard
while many of his fellow officers cooled their heels on
shore at half pay. Since hostilities had resumed, he had
risen rapidly to a command of his own. While it was assumed
that his aristocratic lineage had aided his advancement,
even his most grudging critics could not deny his brilliance,
courage, and luck.

Tightening the sash of his blue robe around his lean
waist, Alex crossed the room to the window and back with
hardly any resort to the cane. "See?" he said triumphantly
as he lowered himself onto the edge of the bed. "It should

be obvious even to a fusty old medical man like yourself that I am as good as new. When are you going to let me go back to my ship? She's almost refitted, and so am I."

"You've been practicing," Peter said judiciously, then paused, his mouth a little dry. He had avoided this moment for weeks but could no longer. Looking his old friend in the eye, he said quietly, "You're not going back to the *Antagonist*. Not right now, and perhaps not ever."

"Why not? Am I up for court-martial?" Alex said. His words were flippant, but his eyes were very still.

Peter followed his friend's cue and kept his tone light. "You remember how long I had to operate, picking pieces of your precious ship out of your hide?"

Alex grimaced. "Remember? Every day of that operation is graven on my liver."

Peter chuckled. "I suppose it felt like days, but after all the brandy you put away before and during the operation, I'm surprised you remember anything. I'm sure the head you had next day had more to do with your brandy than my knife." He paused, then said gravely, "I did my best, but I'm positive there is at least one large shell fragment left in your chest. That's why you still feel so much pain." At Alex's instinctive movement of negation, he said acidly, "Don't bother trying to lie to me. I noticed it was your right arm you used most in that pillow fight."

Alex shrugged. "What does it matter? Half the old salts in the navy have a musket ball in them somewhere. Helps 'em predict weather."

Pete sighed. He had known Alex wouldn't make this easy. "The difference is the location. I couldn't risk any more probing around in the area. You would have died on the table." He stopped a moment, then continued, "You know that musket balls and shell fragments can migrate away from their original location?"

At Alex's nod, he continued, "There is a good likelihood that the fragment may settle down and stay where it is for the next fifty years, just giving you twinges. Or it may move outward to where it can be removed surgically, or even work its own way out. It isn't as if a body *wants* that kind of thing inside." He stopped once more, then said baldly, "Or it may migrate inward until it hits an organ or a major blood vessel."

Alex looked at him levelly. "In which case I die."

Peter held his eye and nodded. "Exactly so."

Alex shifted his gaze out the window to the rock that dominated the colony. After a minute he said, "I'll admit it would hardly be fair to my crew to drop dead suddenly. Bad for morale. Sailors are a superstitious lot."

Peter broke the silence after another few moments had passed. "I'm sorry. I know how much you love the navy. A year from now, if your condition is stable, you can take a new command. But for the moment, I can't in good conscience release you to active duty."

Alex swung his head back, a devilish light in his eyes. "You must be joking! A man would have to be *mad* to love the navy! Weevily biscuits, endless boring patrols, living packed together closer than rats in Seven Dials, no women for months on end . . . and ships aren't built for men my height—I still seem to bang my head at least once a day." He inspected his scarred left forearm, then said quietly, "The navy doesn't own the sea. No one can take that away from me."

"I suppose you'll be going back to England?"

"It looks like I can't avoid it." The note in Alex's voice was so odd that Peter glanced at him sharply. Still looking down, his friend said, "Remember the letter that was delivered yesterday—the one that had been following me all over the Mediterranean for months?"' He looked up to see Peter's nod, then said flatly, "My mother is dead."

Peter exhaled sharply. Lady Serena Kingsley had been one of the most notorious women of her generation, a legendary beauty whose amorality was exceeded only by her cold-blooded selfishness. She had made the Kingsley household a hell for her family and servants, while her husband, Arthur, withdrew from the unpleasantness as much as possible, leaving his children to her vicious moods.

Alex said dryly, "You needn't bother to grope for condolences. Her demise has been greeted with near-universal relief, particularly by those of her lovers who feared she might pen her memoirs someday. And don't look so crushingly sympathetic—I accepted what she was years ago."

He knit his fingers together and looked down at them broodingly. "I'm a coward, Peter." He looked up at his friend's small exclamation with a lopsided smile. "Oh, not in the usual way. It isn't all that hard to face death. After all, life is invariably a fatal condition. But when it comes to people, I've been a coward all my life. I'm sure you know that a major reason I entered the navy at fourteen was to get away from home."

He accepted Peter's nod, then continued, "I ran then, and I would have kept on running if you hadn't just closed the door. I've scarcely spent three months in London over the last fifteen years. My brother and sister are near strangers. They have every right to hate me."

"Why should they do that?" Peter asked quietly.

"Because I left them alone with that . . . that"—he searched for a term—"black widow spider. And I never did a damned thing to help them."

Peter's voice was gentle. "You're too hard on yourself. Lady Serena was the most difficult woman I have ever known. You were a boy then—what could you do about her? It was your father's job to control his wife, not yours."

Alex refused the comfort. "I could have done more. And I certainly ought to have gone home two years ago when my father died. Annabelle and Jonathan are my responsibility, and I have failed them."

"Your service in the navy has been of value to the country."

Alex shrugged. "There is no shortage of eager lieutenants panting for their own commands. Any of them could do what I have done."

"You underrate your own achievements, and your brother and sister's good sense. Remember what a sweet little thing Annabelle was? How she used to follow us around and you would take her up with you on your horse?" Alex started to smile reminiscently, but Peter made the mistake of adding, "How could she possibly hate you? I doubt anyone has ever hated you in your life."

Alex stood again and crossed to the window, leaning heavily on the cane this time. "Wrong. My mother did. Used to tell me that my birth ruined her figure." He settled himself on the window seat and smiled ironically at his friend. "Although half the men in London appeared to find nothing wrong with her figure. Did you know my father kept me back from the navy until he was sure that Jonathan must be a true Kingsley? So that when I got killed the title would still go to a son of his own blood. Sentimental man, my father."

Peter was silenced. Alex had been such a cheerful, hey-go-mad boy. Two years younger than Peter, Alex was the natural leader whose imaginative antics often led them into trouble, while it was left to the quieter, more studious Peter to get them out. As close as they had been then, as many letters as they had exchanged over the years, only now did Peter understand how unhappy his friend must have been.

Alex folded his hands on the brass head of the cane in front of him and his smile softened to a real one. "You shouldn't have gotten me talking about that. Don't look so sad, Peter. It's all history now. We are as much a product of our problems as our triumphs. I am reasonably happy with myself, except for how I've neglected my brother and sister. I may be skittish, but now I will have the chance to make amends for that." He laughed suddenly. "But you must bear the responsibility for sending me back into deadly danger."

"Deadly danger?" Peter repeated in confusion.

"The ladies, Peter." Alex rolled his eyes in comic horror. "They terrify me! All those fluttering fans and sly, catlike eyes—I never know what to say to fashionable women. They make these purring remarks and bare their sharp little teeth, and I don't know whether they are flirting or insulting me or attempting to compromise my virtue." His deep voice took on a mournful note. "It's a hard prospect for a simple sailor."

Peter laughed, glad the familiar Alex was back. "A simple sailor, indeed! I have yet to see you show the slightest sign of shyness around any woman in this house."

"It's not *women* I have problems with," Alex said. "It's *ladies*."

"So avoid the fashionable world," Peter said promptly. "You're a peer of the realm—no one can force you into polite society."

Alex stretched luxuriously. "I'm afraid it can't be avoided entirely. Poor Belle is twenty and hasn't even been presented yet because she has spent the last two years in mourning. I shall have to rescue her from my appalling Aunt Agatha and open up Kingsley House again. The least

I can do is give her a ball that will be remembered for years. But be warned," he added with a baleful glare, "if I become a casualty of the social wars, it will be *your* fault for not letting me go back to the navy."

Peter chuckled and stood up. "You can sit and bemoan your cruel future, but I am ready to eat. Care to join Sarah and me?"

Alex stood up and limped across the floor. "If there is one thing I've learned in the navy, it is to take advantage of a good meal. Lead on!" As he came up to Peter, he briefly put one hand on his friend's shoulder and squeezed, grateful for his quiet understanding. He wished he could take the Harringtons back to England with him, but he knew that coming to terms with his past was one battle he must fight alone.

Chapter 2

Radcliffe Hall

March 17, 1795

Ordinarily Christa started the day with a cup of hot chocolate and a bread roll in her bedchamber, declaring that the British custom of devouring animal flesh in the morning was too much to be borne. On this day, however, she rang early for her maid, Annie, so she could dress in time to meet Lord Radcliffe at his breakfast. After wearing black for a year, it was a pleasure to slip into a white muslin gown with embroidered sprigs of roses. She had made it from a new pattern book, and it was daringly fashionable.

Annie nodded approvingly as she laced the high-waisted dress tightly around her mistress's curves. "High time you put off your mourning, Lady Christa," she said with a vigorous nod. She was a plump, pretty girl, brown as a wren. "You'll never catch a husband if you stay hidden here in the country."

"It *has* turned out well, no?" Christa gave a half turn, admiring the simple flowing lines of the gown. She approved of the new fashions based on the styles of ancient Greece and Rome; they were one of the most positive results of the French Revolution. She had always loved clothes and in this last quiet year she had spent much time designing and sewing. While it was an odd occupation for a lady of quality, she found it soothing, and she was as skilled as a professional seamstress.

Annie threaded a matching rose velvet ribbon through Christa's glossy black curls, cut short *à la Titus*, then handed her mistress a fine cashmere shawl for protection against the great house's drafty corridors.

It was a very large house, built in the ponderous style known as English Baroque, and by the time Christa reached the breakfast parlor she had worked up an appetite. "Pray do not disturb yourself, Uncle Lewis," she said gaily to the man who started to rise at her entrance. "My papa always told me never to come between a man and his breakfast."

"Good morning, Marie-Christine. You are looking very well." Lewis Radleigh nodded approval of her bright dress, then seated himself while Christa poured hot chocolate and recklessly helped herself to a coddled egg and two pieces of fruitcake. After all, she was opening a new chapter of her life.

Silence reigned for the next few minutes as both concentrated on their food. Swallowing the last bite of egg and finishing her chocolate, Christa covertly studied her companion. Portraits showed that the Radleigh men had always been a magnificent lot—tall, broad-shouldered, as blond and confident as lions. Lewis Radleigh was the younger brother of Charles's father, and he had the family height and looks. His blond hair was barely touched with silver and his impassive features could be judged handsome.

But the blood ran thin in him—he was a repressed, colorless shadow of his magnificent relatives. Lewis and Charles's mother, Marie-Claire, had become joint guardians of the infant earl after Charles's father died in a carriage accident, with Lewis managing the Radcliffe properties during his nephew's minority. After Charles's death, he inherited the title in his own right, executing his duties conscientiously but with no obvious signs of pleasure.

Observing that he had finished his ham, Christa said, "Uncle Lewis, I should like to speak with you today. Now that I am out of mourning, it is time I planned my future."

Lord Radcliffe regarded her thoughtfully. "Quite right. I fear I must spend the morning with my agent, but I shall be free this afternoon. Would it be convenient for you to come to my study at two o'clock?"

Christa nodded, then pushed away from the table and stood. "*Très bien*. I shall see you then." As she left the room, she thought with amusement that it was typical of him to make a formal appointment to meet someone he had lived with for the last year. Christa knew Charles had been fond of his uncle and relied heavily on his business judgment, but she herself scarcely knew the man, even though they had first met when she was in leading strings. Perhaps Lewis felt passion for the mathematical articles he published in learned journals. He showed none of that quality in daily life.

For all his stuffiness, he had responded admirably when Captain Brown summoned him to Ramsgate. Christa had arrived in England dangerously ill from fever and shock and had little memory of her first weeks in the country. One image that remained burned on her brain was Lewis's agonized face when he learned what had happened, for he'd been very nearly a father to Charles. Rigidly controlling his personal grief, he had summoned a London doctor to treat her and waited in Ramsgate until she could be moved. By the time she was fully aware of her surroundings, she was safe in Radcliffe Hall.

She was grateful that Uncle Lewis had left her alone to mourn in her own fashion. Anything she wished had been ordered for her, and he had let her ride and walk about the estate alone. They generally dined together, but conversation was always sparse and superficial; wrapped in their separate grief, they were like two ghosts that coexisted without touching. She doubted he would miss her when she went to London.

The inlaid hall clock was striking two when she entered Lord Radcliffe's study. He rose behind his desk and made a slight, formal bow. "Please have a seat. I am glad to see you have put off your mourning." He studied the lively face with its healthy color and sparkling gray eyes, then added, "You look very much like your mother."

"Alas, I will never be so beautiful as she," Christa said regretfully as she chose one of the leather wing chairs in front of his desk.

"That is true," Lewis said soberly.

Christa shot him a glance that blended amusement with irritation. Protocol demanded he assure her that she was equally beautiful. It wouldn't have been true, of course, but most gentlemen would have lied gallantly. No wonder he was in his forties and had never married! One of the maids had gossiped that a widow in a nearby town took care of his "masculine needs," but he seemed too cold a man to really love a woman.

As she now studied his closed face, so like Charles's but without the vital charm, she wondered what he really felt. Was he happy to be an earl? Did he miss his nephew? Was he capable of missing anyone?

Lord Radcliffe sat down again. "What did you wish to discuss?"

"I have been a year now in Berkshire, Uncle Lewis," Christa began. "Since I am out of mourning, it's time I

went to London and entered society. Your cousin Clarissa
has written and invited me to stay with her. She is worried
because I am twenty-three, almost too old to find a husband." She smiled at him teasingly, but his answer was
grave.

"Marriage is the only proper goal for a young lady, but
a dowerless girl is at a great disadvantage, particularly in
London."

She looked at him in surprise. "Dowerless? But Papa
was one of the richest men in France! I know much of the
family property is forfeit, but he sent a considerable sum of
money to Charles."

Lewis shook his head. "That may have been his intention, but it was never fulfilled. He may have delayed too
long, or perhaps he tried, and his arrangements were never
carried out because of the revolution and the war with
England."

Christa stood suddenly, unable to sit still in the face of
this news. "You are *sure* there is no account set up in my
name? Papa had spoken of his intentions perhaps four
years ago, and England did not declare war on France till
more than a year later."

He shook his head again. "Quite sure. I assumed your
father would have provided for you, but when I checked
the bank records of the last six years, ever since the revolution began, there was no money transferred from
France during that whole period." The expression in his
cool blue eyes was unreadable as he added, "I'm afraid
you have nothing."

Christa paced over to the window and stared out at
the bare dripping trees of the park while she struggled to
absorb this information. Her hands were clenched as she
said, "Do you mean that for this last year, all the clothes,

the books, the pin money you gave me—everything was *charity*?"

Lewis stood and followed her to the window. "Please, you must not think of it as such. You are Charles's sister, and there will always be a home for you here." He paused, then said, "But you know what the world is like. Even though you are a countess, a penniless young woman has almost no chance of contracting a suitable alliance. And you are a foreigner—that would count against you even if our countries were not at war."

She turned to face him, her eyes challenging the impenetrable face as a cool finger of alarm touched the back of her neck. There was something odd, very odd, about the way he was emphasizing her unmarriageability. While he was under no obligation to provide for her, he could, if he chose, give her a dowry with the stroke of a pen and scarcely notice the cost. Charles would certainly have done so.

Her voice was dry as she said, "It is true that you English are an insular lot in every sense of the word. But if I wish for a husband, I am not wholly without the ability to find one." Ever since she had reached her fifteenth year, she had been showered with sonnets, flowers, marriage proposals, and scores of less honorable propositions. She was confident that not all had been due to her father's wealth.

A flare of emotion sparked the pale eyes as he stared down at her, and for the first time she was uneasily aware how close he was standing. The earl said softly, "You are a very lovely girl. In fact, I have a solution that will benefit both of us."

She swished around him to her leather chair, but he came and sat next to her rather than returning to his desk. Uncomfortable with his proximity, she leaned back and stared in silence, daring him to continue. Lewis said awkwardly, "It was never necessary that I marry in the past, but as earl I owe it to my name to provide an heir. You are in need of a husband, and I am in need of a wife." His voice faltered under her steel-gray gaze, then he continued more strongly, "Marie-Christine, I would be very honored if you would consent to marry me."

"But you are my *uncle*!" Though she had sensed some strange mood in him, she had trouble believing the words he spoke.

The earl smiled, more sure of himself. "Uncle by courtesy only. You know there is no blood relationship between us. I am perhaps a little old for you, but I am in good health. I am sure we could have many years together."

Christa almost spat at him. "Always you have been Uncle Lewis to me. Though we may not be truly related, to me it feels like *incest*!"

He winced at her plain speaking. "I realize it will take time for you to accustom yourself to the idea, but I am sure you will see the advantages when you think on it. As the Countess of Radcliffe, you will once more have the position and luxury you are accustomed to. You can stay here where you are known and not have to go among strangers."

She stood so suddenly that the heavy chair skidded away behind her. Glaring down at him, she said tightly, "It is most kind of you to sacrifice yourself to help a poor relation. After all, as the Earl of Radcliffe you may look as high as you choose. But if I refuse your so-generous offer, what then? The poorhouse, *mon oncle*? Or will you throw me out to sell myself on the streets of London?"

He stood also, frowning as if she were a willful child. "This has been a shock and you are overwrought. We will speak again when you have had time to consider."

Taking her right hand, Lewis continued more earnestly

than she had ever heard him. "I have spoken badly. Marrying you would be no duty, but a very great pleasure." He pressed a kiss onto her hand, and she stared at the bent blond head with dawning horror. The earl's lips burned as intensely as his eyes had when he stared into hers, and she wondered how she could have ever thought he lacked passion. *Mon Dieu*, but he wanted her indeed! Christa felt a shadow of pity at the desperation in his touch, but it was swept away in a flood of revulsion. Jerking her hand free, she fled the room.

Lord Radcliffe made no attempt to stop her, merely watching, his face once more expressionless. He had expected Christa to be surprised, even shocked, at the news of her poverty and at his proposal, but she should come around soon. After all, what other choice did the girl have?

Even an hour's walking in the raw March day could not cool Christa's outrage. She had paused only to grab a cloak and change her indoor slippers to half boots before storming outside. Her path took her through the home wood and looped back till she stood now on the edge of the ornamental lake. The spot was one where she and Charles would come to skip stones as children. Since flat shale was not common in the area, her brother had used his lordly powers to order that a supply of the stones be perpetually kept on the site.

Prompted by the memory, she poked around in the bushes until, to her delight, she found a pile of shale perfect for skipping. She gathered a handful and moved to the edge of the water. Picking up the first piece of stone, she tossed it in her hand to get the heft, then hurled it across the lake. It crashed into the gray waters without a single skip.

"That is so *typical* of this day! First that . . . that *cochon*, that *pig*, tells me I am a pauper." Christa had always enjoyed talking aloud to herself; usually, though by no means always, she indulged in it when she was alone. She frowned now, and said slowly as she picked up another stone, "It was not like Papa to forget something as important as providing for the future. To be sure, he was a philosopher, but he was also French and a practical man. So, do I believe in my father? Or this pig of an uncle?" She nodded in satisfaction as the stone managed two skips before sinking.

"But the money . . . that is less important than what he tries to do to me. That he should try to *compel* me to marry him . . . me! My ancestors fought with Charles the Hammer at Poitiers a thousand years ago! I am a d'Estelle, a countess of France!"

This sounded so unbearably pompous, even to herself, that Christa laughed out loud and flung another stone. As always, laughter returned her sense of perspective. She said regretfully, "I am no credit to your teaching, Papa. You, who always taught that all were equal in the eyes of God and should be in the eyes of men. As soon as I lose my temper, I forget I am a democrat. And I am not even a true countess, since the Assembly abolished all noble titles five years ago."

The old skills were definitely returning; she couldn't be quite sure because of the rain spattering the lake, but she thought the latest stone skipped five times. Staring at the pockmarked water, she added, "How could I possibly marry a man who calls me 'Marie-Christine'? Even *Maman* only called me that when she was very disappointed in me."

She had acquired her nickname from Charles, the imperious five-year-old who declared "Marie-Christine" far too long for such a small scrap of baby. "Christa" had stuck and was used by almost everyone who knew her well. It was typical of Lord Radcliffe's stuffiness that he used her formal name.

She shivered suddenly, feeling the damp cold for the first time. It was easy to mock the stiff man whom she had known all her life, but his intensity today made him seem a different person, one who frightened her a little. She was uncomfortably aware how much she was in his power—alone in the world, with the man who should have been her protector, a threat.

Christa wrapped her cloak tightly around her and sat on a stone bench near the water's edge for some serious thinking. Only her intimates knew that under the bubbling vivacity of her personality ran a vein of pure, dispassionate logic. She started to tick off points on her fingers as she mused aloud.

"Item the first: Could the honest Lord Radcliffe be lying about the money? Charles always said he was incorruptible. But men are not rational beings. Since he appears to have conceived a foolish passion for me, that could change his behavior. *Maman* once said that middle-aged men can be quite hopeless about young women." Christa paused for a moment to consider with satisfaction the superior mental powers of women before continuing.

"Item the second: Whether he is telling the truth or lying like Reynard the Fox, there is nothing I can do. Absolutely nothing. He is an earl while I have neither money nor influence nor evidence of wrongdoing. And who knows? He might even be telling the truth.

"Item the third: I cannot refuse him and stay at Radcliffe Hall, with him . . . *lusting* after me. It would not be right to live on his charity under those conditions. Besides, he might wear down my resolve." She felt once more those hot, demanding lips on her hand and unconsciously wiped her palm on her cloak. He was not unattractive for a middle-aged man, but he was old enough to be her father, quite apart from the fact that she really did regard him in the light of a blood relative.

Her mind reached a logical corollary and halted in shock. Might he consider *forcing* her to the altar, with threats or drugs or violence? Christa would not have dreamed it possible in England, but now she had no idea what Lord Radcliffe might be capable of. Aloud she said acidly, "I suppose I should be grateful it is marriage he wants. As long as I am in his power, only his own conscience controls him. Therefore, I must leave here quickly, and in secret. My bones tell me his gracious lordship will not want to let me go.

"Item the fourth: Where can I go? Even if I knew another man who wished to marry me, it would be a marriage of convenience only, and if I wished *that*, I might stay here. No, unless I meet a man who is the equal of Charles and Papa, I will never marry. Where else might I go?" She mentally reviewed her acquaintances in England, but quickly realized that apart from a handful of émigré families as poor as herself, there was no one she knew really well. "Neither Lewis's cousin Clarissa nor any other Radleigh would wish to have me with the head of the family disapproving—especially now that I am penniless. I am scarcely acquainted with the neighbors here. There is no one else."

With a quickening of her pulse that was more excitement than alarm, she said slowly. "There is only one possible conclusion: if I cannot stay here, and have no one to go to, I must find work. Is my logic not faultless, Papa?"

Christa stood and shook loose the sodden folds of her cloak while she reached down for one last piece of shale. Hurling it flat away with all the strength of her arm, she watched as it skipped seven times, then nodded approvingly. "A sign of good luck, no?" Then she turned away from the little lake and headed back to the house to plan her strategy.

Christa sent a message down that she was indisposed and unable to dine with Lord Radcliffe. He would probably think she was sulking, but she didn't care as long as he left her alone. She was packing her portmanteau when Annie entered with a tray.

"I thought you might like some nice soup and cold meat, Lady Christa. You need to keep your strength up if you're sickening. Oh!" Annie gasped, her eyes widening.

Christa straightened from her packing and caught the maid's eye with her own. "I am leaving tonight. Will you betray me?"

"Oh, Lady Christa! You're never leaving!" The two were much of an age and had become good friends; the past year had begun with Annie nursing her and ended with the two sewing and laughing together. Christa had even taught Annie to read and write.

Christa sighed. "I must. It is very simple: Lord Radcliffe wishes to marry me. I do not wish to oblige. Under the circumstances, it is best I depart quickly. Will you help me?"

Annie lifted her chin. "Need you ask? Just tell me what I must do."

Christa came around the bed and gave her a quick hug. "Just don't let my uncle know I am leaving. When he finds out tomorrow, say that I ordered you not to disturb me in the morning. With luck, he might not miss me for a full day."

"Is that all?" Annie looked disappointed. She was a secret romantic and had always believed a suitable crisis would prove she had the stuff of heroines.

Christa shook her head. "I cannot involve you more. You live here. I daren't give his lordship grounds to punish you."

"Why not take me? You will need a companion to protect your reputation." Annie's eyes were pleading, but Christa stood firm.

"I could not afford a maid, even if you would leave your William. Indeed, I do not know how I will be keeping myself." She paused as a thought struck her, then said slowly, "There is another way you could help me. Can you find the names of some London registry offices—the sorts of places that might find employment for governesses?"

"You're never going to look for a *job*, miss!" Annie's round eyes could not have shown more horror if Christa had proclaimed an ambition to walk naked through the Court of St. James. "Why, you're a *lady*!"

Christa gave an irrepressible chuckle. "Even ladies must eat, *ma petite*. Work is the lot of most of womankind, and I think I am capable of it." Since Annie appeared too flustered to respond, she patted the maid's arm and said soothingly, "Indeed, I rather look forward to it. I have always found inactivity *très ennuyante*. Very boring."

Annie still looked dubious but said, "I shall ask Mrs. Harris, the housekeeper. She came to us from London and should know some agencies. Can I help you pack?"

Christa shook her head. "I am almost finished. It is time I began taking care of myself."

"Is that all you are taking? You're never leaving all your lovely clothes behind!" Poor Annie found this the saddest idea of all. The portmanteau was scarcely large enough for half a dozen garments.

"Well, a pretty fool I should be to try to carry more," Christa said patiently. "Get you downstairs now to talk to Mrs. Harris. I am relying on you!" She escorted Annie to the door and firmly ushered her out, then leaned against the carved door for a moment, her shoulders sagging.

For all her show of confidence, Christa was worried about leaving this secure existence to brave the world. Although she was more capable and self-reliant than most women of her station, she was going forth into a foreign country as well as a new and demanding way of life. She had spent perhaps thirty months of her life in England, almost entirely in the pampered isolation of Radcliffe Hall. Christa could only guess at what life was like among the common people.

She turned to look in the mirror, saying sternly, "Eh, Countess, enough of the self-pity! You speak English fluently and you have over a hundred pounds of pin money that you haven't spent—that is a fortune for a working person. Enough to support you for many months if you are careful."

Her step had lightened when she returned to her packing. The sterile luxury of Radcliffe Hall had been smothering her even before Lewis made his unwelcome advances. An independent future might hold difficulties undreamed of, but it was a direction that promised new life. After all, Christa was young and strong, and embarking on a great adventure!

She chose her plainest and most durable clothes and shoes. They were really too fashionable for a governess, but she had no choice. Her only jewelry was the antique picture locket that held miniatures of her family.

Christa hesitated before packing the boy's clothes she had worn on her escape. She was unlikely to need them, but they were a tangible link with her past. Last, she went to her chest and took out a small leather pouch containing Charles's gold watch. The provincial assembly in Nor-

mandy had trumpeted proudly about the English spies they
had killed, proof of the wicked British plots against the
revolution.

Lewis had pulled some diplomatic strings and eventually a packet of personal effects crossed the Channel to
Radcliffe Hall. It contained Charles's identification papers,
the watch, and a signet ring with the Radcliffe arms. At the
sight of them, Christa's last faint hope that he and her
mother might have survived had flickered and died. Lord
Radcliffe had taken the ring and given her the watch.
She had been grateful for his generosity; the watch had
belonged to Charles's father, and she would not have
blamed Lewis for keeping it.

She slipped the watch and most of her money into a
belted pouch that could be tied under her dress; no one was
stealing either while she had breath in her body! Then she
snapped the case shut and lifted it experimentally. It was
a little heavy, but Christa could carry it the five miles to
the main coaching route. With her preparations complete,
she attacked Annie's tray of food with gusto.

The last of the apple tart had just disappeared when the
maid returned. "I've got five names and addresses for you,
Lady Christa," she said proudly. "And here's a packet of
bread, meat, and fruit for your journey."

Christa accepted the offerings gratefully. "You are a
splendid help, Annie. *Merci*."

Annie blushed. "It's my pleasure, I'm sure, miss." She
hesitated, then said shyly, "Is there any place I could get in
touch with you? If . . . if anything should change here."

Christa said regretfully, "It is better you not know where I
am going. I promise I shall be safe, and perhaps sometime in
the future I will be able to write to you. But for now . . ." She
gave a Gallic shrug, then went to the wardrobe and took out

several lengths of fabric. "I have a present for you, Annie. My dresses would not fit you, but here are some pieces of silk and velvet for your trousseau. I am sure that you will have persuaded William to the altar by this summer."

"Oh, Lady Christa!" Annie reached out in awe and stroked the beautiful fabric, then looked up with tears in her eyes. "I will miss you ever so much. Sometimes . . . it was like we were friends, not that I was just a servant."

Christa gave her a last hug, then said shakily, "You have been a good friend, Annie. I will miss you too. Now, go quickly, before my resolve weakens."

After the maid left, she lay down to attempt some rest. She had six hours left to enjoy the fine feather mattress.

Chapter 3

Christa had given herself ample time to reach the crossroads where the coach could be stopped, and had a long, cold wait before the winter dark began to lighten. When the coach's arrival was heralded by the pounding of heavy hooves, she started waving, holding her ground even when it appeared she might be run over. In a jumble of curses, the thickset driver pulled up and glared down at her.

"Please, *monsieur*, I wish passage to London."

He considered for a few moments, then nodded. "Pass your box up." As Christa boosted it in the air, she was grateful she had packed no more. Pushing the long-suffering outside passengers aside, the driver precariously fastened the portmanteau atop the pile of existing luggage. As he did so, a red face appeared at the window to bawl, "You can't take her! There's no room inside."

Another voice chimed in, "Aye, another passenger will burst the sides of the coach."

Christa was starting to worry when the driver yelled, "There's always space for a little dab like her. One of you gents might like to carry her on yer lap." He cackled at his own wit.

The red-faced man, unabashed, yelled back, "She's not

on the waybill. Us who is already here have our rights! I'll report it to the company!"

The driver spat contemptuously, narrowly missing the man in the window. "There 'ud be plenty of space if we left *you* here. Get in, miss. We've a shedjool to meet!"

More voices sounded, agreeing that time was a-wasting, and if the red-faced man didn't like it, he could *walk* to London. As Christa scrambled up, she suspected the driver's championship stemmed from a desire to keep her fare for himself, but she was too grateful to care.

Inside, the red-faced man glared at her while a plump, motherly looking woman smiled encouragingly. The coach jerked into motion before she could be seated, and she very nearly did end up in someone's lap before squeezing herself between a grossly overweight woman who apparently considered bathing unhealthy, and a greasy-looking clerk who tried to engage her in conversation. His eyes bulged slightly, and he licked his lips as he stared at her. Christa said several times in her heaviest accent that she did not speak the English, but he persisted.

Tired from lack of sleep, she dozed later in the morning but awoke at the feel of a furtive hand on her breast. Her outraged *"Monsieur!"* was accompanied by such a glare that the clerk shrank as far back from her as possible. Ostentatiously turning away, she refused to look at him for the rest of the journey.

It seemed an endless day of jolting and tight quarters; on muddy, rutted late-winter roads. A coach ride was an exhausting business. *At least all of these bodies together keep us from the cold,* she thought philosophically. *As long as I don't breathe too deeply I shall do very well.* Of course, travel was always tiring, but Christa now better appreciated the roomy, well-sprung private carriages she had enjoyed in the past.

She made the most of the short stops to stretch her legs and nibble on the food Annie had packed. The trip helped Christa to distance herself from Comtesse Marie-Christine d'Estelle. She must forget that that usually pampered young lady had ever existed and think of her new life as a role in a theatrical. If she could not convince herself that she was of common birth, she would be unable to convince anyone else. When they finally reached the London inn that was the end of the line, she stretched her aching body and told herself in amusement that a stagecoach had been a splendid place to begin her new life; she now felt very common indeed!

Christa's spirits rose as she looked around at the brawl and bustle of the city. Had not an Englishman once said that a man who was tired of London was tired of life? Surely she could find a place in this teeming capital—perhaps someday she might even find a man to share her life. Ignoring a seedy-looking fellow who asked if the young country miss needed a place to spend the night, she lifted her bag and set off to find her cousin Suzanne.

It was early afternoon of the next day when Lord Radcliffe decided to summon Christa for another discussion. Her absence from dinner hadn't surprised him but he thought twenty-four hours should have begun to reconcile her to his proposal. When her maid, Annie, came down and stammered that Lady Christa wasn't in her room, he first thought she must have taken a walk. "When did she go out?"

"I . . . I don't know, my lord."

Something about her guilty look triggered his suspicions. Damnation, surely the chit wouldn't be foolish enough to run away! His brows drew together, and he demanded curtly, "When did you last see her?"

"L-last night, my lord. She said she didn't want to be disturbed this morning."

The ever-calm Lord Radcliffe began to swear with startling fluency, then stood, towering over the frightened girl. "She has run away, and you have helped her. *Where did she go?*"

"I don't know, my lord," she said in a trembling voice.

The earl held her eyes with his and spoke softly, every word wielded like a weapon. "Anne Wilson, your father, your brothers, and your sister all work for me, as does your lover. He, I believe, is the sole support of an invalid mother and three younger children. I will ask you once more: *Where is she?*"

Annie started crying. She might have been a heroine if only her own welfare was involved, but the man in front of her had the power to beggar her entire family. How had he known about her and Will, cold stick of a man that he was? She had always thought him a good enough master who paid reasonable wages and never beat a servant, but now he terrified her. With a silent prayer for forgiveness, she quavered, "She's gone to London, my lord."

He nodded; it was the logical move. "Whom was she going to stay with?"

"I don't know, my lord." As his brow furrowed angrily, she said desperately, "As God as my witness, my lord, she wouldn't tell me! Lady Christa was going to look for work. She asked me to find the names of registry offices."

The earl looked at her anguished face and nodded in acceptance. "Whom did you ask for that information?"

"Mrs. Harris, my lord."

"Send her in. If you wish to stay in this house, it will be as a parlor maid. Now, go, while I am still feeling merciful."

Lord Radcliffe watched broodingly as she scuttled out

of the room. Marie-Christine had often asked him to frank letters to émigré friends in London; he could remember most of the names and addresses if he tried, and Mrs. Harris could tell him what registry offices she had named. He rang for his valet. When that gentleman appeared, the earl said shortly, "Pack my clothes. We leave for London in an hour." The valet bowed and left the room as quickly as possible. He had never seen his controlled, remote master with a face like *that* before.

Suzanne de Savary had had a long day at the shop, followed by an overstimulating supper with her four children. It was not surprising that it took her several moments to recognize the figure at her door who managed to be both jaunty and disheveled at the same time. "Eh, Suzanne, I know I am déclassé, but surely you will not keep me on your doorstep?"

"Christa!" Suzanne shrieked before sweeping her into an embrace. When the children realized that their favorite cousin had arrived, pandemonium reigned for some time. The four children ranged in age from thirteen to six. Suzanne herself was a darkly handsome woman in her mid-thirties with the supremely stylish look of a certain kind of Frenchwoman. She was a first cousin of Christa's mother and had known Christa all her life.

"We have just finished our evening meal, Christa, but there is bread and soup. You must be hungry." Suzanne looked apologetic but Christa absolved her with a smile. Times were not easy for her cousin—this tiny flat above a draper's shop was a far cry from the luxurious home she had known in Paris. Suzanne had fled to London three years before, when her husband was arrested. He was a

Girondist who eventually went to the guillotine when his politics were declared too moderate.

"Some of your wonderful soup would be exactly right. And for these greedy urchins, I have some candied plums." She stroked the spun-floss head of the smallest de Savary, Helene, as a ragged cheer went up. Even Suzanne looked pleased as Christa produced a packet acquired from a street vendor. Everyone in the de Savary household had a too-seldom-indulged sweet tooth.

A place was set at the table for Christa; if the amount of soup seemed meager, she made no complaint. While she ate, the children devoured the sticky plums and told her of their trials and triumphs since last they had met. After she had wiped up the last drop of soup with a piece of crusty bread, her cousin set a steaming pitcher on the table with a flourish.

"Oh, Suzanne!" Christa said as she inhaled reverently. "A proper pot of French coffee! For this I would have *walked* to London. These barbaric northerners have a way with tea, I admit, but their coffee . . . *mon Dieu*!"

Her cousin waved her hand grandly. "For you, *ma petite*, the best that Chateau de Savary has to offer."

Another hour was spent in general conversation before the children's heads began to nod. Only after they had been put to bed in the small back room did the two women start to talk seriously.

"Now, little cousin, you will tell me why you appear at my door, after dark, covered with mud, and without proper escort," Suzanne said as she put the coffee on the stove to reheat; it was too precious to waste.

Christa sighed, feeling the weariness of her long day. "I am here to look for work. I know you have little space, but I hope I can stay a few nights while I visit the registry offices."

Suzanne poured the last of the coffee into two mugs,

then sat and eyed Christa thoughtfully while she sipped. Finally she said, "You are welcome to stay as long as you need, but you seemed to be very comfortably situated at Radcliffe Hall." Her rising inflection made it more of a question.

"Charles's uncle, the present Lord Radcliffe, tells me that I am destitute and that he wishes to marry me. I do not like the way he asks." Christa shrugged. "So here I am."

Suzanne studied her young cousin. It was hardly surprising the uncle was taken with the girl; her combination of blithe intelligence and delectable curves had won her many admirers. "I have never met this Lord Radcliffe, but he is said to be an honorable man as well as a very wealthy one. Did you not even consider his proposal?"

"No," Christa said shortly. "I will marry for love or not at all."

Suzanne raised her eyebrows. "You are sure? Love is all very well, but there is much to be said for wealth. It is a hard world for a woman alone." Her eyes clouded as she was reminded of her own dilemma, then she continued, "What will you do?"

"I will find a position as a governess." Christa leaned forward eagerly. "You know how Papa was about education! I know far more about history, literature, philosophy, and mathematics than most men who have been to university." She grinned. "My *accomplishments* are not so good, but I am competent with music and drawing, and of course my French and my needlework."

Suzanne looked dubious. "I do not doubt your learning, but you are young and have no experience."

"I have taught children and servants on Papa's estates many times, and it was a great pleasure. I thought you and some of our émigré friends might write letters for me."

Her cousin nodded thoughtfully. "Perhaps it can be

done. Certainly I can give you a character. But jobs are scarce." Her eyes rested on the plain white wall without focusing. Christa leaned forward and took her hand.

"And now will you tell me what is troubling you?"

Her cousin started guiltily. "Is it so obvious? It is of no importance—nothing can be done."

"Tell me anyhow," Christa coaxed.

"Well . . . you know the *modiste* I have been working for, Mme. Bouchet? Though she has never been closer to Paris than Greenwich, she has been a good employer. I have become her chief assistant this last year." Christa nodded. The two had corresponded regularly, and she knew her cousin had been pleased with the situation.

"Madame's hands have been bothering her. They are too swollen now for her to work easily, and she has decided to sell the shop and move to Canterbury to live with her sister. She would like to sell it to me, but . . ." Her voice trailed off.

"You cannot afford it?" Christa questioned.

"*Exactement.* There is an Austrian woman interested and she can meet Mme. Bouchet's price. Madame gave me some time to see if I could raise more, but I sold everything I could, even my wedding band, and it is still not enough. I even thought of writing to you, to see if I could borrow some, but now . . ." She raised her head proudly. "I shall manage. I will find another situation. Soon I will be chief assistant again. And in a few years, perhaps I can open my own shop."

Christa knit her brows. Suzanne must have been desperate indeed to consider borrowing—she had refused Christa's help in the past. *In the days when I thought I had money.*

"How much more do you need?"

"A fortune . . . a hundred pounds."

Christa reached under her skirt and wrestled with the pouch hanging from her waist while Suzanne watched in bemusement. Finally unfastening it, Christa pulled it free of her petticoats and poured the golden coins inside onto the scrubbed deal table. "*Voila*! The shop is yours."

Suzanne gasped. "Marie-Christine, I cannot! It may be years before I can repay you. Perhaps never." She reached one hand out longingly, her once-white fingertips roughened from constant manual labor. If she accepted the money, it would mean a future for her children . . .

Christa said severely, "It is not a gift, it is an investment. You will buy the shop and call it 'Suzanne's' and work very hard. A year or two from now, when you are the premier *modiste* in London and can afford to pay me, I shall come work for you. We shall be partners."

"You could become my partner now," Suzanne offered.

Christa shook her head firmly. "That would strain your resources too much. You will want to make changes in the shop, won't you?" At Suzanne's nod she continued, "That will cost money. And you must support yourself and the children and be able to weather slow spells and customers who do not pay quickly. Money will be in very short supply at first. You do not need another mouth to feed. And your flat here is too small for another person."

Suzanne was silent, unable to refute her cousin's logic.

"And there is another thing," Christa said slowly. "It is very strange of me, but . . . I want to know that I can stand alone, without help. If I work with you, once again I would be sheltered." She smiled with a trace of embarrassment. "I know I am foolish—but the time to become your partner is in a year or two, when you are a success."

Suzanne was silent for a moment. "I think I understand. But if I am not a success—"

"Of *course* you will be!" Christa laughed. "You have

more style and fashion in your little finger than any woman I ever met. And will it not be amusing to work together?"

Suzanne came around the table and hugged her, tears of gratitude in her eyes. "You are my good angel!"

Christa wrinkled her nose in embarrassment. "*Eh, bien,* but even angels need sleep. We must both be up early in the morning."

When Suzanne arrived home the next evening, she paid little attention to the carriage standing in front of the draper's shop until a man stepped from it to address her. "Mme. de Savary?"

She whirled and looked at him suspiciously, seeing a tall, fair man with a cold face and impeccable tailoring. "Monsieur? I do not believe I know you."

He bowed. "Permit me to introduce myself. I am Lord Radcliffe, and I would like speech with you."

She looked at him with interest. So this was the wicked uncle! "Very well," she agreed. "But it must be while I begin the evening meal. My children will be home from school soon."

The earl nodded, then followed her up the dark stairs to the low-ceilinged flat. She removed her cloak and went to the stove to build a fire. "What did you wish to speak of, Lord Radcliffe?" she asked without looking at him.

"I am seeking your cousin, Marie-Christine d'Estelle."

She looked over her shoulder. "You have misplaced her? I thought she was living under your protection at Radcliffe Hall."

His lips tightened and he said, "She left two days ago."

Suzanne lifted one eyebrow. "So? Christa is of age."

The earl said smoothly, as if it had been said several times before, "Yes, but she had been unwell, feverish, and

I am worried about her. She has never recovered from the loss of her family."

"And of course, you wish to rescue her?" The irony in Suzanne's tone was so gentle it might have been imagined.

Lord Radcliffe nodded stiffly. "Of course. I am very worried about her. Here is my card," he said as he drew out his card case. "If you hear any word of her, I would be very appreciative if you would inform me as quickly as possible." He looked around the shabby room significantly. "*Very* appreciative."

Suzanne's initially open mind closed with a snap. Why, the man wanted her to *sell* information about her little cousin, her good angel! No wonder Christa wanted nothing to do with him.

Fortunately, the children arrived at that moment and their noisy entrance prevented her from any rash statements. Lord Radcliffe took his leave; Suzanne hoped that Christa would not choose that moment to return.

Footsore and bemused, Christa very nearly walked into the carriage parked in front of Suzanne's. Swerving around it, she saw the coat of arms painted on the door—a golden lion, rampant, a silver stag—and gasped with sudden shock. Fortunately, there was considerable foot traffic as people made their way home in the gathering dusk, and she let the movement carry her along until she could dart into an alley. Drawing several deep breaths to calm herself, she peered cautiously out, just in time to see Lord Radcliffe emerging from Suzanne's door. He had a black look on his face, and she could only be grateful he did not glance in her direction.

Her relief was checked when the earl spoke to one of his footmen before entering the carriage. The footman nodded and dropped off the back of the vehicle, then crossed the street to stand in the shadow of the building opposite Suzanne's.

Christa felt a chill. She had passed unnoticed when she was part of a group, but the man set to watch would certainly have seen her enter her cousin's if she had returned a few minutes later. What would he have done then—sent for her uncle? Captured her in the dark passage outside Suzanne's, then carried her away?

Luckily, her cousin had a rear entrance. By working her way through the maze of odoriferous alleys, Christa was able to safely reach the rickety outside stairs that led to the flat.

Suzanne answered her knock quickly. "Thank *le bon Dieu* you are safe!" she exclaimed. "You saw Lord Radcliffe leaving?"

"*Oui*," Christa confirmed as she removed her voluminous cloak and shook out her dark curls. "And he has left a man outside to watch. I hope it will be a *very* cold night!"

"I do not like your Lord Radcliffe," Suzanne said as they walked toward the combination kitchen/sitting room/dining room. "He seems a determined man, perhaps a dangerous one."

"'He is not *my* Lord Radcliffe, and I do not intend he ever shall be!"

The children's enthusiastic welcome prevented further discussion, and once again it was late in the evening before the two could speak privately. Since coffee was too precious to drink two nights in a row, they sipped hot cider as Christa described her day.

"In the morning I went to visit the friends we thought might write characters for me. Mme. Gerard, the d'Aubossons, the Comtesse du Thonon. *Mon Dieu*, but it was sad to see them in such reduced circumstances! Yet they are bearing up well. In fact, Mme. d'Aubosson sent some sweets for the children."

Christa drew a carefully wrapped parcel from the cloak she had hung earlier and handed it to her cousin. "She owns a sweet shop and made these with her own hands—she, who could not pick up her scarf when it fell to the floor! I think she has pride in her accomplishments—not altogether a bad compensation for what she has lost."

"How kind of her," Suzanne said. "I shall save these until Pierre's name day—it's next week." She looked searchingly at Christa. "You had no other luck?"

Christa gave a wry half smile. "I didn't expect it to be easy! Two of the offices were disgraceful places, best suited to luring young girls from the path of virtue. The others were respectable but gave no hope for a position soon. The gentleman at the last agency was most kind and gave me the addresses of more offices to visit tomorrow, ones he said were safe." She sipped her cider and said, "Were you able to complete your arrangement with Mme. Bouchet?"

Suzanne's face lit up. "Oh yes! It made us both very happy. She will stay another fortnight to teach me more about keeping the accounts. Mme. Bouchet was kind enough to say that my fashion sense was superior to hers."

"Very proper of her."

"What will you do? It will not be safe for you to stay here if Lord Radcliffe maintains a watch." Suzanne shivered slightly. "I think he had called on others before he came here. How did he know whom to visit?"

"He must have remembered the addresses of letters he franked for me. I could admire his lordship's efficiency more if he did not remind me of a cat in pursuit of a mouse." She chuckled. "But more often than not the mouse gets away. I will just have to find a situation quickly."

Christa stood and yawned. "When I have disappeared into one of these great London households, he will never find me."

The afternoon was well advanced when Christa reached Mrs. Haywood's Select Domestic Establishment in Hans Town. When she entered, the prim young woman writing at a desk in the front room looked at her disapprovingly. "Do you have an appointment?" The eyes that raked her implied that Covent Garden was more suited to the likes of *her*.

"No, I fear not. I realize it is very forward of me, but is it possible that Mrs. Haywood might be able to see me this afternoon?" Christa accompanied the remark with her sweetest smile and had the satisfaction of seeing the young woman thaw a bit.

She nibbled on her quill, then stood and said, "I'll see what I can do. You may take a seat."

Christa gratefully accepted her invitation. She had already visited five registries today and been rebuffed at all of them, sometimes without even a semblance of politeness, and always after a lengthy wait. This particular office had an air of almost oppressive gentility, with quietly expensive furnishings and an atmosphere calculated to intimidate the average scullery maid or hall boy. Christa tried to convince herself that Mrs. Haywood would have something for her, but the empty waiting room did not nourish hope.

The young woman came back with a look of mild surprise on her face. "Mrs. Haywood will see you now. Follow me."

Mrs. Haywood had once been housekeeper at the town mansion of a duke, and her black dress and severely pulled back hair bespoke discreet efficiency. She looked up from her desk when Christa entered, openly judging. She said crisply, "You may be seated. Tell me who you are and what kind of position you seek."

Christa inclined her head politely, then sat. "My name is Christine Bohnet, and I seek a position as governess. Here are my letters of reference." Christa waited anxiously while Mrs. Haywood perused them. She had chosen to keep the name "Christine" and coupled it with the surname of the two servants who had fled Paris with them; the Bohnets had been almost like her own family.

Mrs. Haywood handed back the letters and said, "I'm afraid I can do nothing for you."

Frustrated again, Christa raised her chin and said, "May I ask you a question, madam?"

The woman raised a brow but said, "You may."

"What is wrong? Is it that there is no work, or is it me?" Christa said. "I must know."

Mrs. Haywood sighed but decided to give her an honest answer—those clear gray eyes deserved nothing less. "In a sense, it is you. The only situation an émigré is likely to be considered for is teaching French, and many of your compatriots seek those same few places. For other teaching work, you face resentment and prejudice. There is a war on, remember, and France has always been our traditional enemy, admired and despised at one and the same time.

"While you have excellent references, you are unlikely to find a position. You are too young, too pretty, too French, and few families want their daughters to learn the academic subjects you have mastered." Mrs. Haywood's voice was sympathetic as she added, "You would be better advised to seek another kind of employment."

It was the answer Christa had begun to suspect. "Thank you for your candor. Do you have any suggestions of schools I might approach? Surely there are some that would wish a French mistress."

Mrs. Haywood was starting to reply when her young employee entered with an officious footman following closely. The girl gave a scathing glance at the man and said, "This *person* wishes to hand deliver a message to you."

The footman, a bluff fellow whose height and well-formed calves probably doubled his annual salary, said righteously, "Lady Pomfret said I was to deliver this into your own hands and wait for a reply."

Mrs. Haywood broke the seal and quickly scanned the note. Looking up, she said, "Give Lady Pomfret my regrets. At the moment I do not have on my books an abigail suitable to her ladyship's station."

A mad idea struck Christa. Since she must find work as soon as possible and no one would have her as a teacher, why should she not be a lady's maid? The thought was a radical one. Teachers came from the educated classes and commanded some respect; an abigail was at the top of the domestic hierarchy but very much a servant. And yet . . . did not Papa say all work had dignity? She spoke quickly before she could change her mind.

"Mrs. Haywood, I may know someone for her ladyship. May I speak with you privately?"

The proprietress considered, then turned to the footman. "Will you take a glass of ale? I will see what this young person has to say."

A greedy light showed in the footman's eye and he followed the assistant out of the room. Turning to Christa, she said, "You know an abigail who is at liberty? She must be a woman of very high skills—Lady Pomfret is most particular."

"Please, Mrs. Haywood, let *me* have the position." Christa's eyes were pleading.

"Out of the question!" the proprietress said, her deep voice abrupt. "You are obviously a young woman of gentle birth. It is difficult to imagine you teaching, but impossible to imagine you as a servant. My business is built on providing skilled workers. I cannot afford to send out a novice."

"But I can do the work! I can sew and alter dresses and care for milady's jewels. I know how to style hair, and I make very fine cosmetics. I can write letters or read aloud or play the harpsichord to soothe the mistress." The words came out in a rush as she tried to head off the disapproving look on Mrs. Haywood's face.

"A lady's maid is one situation where being French is an advantage—France has always led fashion." Christa stood, almost quivering with determination. "If you will let me work with you for ten minutes, I will *prove* what I can do!"

Intrigued by the proposition, Mrs. Haywood decided to let this unusual young lady have her chance; today was becoming much more amusing than she had expected. She said, "Very well, convince me."

Christa moved behind the proprietress and said in her pretty French accent, "If Madame will permit . . ." and started to remove hairpins. A born mimic, she fell automatically into the deferential firmness common to lady's maids.

Taking her comb from her reticule, she used it to loosen and reshape Mrs. Haywood's dark hair. An elaborate style was not possible without more time and equipment, so Christa pulled the thick hair back in a way that created soft waves around the woman's face, then knotted it lightly at the crown. The long tresses below were pulled into a loop and pinned under the knot.

"Madame's hair is *magnifique*," she murmured as her hands skillfully finished the styling. Christa gave thanks that the day had been warm enough for her to wear a long cashmere shawl rather than her cloak; the garment was a vivid periwinkle blue that would suit Mrs. Haywood's coloring to perfection. She draped it around Mrs. Haywood's shoulders, then gently rubbed the woman's cheeks to give her more color. Pleased with the results, she asked, "If Madame has a mirror?"

Madame did have a hand mirror concealed in a lower drawer of the massive desk. Mrs. Haywood pulled it out, then looked at her image and gasped. The face looking back was not the stern widowed businesswoman that circumstances had created, but the eager young girl she had been, in love with Thomas Haywood and facing a life of infinite possibilities. The soft hairstyle removed fifteen years from her age, and her skin glowed above the rich blue cashmere. She was shaken. The face she showed the world was so formidable that she herself had almost forgotten that young girl.

Mrs. Haywood needed a moment to collect herself before saying, "You are indeed very skilled. You can also mend and wash and starch fine fabrics?" At Christa's nod she said rather dryly, "I do not doubt you know how to supervise the lower staff. Sit down again and I will tell you more about Lady Pomfret."

Christa looked so young and hopeful that Mrs. Haywood regretted the warnings she must give. "You cannot possibly know how different life is belowstairs. The abigail of the mistress has a great deal of status but is the target of resentment because of her privileges and suspicion because of her closeness to the family. The hours are very long, and you will have almost no freedom.

"Moreover, Lady Pomfret is not an easy woman to work for. I believe half the legitimate registry offices in London have provided her with abigails—in the last five years I have sent her two myself. She pays only twenty-five pounds a year, which is ridiculously low for the skill required. And her husband . . . there have been complaints about her husband." Mrs. Haywood hesitated, wondering whether to elaborate, but decided not to. The girl looked intelligent enough to deduce what kind of complaints. "You are positive you wish to undertake this?"

Christa's gaze was steady. "I must."

"Very well, if you are sure. Can you start this evening?" At Christa's nod Mrs. Haywood continued, "My usual commission is a shilling on the pound for the first year's wages, but since it is Lady Pomfret, I will charge only a crown." Her voice was wry as she added, "If you are still there in a year, you can pay me the rest." She wrote the address on a slip of paper, then handed it across the desk.

Christa stood, her eyes shining. "Oh, *thank you*, Mrs. Haywood. I shall never forget your kindness."

"I only hope you will not regret this day's work." The woman stood and extended her hand. "If you are in need of another situation in the future, I hope you will come to me again. Good luck."

Christa refused to be worried by Mrs. Haywood's pessimism as she returned to Suzanne's to collect her things and say good-bye. She was excited at having successfully crossed the first hurdle. She would work hard and give Lady Pomfret no grounds for complaint. Life was good, *n'est-ce pas*?

Chapter 4

Before she left Suzanne's, Christa noticed with amusement that one of Lewis's flunkies still lurked in the shadows across the street; if the earl wanted inconspicuous watchers, he shouldn't dress his servants in silver livery. Luckily her route through the alleys had not been discovered, and she was able to come and go without detection.

For the sake of both speed and safety, Christa used some of her small amount of money for a hackney ride to Lady Pomfret's town house on Bedford Row. It was a handsome three-story building, though nothing so imposing as Radcliffe House in Mayfair. The evening was well advanced when she lifted the heavy brass knocker and rapped sharply.

The footman who answered proved to be the same one who had carried the message to Mrs. Haywood's. Since the primary purpose of footmen was ostentation, tall handsome oafs like this one commanded higher wages than men who were shorter or more intelligent. Christa had not been impressed by him earlier, and further study showed no reason to improve her opinion. With a polite nod she said, "Good evening. I am the new lady's maid. To whom shall I announce myself?"

The footman stared at her blankly for a moment, then a lewd smile spread over his face as he recognized the pretty little Frenchy from the registry office. This one looked much better than the horse-faced Yorkshire woman who had preceded her, and he was anxious to find out if it was true what they said about French women.

Standing aside so she could enter, he said, "That would be Mrs. Higgins, the housekeeper. Follow me, miss."

The footman led her through a series of halls and passages; the house was very deep to compensate for the narrow street frontage. A stair at the back took them down to the main service area. At the bottom, he gestured at a closed door. "That's Mrs. Higgins's parlor. By the way, my name is James."

Giving her a gap-toothed smile, he stood aside to let her pass. Christa was suspicious of his politeness, and with reason: the footman gave her a sharp pinch on the buttock as she passed. Since she thought it wise to establish an aura of untouchability as soon as possible, Christa swung the portmanteau back sharply without even turning her head. She judged it hit just below the kneecap, and from the strength of his muffled oath, it must have connected well. As she knocked on the indicated door, she looked at him coolly and said, "Thank you, James," then entered the comfortably furnished housekeeper's room.

Mrs. Higgins had been working at her account books and was not best pleased to be interrupted. A pinch-mouthed creature who dressed entirely in black, she seemed singularly unimpressed by the new addition to the household. Her mouth tightened even further as she looked Christa up and down, and she did not suggest the girl sit in the extra chair. "You're the chit from the agency? I'll show you your room, then take you to Lady Pomfret's chambers to await her ladyship's retiring. The last abigail left in a hurry and her ladyship's things need a great deal of work, so you needn't be idle while you wait.

"The upper servants eat in the steward's dining room. The second housemaid, Betsy, takes care of the water and coal for her ladyship's chambers. You can order her on matters pertaining to the mistress's comfort, but remember, she has other duties as well. I will introduce you to the laundry maids tomorrow. I have Lady Pomfret's jewel box here for safekeeping. You may take charge of it only if the mistress approves you. Now, come along." Mrs. Higgins rose with a jingle of the key ring that was the badge of the housekeeper.

Christa counted one hundred and ten steps from the basement to the attic as she followed Mrs. Higgins up the narrow service stairs. Her new home was cramped and bare floored, containing only a narrow wooden bed, a two-drawered storage chest, and a washstand with a chipped pitcher and a bowl that didn't match.

Mrs. Higgins barely gave her time to set down her portmanteau before leading her back downstairs. Lady Pomfret's suite took up half the second floor, and consisted of a sitting room, a bedchamber, a dressing room, and several small rooms for her wardrobe. The three main chambers had fireplaces, a comfort not to be found in the attic.

"Use the time to familiarize yourself. Lady Pomfret will expect you to know where everything is kept, even on your first evening. I will see you in the morning. The staff breakfast is at seven o'clock." With a curt nod the housekeeper turned and went out, leaving Christa alone to explore.

After two hours of sorting through gowns, shawls, wigs, silk stockings, slippers, and perfumes, she was reasonably sure where everything was kept and had developed a low opinion of her new employer's taste. In spite of the housekeeper's pessimistic comments, things were in reasonable order. Christa was mending a rent stocking with tiny, nearly invisible stitches when Lady Pomfret returned to her room.

Her ladyship stopped and gave her a baleful look as Christa stood quickly and curtsied. "You must be Bonnet." Her new mistress had a grating voice that was in keeping with her coarse appearance. The woman must have been handsome when she was younger, but the buxom girl had become a stout matron in her forties. Lady Pomfret wore an elaborately powdered wig, a style that was now passé but still seen sometimes on older women.

Christa inclined her head respectfully and said, "*Oui*, my name is Christine Bohnet, your ladyship."

The woman snorted. "Bow*nay*? I'll have no such foreign names around me. You're 'Bonnet' from now on." She examined her new maid pessimistically, a process that Christa was getting heartily sick of. "Unlace me."

Her ladyship lifted her arms so Christa could remove the silk polonaise and skirt. Then Christa unlaced the heavily boned corset, a process that changed her ladyship's silhouette amazingly. "I'll have my green nightgown now."

Fortunately Christa had found the garment in her explorations. "Shall I remove your wig now, madam?" she asked.

"Of course!" Lady Pomfret snapped as she plumped herself down before the dressing table. "Are you going to be another of those imbeciles who don't know their job? It's impossible to get decent servants these days—they're all thieves or sluts or drunkards or all three. Which are you, Bonnet?" she finished, her watery gaze meeting Christa's eyes in the mirror.

"None, your ladyship," Christa said soothingly. "I desire only to learn what pleases you. Forgive me if I do not

always know, but I promise I shall attend to your comfort
as best I can."

Mollified, Lady Pomfret started to relax as Christa deftly
removed the heavy wig and began to brush out her mousy
hair. Its sparseness might explain why Lady Pomfret preferred the older styles.

"The most important thing my abigail must have is discretion. There will be no tales of me leaving this chamber,
or I'll have your head." At Christa's involuntary shiver,
Lady Pomfret's small blue eyes brightened and she asked
with some animation, "Have you ever seen someone guillotined, Bonnet? I hope so. I've always wondered if it is
true the blood spurts over fifteen feet. Fetch my *dormeuse*."

Revolted by the woman's morbid curiosity, Christa went
to fetch the sleeping cap but disclaimed any personal experience of the guillotine. It was not the truth; she had gone
once when a young girl she knew was executed. It had
made her feel ill for days, but she had felt a duty to go, that
her friend should not die with no one there who cared. It
was not a memory Christa would share with Lady Pomfret.

"I'll have my cup of chocolate at eleven o'clock, not a
moment sooner. Mind you don't wake me when you come
in to start the mending."

Waving her hand dismissively, she climbed into the
high-canopied bed. A housemaid had slipped in with a
copper bed-warming pan while Lady Pomfret was having
her heavy white-lead makeup removed; the servants of the
house had learned well the lesson of being unobtrusive.

Christa turned out the lights and banked the fire so it
would burn through the night. Leaving the bedchamber,
she was assailed by the gloomy feeling that it was going to
be very difficult to like Lady Pomfret.

Christa was bone tired by the time she reached her bleak
room. She was lucky to have any kind of private chamber,

but as she looked at her cheerless surroundings by the light of the one candle stub allowed, it was much harder to be enthusiastic about her new adventure than when she had contemplated it at Radcliffe Hall.

Swallowing hard, she whispered fiercely, "I will *not* feel sorry for myself! This is not for always, and I can survive it very well." But when Christa slipped into the lumpy, narrow bed, it was a long time before sleep claimed her.

Mrs. Haywood was interviewing a cook—self-described as *plain, very good*—when her assistant hurried in with a card. "His lordship would like to speak with you."

Glancing at the card, Mrs. Haywood raised an eyebrow at the elegantly engraved words, "Lewis Radleigh, Earl of Radcliffe." Unusual, most unusual.

The cook was happy to step outside while the Quality conducted its business; it confirmed her belief that Mrs. Haywood's Select Domestic Establishment was the best place to improve her own situation.

Mrs. Haywood stood as the tall, fair-haired nobleman entered, noting the remote eyes and tense lips; the man was not here on ordinary business. "This is an honor, Lord Radcliffe. Pray be seated. How may I serve you?"

The earl did not avail himself of the invitation until she was seated. "I am looking for a French girl, a little below medium height, short, curly dark hair, gray eyes, very pretty."

"This is not that sort of agency, your lordship," Mrs. Haywood said dryly. "I believe there are houses near Covent Garden that can better fulfill your desires."

Flushing, he said stiffly, "You misunderstand me. I am looking for a particular young woman who may have come here seeking a teaching situation."

Mrs. Haywood frowned slightly and said, "All our work is done with the utmost discretion. Even had I seen such a young woman, it would be inappropriate for me to discuss her."

"Even if she is wanted by the law for theft?" Lord Radcliffe's voice was wooden.

Mrs. Haywood studied him thoughtfully. She did not know what Mademoiselle Christine Bohnet was about, but she would go long odds the girl was no thief and that this nobleman's interest was one the chit had no desire to encourage. In a hard world, women must stand together.

The proprietress clasped her hands together in front of her on the desk. "Should you wish servants for your household, Lord Radcliffe, I would be happy to be of assistance, but I fear I cannot help you in this."

The earl seemed to swell before her eyes and he said threateningly, "If you are withholding information from me, I am sure you realize I have the power to destroy you and your agency!"

Mrs. Haywood held his eyes, unabashed. "I know your reputation, Lord Radcliffe. You are said to be a man of fairness and good sense. Would you really beggar a widow with three children for no reason at all?"

He seemed to diminish and age right in front of her eyes. "No. No, I would not," he said in a voice scarcely above a whisper.

She felt a trace of pity for him. "Come, my lord, if your mistress has left you after a lovers' quarrel, give her time to recover her senses and she may return on her own."

The earl stood, his eyes hooded and unfathomable. "It is not what you think." Then he turned and left the room, his dark blue redingote swirling wide. Mrs. Haywood watched him, regretful that she might never know the story's ending.

* * *

Lewis Radleigh sat up late that night in his library, lowering the level of a brandy decanter with workmanlike efficiency. He and his secretary had been separately seeking Marie-Christine throughout the metropolis for the last week. The earl had visited all her friends and relatives himself, but none would admit to having seen her. Watchers set at three of the most likely households found no trace of the girl. Either she had visited none of them or she had a gift for inspiring loyalty that sealed the émigrés' lips even in the face of substantial bribes.

Lord Radcliffe knew exactly how dangerous London could be for an innocent young girl, and every passing day increased his fears. He no longer knew where to look; between them, he and his secretary must have visited every registry office in the city. Several people thought Marie-Christine had been there; one office gave what appeared to be a good lead. It was a crushing disappointment when it proved to be the wrong woman, another émigré. Other establishments seemed to be blatant procurers, and the earl could only pray she had not fallen into such hands. By this time, the girl might be in a brothel where he would never find her.

Or she could be dead.

The earl swirled the brandy in his balloon glass, watching the candlelight refract through it. Excellent brandy, doubtless smuggled from France. He took a deep draft, no longer feeling it burn as it went down his throat. Lewis suspected that Mrs. Haywood might have seen her, but the infernal woman had judged rightly—the earl could no more injure her than he could have ruined his maid's family in Berkshire. With Annie, the threat had gotten him the information he needed, but threats hadn't worked with the more worldly Mrs. Haywood.

Lord Radcliffe was unable to blot out pictures of Marie-Christine—her warmth and good nature, the gray eyes so much like those of Charles and Marie-Claire, her lively intelligence. He would see that laughing face, and then, with gut-wrenching clarity, he would imagine her body violated in some back-street stew.

Burying his face in his hands, he sought to obliterate his inner vision. Alone in his great London mansion, the Earl of Radcliffe wept for what he had done.

"Get out, you slut! Don't come back till you've delivered those notes. And mind you wait for answers!"

Christa avoided the hurled silver-backed hairbrush with ease. Dodging thrown objects was one of the more amusing parts of the job; the servant's code did not say that she had to stand still to be hit. Considering Lady Pomfret's aim, there was no great danger. With a sweet smile, she slipped out the back door of the suite into the servants' passage.

In the last three weeks, Christa had found that the long hours were tiring but bearable, as were the Spartan living conditions. The poisonous gossip among the other servants was more unpleasant, and Mrs. Haywood had been correct in her warning—a lady's maid was an object of suspicion and resentment. She was too well dressed, too well paid, too close to the mistress. Nonetheless, that also was tolerable, though she missed normal human companionship.

Christa had survived by burying her memories of her past. Except for occasional moments late at night, she thought of herself as Christine Bohnet, a young girl of peasant stock, trained to serve. It was now second nature for her to guard her tongue, avoiding any reference to her exalted birth. She was not sure how the household would react to the news that she was an aristocrat fallen on hard times. Either she would be dismissed as being too grand for her position, or, more likely, Lady Pomfret would take a gloating satisfaction in humiliating a woman of superior birth. Either alternative was repellent. Christa found that her pride would not accept anyone pitying her loss of consequence—far better to appear born to the servant class.

She no longer felt herself to be in danger from Lord Radcliffe—if he had been able to trace her, it would have happened already. Now that Christa was hidden in this household, he would never find her unless they walked into each other on the street. Even then, the earl might not truly see her—she would be dismissed as just another mob-capped servant.

The greatest burden was lack of freedom to come and go. Were it not for her ladyship's messages to her two lovers, Christa would go mad with confinement. The lovers were the reason Lady Pomfret placed such emphasis on discretion—it was more important to keep them from learning about each other than to keep her affairs from her husband.

It was a source of astonishment that Lady Pomfret had two lovers; truly, some men had no discrimination! Both men made casual advances to Christa when she delivered notes but accepted her rebuffs easily.

Before setting out, Christa went to her attic room for a shawl against the brisk April air. When she had a free moment during the day, she would often open the window and lean out, enjoying the sense of space and freedom and the fascinating jumble of rooftops. Today, however, she stopped on the threshold, surprised at the sight of a very small girl scrubbing the floor.

Because Christa ate with the upper servants, she was unfamiliar with most of the staff. She knew someone cleaned her room but had never seen who. "Good day, young lady," she said cheerfully. "I haven't the pleasure of your name."

The plain little face that turned to her was terrified. "Oh,

I'm dreadful sorry, miss! I'll get out." The child grabbed her bucket and mop and tried to dart toward the door.

Christa put out one hand to stop her. "You need not run. My name is Christa. What is yours?"

The huge eyes dominated the peaked face; she looked to be no more than nine or ten. She stammered, "Please, you won't tell Mrs. Higgins, will you? I'm not supposed to talk to anyone, nor be seen, neither."

Concerned for the child's obvious fear, Christa knelt and put her arms around the girl's thin shoulders. "*Ma pauvre*, do not worry! I shall not hurt you, nor report you to Mrs. Higgins." To her shock, the child burst into tears, burying herself in Christa's arms and shaking violently.

It was several minutes before the storm subsided. By then they were seated side by side on the bed and Christa had found a handkerchief for her guest. "Now, tell me your name, and why you were crying."

The child said, "I'm dreadful sorry, miss. It's just that you're the first person to say a kind word to me since I came here." Her face started to pucker, then with a valiant sniff she continued, "My name is Miranda."

"What a splendid name!" Christa said admiringly.

Miranda nodded vigorously. "Isn't it lovely? Mrs. Willason at the foundling home chose ever such lovely names—there was Prospero and Portia and Romeo and . . . lots of others."

Christa smiled with amusement; obviously Mrs. Willason enjoyed Shakespeare. "But Miranda is one of the best."

"Oh, it is. Since I'm only the scullery maid, I get to keep my own name, too." At Christa's look of puzzlement, she explained, "Didn't you know that in this house most of the servants are named for their position? The head housemaid is always Lily, the first footman is William, the second footman is James. Like that."

"You mean, if one is promoted, one gets a new name?" Christa asked in fascination.

Another nod. "Yes. The scullery maid has no name 'cause I'm the least important. And upper servants like you and the butler and the housekeeper and Sir Horace's valet can use your own names. That's why you get to be called Miss Bonnet—because you're one of the most important people in the house."

Christa digested this, then asked, "What do you do?"

"Wash things, mostly. I get up at four in the morning to do the flagstone floor in the kitchen, then the back stairs, and I black lead the grates and clean the rooms of the upper servants."

Christa frowned slightly, noticed how Miranda's hands and arms were chapped raw from too much scrubbing in cold places. "It sounds like very hard work."

"Oh, it is, miss," the child sighed. "Sometimes when my hands are bleeding on the floor, I think I'll never get it clean."

Christa repressed a shudder. It was abominable! And yet, this child had clothes and food and a roof. There must be thousands like her on the streets of London, scavenging to survive.

"I must run some errands for her ladyship, Miranda. But perhaps we can visit another time?"

"That would be ever so nice, miss," the child said wistfully.

"I would take it as a great favor if you would call me Christa." She smiled.

Miranda bobbed a curtsy and said shyly, "I would like that, Christa. Very much."

Chapter 5

Alex straightened his cravat a trifle nervously before opening Vice Admiral Hutchinson's heavy door. As a bluff captain more than a dozen years earlier, Hutchinson had been one of the board members who had examined Alex for promotion from midshipman to lieutenant, and he had left an impression of bullheaded ferocity. As one of the three professional sea lords of the Admiralty, Hutchinson was now one of the most influential men in the navy, and it was a shock when the admiral greeted him with an affable "Come in, my boy. Would you like a bit of sherry while I examine your dispatches?"

Alex loathed sherry but politely accepted a glass along with a comfortable wing chair in a corner of the large office. After Peter Harrington had certified him for travel, the viscount had been sent back to England on the first available ship. As was customary in such cases, he had also been entrusted with a case of dispatches for the Admiralty. Alex posted up to London as soon as he arrived in Portsmouth and had arrived before the Admiralty offices closed for the day.

After skimming through the official papers, Admiral Hutchinson then questioned Alex on his opinions of how the war was progressing in the Mediterranean. He occasionally made notes himself, apparently preferring not to have a secretary present. After nearly two hours had passed, the admiral leaned back in his own chair and said, "For someone who barely made lieutenant, you've acquitted yourself very well."

Alex colored a little. "When action is required, I have no problem, but I've always done badly with oral exams, Admiral. My brain seems to disconnect from my mouth. Even if I know the answer, I can't find the words for it."

"I noticed," the admiral said dryly. "You also reverse numbers in your calculations. Fortunately for you, I once had a captain with the same problem. He was a brilliant officer in spite of that, and I learned to trust his ability. You had a good enough record in action that the other board members were persuaded to give you the benefit of the doubt."

Alex blinked in surprise; Captain "Cannonball" Hutchinson had been legendary for his toughness. It was remarkable to think he had been Alex's advocate. "Then I must thank you for my naval career. If I had had to rely on examinations, I would still be a midshipman."

The admiral waved his hand deprecatingly. "Part of an officer's job is to recognize talent, and you've amply repaid my faith. Anyone who can capture a hundred-gun French blockade runner with a frigate the size of the *Antagonist* is a credit to the navy. How are you feeling?"

"Very well, sir."

The admiral tapped the pile of papers on the table next to him. "According to your medical report, that's not quite true."

Alex shifted in his chair, uneasy at having attention focused on his injury. Admiral Hutchinson noticed his movement and said, "I have a legitimate interest. The navy is going to need all of her experienced captains in the years ahead. I think you're ready for a ship of the line."

Alex straightened up, his attention engaged, but he refrained from comment. One of the first things one learned in the navy was not to volunteer conversation.

Pulling a pipe and tobacco pouch from a drawer in the side table, the admiral said, "What are your plans? You'll be off active duty until next year, but what then?"

Alex paused, uncomfortable with having to make even a tentative commitment. "Sir, I really don't know. My father has died, and I have a good deal of personal business to take care of here in England."

He halted as a vision of the Harringtons' household flashed before his inner eye. He had found himself envying the warmth and companionship his friend had found. The viscount considered remaining silent but decided to make a clean breast of it. "I may not want to return to the navy. There is a part of me that finds the idea of a settled life on land appealing. The navy is a world of its own, compelling, but also very strange."

The admiral gave a short bark of laughter. "I always found I missed the land when I was at sea, and now that I'm permanently docked, I miss the sea. I realize it's early days for you to be making a decision, but I wanted to talk before you disappeared into civilian life. If you do return to active command, we should be able to find you a ship very quickly."

The admiral paused and drew on his pipe, attempting to improve its feeble glow. "My personal belief is that we may be at war with the French for a long time to come. This citizens' army of theirs is like nothing else in Europe. They're fighting for something they believe in, not as mercenaries, and there is great power in that. Look at what the American colonies did."

Hutchinson inhaled a deep lungful of smoke, then let it out with satisfaction. "That's two things the Americans do well—fight in the woods and grow tobacco. But to return to the subject at hand. If I'm right, we will need all our resources."

He looked at Alex's carefully neutral expression. "I think it unlikely that you will wish to return to sea since you are a peer and have numerous responsibilities, and you need the prize money less than most. But if you stay ashore, there are times the Admiralty might want to call on you for some advice—you are one of the best tacticians I've ever seen. Can we do that?"

Alex stammered, "Yes, sir. Of course, sir!" This was one of the most surprising interviews of his life—it was distinctly unnerving to hear that the august Lords of the Admiralty might value his opinion.

Admiral Hutchinson stood and extended his hand in farewell. "You will want some time to get your land legs, but please keep in touch with me. I can always be reached through this office."

Alex was in a daze as he walked out of the Admiralty into the mild May evening. The great ships of the line were Britain's finest fighting vessels, carrying twice the guns of a frigate like the *Antagonist*, and to command one was the dream of every young naval officer. Hutchinson's offer was a tremendous compliment, and the prospect appealed in spite of Alex's nascent yen for a settled life. He mentally kicked himself back to reality; there was no point in thinking much about it since he would get a ship of the line only if he didn't expire as Peter had so gloomily suggested. At the moment, dinner and a place to sleep were of much greater relevance.

Unable to face his family quite yet, Alex bespoke a bed at a snug inn called The Anchor that was a nearby favorite of naval officers. Over a leisurely meal he considered his tasks for the next day. First, visit the family lawyers and announce that he was finally taking the helm of the Kingsley interests. Then, a visit to Kingsley House to see about opening it again. Several of the servants had been kept on after his mother died. The longtime family butler, Morrison, should be able to get the place staffed properly without much delay.

Then would come the hard part: he must go to Aunt Agatha's to find Annabelle. Jonathan was at Eton, so he'd go there later. Alex flinched at the thought of the scorn he would see in their faces, their justified anger at the way he had run away from his responsibilities.

But there was no help for it. Without being able to express the thought in words, Alex knew there was a flaw in his maturing that could only be healed in service to his family.

When he retired, he had trouble falling asleep in a bed that wasn't moving.

Like many greatly feared confrontations, Alex's homecoming turned out to be far easier than expected. He had steeled himself before raising the heavy brass knocker at his Aunt Agatha's Portman Square house. When the footman admitted him, there was scarcely time to hand over his hat and request the presence of Miss Annabelle before he heard an excited voice from the top of the stairs leading into the wide vestibule.

Alex looked up to see his sister calling to a maid behind her, "Quickly! Find Jonathan and tell him Alex is home!"

Then she was flying down the stairs—her light slippers moving so quickly he feared for her safety—and into his arms, hugging him fiercely. Alex looked into the huge blue eyes swimming with tears and realized with awed humility that she didn't hate him at all—by some miracle and for reasons he couldn't fathom, she loved him.

Annabelle blinked back her tears and said shyly, "I'm sorry to be such a watering pot, Alex. But . . . but will you be staying this time? For at least a while?"

He felt a rush of tenderness as he gazed into her lovely face, as beautiful as their mother's but with a sweetness that angry woman had never known. "Yes, Belle," Alex said huskily. "This time I'll stay as long as you want me."

Larger feet thundered down the marble steps and he looked up to see his younger brother skid uncertainly to a halt an arm's length away. Alex would hardly have recognized Jonathan; at their last meeting, three years before, he had still been a boy. Now he was a gangling fifteen, as blond as both his siblings and bidding fair to be as tall as his older brother. Alex impulsively reached out his hand, and suddenly the three were embracing in one confused tangle of arms and legs and blond hair, laughing and crying together.

For the first time, and against all odds, the three children of Lady Serena Kingsley were a family.

Half an hour later they were sharing tea and cakes in the small drawing room, where Aunt Agatha had shown the rare good sense to leave them alone. Annabelle automatically fell into the hostess role, pouring tea and offering cakes to her brothers.

Alex saw that she'd grown into a lovely young woman with the height of the Kingsleys and a grace all her own, but there was a shyness and uncertainty in her demeanor that must be the result of too many scoldings and criticisms. His sister still wore mourning for her mother, and he could not decide if her slightly haggard look came from the black dress or from some other source.

"Are you ready to be presented this fall, Belle, during the Little Season? The mourning period for Lady Serena will be over within the next couple of weeks," Alex said.

His sister wrinkled her nose a bit and handed him his tea. "I suppose I shall have to be. After all, I'm twenty and almost on the shelf. Do you have a naval friend who will marry me sight unseen so I can avoid going to the marriage mart?"

He chuckled. "Really, Annabelle, you can do much better than a salty old sea dog! I expect there will be dozens of swains begging my permission to pay their addresses. There can't be many prettier girls in London."

Annabelle shot him a startled look. "It's kind of you to say so, Alex, though I know that isn't true." The last sentence fell away under her breath, almost inaudible.

Alex wondered why she couldn't believe the evidence of her mirror, but as he studied her more closely, he realized that while the delicate face, slim body, and long golden hair were beautiful, the overall effect did her less than justice. "We shall need to get you a whole new wardrobe. The styles have changed considerably since you first went into mourning after Father's death."

"Aunt Agatha didn't think it right to waste money on mourning clothes when no one would see them." His sister sighed. "Wilkens says fashionable gowns would be wasted on me. She says I have no sense of style, not like Mother at all."

Alex raised a brow questioningly. "Have you kept Wilkens on? I know she was Lady Serena's dresser for over thirty years and you must be fond of her, but wouldn't you prefer a younger abigail, someone more your age?"

She faltered. "I'm not at all fond of her, actually, but Aunt Agatha said I had a duty to keep her on."

Alex frowned. Wilkens probably bullied Annabelle unmercifully. She was a bad-tempered old biddy, completely devoted to Lady Serena but loathing the rest of the human race, particularly her mistress's children since they might be expected to hold some share of their mother's affection. The dresser's jealousy was unwarranted; Alex could remember no instance of motherly regard from Lady Serena.

Their father's sister, Aunt Agatha, had a certain fair-mindedness but was elderly and self-absorbed. She would have made no attempt to enter into the feelings of a shy young girl. The sooner Alex got Belle away from both of them, the better.

"In that case, we shall pension her off," he said cheerfully. "She can go to her well-earned reward in whatever that place was that she used to mutter about."

Annabelle giggled. "You mean Scunthorpe?"

"Exactly. It is a good name for muttering. I hope the village can survive Wilkens's return. If she misses her old life, she can harass whatever relatives she has left. Meanwhile, you shall have a new maid."

"Shall I have to choose her myself?" Annabelle looked alarmed.

Alex was beginning to suspect that almost everything alarmed his sister. He gave an inward sigh but smiled reassuringly. "I'll help you. We will advertise for suitable candidates, and you may choose the one you like best—that's all there is to it."

Annabelle still looked intimidated at the thought of exercising such control over her own destiny, so Alex turned his attention to Jonathan, who was putting away cakes with the dispatch and vigor that only a growing boy possessed.

Jonathan colored slightly under his brother's regard and hastily swallowed the rest of his cream cake. "You're probably wondering why I'm not at Eton."

"The question had occurred to me," Alex admitted.

"I was expelled for the rest of the term." At Alex's questioning look, Jonathan said with a mixture of pride and embarrassment, "I put a cow in the chapel bell tower. Some of my friends said it couldn't be done, so I said it could."

With sudden foreboding, Alex knew what was coming next. "Don't tell me," he groaned. "You said it was possible because your brother had done it."

"Of course!" Jonathan said proudly. "I couldn't have them making a liar of you, could I?"

Jonathan seemed so proud of his older brother that Alex felt a shade uneasy, fearing that he was not cut out to be a proper hero. Pushing aside the thought, he said. "I presume you discovered the problem with putting a cow in a tower?"

Jonathan tried to look ashamed of himself, but without success. "The cow will walk *up* steps, but it won't walk down. When they sent me home, the cow was still up there."

Alex started chuckling. "I hope for the cow's sake that someone remembers the solution Peter Harrington came up with."

"What was that?" Jonathan asked curiously.

"A cow won't go headfirst down a stair, and who could blame her? But she can be persuaded to *back* down, if you have someone stationed at each hoof to move it backward." Alex suddenly laughed outright. "It's a slow business and difficult to get volunteers for the back feet."

In a moment they were all whooping with laughter at the thought. In his innocence, Alex decided that being head of a family might not be so difficult after all.

* * *

It was time to work on the wigs again. In the eight weeks since Christa had started her career as an abigail she had cleaned, trimmed, and recurled every one of the heads in her charge. Her ladyship apparently did not object to lice and other fauna infesting her hairpieces, but Christa did.

Lady Pomfret was out much of the time, leaving her maid in peace to mend and alter and refurbish. It was a rather lonely life but not unpleasant. There was satisfaction in a job well done, and Christa would sit in milady's boudoir and read books from the library when her other tasks were done. On a day like today, with the May sunshine flooding in the window, she would succumb to her natural exuberance and sing happily away in French.

Carefully removing the clay rollers from the formal headdress in front of her, Christa patted the plump ringlets into place around the top of the head, then looped a long swath of hair at the nape into a cadogan. Sadly, Lady Pomfret wanted her to attach a coquelicot band, three ostrich plumes, and a bunch of pink roses with green foliage. The thought of them bobbing above her ladyship's beefy countenance did not please; Christa was beginning to understand why a lady's maid would leave a position because her mistress did not reflect creditably on her.

She broke off her song when the front door of the suite opened to reveal Lady Pomfret's husband, Sir Horace. Christa had never seen Sir Horace at close quarters before. The baronet was as beefy as his wife, and as he walked toward her, she heard creaking sounds reminiscent of a ship at sea. It must be a corset. Suppressing a smile, she stood and bobbed a curtsy.

"Good morning, sir. Lady Pomfret is abroad early today. Do you wish to leave a message?"

Sir Horace stared at the abigail, unconscious of the fact that the tip of his tongue had slid out and licked his lower lip. By George, but she was a tasty morsel! The baronet

kept a woman near Covent Garden but liked to have at least
one or two of the maids primed and ready as well. He'd
been mowing the third housemaid for several months, but
she wasn't half so toothsome as this one.

"No need. You must be the new mam'zelle, Bonnet."

Christa nodded. "*Oui*, milord. I am Christine Bohnet."
She pronounced her surname in the French fashion but
without hope; none of the English appeared willing to
tackle foreign sounds.

"You're a pretty little puss," Sir Horace said, moving
around the narrow table where Christa worked on the wigs.
"Sometimes I hear you singing when I'm in the hall."

"I am sorry, sir, I do not always notice that I am singing.
I shall try to be quieter."

"No need to apologize," he said with oppressive bon-
homie. "It does my heart good to hear you sing."

Christa looked at him with distaste. The baronet was
within an arm's length of her, and proximity did not improve his appearance. A number of teeth were missing and
he had smallpox scars. That was not his fault, of course, but
the scars did not improve a countenance that was low
browed and bulbous nosed to begin with.

She did not start to become irritated until the man
reached out and pulled off her mobcap. Christa was proud
of that cap; she thought it gave her the look of a proper
servant. Without it, her simple dresses made her look too
elegant for a maid.

The baronet tweaked a dark curl. "Pretty hair you
have, too."

Christa stood and deftly put the width of the table between them. Really, men were so tiresome! She had found
a book downstairs in the library called *Directions to Servants*,
an amusing satire derived from life belowstairs. The author,
Jonathan Swift, said that the lord of the household often

fancied his wife's maid, even if she were not half so handsome as his own lady. All of Lady Pomfret's men appeared anxious to prove the writer correct; having discouraged the two lovers, apparently Christa would now have to do the same with the husband. "Milord is very kind. If milord does not require anything, I must go out now to purchase some ribbons for Lady Pomfret."

Christa hoped that mention of his wife might deter him, but the baronet pasted on what was intended as a charming smile and moved after her, trapping her between a wing chair and a small table. He was surprisingly quick for such a bulky man; he must have pursued a good few maids in his time.

"No need to run away," he said coaxingly. "It is early yet. Plenty of time for us to have some fun, eh?" The Chinese-blue dress Christa wore had an open neckline and Sir Horace reached out and grasped the bare skin of her neck and shoulder. His damp hand started squeezing and petting, then slid down to her left breast. "Nice," he said with approval. "Is the rest of you just as nice?"

The baronet put his other hand on Christa's shoulder to pull her to him, then tried to force her chin up. She turned her head sharply and the wet kiss landed on her cheek. Using her most aristocratic voice, Christa said sharply, "Sir Horace, let go of me *at once!*"

Her air of authority startled the baronet so much that he released her, but increasing excitement led him to believe that she was just holding off until the business arrangements were settled. "Don't worry, my pretty. I'll make it worth your while."

As Christa tried to slip away, Sir Horace followed until she was backed into a corner of the room. "Swift said the final favor was worth a hundred pounds. I've never paid a servant half so much, but you look to be worth it."

Christa was hard pressed not to burst into laughter at the

farcical scene; she knew now whose book she had found in the library. Didn't the foolish man recognize satire when he read it? Apparently the baronet studied the book to learn his courting techniques!

Her amusement ceased abruptly when Sir Horace grabbed her with one arm and slid his other hand inside the bodice of her dress. At the touch of his clammy hand, Christa abandoned all hope of an easy escape and kicked him on the shin. She would have hit him with her fists, but one arm was held in his grip and the other pinned against the wall. Sir Horace's breath stank of brandy and rotting teeth as he tried to kiss her again. She bit his chin and attempted to wriggle out of his grasp.

Christa had almost pulled free when the baronet lunged and wrapped his arms around her waist, his weight dragging her to the floor. She was knocked breathless, his heavy body pinning her to the carpet. Sir Horace seemed to take her temporary quiescence as consent. He gasped hoarsely, "I'll give you a settlement! You'll have a house till I tire of you, and twenty pounds a year for life."

She twisted frantically but was unable to get free. For the first time Christa realized that this disgusting man might actually rape her. *No*—a thousand times no! She was a d'Estelle and would never let this barbarian defeat her. As Sir Horace lifted his body to reach up her skirt, she jerked her knee up, hitting him hard where a man is most vulnerable.

With a howl of rage and pain, the baronet rolled partially off her as he convulsed around his injury. Christa was pulling herself free of the heavy body when the main door swung open to reveal Lady Pomfret with the footman, James, holding the door open for her.

At the sight of the tableau, her ladyship's beefy face turned a remarkable shade of purple and her hefty body

seemed to swell like a pouter pigeon's. With the awful rage
of a woman wronged, Lady Pomfret thundered, "I knew
you were a slut, Bonnet, as soon as I saw your rouged face
and sly smile, but even a tolerant woman like me is
shocked that you'd wave your muff at my husband in my
own bedchamber!"

Christa scrambled to her feet, so outraged she had
trouble finding the correct English words. "Do you think I
wanted that . . . that *pig*! that *beast* . . . to lay his loathsome
hands on me?"

From his position on the floor, Sir Horace moaned, "The
doxy led me on. Wanted me to set her up with her own
house."

Lady Pomfret's outrage reached awe-inspiring new
heights. She scarcely cared how many trollops her husband
lay with, but deeply resented his spending money on them,
money that could have gone into her own jewel case.
"Why, you little hussy! After all my generosity to you . . .
the purple silk gown, the ribbons and plumes I gave you!
Now you want to steal the bread from my mouth!"

Her temper well and truly lost, Christa spat back, "It
would be better for you if I did! Then perhaps you would
not be shaped like a breeding cow and your husband and
lovers would keep their hands off me! And I would not be
caught in my *coffin* in your castoff clothes . . . I have never
seen a woman with worse taste!"

At these insults Lady Pomfret came perilously close to
expiring of apoplexy. She howled, "Why, you little . . . you
little . . ." Insults failed her; waving her arm at the gawping
James, she shrieked, "Throw her out! Throw her out of the
house this minute!"

"My pleasure, your ladyship," he said with wicked anticipation. The Frenchy had hit him in the knee when he
was just being friendly and treated him like dirt ever since.

Revenge would be sweet. Grabbing Christa's upper arm with cruel tightness, James pulled her through the door into the passage and down the stairs.

Lady Pomfret watched the footman drag her down the steps with satisfaction. She had known the wench was too cooperative and good-natured to be true. Impossible to get good servants, utterly impossible! Then she scowled and returned to her bedchamber to deal with her husband.

James twisted Christa's arm so that she could not maintain her balance. "For heaven's sake, James, let go of me," she said with exasperation. "I will get my things from the attic and leave most gladly."

The footman stopped in front of the massive front door and smiled unpleasantly. "You heard what Lady Pomfret said—you're to go 'this minute.' There's time for only one last thing."

Tightening his grip on her arm, James grabbed Christa's hair with his other hand and pulled her head back, forcing a vicious kiss on her. There was nothing of passion in it, only the desire to humiliate the uppity wench. Releasing her hair, the footman grabbed Christa's buttock and squeezed it with insulting deliberation while he pulled her body against his. "Thought you were too good for the likes of me, did you?"

Christa had not blamed James for removing her from Lady Pomfret's presence since it was his job. But she was no more willing to be mauled by the man than the master. She butted her head up into his jaw and heard the distinct sound of breaking teeth.

"You are as bad as your employers," she gasped. "If a household is rotten at the top, there will be rot clear through!"

Bellowing with the pain of his cracked jaw, James dragged open the heavy front door. As Christa darted outside, he placed his hand between her shoulder blades and, with vicious strength, shoved her down the high stone stairs.

Chapter 6

A lex had decided to dismiss his carriage; the pleasant
May morning was best enjoyed on foot. He had been
in London for only a week and still reveled in the fact that
he could walk more than a hundred paces in any direction.
So far he hadn't missed the navy at all, though he had not
yet become accustomed to being "Lord Kingsley" rather
than "Captain Kingsley."

He was admiring the houses in Portman Square when he
heard a woman cry out, looking up just in time to avoid
being bowled over by a falling female. Shifting his weight
with the quickness of a man who has climbed a ship's rigging in a hurricane, Alex was able to catch her in his arms
while maintaining his own balance.

Christa was not given to strong hysterics but the events
of the last quarter-hour had swept her up in a turmoil of
anger and fear. She had been mauled by two men and had
just escaped a possibly lethal fall. When her tear-filled
eyes registered that a tall blond man had saved her, reason
and memory disappeared in a flood of chaotic emotion.
She cried "*Charles*!" and wrapped her arms around the
strong male body that held her as she succumbed to shud-
dering sobs.

Alex blinked in confusion. As a seaman he had always

been known for his quick grasp of a situation, but having a delightfully soft female in his arms played havoc with his judgment. She had called him "Charles" with a wild, questioning note in her voice, then buried her head against his waistcoat. The girl's sobs started to abate, but a torrent of French words poured from her.

Alex found himself envying the absent Charles who should have been holding this delicious armful. He listened for a few moments, then said, "Sorry, but I'm not Charles. You'll have to slow down—I understand some French, but not at this speed."

She froze in his arms, then raised her head to look at him. He gave a gasp of pure shock. Later—much, much later—Alex would realize that she wasn't really beautiful, but now the impact of the enchanting face hit him like a nine-pound cannonball. Wondrous gray eyes had the clarity of smoky quartz, with dark flecks that flashed silver when her gaze shifted. The longest, blackest lashes he had ever seen set off a flawless complexion and an irresistible pixie face that seemed to be laughing even through her tears.

When she abruptly released him and stepped back, Alex calculated that the top of her head would just fit under his chin. Her agitation vanished and she said with quiet dignity, "Forgive me, *monsieur*. Of course, you are not he. Charles is dead. I did not mean to cast my distress on you. Thank you for your most timely intervention."

Alex thought the girl had an indefinable air of quality to her, and a quiet elegance of dress that marked her as a Frenchwoman even had he not heard her speech. With a start, he realized that she was inspecting him as carefully as he was studying her. Did they raise bolder women on the other side of the Channel? He revised his thought; her gaze was not so much bold as disarmingly frank. A smile lifted one side of his mouth. "Do I pass inspection?"

Christa suppressed a familiar stab of grief as she looked at her rescuer. Of course he was not her brother. Now that her eyes were not blurred by tears, she could see that the blond hair had a more golden cast and an irreverent curl, could hear that the voice was deeper and slower. His dress proclaimed him a gentleman, and he was taller even than Charles had been, with a relaxed, loose-limbed figure. If his long, tanned face was not classically handsome, the laugh lines around the corners of the clear amber-brown eyes made it enormously appealing.

She smiled wryly. "*Oui, monsieur*. I believe you will not attack me, which is my principal requirement of the moment."

"If you are wishing to be attacked, I should be happy to oblige, miss," Alex said helpfully.

Had he not been so disarmingly open, the remark would have sent her fleeing down the street. But it was impossible to feel threatened by this stranger. He seemed the sort who always found humor around him, and she had found that the ability to laugh was a civilizing influence. In her experience, the most unpleasant people were those who took themselves too seriously. So Christa smiled and said, "No, I have been attacked quite enough today. Do I pass *your* inspection?"

"I see no obvious reason why you should be thrown headfirst down those steps," he said seriously. "I realize it's not my business, but might I inquire as to the reason why?"

Christa bit her lip as she remembered the difficulties of her position. "I am—or rather, I *was*—abigail to Lady Pomfret here." She waved her hand up at the blank-windowed house. "Her repellent husband decided that my duties included serving him in a manner I much disagreed with. Her ladyship came on us when I was in the process of rather forcibly extricating myself from Sir Horace. She is a woman of limited understanding, and we"—she paused dramatically—"had words."

Wryly she continued, "As I'm sure you appreciate, arguments between two people of unequal station may not be resolved on merit." She gave a purely Gallic shrug. "And so you see me."

"You are certainly right about arguments between those of unequal station," Alex said feelingly. "I've spent fifteen years in the navy, and the desire to be on the higher side of the power equation is a great incentive to promotion."

Christa looked at him with interest but decided she must pass up that interesting potential conversation for the harsh realities. "*Monsieur*, do you know if there is a magistrate nearby? Perhaps one who can help me recover my possessions from the house? All that I own in the world is still in there."

"You mean they literally threw you out without even letting you get your things? Outrageous!" A wicked gleam came into Alex's eyes. "I assume that time is of the essence. Your possessions may be rifled while you are attempting to get the law to help you. Shall I see if I can persuade them to let you in long enough to collect your clothes?"

The girl's quickly suppressed flash of anxiety gave Alex a sudden insight into what it was to be alone and at the mercy of hostile employers. In the navy, even the humblest sailor had some rights, but an Englishman's home was his castle, and great crimes might occur behind these blandly respectable facades. "I will go with you," he offered.

Relieved, Christa gave a decisive nod. Her instincts said she could trust this man, and he was right that the sooner she reclaimed her possessions, the better. "Lead on, *monsieur*!"

They walked up the steps together and he banged the

heavy knocker. While they waited for the door to open, he asked, "By the way, what is your name?"

She bobbed a quick curtsy. "Christine Bohnet, at your service. I am called Christa by my friends." She was pleased that he pronounced her name correctly when he repeated it; he was the first person in two months to make the effort. At that moment, the door swung open to reveal James: a very angry James, still on duty in spite of a rapidly swelling jaw and a smudge of blood at the corner of his mouth.

Seeing her, he gave a thick-tongued growl, "Why, you little—"

The footman was starting to reach for Christa when her rescuer's voice cut at him like a whiplash. "Permit me to introduce myself. I am Captain Lord Alexander Kingsley, Viscount Kingsley, and a magistrate of the county of Suffolk. We are here to collect Mademoiselle Bohnet's possessions."

James stopped and blinked stupidly at the man he had overlooked. The little trollop had found a protector with amazing speed. His brain, never very quick, ground to a halt as he tried to decide whether to let them in. The law was the law . . .

"One side, my man." Alex's voice had the ring of authority that came of commanding hundreds of roughneck sailors, most of whom would rather not be in the Royal Navy. He brushed past James, with a gleeful Christa skipping along next to him. An officer and a viscount! *Le bon Dieu* had provided for her safety very well.

"This way, my lord." She led him to the back of the house and up the servants' stairs. Alex was amazed at how tight the passage was; he had sneaked up the back stairs of the Kingsley houses when he was a boy but had been considerably smaller then. As they climbed, Christa asked over her shoulder, "Are you really a magistrate?"

"Not exactly, but my father was. Like most men of property. I expect I can become a magistrate if I want to. Besides, I've been administering the king's justice at sea for years."

By the time they reached the attics, Alex was puffing and his left side ached sharply, though Christa showed no signs of strain. The room she led him to reminded him of the minuscule cabin of a junior officer on a frigate. His eyes were still adjusting to the increased light of the room when he saw Christa kneel at the side of a small child who had been cleaning the floor. Putting her arms around the little girl, she said, "I am so glad you are here, Miranda, or I could not have said good-bye."

The child said falteringly, "Good-bye? You are leaving?"

Ignoring Alex's presence, Christa hugged the thin little body. "I have no choice, *ma pauvre*. Lady Pomfret has dismissed me, and I must pack and leave immediately."

There was such a look of stark tragedy on Miranda's little face that Alex shifted uncomfortably. No one should be that vulnerable. He spoke for the first time. "Bring her along, Christa. My sister needs an abigail and I have a whole house to staff. I can certainly find a position for Miranda, and if my sister approves, for you as well."

The two faces turned to him with an identical look of hope. Christa sprang to her feet and asked the child, "Do you wish to come with me?"

"Oh, *yes*, Christa!" There was a look of disbelieving excitement on the child's face.

Christa patted her on the back. "Go quickly and get your things."

Miranda whizzed out of the room and Christa shot a grateful look at Alex as she pulled a portmanteau from beneath the bed and started efficiently packing. "You are very generous, Lord Kingsley. Even if your sister does not engage me, I think Miranda will be better off in a house run by you. The Pomfret residence is . . . not a happy place."

He had no trouble believing her statement. Changing the subject, Alex asked, "Were you responsible for the damage to the footman downstairs?"

She colored guiltily. "Indeed, my lord, I am not usually a troublemaker. But the footman sought to take up where his master had left off, and I was quite out of patience by then."

"An understatement. Your skill at repelling unwanted boarders is impressive—remind me not to attack you."

Christa looked at him a bit uncertainly but decided he was joking. She closed her portmanteau with a snap just as Miranda scurried up, her total worldly goods contained in a wrapped shawl. Leaving Lady Pomfret's purple silk gown and plumes for whoever wished to take them, Christa led the way down the narrow stairs for the last time.

When they reached the street, Alex said, "I'll call a hackney. It's some distance to my house in St. James's Square."

Christa said diffidently, "If you don't mind, my lord, Miranda and I can walk if you give me the direction. It is such a lovely day, and she scarcely ever gets outside." Looking down, she asked, "Would you like that, Miranda?"

"Oh, yes!" Confined first to an orphanage and then to the Pomfrets', Miranda found the city a source of teeming delights.

"You're right—it is far too pleasant a day to be in a stuffy carriage," Alex agreed as he reached for her portmanteau. Christa resisted but he brushed her objections aside. "Take Miranda's bundle. My time is my own, and if you've no objection, I'll join you."

Christa raised an eyebrow and murmured something in French as they started to head south. "Sorry, I didn't hear that," Alex said. He expected that it was not intended for his ears, but she obligingly translated.

"I said that I would have gotten myself thrown out sooner had I known how fortunate I would be in my rescuer."

Alex laughed aloud. She was the sauciest creature! He had always liked females of the lower classes because they were much more natural than their social superiors, but this chit was in a category all her own as she recovered from her traumatic experience with amazing speed. "I begin to understand why you got into trouble with the Pomfrets. Not many households would be prepared for such frankness."

"My wretched tongue!" she said repentantly. She took Miranda's hand as they stopped at a busy street corner, and the child happily continued to hold it. "Indeed, Lord Kingsley, when I am back in service, I promise I shall be a model of discretion. But it feels so *good* to be free of that place!"

The rest of the trip was a pleasure to all three walkers—Captain Lord Kingsley could not remember when he had had such a good time. The streets were an ever changing kaleidoscope of activity, with musicians, peddlers, carriages, and beggars competing for attention. Christa and Miranda shared a childlike enthusiasm for the wonders around them, and Alex found it amusing that through the eyes of a foreigner and a child he was rediscovering the city of his birth. His substantial presence prevented the party from being overly molested by beggars and left him free to enjoy the French girl's imaginative commentary as she explained the shops and businesses to the little girl.

The high point of the journey was Miranda's round-eyed fascination with a good-natured performing bear so plump it could hardly stand on its hind feet to dance. After the dance, its master said, "Now, go into the crowd, Caesar, and find the prettiest lady."

The bear obediently waddled into the crowd, straight to Christa. Alex was impressed that she stood her ground as the huge animal bore down on her, though she moved protectively in front of the child. Caesar was as friendly as the average spaniel, and soon both Christa and Miranda were petting him and scratching his ears.

Alex suspected that the beast was trained to go to the woman his trainer pointed out as having the most affluent escort, but he still tossed a coin to the bear leader. "Your bear has good judgment."

"The best, my lord, the best," the man said complacently as he pocketed the crown.

Miranda had to be persuaded that Kingsley House had no place for a bear before the journey continued. Stopping at a cook shop, Alex bought everyone hot meat pies that they could munch while moving, followed by fresh hot gingerbread in alphabet letters. Miranda solemnly picked out an M, a C, and a K from the vendor's tray, then handed each of the adults an appropriate sweet cake.

They were almost back to Kingsley House when they passed a flower seller and Alex impulsively bought two bunches of violets, presenting them with a flourish to each of the ladies. With that gesture he won Miranda's allegiance for life. Christa's silver-gray eyes flew up to meet his in momentary alarm, but what she saw in his face must have reassured her. With a delicious gamin smile, she said, "*Merci*," and tucked the nosegay into her bodice.

Alex was sorry when they finally reached St. James's Square. Christa was exactly the sort of girl a sailor hopes to meet in a strange port: pretty, friendly, and uninhibited. But since she might become an employee, he curbed his improper thoughts. He hoped Annabelle liked her—the girl would be a pleasant addition to the household. Unfortunately, that would also place her completely off limits to him, more's the pity.

Kingsley House was smaller than the magnificent Norfolk House on the other side of the square, but it was splendid by any reasonable standard. Both Miranda and Christa faltered a bit as they gazed up at the building, their handclasp tightening. The brief enchanted hour of freedom was gone; what kind of life waited inside?

The older man who opened the door appeared far more aristocratic than his easygoing employer. Alex handed over his hat and said, "I've found some people for the staff. May I present Miss Miranda . . . I'm sorry, I don't know your last name."

The child blushed, struck once more with shyness in the high-ceilinged entry hall. Christa intervened. "Her name is Miranda Hampstead, named for the village where she was found. She once told me she aspired to become a kitchen maid, so she might eventually learn to cook. Is that not so, Miranda?" The girl nodded vigorously.

"You heard the young lady, Morrison. Have we a situation for a kitchen maid?"

The bemused butler replied cautiously, "Well, I believe that a vegetable maid will be needed, but she must be approved by Monsieur Sabine, the new French chef." There was a charged silence; cooks were notoriously temperamental even when they weren't French.

Alex said, "Give Monsieur my compliments on his superb dinner of last night and tell him Miss Hampstead is commended to him by one of his countrywomen, Mademoiselle Christine Bohnet."

Morrison looked unconvinced but murmured that they could certainly use more housemaids should Miranda prove unacceptable in the kitchen. The butler was becoming used to his new master's odd starts; if he had decided to pick up new servants in the streets, what was a poor butler to do? He knew the boy was sound, in spite of his parents. Though lions couldn't have drawn the admission from him, Morrison felt thirty years younger since Lord Kingsley had returned and opened the house.

As Miranda trailed trustingly off behind the butler, Alex turned to Christa and said, "Shall we find my sister, Annabelle?" Without waiting for a reply, he started up the sweeping Y-shaped staircase. At this hour of the day Annabelle was almost certainly in her sitting room sketching or writing letters. Sure enough, when he knocked at her door, a soft voice said, "Please come in."

Alex was beginning to question the wisdom of bringing his sister an abigail that he had picked up like a stray kitten, so his voice was particularly breezy when he said, "Good afternoon, Belle. I have found an abigail for your consideration. This is Mademoiselle Christine Bohnet. She is French and comes very highly recommended." He mentally qualified the statement—if nothing else, the girl was skilled at defending her virtue.

As Christa made a respectful curtsy, the two young women examined each other with curiosity and some misgivings. Miss Kingsley wore an unflattering black dress, but the slim figure, lovely face, and wonderful golden blond hair showed that she would be a mistress worthy of an abigail's best efforts. But it was the younger girl's apologetic expression that made Christa instinctively wish to help her. Her rescuer's sister looked as if she needed a friend and ally as well as a skilled abigail, and Christa would be happy to fill those needs.

"It would be a pleasure to work for someone as lovely as Miss Kingsley," Christa said warmly.

Annabelle was disconcerted by the bright-eyed creature her brother had brought home. The French girl had a contagious, elfin charm unlike any abigail Annabelle had ever seen, and she seemed very young. Her curly black hair was cut short in a style that might be au courant in Paris but was unusual in London. But the girl's artless admiration was disarming, and she had none of the haughtiness common among the better lady's maids.

Smiling shyly, Annabelle said, "Do you really think you could give me some town bronze? I fear I am sadly lacking."

Christa said earnestly, "Miss Kingsley, you could not fail to make a maid's efforts shine. My former employer . . ." She stopped and gave a delicate shudder, then began to circle Annabelle with a measuring eye.

"The new styles will suit you to perfection. When you emerge from mourning . . . you will carry all before you." Casting her eyes heavenward, she clasped her heart dramatically. "Men will perish for love of you, and day and night they will beseech your brother for your hand. You will be a *tour de force*!"

Both Kingsleys burst into laughter at the picture. Annabelle felt the first stirrings of excitement. She knew that she was too tall, too thin, too pale, for beauty; had her mother not told her so? Nor had she taken Alex's compliments seriously—after all, he was her brother and doubtless wanted her off his hands. But this energetic young Frenchwoman seemed sincere in her compliments. Perhaps she really could make Annabelle presentable, and such warmth and good nature would be delightful to have around.

"I should be very happy to engage you, if you would truly like the position," Annabelle. said. "Let me show you your room." She stood and crossed to a door in the back of the room.

Relieved that the two young women seemed to have

taken to one another, Alex said heartily, "I'll just put
Christa's bag there and be on my way."

They hardly noticed when he left.

"Christa?" Annabelle said musingly. Though it was
usual to call a lady's maid by her last name, she found herself asking, "That is very pretty. May I call you that instead
of Bohnet? Somehow your surname seems . . . too formal
for you."

"I would like it very much," Christa said. She halted on
the threshold of the small maid's room and said, "Oh, how
lovely!"

It was a very attractive chamber. The furnishings were
not new but were well made and looked mellow rather than
obviously worn. Not only was there a pretty blue-patterned
carpet on the floor, but the pitcher and basin on the washstand matched each other, and a striking watercolor of a
ship at sea hung on the wall. A door in the back of the room
led to the servants' passages. It was not uncommon for a
lady's maid to have a room in her mistress's suite, and this
arrangement meant that Christa could doze in comfort
when Annabelle was out late, yet still be available to undress her mistress when she returned.

She gave Annabelle a shining look. "It makes me very
happy to be here. I hope you will be happy too."

Annabelle smiled. It was an incongruous thought for an
aristocrat hiring a maid, but she had the sudden feeling that
they might become friends.

The servants' hall at Kingsley House was vastly different
from the Pomfrets'. The house was still understaffed, so
everyone ate gathered around one large table, with Mr.
Morrison, the butler, presiding at one end and his wife at
the other. Mary Morrison had been the head housemaid

when she married her husband but had to give up her job because the late Lady Serena did not approve of having couples in her employ. When the butler suggested his wife as the new housekeeper, the new Lord Kingsley had been happy to give his permission.

Together the Morrisons ruled over their domain like firm but affectionate grandparents. While chairs were assigned by rank and the seniors led the conversation, all of the servants were entitled to speak. To her delight, Miranda was no longer the least important person in the household; as the vegetable maid she ranked above the scullery maid, another foundling like herself, named Daisy. Each of the two girls was pleased to find someone her own size, and a fast friendship was in the making.

After a comfortable evening meal, Miranda described her earlier interview with Monsieur Sabine to Christa, explaining how the rotund chef had inspected her with scowling intensity, muttering deeply in French and periodically clapping a red hand to his brow in despair. After some minutes of such carryings-on, he had barked, "Zee green beans—wash them!" before stalking off. Miranda had hopped to the task willingly; oddly, she said she found the Monsieur endearing rather than frightening, and seemed to understand him even when he was raving in French. She had never been happier in her life.

Christa did not meet the Monsieur (as he preferred to be called) until later in the evening of her first day. Though a chair was kept for him at the communal table, he chose to eat alone after the upstairs meal was over. Miranda served him a cold collation in his private belowstairs sitting room while he relaxed and helped himself to a few glasses of the household's best wine. The Monsieur had been with the Kingsleys less than a week, but he believed that it was important to train employers quickly and firmly. Since his sauces were superb, his pastry nearly weightless, and his touch with a joint unexcelled, awed employers had always been desperate to grant him whatever he desired. As Master Jonathan had said in astonishment the night before, even his *vegetables* were good!

On this night, the Monsieur wished to speak with his newly arrived countrywoman. Morrison himself gravely informed Christa of the audience, though it was possible that a twinkle lurked in his old eyes. As she entered the cook's sitting room, Christa thought irrepressibly that there had been less sense of ceremony in meeting poor Louis XVI in the days before the revolution. Admittedly, the king had had more courtiers, but the Monsieur had much more presence!

Since the door to the cook's sitting room was ajar, the servants perched around the hearth listened with unabashed interest. Regrettably, the conversation was entirely in French, but the flavor was unmistakable. It began with the Monsieur gracious but haughty, progressed through a lively dialogue of apparent equals, and ended when he escorted Christa back to the servants' sitting room, reverently kissing her hand before closing the door behind her.

Christa choked back a giggle at the sight of all the curious eyes regarding her. "Is there any more of the coffee, Mrs. Morrison?"

After Mrs. Morrison poured her a cup, Christa joined the circle before the hearth. The housekeeper asked, "What on earth did you say to him, Christa?" Even downstairs, where protocol was more rigid than among the Quality, "Christa" she was and would remain.

Christa sipped her coffee and gave a sigh of pleasure; French standards had prevailed in the brew. "We merely talked. The Monsieur told me of some of the houses he has cooked in. Really, a most impressive list. How did you manage to persuade him to come here?"

Mr. Morrison's eye definitely twinkled. "He informed us that the Prince of Wales wanted him, but that the House of Hanover is too new for his taste."

Christa choked on her coffee while the chief footman, Albert, helpfully patted her on the back.

"He's a rare bedlamite, the Monsieur," Morrison said as she succumbed to a fit of giggles. "But so long as he cooks like an angel and doesn't put one of those great knives of his through anyone, we're happy to have him."

Still chuckling, Christa looked around the ring of faces. Not one of them watched her with jealousy, anger, or resentment. She had come a long, long way today. Finishing her coffee, she gave them all a good night smile and bade them sleep well.

The footman, Albert, might not have been as tall as some of his more expensive Mayfair colleagues, but he was not lacking in temerity. The next morning he asked the Monsieur about *mademoiselle's* background and almost lost an ear to one of the chef's dramatic gestures.

"It is a privilege to have that one in this house!" the Monsieur intoned, with a flourish of his onion chopper.

"Yes, it is," Albert agreed. "But where did she come from?"

Another sweep of the knife, this time cutting loose two bulbs of a garlic rope that hung from the ceiling. "I know what I know," the Monsieur said mysteriously. "But my lips, they are sealed. Begone!"

Being no fool, Albert went.

Chapter 7

The Honorable Jonathan Kingsley felt a slight unease as he presented himself in Lord Kingsley's study. In his experience, a chat with the authorities was apt to prove uncomfortable. Alex seemed like a great gun and his young brother had hero-worshipped him all his life. Nonetheless, Alex's casual invitation to stop by after breakfast was still a summons.

Alex looked up, with an expression of relief, from an account book he was studying. "Good timing, Jon. The family lawyers are generating documents for my inspection faster than I can read them. Much more of this and I'll feel that I'm still shipboard."

Jonathan blinked in surprise. "A captain does accounts?"

His brother laughed. "It's not all standing on the quarter-deck and waving a cutlass, if that's what you mean. An officer has to do navigational mathematics, write reports, maintain the log, keep accounts of supplies and pay, and half a hundred other things. For every half hour of action, there are months of routine work."

Jonathan's face reflected his surprise at this novel thought as he sat down opposite his brother. Alex leaned back in his chair, the quill pen bridged between his fingers. Now that the first flush of enthusiastic reunion was behind them, it was time to start building a real relationship with his brother. It was odd to see someone who looked so much like himself at the same age, but who had a stranger's mind behind the familiar face. But while Alex's experience with brothers was limited, he had commanded a good few midshipmen in the same age group.

His brother flushed slightly under the considering gaze. "Have . . . have I done something wrong?" he said uneasily.

Alex raised an eyebrow in surprise. "Not that I know of. Unless you have some interesting confessions to make?"

Jonathan started to relax. "Nothing lately," he said cautiously.

Alex tossed the quill onto the desk. "As long as you restrict your transgressions to the kinds of youthful folly I committed, it will undercut my ability to give pious lectures. By the way, I wrote to the headmaster at Eton to tell him how to get the cow down, in case they haven't already puzzled it out."

"That's good." Jonathan chuckled. "I had been rather worried on the cow's behalf."

"Actually," Alex said after a brief silence, "I wanted to talk to you about your future." Jon's face promptly shuttered up; Alex noted the fact before continuing, "Do you have any idea what you might like to prepare for?"

"You mean, you're asking me? What I want to do?" Jonathan was so surprised that his voice squeaked. It was one of the unfortunate side effects of being fifteen.

"Who else should I ask?" Alex asked reasonably.

"No one ever consulted *me* before. Father wanted me trained for the Church."

"The *Church*?" Alex asked disbelievingly. He barely knew his brother, but even so, the vicarage seemed a wildly unsuitable choice. "Is that why you've done so badly in school? So you would be thought unworthy of the contemplative life?"

Jonathan had the look of a fox caught in the hen coop. "You figured that out quickly," he muttered with a mixture of respect and sulkiness.

"Probably because I would have done the same if some chaw-bacon had thought to make a priest of me," Alex admitted. "What would *you* like to do?"

A look of hope dawned on the boy's face. "I want to go into the army," Jonathan blurted. "It's not just a passing fancy. I've always wanted that. It's all I've ever wanted!"

"It seems a reasonable ambition, but I'd like to see you finish school first."

"You mean you would buy me a commission?" Jonathan seemed to have trouble absorbing the news.

"I'll buy you a commission in any regiment you like, and as many promotions after that as you deserve. Is the idea so surprising? After all, it's my responsibility to see you established."

Jonathan's face twisted as he desperately tried to keep control. Finally he said unsteadily, "I've never once had what I asked for. I . . ." He stopped, as though unable to continue.

Alex regarded him narrowly. Jonathan's confidence was apparently as nonexistent as Annabelle's, and Alex felt his own guilt twisting inside. When he was fifteen, he had been a year at sea and was already his own man. He thought it was not too late for his brother and could only hope that the same was true for his sister.

"As I said, I want you to finish at Eton. The army has at least as much paperwork as the navy, and you'll be a better officer for knowing how to write and figure and think. I wouldn't dream of asking you to refrain from pranks, but

I expect you to avoid those that will get you expelled. Is that understood?"

"Oh, yes, yes!" Jonathan stood, shaking with his excitement. "And . . . you'll even buy me a commission in the *Hussars*?"

"If they'll have you," Alex said with a half smile.

"You're the best brother anyone ever had!" Jonathan exclaimed. "Can I go now? I want to write to my friend Robbie. *He* wants to go into the Guards," he added scornfully.

Alex snorted with the contempt of a navy man. "I never could tell one regiment from another. Can't see that it makes any difference."

His brother looked momentarily outraged, then laughed out loud when he saw he was being teased. Apparently teasing was as new an experience as being asked his opinion on his future. Beaming joyously, Jonathan left the room with more speed than grace.

Alex watched him go thoughtfully. The boy was already showing some of the exuberance that should be natural at his age. His view of the army was somewhat romanticized, perhaps, but Alex felt the choice was basically sound. It was gratifying to be able to please his brother so easily; really, this head-of-family business wasn't difficult at all!

When Annabelle returned from breakfast with her brothers the next morning, she found her new abigail evaluating her wardrobe. Annabelle watched for a moment, then said apologetically, "I know a great deal of work will be required. What do you suggest?"

Christa turned to her with shining eyes. "Miss Annabelle, we are going to have a most wonderful experience— *everything* must be replaced! When will you be out of mourning?"

Annabelle's face tightened before she said, "My mother

died at the beginning of June, so it's about two weeks more."

"I'm sorry for your loss," Christa said gently.

"I'm not!" Annabelle said defiantly. "I don't miss her *at all*, in spite of what Aunt Agatha said." Then, defiance crumbling, she started to cry. Christa guided her to a brocade chair and produced an embroidered handkerchief. Luckily it was one of the first things she had located earlier.

Annabelle sobbed for several minutes before coming up for air. "I have wanted to say that for so long, but there has been no one to talk to. It would not have been fair to Jonathan to discuss it with him, and my Aunt Agatha would have been appalled at my lack of filial respect, even though she and my mother couldn't abide each other." She twisted her handkerchief and looked up pleadingly. "Do you think I am appalling?"

Christa considered a moment before answering. Her love for her own mother was as natural and unquestioned as the spring rain, but such was not always the case. "I do not think a child *owes* a parent love. It must be earned, like any other love. Not all parents are worthy." She looked at Annabelle's soft blue eyes and gentle face, then went on, "You look to me like a girl who wants to give love. It is a great tragedy if you have had no one willing to receive it."

"You *do* understand!" Annabelle smiled with relief. "But I don't wish to make a Cheltenham tragedy of it. I have been lucky in my brothers. Jonathan and I are closer than if we had had kinder parents. I always miss him dreadfully when he's at school. And Alex has been so good. We didn't get many letters, of course, because he was so much at sea, but it was exciting when they arrived—like a window on a different world.

"Sometimes he would send presents. Always the most wonderful things—Spanish lace, Arabian jewelry, porcelain all the way from China. . . . Once he even sent a monkey—

it was the drollest creature! The lieutenant who delivered it said that the next time he saw Alex he was going to launch him from a cannon for extracting the promise to deliver the beast to Jon and me."

"He sounds a very thoughtful brother," Christa said encouragingly. "Do you still have the monkey?"

Annabelle's amusement vanished as quickly as it had come. "It got into my mother's wardrobe and ruined a dress. She had one of the footmen wring its neck."

Christa was appalled. What could one say in response to such a story? Instead she asked quietly, "How did your mother die?"

"In a carriage accident. She was with one of her lovers." Annabelle tried to appear blasé, but her eyes would not meet those of her maid.

Christa considered retreating to a servant-like discretion but decided it was far too late for that. Besides, she had the feeling that this extraordinary conversation was a much-needed release for her new mistress, a release that would enable Annabelle to start looking forward rather than back.

"You need not live your life as your mother did."

"I could not if I tried," Annabelle replied with brittle nonchalance. "She was beautiful. Men would forgive her anything."

"And women?"

"She did not care what women thought."

"A woman who could not care for other women—she sounds much to be pitied," Christa said seriously.

Annabelle looked startled at that. "In what way?" she asked curiously.

"To be unable to care for other women is to be unable to love oneself. Did she seem a happy woman?"

"I never really thought about it," Annabelle said in surprise. "No, I don't think she was happy. In fact, I know she was not. She was always complaining. Nothing was ever right. She would be a little happy when she had a new lover, but that would quickly pass."

"You see? You are not like her. You may suffer because you care, but that means you have also the capacity for happiness. Have you not known joy?"

"Why, yes . . . yes, I have. There have been times when I thought no one on earth could be so fortunate or happy as I." Annabelle smiled at Christa shyly. "You have given me a great deal to think on."

"That is quite enough seriousness for one day," Christa proclaimed. "One does not hire a French maid because one wishes gravity. It is my job to make you as delectable as one of Monsieur Sabine's pastries. We have four months before your come out to do the job." Cocking her head to one side, she inspected her mistress. "Four weeks would be enough, and only that long to give the *modiste* time to create your wardrobe."

Annabelle almost bounced in her chair. "Do you really think it is possible? I rather like the idea of having men fight for my favors."

Christa waved her hand grandly. "After you are presented in the autumn, St. James's Square will be carpeted with men begging you to walk on them. I, Christine . . . Bohnet, promise it!" She was so carried away with her rhetoric that she had almost used her own rolling name and title. She must be more careful. With this trusting girl treating her more like a friend than a servant, it would be all too easy to forget her role.

No, not her role. Her station in life. She must always remember that.

Their conversation was interrupted by a knock at the door. Christa opened it to find Alex. A most delightful man to find on the threshold, she decided. Those amber eyes were a very unusual shade, warm but mischievous at the same time. Or was it the lurking twinkle that was so appealing?

"Good morning, Christa. Is my sister receiving visitors?"

Annabelle jumped up and ran to give him a hug. Christa found herself envious; she would enjoy having unlimited license to hug such a man. Her body shivered deliciously as it recalled the strength of his grasp the previous day. She firmly repressed the memory; many a maid had been lost after thinking such thoughts.

"Of course! Please come in. Christa has been telling me how she is going to make me beautiful." Annabelle smiled teasingly. "I think that it may be *very* expensive."

Alex entered and straddled one of the chairs, his arms crossed casually on top of the delicate back. It was a totally un-navy-like posture, and it felt good. He studied the two young women for a moment before speaking. His sister was clearly the beauty of the two, with a lovely dreaming face and great sweetness of expression, yet it was Christa who drew the eye. The French girl had a vividness about her that made every other woman he had ever known seem only half-alive by contrast.

"I've been thinking, Annabelle. Shall we go to the Orchard soon? The town will be thin of company by the time we're out of mourning, and I have a desire to see the family seat."

Annabelle exclaimed delightedly, "That would be wonderful! I haven't been there since Father died. You know how Lady Serena hated the country."

Alex glanced at Christa, enjoying her sparkling gray eyes and the dark curls that escaped her cap. She had the most kissable lips. Did Frenchwomen always look like they were either entering or leaving a bed? He pulled his thoughts back to the business at hand. "How long will it take to get new clothes made for my sister? The sooner we burn her present wardrobe, the happier I shall be."

"It will take no more than a week or so for a country summer wardrobe," Christa replied. "The *modiste* can work on the formal gowns for her come out while she is away."

"Very good." He nodded. "Belle, can you be ready to leave on Friday next week? I see no virtue in lingering here." Though he did not speak of it, Alex thought the three Kingsleys would relax more quickly in the informal atmosphere of Suffolk. And it was time to start learning the ways of a gentleman farmer; the Orchard was the principal source of the family income.

Annabelle looked a little uncertain. "Christa, will that be time enough for the sewing?" Now that a new wardrobe was in the offing, she would have been loath to forgo it.

"I think so," Christa affirmed. "At least . . . is there someone who does your dresses now?"

"Yes. And I don't ever want to set foot in her establishment again! Do you have someone you can recommend?"

"Yes, there is a new shop called Suzanne's. I know Mme. de Savary, the owner, and she has the finest fashion sense I have ever seen. Because she is just establishing her business, I think I can promise you that she will give very good service. And her prices are *très* reasonable."

"That isn't critical," Alex commented. "My prize money has accumulated amazingly, and I want my sister to have the best."

"Oh, this will be the best," Christa said with a twinkle. "And if you are determined to spend your money, we will just have to buy twice as many clothes!"

"Very well," he laughed. "Use your judgment. But, mind you, my sister must look splendid."

Tired of being discussed as if she were absent, Annabelle

said sweetly, "Would you like to come with us to Suzanne's? We must begin this undertaking forthwith."

"The devil I will!" Alex said in an appalled tone. "Oh . . . sorry, Belle, you made me forget my language. And no, you little minx," he added with a grin, "you are *not* getting me anywhere near such a place. All I care about is results. The means I leave to you and Christa." He rose to take his leave. "I'll see you at dinner."

He felt even more satisfied than after his talk with Jonathan. It appeared that all his brother and sister needed was the opportunity to stretch their wings. He was pleased with their progress. But as he left the house, it was not his siblings that occupied Alex's mind—it was a pair of sparkling gray eyes and a body whose curves were designed to be touched.

Christa nodded approvingly when she followed Annabelle into Suzanne's. She had visited the shop once or twice when running errands for Lady Pomfret, but the most recent visit had been a month before, and there had been changes since. The cluttered look Mme. Bouchet preferred had been renounced in favor of simplicity. The walls were now covered with a delicate rose wallpaper and several comfortable chairs were grouped by a table with copies of *The Ladies' Magazine*. A few choice garments were displayed in the carpeted salon, and in one corner, several lengths of fabric were twisted into a rosette, then allowed to sweep to the floor. Although little money had been expended, the shop had acquired an air of gentility it previously lacked.

Suzanne herself came to meet them, elegant in a dark blue gown that managed to look as businesslike as it was flattering. She raised her brow questioningly at the sight of her cousin's companion, so Christa hastily performed the introduction. "Miss Annabelle, may I present Mme. de Savary? Suzanne, this is my new employer, Miss Annabelle Kingsley. She will be out of mourning soon and will need an entire wardrobe."

"Indeed?" Suzanne's speaking glance told Christa that explanations would be required later, but for the nonce her attention was focused on her new customer. "Your timing is good, Mademoiselle Kingsley. I have just received Herr Heideloff's *Gallery of Fashion*, and two new fashion dolls from Paris as well. The styles should be very becoming on you. Will you take a seat while I bring them? And perhaps a cup of tea as well?"

Annabelle was delighted to be treated with such attention. When she had visited her mother's *modiste* she had been ignored or treated as a child, except for Lady Serena's occasional unflattering comments on the deficiencies of her daughter's figure. However, Annabelle was shocked when the book of fashion plates was brought for her inspection.

"Mme. de Savary, how could I possibly appear in public dressed like this? Why, these are no more than shifts! My mother said the *robe de chemise* was indecent," Annabelle said falteringly, her eyes fixed in fascinated horror on a plate showing two women in flimsy summer dresses.

Suzanne smiled understandingly. "It is true older women avoid the new styles. They are better suited to slim figures such as yours. Perhaps your mother was a little envious."

Annabelle was much struck by the comment. Could it be that the devastating Lady Serena had not wished to be seen without her stays? Her eyes began to shine with unholy glee. "Madame, do you have a chemise that I might try on?"

Suzanne nodded. "*Oui*, I keep several samples made up for customers to see the effect. Come into the fitting room."

Christa and Suzanne would not let Annabelle look in the mirror until they were satisfied with her appearance. First they removed her stays, then provided a lightweight shift and a soft lawn dress in creamy white. Christa unpinned her mistress's thick blond hair and made some quick adjustments, then did something with a ribbon. Stepping back, she nodded with satisfaction. "What do you think, Miss Annabelle?"

Annabelle turned to face the mirror, then stopped in speechless wonder at the sight of the stranger in front of her. The chemise had a low neckline, light puffed sleeves, and blue ribbon ties at the neck and below the breasts. The ties gracefully hinted at the body beneath the translucent fabric, then the dress fell into gentle, classical folds. The ribbons banding her hair matched those of the dress, and gave her a Grecian look as her golden curls fell simply over her shoulders. She felt half naked; the look was startlingly different from the heavily constructed dresses she had been wearing. Startling, but not unattractive—not unattractive at all. Turning to the women who awaited her verdict with a shining smile, she said, "I think this will do very well."

The rest of the afternoon was spent in an orgy of happy decision making. The fashion dolls were particularly useful because in every detail they were dressed and coiffed exactly like real women. As she gave her mistress the first doll, Christa remarked, "Is it not strange, Miss Annabelle, that England and France are at war, yet frivolities such as these pass freely between the countries?"

Suzanne clucked in mock disapproval. "*Au contraire*, Christa. War is a frivolity, one of those foolish games men indulge in. Fashion—now, *this* is a serious business!"

The three of them laughed together, and even the seamstress taking Annabelle's measurements permitted herself a chuckle. After all, does not a proper dress improve any occasion?

Suzanne stocked some French fragrances, and Annabelle had a pleasurable time sniffing them. She considered Hungary water and *eau de cologne*, and almost bought a vial of *l'eau admirable*, a refreshing blend of citrus, lemon, bergamot, neroli, and lavender that was very different from the musky scents her mother had favored. However, when Christa was consulted, she agreed that it was a fine blend, but perhaps just a bit . . . common? It had been first developed almost a hundred years before and a number of women wore it.

After more sniffing, Annabelle chose a simple essence of violet. Christa gave her approval to this one. "It is unusual, Miss Annabelle. Delicate but with a haunting sweetness— exactly right for you."

Annabelle felt absurdly pleased to have won her maid's approval; she humbly accepted that she had much to learn from these two Frenchwomen.

As Annabelle and Christa prepared to return to St. James's Square, Suzanne said, "Very well then. The first three dresses will be ready the day after tomorrow, and I will have more fabrics then for your approval. Christa has a list of the accessories that will be needed—gloves and slippers and the like. We have made a good beginning, no?"

Annabelle nodded in satisfaction. A very good beginning, indeed!

Chapter 8

The Monday before their departure to Suffolk was chosen for Annabelle's fashion debut. It was only to her brothers at a family dinner, but Annabelle was still nervous, so Christa dedicated most of the afternoon to preparing her mistress. During the previous days she had made several visits to chemist and herb shops to secure the necessary ingredients for making beauty aids. First, she washed Annabelle's hair, then rinsed it repeatedly with a chamomile infusion.

"What will this do?" Annabelle asked.

"It brightens blond hair. If your hair was dark, like mine, we would use rosemary for richer highlights." Christa's strong fingers kneaded Annabelle's scalp gently. "Then, because your hair is very fine, we will end with a beer rinse."

"*Beer*?"

"Yes, it will make your hair seem thicker."

"But I can't face my brothers smelling like the brew-house!"

"I promise the scent will be gone by the time your hair dries." Christa smiled roguishly. "Though smelling ever so slightly of beer would make you attractive to most men."

Annabelle could not help laughing. She had trouble re-membering that Christa was a servant. Aunt Agatha had

said that one must be firm, or servants would take advantage.
Christa had shown no signs of "taking advantage" and her
infectious spirit and tolerant understanding were rapidly
making her into a friend. Annabelle had few friends; she
had been too shy to make many new friends at the select
seminary for young ladies that her mother had packed her off
to when she was nine. She did maintain a correspondence
with two girls she had met there, but both had married soon
after their come outs, and they had the interests of young
matrons with children.

"Now for the complexion," Christa said. She wrapped
a towel around Annabelle's dripping head, then produced a
jar filled with a sticky mush that her mistress eyed dubi-
ously.

"You are sure that will be good for me?"

"This is a mixture of honey and oatmeal—and a secret
ingredient of my own. I will leave it on for fifteen minutes,
then pat it before I rinse it off. Your skin will glow with
color and be very happy. Although, to be honest, your complexion is almost perfect the way it is," Christa admitted.
"But you must remember, part of being beautiful is how
you think of yourself. If hours are spent on the task of
making you lovely, will you not feel lovelier? By the end
of this afternoon, you will feel that you have earned the ac-
colades you will receive."

"What if my brothers don't notice any difference?"
Annabelle asked nervously.

"They will," Christa replied serenely. "And then you
will know that you are beautiful. If a girl can impress her
brother, she can impress *anyone*!"

"You sound very sure." Annabelle giggled. "Do you
have a brother?"

"I did." Christa's answer was terse and invited no comments. Annabelle was suddenly struck by how little she

knew about her abigail apart from the fact that she was French, delightful company, and very skilled at her trade. Why had Christa come to England? Where had she learned to speak the language so well? Did she have any family?

For all the intimacy of their day-to-day association, the gulf between servant and mistress was vast and uncross-able, and Annabelle could not bring herself to ask Christa about her background. A conversation of that sort would not be at all proper. She could almost hear the words Aunt Agatha would use to reprimand her: *Servants aren't like us. They don't feel things the way we do. Don't encourage them to ape their betters.*

It was a statement that Annabelle had never questioned until now, when honesty compelled her to admit that if Christa were dressed up and taken to a ball, her wit and charm would make her a sensation. She was probably more intelligent than her mistress, and certainly more experienced and better informed. As that was the case, which of them was the "better"?

Annabelle put aside her radical and uncomfortable thoughts as Christa started gently patting and pulling the honey face mask. Sure enough, it made her skin very happy. With a blissful sigh, Annabelle forgot social analysis in favor of enjoying the sensation.

Alex chatted with his brother while they waited for their sister to join them. While one part of his mind was listening to Jonathan's detailed analysis of the relative virtues of light and heavy cavalry, another part was aware that he seemed to have been waiting for someone for a long time. Abruptly he realized that he had been watching for Christa. True to her word, she was a model of discretion, and he hadn't seen her for days. The girl had disappeared into the household exactly as she ought. Unfortunately. Perhaps he should call on Annabelle in her boudoir more often?

Annabelle appeared before Alex had fully examined why he was so concerned with the welfare of a mere maid. His sister stood in the doorway for a moment before entering, and he suspected she was late deliberately so she could make a grand entrance.

The effect was everything Annabelle could have wished for; even Jonathan stopped talking about the cavalry to stare at his sister. Alex had never seen her look so lovely. Her hair glowed bright gold as it fell around her face in soft curls, while the long tresses behind her head were caught in a bow that matched the ribbons tying her dress. The low-cut gown was superbly simple and showed his sister's graceful figure in a manner that managed to be both alluring and modest. Its color was a pale lilac that could be considered half-mourning, but the shade was also a perfect foil for Annabelle's delicate coloring. She wore a simple amethyst pendant about her neck, and her expression was a blend of confidence and shy hope.

Alex crossed and took his sister's hand, then bowed over it. "My dear, you are exquisite. Christa was right: I shall have men standing in line outside my study, waiting for the chance to beg for your hand." He smiled into her wide blue eyes, noticing that they looked different. Darker lashes and brows, perhaps? He offered his arm. "Shall we go in for dinner before Monsieur Sabine becomes upset?"

Annabelle lifted her head with a gesture worthy of a queen and took his arm graciously, beauty receiving her due. The royal expression dissolved when Jonathan exclaimed, "You look smashing, Belle. The prettiest sight I've seen since my mare Cinders had her foal."

Alex laughed aloud at how quickly her expression reverted to an older sister tempted to box her brother's ears.

"Christa warned me that brothers were difficult to impress," she said with a mock glare.

"On the contrary," Jonathan said earnestly. "That is the sincerest compliment I have ever made a girl. And you are only my sister!"

As they settled at the polished mahogany table, Alex asked, "I assume from the evidence that Christa is working out well?"

"Christa is wonderful," his sister said enthusiastically. "The best present you ever brought me. It's marvelous fun going to the shops with her. She apparently thinks it is not her place to disagree with me publicly, but if I look at something she thinks unsuitable, she has the most wonderful expressions. She lifts her brows or rolls her eyes. When I admired a truly vulgar beaded headdress, Christa just closed her eyes and firmly shook her head back and forth. I find myself looking at things she will not approve of, just to see what she will do. It is the greatest fun!"

Alex had seen that gift for expression when he brought Christa and Miranda across London. It would almost be worth going to the shops with his sister to see that vividly alive face again. He thought quickly, then said, "Would you care to go walking with me in Hyde Park tomorrow, Belle? You'll have to take Christa, since I will be going on to the Admiralty afterward, but I want to show you off to the polite world."

Annabelle looked so pleased at the invitation that Alex felt a bit guilty for issuing it as a subterfuge. His conscience was soothed with the thought that since he had brought Christa to the house, it was his responsibility to see that she was happy. Duty could be such a convenient crutch.

The next day's walk in the park was a success in terms of showing off Annabelle; Alex swore that she caused a traffic jam in Rotten Row that would not be cleared for a fortnight. A remarkable number of casual acquaintances came to greet him and beg the honor of an introduction to his sister. Annabelle glowed at the attention, but maintained a modest demeanor.

However, as a chance for Alex to further his acquaintance with Christa, the walk was a total failure. She trailed a demure four steps behind, her downcast eyes and mobcap proclaiming her servant's status. When he glanced back at her once or twice, he caught a flash of mischievous eyes. Except for that, he rather fancied that her servant's behavior was *too* good—she reminded him of a Drury Lane actress.

After a turn around the park, Alex left the two young women so he could take care of his business at the Admiralty. An experienced head of household might have been more cautious about leaving a beautiful young woman in the park, even accompanied by her maid. But Alex still had a good deal to learn.

Annabelle watched her brother's tall figure disappear, then said, "I want to walk around the park again before we go home."

"Are you sure, Miss Annabelle? It looks like rain."

"A little water won't hurt me," Annabelle said recklessly. She reveled in the attention she attracted and was loath to return home. Last night, her brothers; today, the social world!

They were in the middle of the park when the fast-gathering clouds decided to give up their water. As raindrops started pelting down, it occurred to Annabelle that her splendor would be considerably dimmed with her golden ringlets hanging like horse tails. Then, shockingly, she realized what her muslin dress would look like soaking wet. She would appear naked!

Christa called, "The trees to the left should shelter us until this passes by!"

The two girls abandoned dignity to run across the grass, and they managed to get under a broad chestnut before becoming totally saturated. The fifteen-minute wait under the tree was filled with Annabelle's chatter about the people they had seen and the men who had admired her. Christa listened tolerantly. Annabelle would soon come to accept the fact that she was attractive, but for the moment it was a new and delicious experience.

The rain blew over quickly and pale sunshine was restored. They were nearly out of the park when Annabelle was stopped by a puddle that filled the shrub-lined path in front of her. She was deciding whether to ruin her slippers, retreat, or risk an unladylike jump when a smooth tenor voice said, "Allow me."

Annabelle looked up and gasped. The gentleman gazing at her so admiringly was the most elegant man she had ever seen. His dark Brutus-cropped hair was a masterpiece of artful disarray, his blue coat tailored to show his shapely torso and numerous gold fobs. He was a veritable pink of the ton, and his fine dark eyes regarded her with worshipful wonder. As Annabelle returned his gaze, the gentleman peeled off his expensive coat and laid it over the puddle in front of her.

"Such a lovely lady should not soil her dainty slippers," he murmured, his voice seductive.

Christa watched in amusement. It was clear why Queen Elizabeth had favored Sir Walter Raleigh; the dramatic gesture could not fail to please. Of course, it had been Sir Walter's original idea; this fop could not claim as much credit.

Annabelle tripped delicately over the coat, which he lifted behind her; clearly his chivalry did not extend to the undainty feet of maids. Looking up at him, she breathed, "Sir, you are too kind. You should not have ruined your coat for me."

The gentleman bowed. "No price is too high if it contributes to your comfort." As he straightened, he said with a pretty show of hesitation, "I know it is too bold of me, but permit me to introduce myself. I am Sir Edward Loaming, very much at your service." He lifted an eyebrow in hopeful question.

"I am Annabelle Kingsley," was the reply. Annabelle was stunned at how fully this man fulfilled her romantic fantasies; if this was a dream, she hoped never to wake.

Really, Christa thought irritably, if Annabelle didn't close her mouth soon, something might fly in. Sir Edward's behavior was very amusing, but surely even a child could see how overdrawn his gestures were, how cold the eyes that overlooked them.

She glanced back at Annabelle; perhaps a child could see through the man, but Annabelle, flushed with the first triumph of maidenly beauty, was dazzled by Sir Edward. Since the two were gazing into each other's eyes with a singular lack of concern for who might be observing, Christa jumped that part of the puddle that was not now absorbed in Sir Edward's coat and said briskly, "It is time we returned home, Miss Annabelle. You will wish to rest and change before dinner."

Annabelle turned her starry eyes to her maid. "Very well," she said obediently. She looked back at her admirer with a coquettish flutter of lashes. Sir Edward seized the opening provided.

"May I escort you home?" he asked with the soulful look most often seen in pets awaiting their dinner.

Annabelle nodded happily and they turned to leave the park. Sir Edward wisely abandoned his ruined coat. While he looked a bit odd in his shirt sleeves and waistcoat, he would have looked a good deal odder carrying the coat at arm's length to prevent its dripping on the rest of his finery.

Christa followed the handsome couple with a slight frown knitting her brows. Annabelle might be overcome by Sir Edward's romantic good looks, but Christa was not impressed at the way he had circumvented polite manners to ingratiate himself. Sir Edward reminded her of some of the exquisites who had fluttered around her in those long-ago days before the revolution. Some were amusing company, but the whole raft of them together was worth less than a real man like her brother or Alex Kingsley.

The trip back to St. James's Square was a dawdling one, delightful for Annabelle, tedious for her maid. Christa was glad that they would soon be repairing to the country—clearly Sir Edward wanted to learn where Annabelle lived so he might call on her. Next autumn he might be one of many, but at the moment he had the value of novelty. If Annabelle became too enamored of his charms, she might ignore more-worthy suitors.

At the door of Kingsley House, Christa whisked her mistress inside before Sir Edward could make too many fatuous remarks. Nonetheless, the interval before dinner was filled with Annabelle's dreamy comments about her escort's handsome face, elegant figure, cultivated voice, and general all-around wonderfulness. Christa confined herself to noncommittal noises at first, but after two hours started losing patience. She was curling Annabelle's hair when her mistress said for the dozenth time, "Isn't he the handsomest man you have ever seen, Christa?"

"Indeed, he is most attractive, Miss Annabelle. Perhaps he has a wife who thinks so, too."

Annabelle's face fell with ludicrous suddenness. "Do you think he is married?"

Christa felt a bit ashamed of her comment, "It's possible. Many of the most *galant* men are married. They can be as outrageous as they wish, for they have nothing to lose and much to gain from their flirtatiousness."

Annabelle looked so woebegone that Christa said encouragingly, "You can ask your brother if he knows of Sir Edward. Then if he calls on you this autumn, you will know if you wish to distinguish him above your other suitors."

Annabelle giggled, once more diverted by the delightful thought of her becoming much sought after. Sir Edward was wonderfully handsome, but there was an abundance of time and opportunity ahead of her.

True to his resolution, Alex called on his sister the next morning as she was completing her toilette. Christa admitted him with a very proper bobbed curtsy, but under her demure facade he sensed the bubbling amusement he remembered from their journey across London. It was as if she saw all life as a game, and it was one of her most appealing qualities.

He smiled at Christa and said cheerily, "Good morning, Belle. If you have no objections, I'd like to visit with you. It should be interesting to observe a few feminine mysteries."

Annabelle laughed from her seat at the vanity. "Surely my big strong brother knows his share of feminine secrets."

Alex chuckled as he seated himself and Christa silently poured him a cup of tea from his sister's breakfast tray. He noted approvingly that she placed a basket of crescent-shaped rolls near to hand—he liked a woman with a good grasp of basics. Alex also liked a woman with a delightfully impertinent derriere, and Christa qualified splendidly on both counts.

He broke and buttered one of the feather-light rolls, then sighed blissfully. "Belle, how have you earned such a delicious breakfast? Nothing like this is served downstairs."

Annabelle turned to face her brother as Christa resumed styling her hair. "Christa said I would like them, and asked Monsieur Sabine to make them for me. Are they not delightful? They are called croissants."

"Remind me to double Monsieur's salary. Whatever I pay him, it isn't enough," Alex said as he reached for another croissant, this time spreading it with orange marmalade.

Returning to his sister's earlier remark, he said, "Actually, Belle, my experience with feminine secrets has been limited. Since I went into the navy at fourteen, I've completely missed the normal social education. Fashionable ladies with their fans terrify me. Why, I don't even know how to dance."

Annabelle pursed her lips in concern. "How strange—I never thought of that. I've always dreamed of your exotic adventures, and never thought of what you were missing. Since you must lead me out for the first dance at my ball next autumn, you will have to take lessons. Jonathan could use some, too—he has always resisted learning! Surely there must be a dancing master in Ipswich who will come out to the Orchard."

Alex's first reaction was to retreat from this threatened female folderol, but then he paused, and a gleam came into his eye; this situation might work to his advantage. "We'll need a second female to make up two couples. Christa, do you dance?"

His quarry raised her eyes from Annabelle's hair and she said demurely, "But of course, Lord Kingsley. A lady's maid must be able to do everything her mistress does."

"And she must do it better, so that she can teach it?" Alex asked teasingly.

"A lady's maid is never more proficient than her mistress," Christa said firmly. "Except for things like starching and cleaning, which no proper lady would have knowledge of."

"Do you ever tire of being discreet, Christa?" he asked.

Her gray eyes opened wide. "Not at all. It is a skill that I have only lately learned, so it has the charm of novelty."

Alex laughed aloud, then addressed both of the girls. "While we are on the subject of the beau monde, is there anything we should be doing now about the ball? I haven't the vaguest idea how one goes about organizing such things."

Annabelle looked uncertain. "I'm afraid I don't either. Lady Serena never included me in any of her entertaining plans, and Aunt Agatha wouldn't have had people in even if we hadn't been in mourning." Her eyes brightened and she said hopefully, "Christa, have you ever been involved in planning a ball?"

"But of course," her maid answered calmly. "It is not so very difficult a task. We must choose a theme, something to make it special—perhaps a Turkish fantasy, or a Roman feast, or a field of flowers. Then a list of the guests you wish to send cards to, and we confer with Monsieur Sabine about the refreshments. And you will need a very special gown. Mme. de Savary will take care of that."

"You make it sound so simple," Annabelle said admiringly.

Christa laughed. "It is simple in theory, but complicated in practice. At the last hour one always finds that the flowers are faded, or that the kitchen cat has gotten into the lobster patties, or that half the guests are not speaking to the other half. It is what makes entertaining such a delightful task.

One never knows quite how things will actually transpire. Nonetheless, we shall contrive."

She paused a moment, her hands automatically patting the last of Annabelle's ringlets into place as a flash of memory pulled her away from the present. *We shall contrive.* It made her think of the d'Estelle family motto, *Vaille que vaille*, which meant "Come what may" or perhaps "At all cost." Christa had been raised with that ideal, and she hoped her ancestors would approve of how she was contriving. She might no longer be a lady, but she was doing her tasks well.

Her attention was brought back to the present by Annabelle's carefully nonchalant description of her meeting with Sir Edward Loaming the day before. Christa could not resist a small snort as her mistress recounted Sir Edward's manifold perfections.

Alex glanced at Christa quickly, then struggled with fair success to suppress a chuckle. Obviously the maid was not as impressed as the mistress. He thought Sir Edward sounded like a coxcomb, but he said obligingly, "I'll ask around, Belle. If he is respectable, there is no reason why he can't call next autumn."

He stood to leave, stretching his muscular frame like a lazy jungle cat before leaving the room. Christa watched his departure with a frustration so intense it was physical. To members of the ton, being acceptable meant having birth and fortune. Neither alone was enough, so she was forever exiled from that charmed circle. She knew the ways of the world she had grown up in—a penniless countess might be an object of pity, but without beauty, wealth, or family backing, she was scarcely better than a tradesman's daughter.

Most of the time Christa was happy in her new lot—she was busy and productive, and she was making friends belowstairs. But whenever she was near Lord Kingsley, she felt an ache of regret for lost possibilities.

Chapter 9

The Kingsley household's removal to Suffolk was accomplished with reasonable efficiency, and they left scarcely two hours after the appointed time. Most of the staff were being left in London for the summer, but the senior servants traveled with the family. These included Christa, the Morrisons, as butler and housekeeper, Lord Kingsley's newly acquired young valet, Fiske, and Monsieur Sabine. Many cooks would have preferred a lazy summer in town, but the Monsieur would have taken it as a mortal insult if the family had not required his skills. As with most artistes, his craft was his passion and fulfillment—leisure had no place in his life.

Christa found the two-day trip into East Anglia to be full of interesting new sights. The only parts of England she knew were London and the rolling hills of Berkshire. Suffolk had quite a different character. It was nearly flat—no, not really flat, but gently undulating in a manner subtle rather than dramatic. Windmills broke the line of the horizon and many of the cottages were half-timbered and thatched.

Alex and Jonathan alternated riding outside the coach and sitting inside with Annabelle and Christa. It was Alex who told Christa the story of the town that was eaten by the sea. "Dunwich is not far north of the Orchard. It was a very ancient town, and a prosperous port until the year 1326. Then a great storm swept away over four hundred houses, and three churches as well. Only a handful of buildings remain."

"Why did the town just fall away like that?" she asked.

"The whole coast of East Anglia is unstable, continually crumbling," Alex replied. "That's why there are no long coast roads in Suffolk. The sea kept claiming them, so the roads run from inland points out to coastal villages. That is also why the Orchard is set back from the water and a band of heath land is left along the shore. There is a local saying that the sea is lovely to visit but dangerous to lie with."

Christa nodded with interest, then pressed her nose to the coach window, eager for a first glimpse of her new home. She gasped in surprise when they emerged from the tree-lined entrance road and pulled to a halt on the circle drive before the house.

"What do you think of it?" Alex asked. "I wager that France has nothing quite like this."

"It's perfectly wonderful!" Christa said as she followed the family out the carriage door after the coachman let down the stairs. "A magpie house!"

It was the largest half-timbered building she had ever seen, and a splendid example of the Tudor passion for pattern-making. The multiple gables had a four-lobed design reminiscent of flowers, while the lower structure was herringboned, the whitewashed wattle and daub making a dazzling contrast with the age-darkened timbers. Huge lantern windows were made of leaded glass, and elaborate plaster patterns called pargeting decorated the spaces above doors and main windows.

Christa said thoughtfully, "It is not grand, or even dignified, but it is the most *playful* house I have ever seen."

Alex chuckled at her frankness; discretion didn't last long when Christa wasn't watching her tongue. "'Playful' is as good a word as any," he agreed as he stared at the lively facade of his ancestral home. "It was originally built in the shape of an E, in honor of the great Elizabeth. There have been additions since then, but always in the same style."

He had not been here in a dozen years, and a curious blend of happiness and unpleasant memories stirred in him at the sight. Alex had spent most of his pre-navy life here, and he fondly recalled riding on the sands, hunting for birds' nests in the marshes, and learning to sail. Peter Harrington had been his constant companion in those early years, and he had spent as much time at his friend's house as at his own. They had even shared a tutor before going off to Eton.

But entwined with those memories were recollections of his mother's periodic depredations as she swept in from London and harassed her servants and children with the casual cruelty of a schoolboy removing the wings of flies. Lady Serena and his father had largely ignored each other except for occasional skirmishes over her spending. However, she had an income of her own and was dependent on her husband only when her extravagance outran her resources.

While Lady Serena was an all-too-vivid memory, Alex's father was almost impossible to recall, a dim, juiceless figure who stayed in his library or estate office. To his credit, he had left the Kingsley estate in thriving prosperity. Lady Serena's fortune was added to the total, making Alex a very wealthy man quite apart from the substantial prize money he had won in the last few years. Even after he had established his brother and sister, there would be an intimidatingly large amount left over. He had the family man of business exploring potential investments. He rather fancied himself as the owner of a fleet of merchant ships.

Alex was recalled from his musings as Annabelle and Jonathan started up the shallow steps to the carved double doors of the main entrance. He found himself looking forward to this summer in the country, although he had a few doubts as to whether there would be enough to keep him occupied. A lifetime of naval activity might not be good preparation for becoming a gentleman of leisure.

Christa liked the low ceilings and rambling rooms of the Orchard even though it lacked the luxury of the St. James town house. The maid's room in Annabelle's suite was hardly more than a closet, with plain whitewashed walls and a simple rug hooked out of scrap fabric. It was fortunate that Suzanne hadn't yet done a major wardrobe for Annabelle for the storage space was quite inadequate.

But there was a light, clean feel to the place, and the old leaded-glass windows looked down into a knot garden that had been laid out when the house was new over two hundred years earlier. The sea lay just over the low ridge beyond the trees that sheltered the house from the wind, and Christa decided to visit it after supper. Annabelle would be sitting with her brothers and wouldn't need her, and Christa found the idea of a fresh sea breeze irresistible.

By the time Christa had unpacked and sorted Annabelle's possessions and readied her mistress for an early dinner, she had worked up a proper country appetite of her own. Down in the servants' hall, she was pleased to discover that the Orchard's staff welcomed the newcomers with no sign of resentment. It helped that the Morrisons had both grown up on the estate, and hence were not "foreigners."

Christa was also amused to see how quickly Monsieur Sabine had bullied the kitchen staff into a form acceptable to him. The Monsieur had been regarded with stunned disbelief as he installed his cherished knives, the sacred never-to-be-washed omelet pans, and the ropes of garlic he had brought from London. Mrs. Ives, the modest country-woman who cooked for the staff when the family was not in residence, had been more than willing to step down in the Frenchman's favor. As she confided to Mrs. Morrison that night, she knew her cooking "warn't fit for the gentry."

The Monsieur had proceeded to put together a divine meal, accompanied by darkly muttered French impreca-tions. Christa heard some of them as she seated herself at the large oval table in the servants' hall and could only be grateful that no one else present understood what he was saying. Even the stable lads might have been shocked by his creative profanity on the subjects of the English, the country, the available food stocks, and the local peasants. Nonetheless, the chef did not appear unhappy; Christa had already decided that he regarded grumbling as a superior form of amusement, second only to concocting exquisite new sauces.

Christa and Fiske, the new valet, had been introduced to the other two dozen servants before the meal. It would be several days before she had the names straight, but Christa sensed friendliness behind the faces of these taciturn Suf-folk natives.

She was sorry Miranda couldn't come here for the summer, but the laws belowstairs were immutable—only upper servants traveled with the family. As usual, Monsieur Sabine did not dine with the rest of the staff; he had already taught the junior kitchen maid to serve him in a small parlor that should have been occupied by the housekeeper.

After the meal, Christa excused herself, saying she wanted to walk down to the shore. As she left the kitchen, Mrs. Ives poured a cup of tea and remarked to Mrs. Morri-son, "Seems a nice enough lass, for a Frenchy."

Mrs. Morrison nodded and sipped her own cup of tea contentedly. It was good to be back home in Suffolk, away from the bustle of town. She and Emma Ives were old friends and she had missed these comfortable cozes when they discussed their colleagues and the Quality. "Aye, she's sweet tempered and willing enough. But she doesn't have a proper sense of her worth. Treats the scullery maid the same as she does you or me."

Emma clucked in disapproval of such improper behavior. Greatly daring, the young valet, Fiske, spoke up. "Lord Kingsley is like that—he behaves the same with everyone."

Both women stared at him until Fiske blushed and cast his eyes down. Speaking in measured tones, Mrs. Morrison intoned, "The *Quality* might forget their proper place, but the likes of *us* never will. And don't you forget it, lad!"

Completely routed, Fiske muttered an apology and moved to less-exacting company at the other end of the hall. Being valet to the master gave him status in the hierarchy, but he knew better than to tangle with those beldames again.

The sea breeze felt exhilaratingly brisk against Christa's face as the long June day faded into dusk, and the firm sand crunching beneath her feet was reminiscent of her lost summer home in Normandy. The haunting cries of circling seabirds echoed across the water, while high overhead, wispy clouds glowed apricot from the setting sun.

The cove was a natural harbor that must have sheltered small boats in the past, and at the far end, a pier stretched into the quiet water. As Christa wandered toward it, she wondered who used this quiet haven, and if it was always so peaceful.

A surge of melancholy threatened to overwhelm her.

Usually Christa could live in the present and not dwell on what she had lost, but she felt intensely alone at this moment, knowing that never again would she share such beauty and peace with those she had loved best. At times like these, Christa could almost wish she had died with them in France. She did her best to obey her promise to Charles and to live fully and happily without sinking into complaint and depression, but sometimes the task seemed an intolerable burden.

Christa had always loved the sea, and some of her most treasured memories were of the tolerant Norman fisher-men. She had been delighted when they allowed her to accompany them on their shorter trips, and in gratitude she learned to haul nets and sail as well as any fisher boy. Her mother did not officially know of the sailing trips; after all, what was a girl-child of the aristocracy doing on a smelly fishing boat? But Christa rather thought Marie-Claire had known and accepted that her active daughter needed an outlet for her energy—her mother had missed very little.

Alex easily identified the small figure ahead of him on the sands. He had slipped away from his brother and sister to have a private reunion with the sea, but the thought of sharing it with the French girl did not distress him. Though she had never been to this shore before, she had an air of belonging.

There was no need to increase his speed, for Alex's longer strides would soon bring him up behind her. The breaking waves drowned out the sound of his footsteps, and while Christa was still unaware of his presence, he could admire the grace of her movements as she drifted along, shifting in and out, one step away from the advancing tide, sometimes stooping to pick up a bright pebble or shell.

When he was nearly on her, she stopped, her face turned to the south. Speaking softly so as not to alarm her, he said, "You are looking toward France?" The slight lift of his voice made it a question.

Christa glanced at him, unsurprised at his presence. "*Oui*, my lord." She turned back to the water and seemed undisposed to comment further. Alex admired the clear-cut line of her profile, the dark curls tumbling in the wind. She had the grave beauty of a sorrowing Madonna. This was the first time he'd seen her face when it was not alive with amused thoughts and feelings.

Two black-and-white birds broke into a squabble over some choice tidbit a few feet beyond her, their long legs and strange turned-up bills giving them a comic air. With an eye to lightening her mood, Alex gestured at the birds and said, "Those are avocets. This coast is their only English home."

She nodded. "Sometimes we would see them in Normandy, but they were rare. They are very droll, *n'est-ce pas*?"

"Normandy was your home?"

Christa did not want to lie outright so she phrased her answer to imply that she had been in service. "We lived there, and in Paris. The family I was with had homes in both places."

"How long have you been in England?"

"Fifteen months. I left at the height of the Terror. Now that Robespierre is gone, perhaps things are better."

"Was it very bad?"

She nodded again. "Yes. The Terror was horrible of itself, but even worse, it was the death of hope. At the beginning of the revolution, six years ago, there was such joy. We believed there would be an end to injustice, and poverty, and the privileges of the wealthy at the expense of the poor. It seemed a chance to begin the world again and make it a better place."

Christa gave him a sidelong glance. "The French are a
race of philosophers and idealists, my lord. Perhaps that is
why we are so quarrelsome."

Alex said gently, "It must be hard to be an exile from
one's homeland."

She shrugged a little. "Perhaps. Yet there is nothing
there for me now. My family is gone, all of them victims of
the revolution in one way or another."

"The guillotine?"

"If my father's heart had not given out, he would have
been sent there. He was a moderate, a believer in compassion and justice. He spoke out against the Terror and was
denounced as an 'enemy of the revolution.' Bah!" she spat.
"It was madness!"

"That is why you left?"

"Yes." Christa pulled her shawl around her shoulders in
the evening chill, unmindful of how odd it would be thought
that a servant should converse so freely with her master. She
felt a need to talk, and she found Alex's presence comforting. "My mother and I were secretly warned by a friend
that the Committee of Public Safety was going to arrest us.
They were angry that my father escaped them. It would not
have been the first time that an innocent family was sent to
Madame Guillotine."

"I thought it was mostly aristocrats who were executed,"
Alex commented.

"No. Perhaps one in ten were, but victims came from all
classes—peasants, craftsmen, merchants. None were spared."
Christa paused, then continued in a voice heavy with sorrow,
"The revolution turned into a mad, raving beast."

"Did your mother escape?"

"No. I pray that she died quickly."

Moved by the sadness in her voice, Alex said gently,
"But you are here and alive, in spite of the revolution."

Christa turned and looked directly at him, then smiled

without reservation. Her rich voice was clear and vibrant, and Alex was again struck by how alluring a French accent could be.

"Yes. I have survived. And I have a debt of living to accomplish. I am much luckier than most of my unhappy countrymen. And what of you, Lord Kingsley? What is it like to come back to your childhood home, no longer a child?"

Accepting the change of subject, Alex considered for several moments before replying, "It's very strange. Everything is the same, and at the same time everything is different. Even though I was the heir, I never really imagined myself as the master here. In fact, I never looked beyond escaping to the sea."

Christa noted his choice of the word "escape," but said merely, "Do you miss the navy?"

"Yes and no." Alex smiled at her ruefully, then started walking back along the beach while she fell into step beside him. "There are no simple answers, are there? The navy has been my work and my family for half my life. And yet there were things about it that I loathed, like press-gangs. A pressed sailor was worse off than a convict, because impressment was often a life sentence. Some of those poor devils would be released from one ship, then pressed before they could even get home to their families. More than once I let a man go if he claimed to have a wife or child he hadn't seen in years." The viscount was silent for a few moments before continuing.

"The sea is a hard life, and a very confined one. A ship of war is one of the most crowded places in the world. As a junior officer, the only spot where I could find any privacy was perched up in the rigging like a gull. Sometimes I thought the confinement, the endless rules, would drive me mad. And yet . . ." He paused, trying to define what he felt.

"Now that it is gone, you miss it?" Christa prompted.

"Exactly, though I hate to admit it after all my complaining about how rigid the life was." Alex gave her a wry smile, grateful for her ability to grasp his thoughts. "It also seems strange to be leaving the navy at a time when the opportunities for promotion will be greater than they have been in the last decade. War is an appalling waste, yet it is a fighting man's great chance. Perhaps I am not enough of a fighting man."

Christa nodded with resignation. "It is the way of the world. There is nothing uglier or less meaningful than war, yet courage and wisdom may flower from that great evil. Men may grow in ways impossible in times of peace." She gave a melancholy smile. "That is the philosopher in me speaking. As a woman, I can only condemn a war that will kill so many. Will you go back to the navy someday?"

"I don't know," Alex said slowly. "Not before Annabelle and Jonathan are settled. Perhaps never. And yet, for all the drawbacks of a naval life, there are times, especially on the night watch, when the ship comes alive around you. The creaking of the timbers, the rigging and sails humming like a great chorus in perfect harmony with the wind and the stars. There is nothing like it."

With French practicality Christa said, "Why not buy a ship here? You are a lord and can do what pleases you."

Alex stopped, much struck by the thought. "Do you know, the thought never occurred to me? I suppose it is because all of my experience has been with working ships." He laughed suddenly. "Or perhaps because one of our English writers, Samuel Johnson, said that 'anyone who goes to sea for pleasure would go to hell for a pastime.' Sailing is not a common pleasure."

Christa stopped walking also and smiled. "Wasn't it also he who said that 'a boat is like a prison, only with the chance of being drowned'? He sounds like a man who had a very bad Channel crossing."

Alex gave her a surprised glance. "You've read Samuel Johnson?"

Christa gave her best look of wide-eyed innocence. "I have been fortunate that former masters have granted me the use of their libraries." She would have to watch her tongue; too much erudition was out of character for a lady's maid.

"Please make yourself free with my library as well," Alex said. Returning to the topic at hand, he said musingly, "I have been wondering what to do with myself all summer. Sailing is something Annabelle and Jonathan might enjoy also. Perhaps one of the local fishing boats would be suitable . . ."

A wistful expression flickered over Christa's face so quickly that a less-attentive eye would have missed it.

"Have you sailed, Christa?"

She nodded. "Yes, as a child I went out on the fishing boats in Normandy."

"Good. I can use you as crew. And you can take care of Annabelle as well. I'll travel into Ipswich tomorrow to see what I might purchase. Thank you for a wonderful idea, Christa."

On impulse, Alex bent over to place a quick kiss on her cheek, but somehow their lips met and suddenly his arms were around her, her soft curves molding into him. Christa's lips parted under his and the whole world narrowed down to the delicious taste of her mouth, the tangy scent of her hair. It was an embrace as natural as the soft splash of the breaking waves, and her response was as free as his own. They stood locked together in the gathering dark, her arms circling beneath Alex's coat, his hands gently exploring Christa's back and richly curving hips.

The spell was broken by a wave from the advancing tide

that raced up the sand and broke over their feet. They separated, each stepping back. Alex reached out one hand and tenderly brushed a dark curl from her face. "I'm sorry. I don't mean to be one of those masters who abuses his authority."

Christa smiled bewitchingly and briefly turned her cheek into his hand. "You know that I enjoyed that as much as you. But better that it not happen again, *n'est-ce pas*? There is only one way that would end, and it is not a way that would do honor to either of us."

Alex laughed a little sadly. "You are right, of course. Are all Frenchwomen so irresistibly practical?"

She gave a saucy smile. "Most of us are practical, but not all of us are irresistible."

Alex laughed again, this time without reservation. "Of all the things one might find thrown out on a London street, you are the best. Come back to the house now, and I shall do my simple male best to keep my hands off you. It won't be easy."

Somehow their arms slipped around each other as they crossed the sands, hers circling his waist, his protective around her shoulders. They ambled their way up the beach and across the heath lands, their steps matching with unconscious harmony until the house was in view. The sight of the Orchard subtly reestablished the social barriers that had dissolved in the sea breezes. Alex halted. "You go on ahead. If we come in together all windblown and sandy it will do neither of our reputations any good."

Christa gave a very Gallic shrug. "I doubt if a French maid has any reputation to begin with, and your reputation would be enhanced rather than injured."

The viscount stepped back and said firmly, "You are a cynical wench. You are also probably correct in your estimate, but I will send you on ahead anyhow. There is no point in being condemned for deeds we haven't even done."

Christa's answering smile was no more than a white flash in the dusk. "Yes, milord." She dipped one hand into her pocket, then held it out, dropping a smooth, cool object into his hand before she turned and entered the gardens.

Alex watched until she was safely inside, his fingers stroking the flat white pebble she had given him. He placed it in his pocket for safekeeping, then turned and walked back to the shore through the darkness. Christa was becoming an unexpected problem. He had never met a woman who attracted him more, and he had opened up to her in a way unique in his experience. Her lively mind and wise understanding were as appealing as her delectable body; had she been a woman of experience, they might have enjoyed each other freely and without guilt. Had Christa been of his own station, he might have courted her.

But for all her sangfroid and delightful lack of missishness, there was an innocence in her response that convinced him that Christa was a virgin, doubtless of God-fearing peasant stock. And she worked for him. Alex had always despised men of his order who took advantage of the women in their households. It was not unknown for alleged gentlemen to throw maids out in the streets after their masters had impregnated them; he'd heard that half the drabs in London began that way.

If Alex indulged his desires with Christa, he would change her life, and not for the better. There were ways to prevent babies, but they were unreliable, particularly over a long affair, and a single night with Christa could not possibly be enough. He had no desire for his firstborn child to be illegitimate, and bearing a bastard might stand in the way of Christa's marrying a man of her own station. Or if she refused to accept that disgrace, she might find a back-street abortionist, with all the risks that entailed.

Alex shuddered at the picture. All of that bright life tarnished or destroyed—it would not happen at his hands.

But he could feel her lips still, and the memory of her warm body pressed into his. . . .

He had been too long without a woman. When they returned to London, perhaps he should look around for a wife. Alex would be thirty soon, a good age to be setting up a nursery. In the meantime, he would enjoy the summer, would take dancing lessons with Christa, have her on his boat, and treat her with as much circumspection as if she were a lady herself.

A sharp pain stabbed near his ribs as he sat down on the shore to watch the pale breaking waves, and Alex smiled without humor. He had no doubt that Peter Harrington had been right in his speculation that a shell fragment was still embedded in Alex's left side. It was there and moving. From what Peter said, the odds were about even whether it would work its way out or kill him. Thoughts of marriage might prove moot.

Christa rolled over on her narrow cot and punched the pillow viciously, seeking an elusive comfort that might let her sleep. She had gone through the motions of putting Annabelle to bed, but her thoughts had been elsewhere. Now, with no distractions, her mind and body were vividly recalling the embrace on the beach.

In the wake of that discussion, it had seemed such a natural thing to let Alex kiss her. He was a most attractive man, and no one would be harmed by it. Her body's traitorous reaction was entirely new in her experience and threatened to sweep away her prized common sense. Even now, hours later, she could taste his lips and the warm depths of his mouth. Alex had been gentle, yet the memory of his tall muscular strength hinted at a power and passion beyond her experience. Christa was aware that no amount of reading could match reality, and she had a sudden craving to supplement her book learning with experience.

She sat up, carefully straightened the blanket and her twisted nightdress, then lay back and smoothed both neatly over her. Prim as a nun, Christa considered the drawbacks and advantages of a love affair. There was something unbearably tawdry about being tumbled by her employer, and the consequences of that could be disastrous in her present situation. She was a d'Estelle and had far too much pride to give herself to a man who found her passingly attractive. While she was sure Alex Kingsley was sincere in his way, Christa knew that men were slaves to their passions—what would be a pleasant interlude for him would be far more significant to her.

Christa felt a brief stab of fury at the circumstances that brought the two together when there was an unbridgeable social gulf between them. Had it not been for the revolution, her birth and fortune would have more than matched his, and they could have met as equals, free to work out a future if they chose.

She ruthlessly suppressed the thought; life had little to do with fairness, and she must work with what it had given her. She would admire her master from afar, keeping her emotions rigidly in check. And when Suzanne's business had grown to the point where it could support them both, Christa would leave the Kingsleys, heart whole and with her pride intact.

The drawbacks of the situation were obvious and conclusive: an affair with Lord Kingsley was out of the question. But for one last languorous moment she allowed herself to think of the advantages. Christa grinned into the darkness. *Sacrebleu*, but he was a *man*!

Chapter 10

Alex left for Ipswich early the next morning. A strenuous day produced satisfactory results and he returned to the Orchard in time for dinner. During the first course, he said teasingly, "I have some news that may be considered a mixed blessing."

Jonathan ceased his annihilation of a lamb chop long enough to question, "Oh?" while Annabelle knit her brows worriedly and asked, "What do you mean?"

Alex sipped a little red wine, grateful that his prudent father had laid down such an excellent cellar before the war with France and the subsequent blockade. "I found a dancing master in Ipswich. He will come out here once a week all summer, or until Jonathan and I have satisfactorily mastered the art, whichever comes first. Annabelle, you will be the judge of when it is safe to turn us loose in a London ballroom."

Annabelle's happy exclamation was drowned by Jonathan's howl of anguish. "Alex, no, not a dashed caper merchant! Surely you aren't going to make me learn to dance?"

"I most certainly will. It is an essential skill to all aspiring army officers. Because the army is not as fair an institution as the navy, dancing ability plays a role in advancement." Alex had to laugh at his young brother's appalled expression.

"Come, Jon, look upon it as a first lesson in military discipline. You will have to learn many things you won't like, and this is merely the first. If it makes you feel any better, I will be there beside you, and probably making more mistakes, which will give you the opportunity to feel superior."

Jonathan had too much adolescent pride to admit that he might enjoy dancing. However, when he had gone that morning to renew his acquaintance with his old friend Tom, the vicar's son, he had noticed that Tom's sister, Sally, had changed out of all recognition, and much for the better. It wouldn't hurt to learn how to dance; Jonathan knew that females set great store by it, and he dimly recognized that someday he might want to impress a girl.

"When is the dancing master coming, Alex?" Annabelle asked.

"Monday, the day before I go to Ipswich for my new boat."

"Your *what*?" This time his siblings were in chorus.

Alex smiled, vastly pleased with himself. "This morning I bought a small boat in Ipswich."

"Whatever for?" Jonathan asked curiously.

"For sailing, of course. And you lucky people are going to learn how to sail too."

There was a long pause while his brother and sister chewed and thought. Unlike his brother, Jonathan's passion had always been for horses and riding rather than the sea. Still, it should be quite fun going out on a boat, and he was in favor of any project that gave him more time in his brother's company. "I think I shall enjoy that, Alex."

Annabelle wasn't so sure. It sounded very strange, and not at all proper, to go sailing for no reason; no young lady of her acquaintance had ever done such a thing. But if her brother wanted her to sail, she would try. "What should I wear, Alex?"

Her brother frowned thoughtfully. "A good point. Jon, do you have some old breeches and shirts that might fit Belle? You were her height not long ago."

"Breeches!" Annabelle squeaked in horror. "I've never done anything so improper in my life!"

Alex smiled at her. "Then it's high time you started. Otherwise, you might be hopelessly missish by the end of this autumn's Season."

He chuckled at her outraged expression, then said coaxingly, "I really think you will enjoy sailing, Belle. If you don't, of course you needn't continue, but it would please me if you at least tried. Besides, I've named the boat *Annabelle*." Alex privately thought that *Christa* would be more appropriate but decided that would invite too many questions.

His sister looked at him fondly, her resistance melted. "If you want me to go sailing, of course I shall. But what if I succumb to mal de mer?"

"We'll take Christa to look after you. She's an experienced sailor and can assure you that you will survive. See if you can find some breeches for her too. Someone on the estate must have a son about her size."

Alex saw the beginnings of a question in his sister's eyes and thought she might be wondering how he had learned so much about her maid. Fortunately, the perfect distraction came to mind. "By the way, Belle, I ran into a navy friend in Ipswich today and asked him about Sir Edward Loaming. The man has an unsavory reputation. If he calls on you in London, refuse him."

Her eyes fixed on her plate, Annabelle murmured in a barely audible tone, "Very well, Alex."

It never occurred to Alex, used to years of giving orders in the navy, that he might not be obeyed.

The dancing lesson turned into a comic disaster. Soon after lunch on Monday, the three Kingsleys and Christa assembled in the Orchard's great hall, which also served as the ballroom. The dancing master, Mr. Rockland, was at heart a composer, but dreary reality forced him to find more lucrative occupations to support his family. He didn't mind teaching young ladies to dance because they were usually enthusiastic, but in his experience, young gentlemen like Master Jonathan were a much less predictable quantity. At least half of them took lessons under duress and seemed to delight in their clumsiness.

What the dancing master had not expected was that the man who had hired him, an adult and a viscount, no less, should prove so hopelessly incompetent. Even the simple country dance Mr. Rockland began with produced missteps, wrong turns, and collisions. The younger brother was little better. The two young ladies—though one, as he later sniffed to his wife, was certainly not a *lady*—were skillful enough, but the expanding chaos of the dance lesson soon reduced the two young Kingsleys to hysterical giggles. Within half an hour the lesson was a complete shambles.

While Jonathan and Annabelle were having a wonderful time, only Christa noticed Alex's tight-lipped frustration. After an hour, Mr. Rockland gathered up his accompanist and stalked out with an air of great injury, while Jon clowned outrageously for his sister's amusement. Under cover of their laughter, Christa went up to Alex and asked quietly, "Lord Kingsley, do you have trouble telling left from right?"

Alex looked at her for a long moment while a muscle in

his jaw jumped. Under most circumstances he was able to conceal the mental quirk that caused him to confuse directions, words, and numbers. He had had trouble learning how to read, and as a student at Eton he was frequently beaten by masters who assumed that any boy so brilliant in some areas must be willfully obtuse to fail in others. Alex had always had trouble with examinations, and under acute emotional stress was often unable to find meaningful words. With maturity he had learned how to work around his problem, chiefly by substituting direct physical action for verbal confusion. It had been years since he had found himself in a situation like this one, where the humiliations of his childhood were painfully resurrected.

"I can tell them apart eventually, but not, unfortunately, quickly enough for this," he said shortly. "It appears that I have no possible future on the dance floor."

"Not necessarily," she said thoughtfully. "Would it help if you were taught with the terms 'port' and 'starboard'?"

Alex chuckled suddenly in appreciation of how ridiculous the situation was. At least Christa accepted his handicap as a matter of course. "No, my dear, the problem is not in the terminology, but rather in the quickness of thought required. The caper merchant says 'left,' my brain apparently hears 'right,' and the next moment I am crashing into my neighbor rather than pivoting gracefully around my partner. And while crashing into you is quite enjoyable, such behavior is not apt to prove acceptable at a London ball."

Christa looked at him with her eyes narrowed thoughtfully. "It is a problem, but not, I think, insurmountable. Have you noticed that your brother has the same problem in lesser degree?"

Alex was startled. He had been so absorbed in his own failure that he had not realized that Jonathan wasn't doing much better than he himself. "You mean we're both hopeless?"

"Not at all, but you will need to be taught in a different way. Are you willing to discuss this with your brother and sister? With Annabelle's help, you and Master Jonathan should soon be dancing well enough."

Alex thought a moment. After years of concealing his nameless affliction, it went against the grain to bring it out in the open. Still, it would be a good way to prove to his siblings that he wasn't infallible.

"Lead on, *mademoiselle*. If you can really teach a hard case like me, you will have a new career ahead of you."

Tired out by laughter, Jonathan and Annabelle had tumbled onto the sofas and settled down to the tea and cakes that Morrison had discreetly brought in moments before. Christa naturally did not join them, but after the Kingsleys had refreshed themselves, she looked expectantly at Alex. This was the kind of occasion for which he often had trouble finding words, but under her encouraging gaze he cleared his throat and said, "I must apologize for ruining our dance lesson. I hadn't realized how necessary it would be to tell right from left. Unfortunately, that particular skill is one I am lacking."

Jonathan shot a startled look at his brother. "You too, Alex? I always thought I was the one who inherited all the family clumsiness."

"We resemble each other more than I realized, Jon," Alex said ruefully. "Belle, can you tell directions?"

She gave a guilty start. "Most of the time," she said cautiously. "It helps that I wear a ring on my" —she stopped and glanced at her hand—"left hand."

There was a long pause before Jonathan said kindly, "Belle, that's your right hand."

The three confused Kingsleys started to laugh together,

and for the next quarter hour they exchanged stories about their past experiences. Listening, Christa decided that Alex was the most afflicted and Annabelle the least, although, as that young lady said, "I scarcely noticed I had a problem because no one expects a young lady to know whether she is coming or going."

That remark produced another round of laughter. As the merriment died down, Alex said, "Christa thinks she may have a teaching method that can help Jon and me. Perhaps if she will explain?"

"It is very simple," Christa replied, her hands turning out. Alex was coming to realize that her hands were as expressive and enjoyable to watch as her face. "After all, Miss Annabelle has learned how to dance. Do you remember how you did it?"

"Well," Annabelle said hesitantly, "I had problems, but I wanted very much to learn, so I practiced a great deal with the other girls at the school. Eventually I knew the movements so well that I didn't have to think about them. All that work," she added wistfully, "and I have yet to show my skills at a ball."

"Then you will be gratified to hear that the Harringtons have invited us to dinner this Thursday," Alex said. "They would like to reintroduce us to our neighbors. Mrs. Harrington said there will be music later if any of the young people want to stand up for a few sets." Ignoring his sister's squeak of pleasure, he continued, "We must hope your teaching technique works, Christa."

"It's not complicated, my lord. If you go through the movements slowly, over and over, eventually your body will remember how to do them and your mind will no longer be needed so you can concentrate on paying extravagant compliments to your partner." Christa made a gesture to her mistress. "Miss Annabelle, if you and I act as partners, and your brothers put their hands on our shoulders . . ."

Christa and Annabelle stood opposite each other in the position for a simple reel. Alex moved behind Christa and put his hands gently on her shoulders while Jonathan did the same behind Annabelle. The two girls hummed the music and slowly moved through the steps. Sure enough, it was easier for Alex to follow the motion transmitted through his fingers than it was to listen to someone speak commands.

Alex had decided that it was his brotherly duty to be the one working with Christa. Being only fifteen, Jonathan might have been so tempted by her satiny skin that he wouldn't have learned anything. Yet in spite of his advanced years, Alex found it difficult to refrain from stroking her neck in a manner that had nothing to do with dancing.

Back and forth, twice to the right. And when Christa turned her head, the same tangy fragrance he had noticed on the beach brought a sharp memory of Malta and a sun-kissed hillside overlooking the azure calm of the Mediter-ranean. *Side to side and turn around.* Rosemary, that's what the scent was. Alex had found a whole hillside covered with it in Malta. Christa must use the herb on her hair. It suited her—piquant and unusual, but at the same time as straightforward as she was.

Absorbed in his thoughts, Alex followed Christa's lead through a number of repetitions of the steps, at progressively faster speeds. He was surprised when he realized the practice had stopped. Christa had certainly done a splendid job of distracting him from thinking about his feet!

The four of them danced again, but this time as couples. After so many repetitions of the steps, the two males could get through the reel without mishap. In another half hour they were dancing with ease and beginning to converse with their partners.

The lesson ended with a late-afternoon tea tray. This time, by unanimous consent, Christa joined them for the refreshments. The Kingsleys all insisted that she had earned the privilege.

A burst of water splashed her face and Christa laughed with the sheer pleasure of it. She was at the tiller of the *Annabelle*, while Alex was forward, instructing his siblings in the intricacies of sails, lines, and the all-important necessity of avoiding the boom when it came about suddenly.

The day after the first dance class, Alex went to Ipswich to collect his new boat, sailing it home with the help of the former owner. Early the next morning, he had his crew down at the cove for their first sailing session. The day promised to be fair and clear—perfect for a new outdoor venture.

Alex started by distributing long-sleeved woolen jerseys to them. An old woman from the Channel Isles lived in Ipswich, and she had knitted the garments out of heavy off-white wool. Alex owned a similar jersey that he had acquired years earlier, and he explained that the natural oil in the yarn kept a sailor warm even when the jersey was soaked. Moreover, the garment allowed free movement. Annabelle had balked a bit at the large shapeless pullover but became a convert to its use when the boat reached open water, where the sea breezes were cool but the sailors stayed comfortably warm.

Christa thought that their captain looked wonderfully dashing with his well-worn jersey stretching across his wide shoulders. Before they set sail, he had questioned her to determine her level of nautical expertise, then made

her second in command as they sailed into the nearby
estuary that led to Ipswich. It was a good place for novice
sailors, calm enough to reduce the possibility of sea-
sickness, and with a steady breeze. After Alex turned the
tiller over to Christa, the sailing lesson for Annabelle and
Jonathan began in earnest.

The salt spray and wind were playing havoc with Christa's
hair, and by the end of the day her curls would be a mad
mass that would require patient disentangling and a wash.
It didn't matter. Christa could not remember when she had
felt so free—certainly not since before the Revolution
began six years before. She might be a servant, but today
she would not have changed places with anyone.

It was also, Christa remembered with a start, her birthday. She was twenty-four years old today and felt half a
century younger than on her last birthday, when she was
living in depressed luxury at Radcliffe Hall. For all her
change in station, life was far better now.

The *Annabelle* was a sweet, responsive boat. Steering
her was easy and left Christa the time to keep a lazy eye
on Alex. Clearly he was in his element, his golden hair
as windblown as her own, his movements unconsciously
graceful as he accommodated himself to the boat's motions.

Raising the jib, he winced slightly. Christa frowned. She
had thought he was favoring his left side and was now
sure of it. The whole household knew the viscount had
been seriously wounded in the Mediterranean, and she
hoped for his sake that the damage would eventually heal.

Having drilled his students enough for one session, Alex
left them to their own devices and went aft to sit by Christa
at the tiller. That morning when he had seen the two girls
in their breeches, it was clear that such garments had a
definite place in the female wardrobe. At least, they had
merit from a man's point of view. Annabelle's long legs

were elegantly slender in Jonathan's old breeches, and she seemed to move with more confidence as she became used to the freedom. As for Christa—if the French fleet at the Battle of the Saintes had sent women with curves like hers into the rigging, they would have carried the day as the British fleet was reduced to lustful wonder.

"What do you think of the *Annabelle*?" Alex asked as he seated himself on the far side of the tiller from her.

"She's a lovely lady," Christa said. "Sails more closely to the wind than any boat I have ever been on. What kind is she?"

"I don't know if this type of boat has a particular name—there are so many kinds of coastal vessels. She is something like the Thames bawleys that work the estuary waters around here, but larger and with more draft so she'll do for deep-water sailing. I suspect someone built her for smuggling, actually. Don't laugh," he said at Christa's chuckle. "That is an important industry around here."

"Do you wish to set up as a smuggler, my lord?" she teased.

"I was thinking of a more legitimate business, actually. Perhaps I'll buy into a merchant fleet. But not for the *Annabelle*. She is just for me. I could sail round the world in her."

"You would need a crew, Captain Kingsley."

"Then you could come with me." The comment was light but the warm look in the clear amber eyes was not. Their gazes locked for a moment before she turned to look forward, where Annabelle was hanging over the bow like an improbably beautiful figurehead, spray flying into her face and hair as the boat cut through the waves. Christa was glad that she had braided her mistress's hair—it would simplify the combing later.

"Your sister is growing lovelier every day. She will be a great success this autumn."

Alex accepted the change of subject, not sure whether to be relieved or sorry that the French girl had ignored his remark about going off with him. When he was around Christa, his tongue took on a life of its own. "I hope so. Belle will enjoy her Season much more if she is confident and sought after. My sister has had few opportunities for pleasure before now."

Christa thought of Annabelle's fascinated reaction to the coxcomb in the park and decided a warning was in order. "For that reason, my lord, you had best keep a close eye on her."

Alex glanced at her appraisingly. "Why do you say that?" In the back of his mind lurked memories of his mother's unbridled promiscuity, but he could not imagine Annabelle following that course. While his sister had her mother's beauty, her temperament was wholly different.

Christa seemed to guess what he was thinking. "She is young; she will be much courted. It is enough to turn any young girl's head, especially one who is not used to being admired. It will be good experience if she goes out socially this summer."

"There will be no lack of opportunities. We have invitations from half the county. Our family is well-known here, and she should come to no harm." Alex hesitated, then said carefully, "I know a lady and her woman often share many secrets. I don't want you to spy on her but . . . I am sure that you and I both have her welfare at heart." His tone held a slight question.

Christa nodded, aware of what he was asking. "You need have no fears on that head, my lord. I have seen my share of the world's wolves and will do my best to keep them from your lamb." She rose, effortlessly keeping her balance on the moving deck. "The sun is well past its zenith. With your permission, I will serve the luncheon Monsieur Sabine sent with us."

"Excellent. Sea air is always a good excuse for appetite." Alex watched Christa go forward, admiring her deft movements. Not only was she attractive, intelligent, and exuberantly alive but she was at home on a ship. He had the dismal feeling that it would be hard to find a woman her equal among the pampered ladies of the beau monde.

Annabelle was supposed to be resting before her first evening party at the Harringtons', but instead she tossed fretfully, envisioning scenarios of social disaster. It was one thing to confront her brothers, quite another to face a roomful of strangers.

"But they are not strangers," Christa said patiently as she sat by her mistress's bed repairing a flounce with tiny stitches. "Most have known you since you were in leading strings."

"That makes it worse!" Annabelle wailed. "They will be remembering Lady Serena and wondering how she came to have such an ugly-duckling daughter." She pressed one hand to her forehead and closed her eyes. "Christa, how will I be able to face them?"

Christa tied a knot in her thread and clipped it with her scissors. "Don't you think you are succumbing to vanity? It is one of the seven deadly sins, you know."

"Vanity!" Annabelle's eyes flew open in indignation. "When my fear is that the whole neighborhood will think I am dreadful?"

"What is it but vanity to assume that everyone there will be so interested in you? Most people are concerned first of all with themselves, second with those they care

about. Since they hardly know you, most will not be very
interested in you."

She laid the repaired dress aside and picked up a stocking that needed darning. "More than that, many of them
will be worried about *your* opinion. After all, you are the
only daughter of the most important family in the district.
You are coming from London, you will be wearing a gown
that cost more than some of the girls' annual dress al-
lowances, and you will be escorted by a distinguished and
indulgent brother. You will be much envied. It will be easy
to become popular."

Annabelle turned her head to look at her maid, fascinated by this novel view of the world. "How will I accomplish that?"

Christa looked up at her, the mending temporarily
forgotten in her lap. "Simply be good-natured and not
proud. Those who are disposed to like you will be pleased
at your friendliness, and the toadeaters will be enthralled
by your condescension. Those who are *not* disposed to like
you will find a reason to condemn you no matter what you
do, so they are of no account."

Annabelle giggled. "You make it sound so easy. Where
did you learn to be so wise?"

"I had good teachers." Christa thought for a moment,
then said, "This evening is really your introduction to society, more so than the ball you will have in London. Because
that is so, I will tell you a very great secret."

"What is that?" Annabelle asked eagerly.

"The secret of being beautiful. It was known by Cleopa-
tra, by Helen of Troy, by Aphrodite herself."

"What can you possibly mean?" Annabelle asked, intrigued.

"Beauty begins in the mind. It helps to have hair and a
face and a figure like yours, but it is the *belief* that one is

beautiful that carries all before you. Everyone is beautiful sometimes, when the heart and soul are in harmony. When you have a very special need to be lovely, like tonight, just close your eyes and think of that."

Annabelle obediently shut her eyes while Christa continued to speak, her voice soothing. "Think 'I am beautiful, in my heart, in my mind, in my soul. It is a gift to those around me, and no one can take it from me. Tonight I will know that I am at my loveliest, and that will free me to make others feel beautiful too.' Think of yourself as you wish to be, loving yourself, helping others love themselves and be beautiful too."

Christa softly repeated such sentences until the lines of anxiety had smoothed from Annabelle's face and she fell asleep. After straightening a blanket over the girl, Christa went into her own room to complete the mending. It was beastly how thoroughly Lady Serena had blighted her daughter's confidence. Some might think Annabelle's fears ludicrous, but her fear was nonetheless real for having no basis in fact. When Annabelle looked in the mirror, she saw not her own lovely face, but her belief that she was unlovable. That would not be eradicated overnight, but in time . . . in time.

Christa took special care with Annabelle's toilette and had the satisfaction of seeing her mistress go off in her best looks and with her nerves under reasonable control. Alex had come to his sister's chamber to escort her down to the carriage, and he praised his sister's apple-green dress and fashionable coiffure effusively. Just before leaving the room after Annabelle, he glanced at Christa and gave her a broad wink that clearly linked them in a conspiracy to ensure his sister's success. She chuckled as his elegantly tailored back disappeared; he seemed to know exactly what Annabelle needed.

Christa spent most of her evening teaching reading and writing to those of the staff who desired to learn. She had started with four students the week before, and her class had now grown to seven. The butler, Mr. Morrison, had found funds to pay for primers and slates, and now every quiet evening after supper Christa and her students would take over one end of the servants' dining table. Many of them were motivated by a desire to improve their positions, since most upper servants had to know how to read and write. However, a few were like the head groom, there for the pure pleasure of learning, and Christa took special pride in their progress.

The evening passed quickly, and Christa retired to lie down and doze until Annabelle returned. It was past midnight when the Kingsleys returned, and Annabelle was bubbling with excited chatter. Christa had anticipated this and had a kettle of hot water ready to make her mistress a cup of relaxing herb tea.

"Oh, Christa, you were right, everyone was so kind!" Annabelle sat in front of her dressing table, her eyes bright with happiness. "They seemed happy to see me, and when I went out of my way to talk to some of the shyer girls, they acted so pleased, as if I was doing them a favor! It was remarkable. And when we danced after the dinner, I stood up for every set. Why, Alex said every unattached man there was fluttering around me." She giggled in pure delight.

Christa smiled at her mistress's reflection as she removed the pins that held twists of golden hair at the back of Annabelle's head. "So your evening was a success?"

Annabelle nodded vigorously. "It was more fun than I ever imagined. And you were right. When I stopped worrying about what people thought about *me*, and started thinking about *them*, they responded so well! It was remarkable."

Christa chuckled and started brushing Annabelle's long tresses down over her shoulders. "Congratulations. Besides having learned the secret of beauty today, you have also learned the secret of charm."

"Which is . . . ?" Annabelle's eyes were dancing as she met Christa's gaze in the mirror.

"To let the other person think that he is the most interesting person in the world. With those two secrets, London will be at your feet." Christa flourished the brush grandly before returning to her task.

"It is going to be at Alex's feet, actually," Annabelle laughed. "The women there wouldn't leave him alone. Ouch!" She squeaked as the hairbrush jerked painfully in a snarl.

"Forgive me, Miss Annabelle," Christa murmured, her lips a trifle stiff. She resumed the smooth, gentle brush strokes, then said carefully, "It is only to be expected that your brother would be popular. He is handsome, a hero, wealthy, and available. An answer to a maiden's prayer, in fact."

"It wasn't just maidens who were after him. Twice I had to rescue him from a particular predatory matron who acted as if Alex were catnip and she the cat."

"Me-o-o-w," Christa said with a twinkle.

"That may sound unkind, but it's true. It was surprising, actually. My big strong brother seemed to become paralyzed when that woman was around. Alex was comfortable enough with the men, but he seemed to avoid most of the ladies."

"Perhaps he has some of the same shyness you had," Christa suggested.

Annabelle frowned thoughtfully. "You may be right, though it's a difficult idea to accept. Well, Alex and I must learn to conquer London together." She yawned. "That tea doesn't have much flavor but it's effective! What's in it?"

"Oh, valerian, anise seed, hops."

"It certainly made me ready for bed. Good night, Christa."

"Dream of your triumphs," Christa said as she quietly closed the door to her own little room. It looked as if Annabelle was making excellent progress. And Christa had no right to find the news of Alex's success so depressing.

The pattern established in the first week lasted all summer. East Anglia has drier summers and colder winters than most of Great Britain, and this summer of 1795 was particularly fine, each long golden day succeeded by another. While conditions were hard on crops, for the Kingsleys it was the stuff memories are made of.

Alex took his crew sailing two or three times a week. Soon both Jonathan and Annabelle were adept at handling sails and rigging, though neither had the intuitive affinity for wind and sea that Alex and Christa shared. The three blond Kingsleys found their hair bleaching to white gold, and even Annabelle's alabaster skin acquired a light tan in spite of Christa's best efforts with bonnets and cucumber lotion.

Christa herself was brown as a nut, her gray eyes startlingly light against her tanned skin and black curls. Alex found his eyes following her when no one was watching. He admired how she blended in, seldom volunteering comments but always ready with a merry quip when someone addressed her. She seemed almost a part of the family, yet never crossed the line of what was proper for a servant.

Alex was unquestionably the captain at sea, but the dance lessons were another story. There Christa was firmly in charge. A local music teacher played the pianoforte while Christa drilled her fumble-footed charges. By the third week, Alex and Jonathan had mastered several dances so Christa added a new dimension to the lessons by requiring that they converse. There is an art to speaking with a partner while whirling in opposite directions, and by the end of the summer the Kingsley menfolk had mastered it. In fact, after an initial relapse into cross-purposes and collisions, they found that talking made dancing easier because it kept them from thinking about the movements.

The twice-weekly sessions were filled with laughter as the participants chatted about what they knew best. Alex regaled them with tales of the navy and foreign lands, convulsing his partners with anecdotes that always seemed to make him the hapless victim. A listener could have been forgiven for assuming that he was an outrageous incompetent rather than a highly regarded naval officer who had distinguished himself from the Battle of St. Vincent, when he had been a scant fifteen years old, through the Glorious First of June and beyond.

Annabelle's shyness had made her a keen observer of her neighbors, and her increasingly forthright comments were shrewd and amusing without ever being unkind. The biggest surprise was Jonathan, who turned out to have a passion for poetry in addition to his undoubted expertise about horses and the army.

If any of the Kingsleys had stopped to think of it, they might have been surprised at how fluently the lady's maid could converse on every topic offered. Had they but known, their teacher had been acclaimed as one of the best dancers and conversationalists in Paris in the days when frivolity reigned in that capital. Instead, the dancers merely enjoyed the discussions, and they all learned a great deal.

By the time they packed to return to London, the two younger Kingsleys no longer kept the head of the family on quite so high a pedestal, and the three siblings had developed deep bonds of affection that would last the rest of their lives. Jonathan had grown two inches and his voice made a permanent transition to the lower registers. As his gangling frame filled out, his resemblance to his older brother became even more pronounced.

Annabelle became the belle of the neighborhood. It was the fashion among the young men that summer to languish after her, and she developed a latent talent for flirting to elegant perfection. Soon she could accept compliments gracefully, put a bashful swain at his ease, and make an older man feel young again. Her natural sweetness prevented any hearts from being seriously damaged and made her popular with her own sex as well. The prospect of the Season no longer held terrors for her.

Alex was satisfied with how the summer had passed, and deeply grateful to discover that his younger brother and sister had not been irrevocably damaged by their mother. Their growing confidence was a source of pride to him, and much of his guilt over neglecting them had been assuaged.

Yet when Alex thought back over the months in the country, it was Christa that occupied his thoughts, Christa scampering around the *Annabelle* in her all-too-revealing breeches, Christa's warm shoulders beneath his hands as she walked him through new dance steps, Christa glancing up through those glorious black lashes to make some devastatingly acute comment as they chatted their way through reels and country dances.

Alex's resolution not to lead her astray was coming under increasing pressure. He had never known a female who attracted him more, and on nights when sleep eluded him, he lay and wondered if she would accept a carte blanche. He was more than willing to make a settlement that would give her security for life, and he found himself wrestling with the ethical question of whether her situation would be better or worse as his mistress.

Many girls of her station would be delighted at such an offer, but Alex had an uneasy suspicion that she would not be one of that number. Besides, if he did start keeping Christa, Annabelle would be deprived of a superlative abigail.

Christa felt restless the last night before leaving for London. All of Annabelle's packing was done, as well as the extremely modest amount required for Christa's own possessions. The reading class had done so well over the summer that the more advanced students now taught the others, and her services were no longer needed. Annabelle was fixed for the evening at the home of a female friend and would not need her until late, so Christa decided to stroll down to the shore.

She hadn't walked here at night since the first evening when she had met Alex and shared that kiss. The memory was sweet, but her practical French nature led her to avoid temptation for the rest of the summer. On this particular evening she felt a little reckless. When the household was settled in London, she would see almost nothing of her master, and she was already missing the playful companionship they had shared.

The moon was full, and Christa easily picked out his dark figure silhouetted against the shining waves as he sat on the end of the pier that thrust its way into the cove. The moonlight reflected off his hair, turning its gold to silver. She had known he would be here, would almost have sworn he had been calling her.

Alex looked up at the sound of her soft steps on the oak

planking and smiled a greeting. "I thought you would come here tonight to say your farewells to the sea."

She smiled a reply and seated herself next to him, close, but not too close, her legs swinging over the water. "Yes. It makes me sad to leave here, my lord. There will never be another summer like it."

"True. Next summer no dance lessons will be required. I would never have believed that I could be made presentable for a ballroom. You're a remarkable teacher."

She ignored the compliment. "The credit belongs to you and your brother. You both worked most diligently."

"You made it a pleasure for all of us. Anyone who can convince a fifteen-year-old boy to spend afternoons indoors should be in the diplomatic corps."

"As I recall, you first used your lordly authority to *order* his presence." She chuckled. "But it was in a good cause. That one will be a heartbreaker when he is a few years older. Put him in a Hussar uniform and there won't be a maiden in England whose heart will be safe."

"I'm afraid you're right," the proud brother said gloomily. "Before he returns to Eton, I must have a talk with him about responsible behavior, or I'll be having irate fathers seeking me out. This head-of-family business can be heavy going."

"You seem to take to it well, my lord. Teaching your brother and sister to sail was inspired. Miss Annabelle is much more confident now that she has learned to do something well."

"I think a good deal more credit goes to what you have done with her hair and wardrobe. What was all the giggling I heard yesterday morning? I would have investigated, but I was due at one of the tenant farms."

"Oh, that!" Christa laughed reminiscently. "I was showing her how to wear a shawl gracefully. It was very long, six yards by two yards, I think. There is a real art to wearing one without falling over it or looking like a gin-soaked street woman."

"Hmm, I can see the problem. Fashion has unsuspected hazards. Did she learn the skill?"

"Eventually. But not without some trial and error. That must be when you heard us giggling."

"I'm sorry I missed it!" He chuckled. "London will require more dignity, I fear. But there will be another summer next year."

Christa shrugged. "Things will have changed. Perhaps Miss Annabelle will be married by then."

Alex was silent for a long moment, his face hidden in shadow. "It won't be the same with Jonathan and me here in a bachelor establishment."

"Nothing is ever the same. That is why we must live each moment we are given."

He laughed, a warm sound in the night. "I have never known anyone else who approached life as a study in philosophy."

"I warned you before that we French are a philosophical race."

"Tell me," Alex asked curiously, "are all Frenchwomen as politically knowledgeable as you?"

Christa considered a moment to find an answer that would be true without being too revealing. "My country is different from yours in many ways. For example, a third of our peasants own their own land, not like here, where almost everyone is a tenant or laborer. And if one owns something, is there not a greater desire to understand, to participate in what is happening?"

"I never really thought about it," he answered slowly. "But it makes sense. I feel a responsibility to study the issues and use my seat in the Lords on behalf of myself and my tenants. Any man would feel the same."

"And any woman," was her tart reply. "Someday, perhaps we shall have the same power over our destinies as men."

"You are a proper revolutionary, aren't you?" Alex said admiringly. "I begin to fear that one morning I will come down and find a mob led by you and Monsieur Sabine demanding new laws and better wages."

Christa laughed. "No need to worry, the Monsieur is a royalist. Besides, there is no one in your household who feels ill-used. Most of your servants believe themselves singularly fortunate to be in your employ."

He turned toward her, his face suddenly serious. "And how do you feel, Christa? Are you happy to be in my household?"

Her heart accelerated its beat, but her reply was calm. "Of course. Your rescuing me from the streets of London was the best thing that has happened to me in years."

The first time Alex had kissed her on impulse, but this time he seemed entirely deliberate. He reached out and cupped her cheek gently, then moved his hand behind her head and turned her face to his. She could easily have eluded him but made no attempt to do so. This moonlit night was for romance, not reason.

What began as a leisurely embrace flared into passion with stunning force. How could she have forgotten the taste of his mouth, the warmth of his body pressed into hers? Her gossamer-thin muslin dress and shift were scarcely a barrier, and she could feel the escalating beat of his heart, the tensing of his muscles as he fitted her curves into his angles. Christa was hazily aware that they were lying on the hard planks of the pier and Alex's body half covered hers, protecting her from the cool sea breeze.

They lay locked together for long minutes, exploring all the subtle variations of lips and tongues. At length, Alex rolled onto his side, his arms pulling her close against him. "Oh, Christa, Christa, what am I going to do with you?" he said softly, his voice nearly a groan.

Christa buried her face against his chest, unable to reply. You fool, she thought despairingly, you unutterably smug fool! At what point in this perfect summer had respect and affection insidiously turned to love? She had been so sure that her mind controlled her heart, that a moonlight kiss with a man who could be trusted not to go too far was a simple, harmless diversion.

Instead, she found herself wracked by waves of unfamiliar emotion. Christa had always known that Alex was attractive, that he was a considerate master, a loving brother, a hero who could laugh at himself. She had enjoyed sailing and dancing and talking with him, admiring the way their minds fitted. But the feeling sweeping through her now was so much more than the sum of those things; it was a profound sense of physical and emotional attunement beyond anything she had ever known.

The loss of her family in the revolution had outweighed all other deprivations, but now Christa found herself raging against the cruel fortune that had taken her name, her wealth, and her right to meet this man as an equal. She knew that Alex cared for her and there was no doubt that he found her attractive, but that would be an end to it. It would not occur to him that he might love a maid, any more than Christa would have thought to fall in love with a footman in the long-ago days when she was a wealthy countess. Lust there might be between master and servant, but mutual love? Unthinkable.

Alex stroked her back and said tenderly, "Are you trying to burrow your way through me, *ma chérie?*"

The French endearment almost overset her composure before pride came to her rescue. If Christa told him of her feelings, he would be kind, but also embarrassed, perhaps even secretly amused at her presumption. If she said her birth was equal to his own, that would be even worse—he might doubt her or he might pity her, but neither of those unpalatable alternatives would be the love she craved from him.

Christa raised her head and rolled away from his embrace, lifting herself on one elbow. She was proud of the steadiness of her voice when she said, "I think I was trying to hold onto a moment that should never have happened, my lord."

He brushed the silky curls from her cheek, his fingers lingering, then trailing down her smooth neck. "I wish that once you would call me Alex."

"For this moment only, Alex." Christa leaned over and placed a light kiss on his forehead, then stood before he could embrace her again, an embrace that could easily destroy her pride and sense of self preservation. She was grateful that he was a gentleman; if he seriously attempted to seduce her, she doubted her ability to withstand him. But then, if he were not honorable, she would not love him.

Alex stood also, then placed both hands on her shoulders and looked down, his eyes searching as he spoke with unconscious poetry. "You are such a blend of contradictions. You can enjoy life with the simplicity of a child, yet have a wisdom rare at any age. The logical mind of a lawyer with a body to drive a man wild. Child and woman, ice and fire."

Her gray eyes were quartz-clear in the moonlight as he continued. "What kinds of plans and dreams do you have, Christa?"

She gazed back, sadness in her voice. "Plans? I think the gods mock those mortals who think they control their own lives. I try to sail where the wind sends me." She shrugged. "For now, I'll continue with Miss Annabelle. If I have a dream, it is to have my own business, perhaps be a *modiste* with my cousin, Suzanne de Savary, who makes your sister's gowns. To be independent, to have a little comfort and a little freedom."

Alex chided himself for his sharp surge of disappointment. After all, was it likely she would answer that she sought a rich man to keep her? "And what of marriage and children?"

There was a slight catch in Christa's voice as she answered, "That least of all can be planned for. But I think I am too particular in my tastes and may never marry." Uncomfortable under his intent stare, she asked, "What will you do when we return to London, my . . . Alex? Do you aspire to become a man of leisure rather than a man of action?"

He shook his head. "As much as I have enjoyed this summer, I will be ready for more employment in London. It was suggested that I might be of value at the Admiralty, so I intend to volunteer my services there. The Royal Navy is growing rapidly to fight the French and my experience may be useful." Alex glanced at the moon, calculating the hour, then said, "It's time to go back to the house if we are to make an early start tomorrow. I will walk you back."

Christa glanced up at him as he slid his arm around her waist, and they walked along the pier toward the beach. "You think I would not be safe on your land, Alex?" She liked saying his name, rolling it on her tongue in a distinctively French manner.

"I must admit that you are in more danger from me than from bandits or wild beasts."

"Do you truly expect me to believe that?" Christa asked softly.

"You should," Alex said wryly. The moonlight burnished his bright hair.

The rest of the walk was made in companionable silence, at as slow a pace as two healthy adults could manage. Once again, it was the sight of the house, a black-and-white mosaic in the moonlight, that brought them back to awareness.

Christa stopped, the breath caught in her throat at Alex's expression before he wrapped his arms around her in a bear hug. "It is so hard to let you go . . ."

"But you must, my lord. It is time for the princess to become once more a scullery maid."

Alex laughed ruefully as he released her. "You have a talent for bringing things down to earth." Once more he asked, "What should I do about you, Christa?"

"Nothing, my lord," she said firmly. "I am not yours to dispose of."

He sighed. "I know. You belong to yourself . . ."

"And I intend to keep it that way." Christa's voice was low, but the message was unmistakable.

Alex was unprepared for the wave of desolation that swept over him as he watched her graceful passage down the gentle slope to the house. It took every ounce of his willpower not to follow her and beg that she become his mistress. The desire that Christa had always aroused in him was now an inferno, and he doubted that any other woman would be able to extinguish it.

But he was afraid to make the offer. Alex wanted to believe that her steely integrity and independent spirit could not be corrupted. It was a romantic fancy on his part, since part of her charm was the irresistible combination of cool logic and sensuality. The same practicality that led

Christa to avoid a casual entanglement might make her willing to sell her body in return for the money to finance her future. If so, he didn't want to know it—if she would not give herself freely, he would not buy her with gold. As he watched her enter the rear door of the house, Alex damned himself for an idealistic fool.

Chapter 11

The cavalcade to London might have left on time had it not been for complications from an unexpected source. Monsieur Sabine had been more than usually moody the last few days, and on this morning he crossed his arms on his chest and flatly refused to leave. When the butler, Morrison, attempted to determine why, the Monsieur managed only to convey that he could not leave the Orchard before his speech deteriorated into a babble of French imprecations and sweeping gestures.

Grateful that the Monsieur did not have his carving knife in hand, Morrison sent for Lord Kingsley. While it was unusual for the master to concern himself with the details of belowstairs life, cooks were personages of great importance. After a moment's thought, Morrison also sent for Christa to translate, suspecting that his lordship's French might not be up to the torrent of invective pouring from the Monsieur.

Christa arrived in the kitchen to find Alex attempting to make sense out of Monsieur Sabine. The cook was waving his arms and periodically grasping at his plump chest. Alex greeted her entrance with relief.

"Thank heaven you're here! Can you understand what

he is saying? I'm afraid he may be having some kind of heart attack."

There followed several minutes of Christa asking patient questions, then listening to voluble replies. Struggling to keep a straight face, she turned to Alex and said, "It *is* an attack of the heart, in a manner of speaking. Monsieur Sabine refuses to leave because of Mrs. Ives. The cook, you know," she said helpfully.

"Of course I know Emma Ives," he said with bafflement. "But what has she to do with Monsieur Sabine?" Alex glanced at the chef, who had crossed his arms on his chest and was waiting like a Buddha for matters to be resolved to his satisfaction.

Christa lowered her voice and said confidentially, "Apparently he feels that Mrs. Ives is necessary to his art. He says the soufflés don't fall as quickly and the sauces don't curdle when she is around. So either you must persuade her to go with us to London or resign yourself to eating his cooking only when you are in Suffolk."

When the viscount still looked puzzled, Christa shook her head in resignation. Really, men were so slow. Carefully she said, "She is a comely woman, you would agree?"

Laughter showed in Alex's eyes as he caught her meaning. "And she has been a widow for some years now. I shall see if she is willing to go to London."

Mrs. Ives blushed like a schoolgirl. The good lady had never been out of Suffolk in her life, but she "wouldn't mind, if that's what Pierre wants." Alex and Christa exchanged a speaking glance that almost sent them both off into whoops. Pierre, indeed! Obviously something had been going on amongst the garlic ropes.

One of the baggage coaches was detailed to wait while Mrs. Ives packed her possessions and the Monsieur's special knives and omelet pans. Monsieur Sabine was so pleased that he handsomely offered to leave two ropes of garlic. The offer was received with faint enthusiasm; garlic was all very well in heathenish French delicacies but had no place in honest Suffolk fare. Meanwhile, the Kingsleys finally left for London.

Christa was grateful for the bustle of activity that awaited her in the city. All of the other servants welcomed her back warmly; her young friend Miranda, looking healthy and happy compared to the peaked waif of last spring, was delighted to see her and demonstrate how she had practiced her letters over the summer.

After a frenzied week of updating his wardrobe to his new dimensions, Jonathan was off to Eton for the Michaelmas term. And true to his word, Alex volunteered his services to Admiral Hutchinson at the Admiralty. He was gone from the house early most days, and his casual morning visits to his sister's room were a thing of the past. It would have been difficult to determine whether Annabelle or Christa missed the visits more.

It was remarkable, Christa decided, how two people could live under the same roof without ever seeing each other, but of course a servant and a master lived in different worlds. The informal companionship of the summer had been an aberration; the present lack of contact was the norm. Resolutely she pushed aside all thoughts of Alex the man, and dedicated herself to making Lord Kingsley's sister happy and successful. Only in the reaches of the night would she feel his touch, remember how the laughter in those amber eyes always kindled a response in her.

Luckily arranging Annabelle's ball was a demanding task. Nominally, Annabelle's Aunt Agatha was the hostess and organizer, but, in fact, Christa made all the arrangements after discussing the possibilities with her mistress.

Over the summer, the girls had considered numerous themes and settled on an Arabian Nights fantasy. The ballroom would have panels of gauzy fabric sweeping from the center to the walls in simulation of a tent, and the refreshments would include honey and nut pastries and spicy lamb dishes as well as the usual ices and lobster patties. The date chosen was October 15, Annabelle's twenty-first birthday, and they had five weeks to clean and polish, send out cards, and see to the other minutiae of entertaining.

On the fourth day after their return to London, Christa went to her cousin Suzanne's shop, ostensibly on behalf of Annabelle's wardrobe but in reality because she felt the need to visit a friend. By arriving early, she caught Suzanne before the shop became busy, and they were able to retire for a proper cup of French coffee.

After exchanging hugs and commonplaces, Christa asked, "How is the business doing?"

"Quite well. I have retained almost all of Mme. Bouchet's customers and acquired a number of others as well. Except for your Miss Kingsley, there are no aristocrats, but that is not altogether a bad thing. I understand that merchants' wives pay their bills more promptly than members of the beau monde."

"Your clientele should increase soon. Yesterday Miss Annabelle and I were walking in the park when she fell in with a friend of her aunt's, Lady Camwell. While they were chatting, I walked with Lady Camwell's maid, who was most curious to find out who made Annabelle's gown. It was the pomona-green walking dress, you remember it?"

"Of course," Suzanne said eagerly. "Then what happened?"

"Naturally I was *most* reluctant to divulge the information, but after much coaxing, I told her. In the strictest confidence, *naturellement*."

Suzanne started to laugh so hard she choked on her coffee. "*Naturellement*, indeed, you minx. You could not have picked a better method to publicize the shop if you had run advertisements. I've heard of this Lady Camwell— five daughters, and one of the biggest gossips in London."

"Exactly so," Christa said complacently. "Soon you will be everyone's favorite little dressmaker. 'Such an unfashionable address, my dear, but a marvelous way with style.'" Christa mimicked the bored tones of a lady of fashion with wicked accuracy. "And soon you will be busy enough to take me on."

Suzanne looked at her with a slight frown. "You know that we can always find a place for you, *ma petite*. Are you unhappy in the Kingsley household?"

"Oh, no, no," Christa quickly reassured her. "Miss Annabelle is kindness itself, and the work is pleasant. But I can foresee the time when I will be ready for something more . . . challenging. Perhaps in the spring. I will have been in service for a year then, long enough to prove that I can do it."

Suzanne relaxed a trifle. "That would be better for me. I have just paid the children's school fees, and I am negotiating for the lease of the shop next door. Henry assures me that my business will be expanding, and I will need the space soon."

"And who is this Henry?" Christa asked as she sipped her coffee. She was interested to note a faint tinge of color rising on her cousin's cheekbones.

"Henry Worth, the draper who supplies my fabrics. He has been a great support to me these last months."

"Hmm?" Christa said with a twinkle.

Her blush deepening, Suzanne said, "His wife died last

year, leaving him with two little ones. *Les pauvres* were so
sad. They like to come and play with my children."

"And what do their parents do when the children are
engaged in their play?"

"Henry has behaved with complete propriety," Suzanne
said with austerity, then burst into giggles. "But it is not for
my lack of trying to make it otherwise. He is a perfect
gentleman. Too perfect." She reached for the coffeepot to
refill the cups, then said happily, "Henry doesn't want to
compromise my reputation. He thinks it is better to wait
until we are married."

Christa jumped up to give her cousin another hug. "That
is wonderful! Have you set a date?"

"Not yet. Next summer, perhaps. But he will not be a
perfect gentleman all that time, or my name is not Suzanne
de Savary!"

They laughed together, but under her happiness for her
cousin, Christa felt a pang of envy for Suzanne. "He will
make you happy, Suzanne?"

"Yes. Henry is a truly good man. And he is proud of me.
He thinks I'm very clever! He says our businesses will do
well together. I get first choice of his fabrics, he refers customers, and of course I am already one of his best clients."

Christa gave her cousin a serious look. "Do you miss
your old life, Suzanne? The gaiety of Paris, being an
aristocrat?"

A firm shake of the head was her reply. "Not at all. It
was different for you when you were at the center of
everything. You were born for the political salons, the
balls. But my branch of the family did not have a fraction
of the money that yours did. My dear, foolish husband,
Guy, refused to live within our means, and sometimes it
was a nightmare of placating creditors, of making sure the
children were taken care of. We lived on the fringes of

the haut monde, pretending that we belonged in the center.
It was exhausting."

"I didn't know that," Christa said with surprise.

"I am glad. That means I was successful at keeping up
appearances. But all that is over now. I shall be happier as
an honest tradesman's wife, managing a household, and
doing something I am good at."

The girl who was minding the shop put her head between the curtains and said, "There is a Lady Camwell here
with her daughters and two friends. She insists on seeing
you personally."

The cousins' eyes met in a mirth-filled glance before
Suzanne drained her coffee cup and stood. "Christa, here is
the package of ribbons and gloves you came for. Be sure to
have Miss Annabelle come within the next week for the
final fitting of her court dress."

Christa stood also and smiled as she made her farewell.
She was happy for her cousin, but Suzanne's marriage
would certainly affect their future partnership plans. As she
made her way through the busy streets, Christa wondered
if she herself would be content to marry a draper. *If he were
like Alex Kingsley, she would be.* Her mouth tightened at
the unbidden thought; it was impossible to imagine Lord
Kingsley as anything other than he was, and that was far
above her touch.

While Christa chatted with her cousin, Annabelle received an unexpected caller. Her heart started beating faster
when a footman brought her the card and an exquisite
nosegay of late-summer flowers. *Sir Edward Loaming, Bart.*
All summer Annabelle had remembered that meeting with
him in the park. He was so handsome, so romantic. . . .

She sighed happily in remembrance before her brow

clouded over. Alex had said she was not to let him call. She fingered the card. Surely it would be wrong to refuse to see him without explaining why? Yes, definitely, explaining in person why she could not receive Sir Edward was the most honorable course of action. Her rationalizations firmly in place, Annabelle went down to her visitor.

Sir Edward stood when she entered the drawing room, gazing at her admiringly. Today he was resplendent in a bottle-green jacket and pale yellow inexpressibles, a collection of gold watch fobs and a quizzing glass adorning his elegant person. He executed a faultless bow, then said throatily, "Miss Kingsley, you are even lovelier than my memory of you! Dare I hope that you remember me?"

Annabelle stared at him, a moth to his candle. The adoring youths of the summer had been pleasant companions, but mere boys. *This* was a mature man, virile and confident. Her memory had not played her false—he really *was* the handsomest man she had ever seen. The dark curls and profile were reminiscent of one of the more scandalous Greek gods, and those liquid dark eyes were fixed adoringly on *her*, plain Annabelle Kingsley.

"Sir Edward," she said falteringly, "it's a pleasure to see you again, but . . . I fear I will not be able to receive you in the future. My brother has told me not to continue the association."

Sir Edward's brow darkened, and only partially for effect. The adored only child of elderly parents, he had been raised to believe that even the best was barely good enough for him. It was a great shock to discover after his parents' deaths that his inheritance was a mere competence, scarcely adequate to keep a gentleman in clothes, much less in gaming.

For five years, Sir Edward had been on a collision course with disaster as his debts mounted and his heavily encumbered estate was squeezed to the last farthing. Then three years earlier he had found a measure of financial relief when he courted and won favor with the bran-faced daughter of a banker. To the baronet's delight, before he could persuade her to elope, her disgusted but pragmatic father offered him a substantial amount of money to take his handsome hide out of the heiress's vicinity. Nobly proclaiming the purity of his love, Sir Edward had taken the money and run.

The experience had provided him with a new source of income, and three more heiresses followed the banker's daughter. The last time, he and the young lady had actually made it halfway to Gretna Green before the outraged guardian caught up with them. Prior to taking the weeping girl home, the guardian had signed over a substantial amount of money to ensure that no word of the elopement would issue from Sir Edward's well-chiseled lips.

Details of the affairs did not become known because it was also in Sir Edward's interest to suppress them. Even so, the baronet's name had acquired an unfortunate aura of scandal, and it had become well-nigh impossible for him to get near an heiress.

On principle, the baronet would be charming to any young girl who was expensively dressed and inadequately chaperoned, then investigate to see if she were worth pursuing. A democrat in his way, Sir Edward was willing to extort money impartially from both aristocrats and those commoners who indulged in trade. Annabelle Kingsley had passed his tests easily: she was from an extremely wealthy family, she seemed impressionable, she would soon be twenty-one and free to marry whom she chose, and her guardian was an older brother who had been out of the country for years and would not be up to snuff socially.

The situation was ripe for Sir Edward's exploitation, and

it was regrettable that the girl had left town in June. Even more regrettably, he became badly dipped over the summer and was in dire need of new money. Annabelle was his only prospect at the moment, and he daren't let her slip between his fingers. Wrinkling his brow artistically, he said with a touch of vibrato in his smooth voice, "Oh, the unfairness of it!"

"What is unfair?" Annabelle said uncertainly as she seated herself and gestured for her visitor to do the same.

"That your mind should have been poisoned against me." Sir Edward carefully picked a chair that showed his noble profile to best advantage.

"My brother didn't poison my mind, he just said not to see you." From the tartness of the reply, Sir Edward deduced that the girl didn't like the implied criticism of her brother, and he adjusted his strategy accordingly.

"It's not his fault. He has been out of the country for so long. No doubt he made inquiries about me and was told that old tale. Can a man never live down the mistakes of his youth?"

It didn't occur to Annabelle to wonder at his knowledge of her brother. Intrigued, she asked, "What old tale is that?"

Sir Edward thought rapidly. "It was a duel." He sighed mournfully, then continued, "A man claimed I had dishonored his wife. It was a foul lie, of course. The lady had merely been in need of friendship because of her husband's unkindness. But I could not see her name dragged in the mud."

Her eyes like saucers, Annabelle asked, "What happened?"

Sir Edward shrugged deprecatingly. "The inevitable. The brute was no proof against my swordsmanship. I should have killed him. He rewarded my mercy by spreading slander about me. Lies that I am paying for even now, ten years later."

"Surely if you called on Alex and explained the situation, he would change his mind."

Sir Edward gave an inward smile of satisfaction. She had taken the bait; really a most gullible chit, perfect for his purposes. Standing, he shook his head sorrowfully. "No. Why should he bother to listen to the explanation of one disgraced man when so many others must be begging for permission to pay their addresses? Lord Kingsley will want only the best for you." He stopped and gazed into her blue eyes. "What man would not?"

Annabelle looked back unhappily. It was unfair that a man of such noble character be so maligned! And now he was going to walk out of her life forever. It did not occur to her to discuss the matter directly with Alex; she had never openly questioned an order in her life. But years with her mother had schooled Annabelle in keeping her own counsel. She stood, her mind rapidly considering the possibilities.

Sir Edward regarded her face with satisfaction, then moved in for the coup de grâce. "Just this once, may I kiss your hand?" he said, his voice soft and thrilling. He chose the piece of anatomy carefully. An innocent miss might not enjoy a first kiss on the lips, and it was important that she be affected.

Without waiting for her reply, he reached out and took her hand. Holding it, Sir Edward murmured, "So graceful, like a bird."

Originality in metaphor was not the baronet's forte. But he knew how to get the most out of kissing a hand, starting with the back, then turning it over to press his lips into the palm. He could feel Annabelle's hand trembling in response. Most satisfactory; it was probably the first time a man had ever touched her with carnal intent. After brushing her fingertips with his tongue, Sir Edward pressed her hand to his cheek, whispering brokenly, "Oh, Annabelle, that I should find you, only to lose you so soon!"

Annabelle was helpless in the face of his adroit manipulation. Unable to distinguish between the first stirrings of sexuality and Sir Edward as an individual, she saw him as the personification of romantic love. Surely it would be thwarting her destiny to let him leave her. . . .

With a catch in her voice, Annabelle said feebly, "Sir Edward, you mustn't . . ." Her hand was still pressed against his cheek, the prickly masculinity of subliminal whiskers so different from feminine skin.

The baronet looked at her with dark, haunted eyes. "You are right, my angel. No shadow of scandal must ever dim the luster of your name. So now I will say farewell, forever."

"No!" As Annabelle looked at him, the solution occurred to her. "I cannot disobey my brother and let you call. But if we should happen to meet in the park? I often walk there with my maid. Early in the afternoon, before the fashionable hour."

"My angel, you are a woman in ten thousand! In a million!"

The happiness that suffused his face dimmed any stirrings of guilt. If this man was Annabelle's destiny, surely when the time was right, Alex would give his blessing.

Alex was finding an unexpected satisfaction in his work at the Admiralty. Over the years he had had his share of contact with that august body, from dealing with the tyrannical porters to anxious intervals in the infamous waiting room, where even admirals came to petition for appointments and commands. The ten years of peace between 1783 and 1793 had put many navy officers on the shore at half pay, and Alex counted himself lucky to have been continuously employed through that period. The Kingsleys had money and influence, but so did many other officers.

The resumption of hostilities with France two years earlier had led to a massive expansion of the navy, with hundreds of officers being returned to active duty. Sometimes he thought that if the French hadn't existed, it would have been necessary to invent them—otherwise England would not have an opponent worthy of her mettle. It was ironic that the French and Spanish built better ships, while the British were undeniably superior seamen. Alex had no doubt that once again his country's naval supremacy would enable her to defeat her cross-Channel enemy.

Thoughts of the French inevitably led him to Christa. Alex had rigorously avoided seeing her, even at the cost of reducing his intimacy with his sister. The French girl was bewitchingly attractive and the feel of her soft body haunted him. She responded so sweetly, without apology or missishness. . . .

Alex gazed absently out the window of the small office he had been given. It was late September, and below, Whitehall was thronged with carriages, drays, and peddlers. At the moment, a detachment of soldiers was marching past toward the Horse Guards just up the street. He found himself rubbing at the chronic stab of pain in his left side and smiled without humor—like death and taxes, the pain was always with him, and he wished the devilish shell fragment would just decide where it wanted to go.

With a sigh, Alex returned to his desk. It wasn't only Christa's body; he'd never enjoyed another woman's company as much, nor felt as relaxed in her presence. The fact that he found a servant so appealing proved his father's complaint that Alex had inadequate respect for what was due his name.

To counteract Christa's insidious influence, Alex had decided it was time to meet eligible females of his own station. There was no shortage of potential mates at the numerous entertainments he and Annabelle attended; with male naiveté, it didn't occur to him that some of those invitations to his sister were inspired by the knowledge that he would be her escort. A handsome, wealthy viscount in need of a wife was a prize indeed.

In the meantime, Alex was writing about tactics at Admiral Hutchinson's request. He and the bluff old sea dog had become good friends. Hutchinson was the third professional sea lord, and his duties involved the placement of commissioned and warrant officers; he often conferred with Alex about potential appointments. For all the role of influence and money, the Admiralty took its duties seriously, and it was rare for an incompetent to receive a command.

Alex was pleased at how his work on tactics was progressing; he knew more than he had realized and had developed some strong opinions. He also knew that the clerks who made fair copies from his drafts thought his spelling was a joke, but senior officers who read the work in progress were pleased at the results. And writing kept him from thinking about Christa. At least, very often.

In a lavish town house on Curzon Street, Sybil Debenham gazed at her reflection with profound satisfaction. Tonight was the Wincastles' ball and she intended to make her move on Lord Kingsley. She had worked carefully toward this moment, surveying the eligible males, then evaluating them as to quality of title, wealth, and personal characteristics. Of the three, title was by far the most important; Sybil had quite an adequate share of the world's goods herself, inherited from her vulgar mill-owner grandfather.

She turned her head slightly to one side, admiring the perfect line of profile that ran from brow to décolletage. Her brow puckered in a small frown. "Merrier, one of the back curls is askew. Fix it."

"But Mademoiselle requested that I pin it that way, for a more frolicsome look." The French maid's voice was carefully neutral.

Sybil's exquisite Cupid's-bow mouth thinned. "I'm not interested in your excuses. Fix it!" While the maid's deft hands repinned the coiffure, Sybil returned to rapt contemplation of her image. It was universally acknowledged that she was a diamond of the first water, with a perfect heart-shaped face, guinea-gold curls, and exquisitely sculptured features.

Critics might say that her aquamarine eyes were too small and close together for perfect beauty, but she dismissed such carping as sheer spite. Besides, that fool of a maid was very good with cosmetics and was able to transform the merely beautiful into the sublime. Sybil lowered her lashes, admiring how the shimmer of gold dust on her eyelids matched her gilded fingernails. This time she could not possibly fail.

The satisfied self-examination faltered a bit. For some reason Sybil had never fathomed, she always excited feverish admiration but had never received the superior offer she so clearly deserved. Her fortune was excellent, her beauty without peer, so she could only conclude it was her breeding that stood between her and the heights of the beau monde. That dratted mill-owner grandfather. Of course, the Gunning sisters' births had been inferior to hers, and they had been fabulously successful on the Marriage Mart. She suppressed the thought quickly.

The fact that Sybil was twenty-two and in her fourth Season had caused her to lower her sights; if she didn't accept an offer soon, she was in danger of becoming a laughingstock. Her first Season she had intended to accept only a duke but was reluctantly forced to admit that there were too few eligible dukes to choose from. Two of the Royal Dukes had made propositions, but of the wrong kind.

The second year, Miss Debenham had added marquesses to the list of availables; in the spring of 1794 she had expanded to earls. If only the Earl of Radcliffe had not gotten himself killed just before that Season began . . . Lord Radcliffe's attentions had been most flattering the previous two Seasons. Why, if she had encouraged him in her second Season, Sybil might be a widowed countess now, with the wealth and title, and no nasty physical duties required.

The present Earl of Radcliffe was also single and stricken enough in years that he might not paw too much, but the dratted man was scarcely ever in society. Really most unfair that Sybil had not been given an adequate chance to show him what he was missing out there in the country.

She stood and lifted her arms so Merrier could remove the silk wrapper that protected Sybil's gown during makeup and hairdressing. She slid one hand lovingly down the gold lace overdress. The Parisian style setters might be advocating simplicity, but men still appreciated grandeur. Kingsley didn't have a chance.

This past spring, Miss Debenham had reluctantly decided

that she might have to accept a viscount, though she still would not stoop to a baron. She had been running out of possibles when Kingsley had appeared on the scene. One saw him everywhere this autumn, and while Sybil knew that some other girls had set their caps for him, there wasn't one that could compete with her. She had taken her time studying him cultivating his dim little sister Annabelle, observing how he interacted with people.

Kingsley was annoyingly informal, with no proper sense of his own dignity, but that was a minor failing. He was attractive enough to be a credit to her, and surprisingly, he seemed rather shy around women. It must come from spending so much time with a bunch of seagoing ruffians. Perhaps the viscount would return to sea after they were married. Then he wouldn't be in her way, and he looked to be the heroic sort, which would increase her own consequence. If he did well enough, Kingsley might even be elevated to earl. That would be a good reward for her condescension in accepting a viscount.

Her maid fastened the diamond necklace about her neck and Sybil nodded with satisfaction. It was the perfect touch. Tonight she would bring herself to Kingsley's attention. Shy as he was, the viscount would be awed by her beauty and dazzled by her favor. By the end of the month, he would make her an offer, there was no doubt of it.

Claudia Debenham nodded approvingly as her daughter came down the stairs, one hand gracefully trailing along the curving banister. It was always good to practice artful gestures; one never knew who might be watching.

"Very good, my dear. That dress suits you very well. Kingsley will be quite smitten." The two women were co-conspirators in pursuit of the elusive title; in fact, the daughter's obsession stemmed from the mother's failure to achieve the social heights she had desired for herself. Claudia had been a well-looking girl but was nothing like the dazzler her daughter was. The older woman had counted herself lucky to catch the second son of a baron. Of course, her husband Leo's elder brother had been sickly, and she had had hopes that Leo would inherit the title. Instead, the sickly brother was flourishing, with four healthy sons, while Leo had declined into an early grave. It never occurred to Claudia to wonder if she herself had contributed to his premature demise.

"Now, tell me again what you will do," Claudia commanded.

Sybil rolled her eyes in irritation. "*You* know, Mother," she said petulantly. "When Kingsley enters with his sister, I wait a few minutes while they get settled, then go over and tell her I have found an outstanding milliner and ask her to go with me tomorrow. Annabelle will have to introduce me to her brother. Then when her court is rushing up to claim dances with her, I put him at his ease. Lord Kingsley will certainly ask me to dance. I will tell him how I adore his insipid little sister, which will please him. And I'll ask him about his adventures in the navy. Men love talking about such things. It should go perfectly smoothly; he has shown no preference for any other girl."

"None of them can outshine you, my dear," her mother said complacently. "Shall we be on our way?"

"Lord Kingsley and Miss Kingsley," the footman intoned.

Annabelle looked around the Wincastles' ballroom in happy anticipation. It was one of the grandest of the autumn's entertainments, and she had been looking forward to it. Parties were quite enjoyable now that she was dressed well and more confident.

"Enjoy your moment of peace, Belle," her brother said with a grin. "I see one or two of your admirers looking in this direction, and they will be elbowing me out of the way soon."

"Oh, Alex, you exaggerate," Annabelle said with a laugh. "They are always most respectful to you. After all, you are my guardian, and they want to turn you up sweet."

"Where *do* you pick up such language, Belle?" Alex said as he led them toward a row of chairs on the opposite side of the ballroom.

"Where else but in the bosom of my family, O brother mine," Annabelle said demurely.

"If you don't show some respect for your elders, I'll start larding my speech with navy terms. If you use *them*, you'll be like the sailor's parrot. Unfit for mixed company."

Annabelle laughed as she settled into a chair, then suppressed a sigh when she saw that Sybil Debenham was bearing down on them. Miss Debenham had been most kind in her attentions, but Belle had trouble warming to her. Sybil's conversation was paralyzingly empty, and her relentlessly fashionable style made the younger girl feel too tall, too gawky, and hopelessly countrified. But it was not in Annabelle to refuse proffered friendship, so she looked up with a smile and said, "Good evening, Miss Debenham. You are in particularly good looks this evening."

"Please, my dear, do call me Sybil. I've asked you a thousand times!" Miss Debenham fluttered her fan, artlessly overlooking Lord Kingsley's substantial presence. "I want to tell you about this *superb* milliner I've discovered. An absolute marvel! Do say you will come with me to see her tomorrow." Her gracious invitation managed to convey that Annabelle was in dire need of the ministrations of any and all purveyors of fashion.

Alex was watching the new arrival with fascination; she was the most highly finished piece of nature he had ever seen! Every curl was perfectly placed, every gesture, a study in graceful composition. He was wondering if she practiced her movements in front of a mirror when Annabelle made the introduction. "Alex, this is Miss Sybil Debenham. Miss Debenham, my brother, Lord Kingsley."

Alex blinked under the force of the aquamarine eyes turned in his direction. Making a bow, he murmured his pleasure at the honor done him. Miss Debenham giggled. "Oh, the honor is mine, my lord. I have been *longing* this age to meet the hero."

Alex swallowed uncomfortably and murmured that she must have confused him with someone else. Treating his response as a piece of wit, Sybil giggled again. "And modest too! How naughty of you to have deprived London of your presence for so long."

Unable to respond adequately to such effusiveness, Alex asked, "Would you care to dance?" A glance at Annabelle showed that she was rapidly disappearing into a circle of admirers and was in no need of his support.

"I would be *delighted*, my lord," Miss Debenham said promptly. Had Alex looked more closely, he might have seen a triumphant gleam in the Incomparable's eyes.

Alex was grateful that Christa had managed to teach him to dance. Now he enjoyed it, and dancing reduced the necessity of speech to an absolute minimum. He decided that Miss Debenham was a gorgeous widgeon—certainly gorgeous, and decidedly a widgeon. But a man would have to be blind not to enjoy looking at her, so he asked her for another dance later in the evening. And without quite understanding how, the viscount found that he had engaged to take her for a ride in the park two days hence. Well, he had wanted to meet suitable women, and what man wouldn't be flattered that a stunner like this indicated that she found him appealing?

Chapter 12

Christa looked at her mistress with a frown. Sir Edward Loaming had "happened" on them in the park with great frequency in the last several weeks, and it was obvious to the meanest intelligence that something was afoot. She fell back to a distance out of earshot of Annabelle and her swain, but carefully kept them in sight. Annabelle glowed with infatuation; Sir Edward was merely fatuous, she thought uncharitably.

There was no real harm in their meetings, Christa admitted to herself. Although Sir Edward took every opportunity to touch Annabelle's elbow or take her hand to help her around the most minor of obstacles—such as large blades of grass—he stayed within the limits of propriety. It was just that Christa had taken a dislike to Sir Edward and wished that Lord Kingsley would tell his sister to keep away from the man.

But doubtless Alex had checked and discovered that the baronet was perfectly respectable. Every woman falls in love with a handsome face at least once in her life; Christa herself had been enthralled with a farrier the whole of her thirteenth summer. She could only hope that Annabelle would recover from her *tendre* quickly—

She hastened forward when Annabelle stopped and

beckoned to her. "Yes, Miss Annabelle?" Christa asked respectfully.

"I would like you to go to the book shop and pick up that volume I ordered. It is such a fine day that I prefer to stay in the park with Sir Edward."

"I should not leave you, miss," Christa said firmly.

Annabelle gave her a look that was part plea, part command. "I shall be quite safe with Sir Edward, Christa," she said.

Christa complied unhappily; Annabelle was her employer and it wouldn't be fitting to argue with her in front of a third party. "Very well, Miss Annabelle. I should be back here within the hour."

She was still brooding about the situation after she picked up the book. It was, inevitably, one of the romances Annabelle favored. Christa was beginning to suspect that the moralists were right: novels did implant improper thoughts in susceptible female minds. Why else would her mistress take Sir Edward's florid utterances seriously?

Absorbed in her thoughts, Christa dodged through the usual jumble of foot and carriage traffic with the nonchalance of a true city dweller. She was snapped out of her reverie by the sound of a familiar voice shouting, "Stop!"

She turned her head toward the voice, then froze in shock. It was Lord Radcliffe, her unwelcome uncle by marriage! He was halfway down the block, caught behind a heavy dray, and she doubted he was close enough to be sure of her identity. But the earl obviously had seen enough to suspect who she was. The tall, fair gentleman pulled up the curricle and tossed the reins to his groom, then jumped to the cobblestones and headed in her direction.

Without waiting to see more, Christa whirled and darted between two fashionable carriages, narrowly missing the hooves of the leaders. On the other side of the street she turned into an alley, moving fast enough to cover the ground rapidly but not so fast as to appear suspicious. The alley branched into a network of back streets, and within a few minutes she was sure that no one could have followed her. Christa paused to catch her breath after attaining the safety of a quiet residential square, her heart pounding from the near escape. She had almost forgotten about Lord Radcliffe in these last months, and the sight of him brought back all her fears of the previous spring.

Now that Christa knew he was in the city, she would have to be more careful. As she walked slowly back to the park, her fear was replaced with anger. Had it not been for the threat of Lord Radcliffe, she would still be the Comtesse d'Estelle, a lady at home in the highest society. But would she have ever met Alex? Would they have developed the same kind of relationship in the brittle setting of the beau monde?

Christa sighed at the thought—even if she never had any more of Alex than she had had already, she was better off than if she had never known him at all. She lifted her chin and entered the park to find Annabelle.

Lord Radcliffe gave up the chase after a quarter hour in the back alleys where scurrilous residents eyed him measuringly. He was following a mirage. This particular phantom was not Christa. He'd realized after stopping his curricle that the girl was just a mob-capped servant, not his elegant niece.

As Lewis retraced his steps to the carriage, he tried not to think of all the ghosts he had seen in the last months. Not just Christa; once at White's he had seen a man who looked so much like Charles that he had rushed across two crowded rooms, only to step back at the last minute when he realized the man was a stranger. A man called Kingsley, with Charles's height and coloring and some indefinable way of carrying himself that reminded Lewis of his nephew—but a stranger nonetheless.

And Marie-Claire? Her he saw everywhere.

Lord Radcliffe let his groom drive the rest of the way to Radcliffe House. He should have known better than to come up to London. Berkshire was full of memories of when the estate had been alive with youth and laughter, but that was easier to deal with than mocking ghosts that disappeared into the swarming streets of London. The sooner he finished his business and went home, the better.

Annabelle found that her much-anticipated tête-à-tête with Sir Edward was not developing as she had planned. His kisses were intoxicating, the stuff of dreams. Unfortunately, they were accompanied by pleas that she elope with him. "Oh, Annabelle, my adored one," he murmured huskily in her ear. "All my life I have dreamed of finding you. Say you will come away with me!"

She pulled away until she was backed up against a tree trunk in the little grove that concealed them. "Edward, I couldn't possibly! Why, the disgrace of it . . ."

Sir Edward's beautiful dark eyes regarded her sorrowfully. "Don't you love me, Annabelle?" He lifted her right hand and lovingly planted a kiss in it.

She shivered in response. "Oh, Edward, you know I do! But why can't we wait? I'll be twenty-one soon and free to marry whom I choose."

"Every day apart from you is agony. Every night alone is endless." It was a good line; Sir Edward had read it in one of the stupid novels Annabelle favored. He saw what might have been a flash of memory in her eyes, so he hastened on, "Why should we wait when we are both so sure? So much in love?" He still held her hand, and his touch almost overwhelmed her rational mind.

"I want to be married with my brother's approval. Surely if you called on him . . ." Her voice trailed off weakly.

Sir Edward shook his head sadly. "You know already that is no use. He dismissed me without a hearing once, and he would again."

Annabelle wasn't sure that her beloved was making sense, but it was impossible to be sure when he was so close. The baronet leaned forward and circled her with his arms again, pressing little kisses on her neck and ear. "Please, Edward, you are making it so hard to think," she said, her voice quavering.

Which was exactly what the baronet intended. Annabelle was naive but she wasn't stupid, and he knew that if he gave her too much time, she might see through his romantic bombast. Worse, Sir Edward's financial affairs were in crisis, with bailiffs seeking him at all his usual haunts. He was staying with a friend to avoid his creditors, but it wouldn't serve for long, he'd have to leave London within a few days. If he took the wealthy Miss Kingsley with him, he would be able to return to town. Otherwise, there would be no alternative but to retreat to his heavily encumbered estate and wait for foreclosure.

Given these facts, the baronet continued his assault on Annabelle's ears, his hands beginning to roam around her body. She was a passionate wench under her Miss Propriety exterior, and arousing her was his best ticket to success.

"Edward, please," she whispered. "How can I run away just before my ball? All the arrangements are made. So many people are coming. My maid, Christa, has worked so hard on it."

Sir Edward had to fight down the urge to shake the peagoose. "You would put the feelings of a maid before mine?" he purred through slightly clenched teeth. He started working his lips toward her mouth.

Turning her head aside, Annabelle said, "It isn't just her, it's my brother Alex, my Aunt Agatha, all of the people I have met this autumn. What will they think of me?"

Sir Edward got an inspiration. "If we left for Gretna in the next few days, we could be back in time for your ball, and use it to announce our marriage. Your come out, your birthday, and your wedding all together. And if we present him with the deed accomplished, I promise your brother will accept me." Lord Kingsley would have to, or see his whole family disgraced.

"Do you really think so?" Annabelle asked doubtfully. "Wouldn't it be better to be married here by special license? An elopement is just so . . . hole-and-corner."

Special licenses were expensive. So were flights to Scotland, but if her brother caught up and offered to buy him off, the cost of the elopement would be minimal. "Think of the romance, my little love," he crooned. "It would be something to remember all our lives."

"That is what I am worried about," she said with a touch of acerbity. "That people *will* remember for the rest of our lives!"

"No one need know," Sir Edward promised with a quick change of tack. "You will leave a message for your brother that you have gone off to be married and will be back the afternoon of the ball. Since you will be twenty-one that day, he can't possibly object. What could be simpler?" This time his mouth muffled any further protests. Luckily, a small boy came bursting into their little glade.

"Have you seen my ball?" the child demanded pugnaciously as the couple sprang apart guiltily.

"We have *not*, you little . . ." Sir Edward held on to his composure—barely—but not to his heiress. Annabelle slipped away from him and headed back to the main park.

"We must go back. Christa will be looking for me." Annabelle was glad to see her abigail in the distance when she emerged from the shrubbery. Her lover said urgently from behind her, "You will consider it?"

"Yes . . . no . . . I don't know!" Annabelle was feeling hunted. How could a love so perfect leave her feeling so anxious? She glanced back at Sir Edward, then found her irritation melting at the sight of his beautiful, concerned face.

"Will you meet me again tomorrow?" Such passion was in his eyes! Of course, he was impetuous; wasn't that what a proper lover was supposed to be?

"Yes, I'll meet you here," she said hastily in the last moment before her maid came within earshot.

"Are you feeling well, Miss Annabelle?" Christa asked solicitously. "Your face is flushed." She didn't add that her mistress looked as if she had been dragged through a bush backward; it took no great intelligence to deduce what Annabelle and Sir Edward had been doing.

"A touch of sun, perhaps. I shall be glad to get home and rest a bit. We are going to three different entertainments this evening, and it will be a very late night." Annabelle was babbling in relief. She had always been terrible at making decisions, and this one facing her promised to be the most difficult of her life.

Sir Edward escorted Annabelle to the edge of the park. Half a dozen steps behind, Christa heard him murmur, "Until tomorrow, my love," before he squeezed Annabelle's hand and departed. Not for the first time, Christa wondered why he didn't take Annabelle for a drive or call on her at the house, as her other admirers did. Moreover, her mistress had been curiously silent about the baronet, not bubbling

happily as she had after their first meeting last spring.
Christa was getting the unhappy suspicion that something
havey-cavey was afoot.

Annabelle made it to the first of the evening's entertainments, but a blinding headache developed and soon she
looked so white that Alex insisted on bringing her home.
He turned his sister over to Christa, who promised that a
cup of willow-bark tea was just the thing for a headache.
Annabelle smiled weakly in reply and retired with hardly
a good night to her brother. He wondered if she were overdoing her socializing; his sister had been so continually
busy that he had scarcely seen her since their return to
London.

Still wakeful, Alex went down to the library. He had
turned one end into his personal study, preferring the
spacious book-lined room to the poky hole his father had
used as an office. Adding some coals to the fire, he poured
himself a glass of smooth Irish whiskey and water, then
settled into a wing chair with his long legs stretched out in
front of him.

The viscount was feeling in charity with the world. His
work at the Admiralty was progressing well, and more
surprisingly, so was his social life. Alex found that he was
much more comfortable consorting with the ton than he
had expected. While he would never be a master of repartee,
he could converse and dance with a fashionable woman
without making a fool of himself, and even find some enjoyment.

Unfortunately, Alex's search for a wife had borne no
fruit. His passionate attraction to Christa over the summer
had convinced him it was time he married, but none of the
available ladies stirred his interest in the least. Some were

very pretty, many were pleasant, a few were both, but there were none he could imagine living with for the rest of his life. Still less could he imagine facing any of them at breakfast.

Alex chuckled to himself, trying and failing to imagine the glorious Sybil Debenham at any hour before noon. It must take hours to produce that look of shimmering perfection. He looked on his mild flirtation with her as something of a challenge—she was exactly the sort of fan-fluttering female who had terrorized him in his younger days. Alex was pleased that she had not yet reduced him to tongue-tied paralysis. By letting Sybil prattle on about her favorite subject—herself—he found he could deal with her tolerably well.

The viscount seemed to enjoy her favor above her other swains and suspected she might be using him to make another suitor jealous. Miss Debenham certainly didn't seem to feel any real warmth for him, which was why he considered their flirtation to be harmless. Impossible to imagine that the immaculate Sybil's heart was engaged, or even that she had a heart.

Since it was flattering to be favored by such a beauty, Alex would ask her for a dance or two if they were at the same evening party, and occasionally he took her for a drive. A pity that her mind was not half so attractive as her face.

Alex sipped at the whiskey, enjoying the peacefulness of the hour. Even the usual ache in his side was quiet for the moment. It was past eleven and all of the servants would be abed except his own valet, Fiske, who had not yet been persuaded that a viscount could undress himself without assistance.

The door opened so noiselessly that Alex didn't realize at first that he had a visitor. Turning his head at the sound of soft footsteps, he saw Christa enter. Concealed in the shadows by the fireplace, Alex was free to watch her browsing through the bookshelves. It was unabashed pleasure seeing her graceful movements, particularly when she reached high above her head for a volume. Her lightweight sprigged-muslin dress molded to her ripe curves and lifted to reveal trim ankles. Intently studying the shelves in the low light, she had moved within a dozen feet of Alex before making a choice and turning to leave the library.

Christa had enjoyed the peace and quiet, savoring the handsome leather bound volumes and reading random paragraphs to counteract the anxiety she had been feeling about Annabelle. It was a shock when the deep, amused voice sounded out of the shadows behind her.

"Looking for some bedtime reading?"

Though she immediately recognized the voice, Christa jumped in startled reflex and blurted out, "You wretch!" as she whirled.

Remembering her station, she said demurely, "I'm very sorry, my lord, I didn't know you were here. You did say that I could use the library."

"Of course. I'm glad someone does. What did you find?" The viscount rose and moved next to her, glancing at the volume. "Voltaire's *Philosophical Letters on the English*. A good choice. It would certainly put me to sleep quickly."

Christa laughed, a clear, bell-like sound. "*Au contraire*, Monsieur Voltaire is always most amusing to read. Actually, his wit is more original than his thinking."

"You've read this book before?"

"*Oui*. He compares the social and philosophical life of the English with that of the French."

"Most useful for an émigré condemned to live on our damp island." Alex looked at her oddly. "You are certainly the best-read servant I have ever met."

Christa shrugged nonchalantly. "Reading is a simple pleasure that fills the hours of waiting. An abigail has many of those."

"So does a sailor, but being crude creatures, we are more apt to fill them with drink. Would you care to join me?"

She said hesitantly, "I really should not."

Alex grimaced. "Because I am the master and you are a maid?" At her nod, he said, "I promise not to tell anyone if you won't. Having removed that barrier, what would you like?" He crossed to a cabinet that concealed bottles of every beverage imaginable.

"If we are to drink like sailors, surely rum would be most proper?"

He laughed. "You can if you like, but I prefer Irish whiskey myself."

"In that case, some cognac would be nice."

Alex located the appropriate bottle and poured some in a cut-crystal goblet. When Christa took it from him, she gently swirled the amber liquid, then sniffed it, giving a soft sigh of pleasure. "Your cellar is very fine."

"It should be. I expect that brandy is older than you are." They drifted back to the fire, sitting in chairs facing each other.

"Do you think so?" she said incautiously. "I should have thought it was made about 1775."

Alex's eyebrows lifted in surprise, golden arcs in the firelight that sculpted his high cheekbones and long jaw. "Your palate is as well educated as your mind. You must also be older than I would have guessed."

"I am twenty-four, my lord."

"You don't look it." Alex eyed her thoughtfully. He'd supposed Christa to be nineteen or twenty. Should it make a difference that she was older, with more experience and judgment? She looked so enticing, her lively hands still, her dark curls for once free of the ubiquitous mobcap.

As she sipped her brandy, Christa pondered whether she should broach the subject of Annabelle and Sir Edward. When she had asked her mistress about him earlier in the day, Annabelle had changed the subject with almost feverish anxiety. Christa felt torn between loyalties: Alex had asked her to watch out for Annabelle, but she hated to carry tales and feared that Annabelle would never forgive her for it.

After some minutes of comfortable silence, Christa said slowly, "I have been worried about Annabelle, my lord."

He knit his brows and admitted, "So have I. She seems strained. I wonder if she is doing too much." Then he gave his devastating smile and added, "Since we are private, I would prefer you called me Alex."

His caressing voice drove all thought of Annabelle from Christa's mind. She should make her good night and leave because staying under such intimate conditions was playing with fire, but while she acknowledged the danger, she made no move to depart. Christa had missed the companionship of the summer and daily contact with the three Kingsleys on an informal basis.

Most of all, she missed Alex—the passing weeks had not made her feel less in love with him. To sit together companionably, talking or not talking as they chose. It might be dangerous, but she was willing to risk the price.

"Very well, Alex," Christa said calmly, her voice reflecting none of her longing. "Are you finding London comfortable?"

"Much more so than I expected," Alex admitted. "To be a ship's captain is one of the loneliest jobs on earth. A captain must never be too familiar because it makes junior officers and sailors uneasy. The quarters are too close, and too much intimacy undermines the respect and authority the captain must have."

"The loneliness of command?"

"Exactly," he agreed. "It's a cliché, but absolutely true nonetheless. A captain eats most meals alone, walks the quarterdeck alone, has no one to talk or joke with. Did you know that a navy captain has more power on a ship than the king himself? I could order a man flogged; Farmer George could not."

"Did you have men flogged often?"

"Not often, but sometimes it was necessary. Sailors are a rough lot. Some come directly from the jails and prisons. I always told them that they started on my ship with a clean slate, and in general that worked well. Most were good men who needed no more than a fair chance and enough to eat. But there were exceptions, and discipline is essential."

Alex stared into the flickering yellow flames for a few moments. "Sea captains are the last of the absolute monarchs, and some are more than a little mad, ordering their crews to share in their madness. Some preach religion, or order the decks scrubbed a dozen times a day, or insist their men wear a particular kind of hat. As long as they do their job, the Admiralty won't interfere."

He smiled wryly. "I'm sure that you can imagine what a pleasure it is to go to White's or Brooks's or a hundred other places and relax without remembering my dignity."

Christa laughed. "I think that standing on your dignity could not have been easy for you."

"Quite right." His laughter blended with hers.

Looking beyond Alex, Christa saw a model ship standing on a walnut table next to a globe and a vase of flowers. Curious, she rose to investigate and found a model of a frigate, over three feet long and perfect in every detail. "This is exquisite, Alex. I had not seen it before."

He rose also and stood behind her as she bent over and read the name painted on the bow. "The *Antagonist*."

Glancing over her shoulder, Christa said, "She is your ship, then? How lovely!"

He nodded. "Yes, this is the original shipyard model. I contacted the man who designed her ten years ago and bought it from him. It arrived two days ago. I am having a stand built."

Alex ran one hand lovingly along the hull. "Designing a ship of war is an art, not a science. The designer spends months working on a model like this, balancing the requirements of speed, stability, and maneuverability to create a ship that can best carry the men and supplies and cannon the Admiralty wants. Then the lines are taken from the hull, and drawings of the cross-sections are made. The *Antagonist* was the fastest, most weatherly ship I ever sailed in. Several more like her have been built since then."

Christa duplicated his motion, her hand sliding the length of the hull, feeling the subtle changes in the form.

Alex said, "You can see why ships are always called 'she.' With both ships and women, a man seeks the fairest curve."

Christa laughed. "I think most men are not so discriminating—any curves will do. Otherwise, I should not have had to defend myself so often over the years. There are many women more beautiful than I, so one can only assume that most men do not care whether they bed a sloop or a light frigate."

"You do yourself a disservice, Christa. There may be some women more beautiful, but few are more alluring."

She said curiously, "I have always wondered why I am singled out, but when one has just kicked a man in the ankles, it's not a good time to ask why he tried his luck. I would swear I do nothing to provoke attack—what is it that men find desirable in a woman?"

Alex looked down at her, his face becoming very still. Thoughtfully he said, "It is not one feature alone, but rather a quality of . . . perhaps 'womanliness' is the best word, or perhaps 'sensuality' is better."

The left side of Christa's body was limned by firelight, emphasizing the richness of form. He continued, "For example, you have one of the smallest waists I have ever seen, almost as if you wore a corset. But you don't."

Alex reached out with his left hand and placed it on her waist, feeling the warmth of her skin through the thin fabric. "And though you are slim, there is a roundness, a fullness to your figure, that cries out to be touched and explored."

Christa gazed up into his amber eyes, golden in the firelight. His words came slowly, as if Alex was as mesmerized as she. His hand glided up until it cupped her breast and she gave a sharp, startled inhalation as sparks seemed to race from his touch. His hand pulsated on her breast; then he gently plucked the nipple that budded under the fabric. The sensation was exquisite, touching off a reaction throughout her body as the world narrowed to the circle of firelight.

Alex moved his hand down again, seeming to feel every rib as he followed the curve to her hip. He set his glass down, and with his other hand lifted her chin. Christa's silver eyes were fearless and open to him, mirroring the same mixture of desire and doubt that he felt himself. When he claimed her lips, it was with an aching passion that drew them both into a storm of desire. Their bodies pressed together, seeking unconsciously to share one space, and his hands explored far beyond the limits he had observed when they had kissed before.

Christa felt her judgment shredding away as her body responded with mindless urgency. Using her last trace of reason, she groped one hand across the table behind her until it encountered a shape her fingers remembered as the vase of flowers. Lifting it, she poured the contents over Alex's head, drenching them both in a shower of water and chrysanthemums.

Alex released her abruptly and backed away as he sputtered with a blend of frustration and unwilling amusement. Wiping wet gold hair from his forehead, he said with admirable mildness, "A simple 'Stop' would have sufficed."

Christa ruefully shook her head, dislodging a blossom from her shoulder. "It was impossible for me to say it. That is why strong measures were needed." Though her body ached with the loss of his closeness, she managed a wry smile. The alternative would have been to weep.

Alex turned abruptly away from her, leaning his forearms on the back of a wing chair and looking down at his laced fingers as he struggled to regain control. When he finally spoke, the words came haltingly, chosen with great care. "Christa, I have never wanted a woman as I want you."

He lifted his gaze to meet hers. "I would like you to be my mistress. You would have a house, and an income that will keep you comfortable for life.

"But I do not want to buy you. If you would accept them, I would be happy to give you the same things even if you would not accept me. I want you to have the freedom and the security you deserve." She saw his fingers tightening as he continued, his voice ragged, "And I want you to want me."

Christa felt a sudden sharp sting of tears behind her eyelids, and she turned quickly away so he couldn't see her face. *Damn the man*! Why did he have to make it so difficult for her, by caring how she felt?

If he had merely offered money in return for her body, this proposition would have been essentially the same as that offered by Lady Pomfret's husband—the oldest bargain on earth, and one she could turn down without doubts or questioning. Alex's terms would be better than Sir Horace's, but the transaction no different. Instead, he cared enough for her to want her desire. If only he wanted her love as much as she wanted his. . . .

She moved aimlessly across the room. Stopping at a table that held a porcelain bowl of potpourri, Christa sifted it with her fingers, feeling the light crispness of dried rose petals, smelling the mixed scents of flowers and spices. Why should she not accept? She loved him, and for a while at least, she would have him. The house of d'Estelle was no more; there were none left to point a finger at how she had fallen. Most of her countrymen in England would applaud her enterprise in finding such a comfortable situation. Who would know or care?

A faintly amusing thought passed through Christa's mind: her mother would know. It was exactly the sort of thing her mother *would* know, wherever her spirit was now. She would not necessarily condemn; Marie-Claire had always followed her heart. But would she approve if her daughter gave her love to someone who didn't love in return? That was the crux of the question.

Christa's voice was very low when she answered. "And how long would it be for, my lord? Till you tired of me? Until you took a wife? Or would you keep me on then, passing from her bed to mine?"

His face was open and vulnerable as he replied, "I cannot imagine any of those things happening. It is more likely that you would tire of me."

Her throat tightened until she could not have spoken to save her life. Tire of Alex, with his humor and mischievous intelligence, his warmth, his beautiful tawny body? She had once heard of an elderly duke who kept the same mistress for over fifty years. They had walked together daily in St. James's Park, elderly lovers, objects of amusement and derision. Was that what would happen to them—Lord Kingsley and his servant-girl mistress?

Or should she say: "I will not be kept by you, but I was born a countess and you may marry me if you wish"? Her resolve stiffened at the thought. Alex had spoken from lust, not love. He was honest, and she admired that, but she was a d'Estelle—her pride was as much a part of her as her blood and marrow.

Christa's voice was stronger now, and she could meet his gaze. "I think I shall regret this all my life, but I cannot accept. I was not raised to be any man's mistress."

Alex was silent for long moments. "Will you let me give you the security and the freedom you said were your dream?"

Her half smile was sad as she answered, "I shall doubtless regret this also, but again, I cannot accept. Whatever security I have, I will earn with my own two hands."

His gaze held hers. "I don't want you to be angry with me."

Christa shook her head. "I'm not angry." She paused, then said steadily, "But it might be better if I left this house."

"No!" Alex caught himself and continued in more moderate tones, "This is your home. Annabelle needs you. I promise I will never ask you again." With a ghost of a smile, he added, "Unless you wish me to."

She sighed. The part of her that still burned with the memory of Alex's touch wished that he had not spoken with her, not treated her as a woman he respected. It would have been so much easier if he had devoured her with kisses, overpowering her logical mind with passion until it was too late to turn back.

"Good night, my lord Alex." On impulse, Christa crossed the room and placed her hands on his shoulders, standing on tiptoe to press her lips to his in one short, fierce kiss filled with all her love and regrets. He made no move to take her in his arms or prevent her from leaving the room.

As the door closed behind Christa's proudly erect figure, Alex retrieved his glass of whiskey and returned to the chair he had abandoned earlier. The pain in his side was back with a vengeance, and he winced as he lowered himself into the seat.

Staring into the dying flames, he felt a perverse pleasure in Christa's integrity, in the honor that could not be bought. And when he closed his eyes, he could remember with painful accuracy the taste of her last kiss, feel the softness of her body under his hands.

With deep sadness, Alex knew she would not change her mind, and as a man of honor, he could not try to persuade her otherwise. With a wintry smile he finished his whiskey in one gulp. A pity he could not consign his honor to the devil.

Chapter 13

Annabelle woke late the next morning, feeling languid and drained. It took her several moments to remember why she felt so oppressed: Edward. She had promised to meet him today, and he would certainly renew his pleas for her to run away. If they were to go to Scotland and return in time for her ball, they would have to leave almost immediately. She propped herself up in the bed and brushed strands of blond hair out of her face. It felt as limp as she did.

An elopement was very romantic in a novel but not at all what Annabelle had envisioned for herself. She would really much rather get married at St. George's, Hanover Square, with half the ton in attendance and Alex to give her away. She could feel traces of headache beginning to return.

But it was very bad of her to be so shallow and selfish. What did the ceremony matter if she was to be united with her darling Edward? Thinking of his Greek-god face, his adoring eyes, made her feel better immediately. Of course she wanted to marry him. And perhaps he was right in saying that it would be easier to present Alex with a fait accompli. Didn't someone once say that it was easier to get forgiveness than permission?

Christa entered carrying a tray with hot chocolate, croissants, and a rose in a crystal bud vase. "You are feeling better, Miss Annabelle?"

Annabelle nodded as Christa arranged the tray. "Yes, your willow tea was a great help. I've often wondered, where did you learn so much about herbs and teas and medicines?"

Christa shook out the linen napkin and spread it for her. "From my grandmother. She worked in the stillroom of an estate and was very skilled in all manner of old country lore. She was also something of an amateur physician, and I often assisted her when people came to her with illness or accidents." Her grandmother had also owned the estate, a fact Christa did not mention.

After observing Annabelle for a moment, Christa said hesitantly, "You have seemed blue-deviled lately, miss. Has it anything to do with Sir Edward Loaming?"

Annabelle concentrated on buttering her croissant, not meeting her maid's eyes. "Why would you say that?" she parried.

"Well, you have"—Christa paused and said ironically—"'happened' to meet him often lately, and you always seem agitated afterward. Has he been behaving improperly?"

"What a foolish thing to ask!" Annabelle's laugh was brittle. "Sir Edward is a perfect gentleman. What could he possibly do that is improper in a public park?"

Christa's snort was answer enough, but it was obvious that Annabelle was not going to confide in her. After a pause she said, "I will get the morning's invitations and messages for you to look at after you have finished eating."

Annabelle's gaze followed Christa from the room. She had been sorely tempted to tell her abigail about Sir Edward; the girl was much more worldly than her mistress, and her insight would be welcome. But the habits of a lifetime are

not easily changed, and Annabelle had always been secretive,
reluctant to tell her mother anything of importance for fear
that Lady Serena would somehow spoil it for her. Besides,
darling Edward had cautioned her about telling anyone of
their love, in case they might be separated. Her temples were
starting to throb again. Why did it have to be so difficult?

Sir Edward came to the park in his phaeton on this day.
Setting his groom down beside Christa, the baronet took
Annabelle up for a turn around the park. Christa stared
after them as they rattled toward Rotten Row. The
baronet's carriage was a conspicuous vehicle in sky blue
with silver trim, pulled by a team of flashy white horses.
She sniffed in contempt—it was exactly the sort of rig she
would have expected of Sir Edward. "All show and no go,"
she said.

The groom next to her said, "Aye, they are, but Sir Edward
took a fancy to 'em, and there was no stoppin' 'im." The
two servants exchanged a look of mutual understanding
about the foolishness of the Quality. Then the groom, a
burly man of middle years, said, "I'm to the tavern for a pot
of ale. Care to join me, missy?"

Christa shook her head. "No, I'll wait here for my mistress."

The groom guffawed. "Ye may have quite a wait. When
the bart is courtin', he takes 'is time about it."

Christa frowned. "Does he court many ladies?"

"Aye, that 'e does, missy. Till he gets what he wants from
'em. Sure you won't join me to lift a few?" The groom's
eyes ran appreciatively over the Frenchy's saucy little
derriere, just the kind he liked, but he stopped abruptly
when he saw the scowl on the maid's face. The girl was in
a rare taking, and no mistake. He'd find no joy there today.

"I'll be on my way then, miss," he said uneasily, tugging his hat before he turned away. He wondered who would be the target of the Frenchy's wrath; he was glad it wouldn't be him.

Annabelle was finding her ride with Sir Edward as uncomfortable as she had expected. His entreaties would have melted a heart of stone, but still . . .

"Why can't we wait just a few weeks longer, Edward?" she asked, near tears.

He gazed at her soulfully, then was called back to his driving by the furious shout of a curricle driver that he'd narrowly missed. Several minutes were spent in regaining control of his skittish team and driving to a less heavily trafficked area. Finally Sir Edward pulled the team up beneath a tree so he could give his nervous prey full attention. Taking her hand in one of his, the other being engaged in holding the reins, the baronet arranged his expression once more into the soulful lines he had found so successful. Some women preferred passion, some responded to command, but he had discovered that Annabelle reacted best to emotional manipulation.

"You cannot know how difficult it is to be a man," he said huskily. "I burn for you. To be so close, and yet not to have you—it is agony!" Sir Edward squeezed her hand hard, then paused and looked away as if he needed to regain control.

After a suitable interval, his gaze returned to her. "The promise in your eyes inflames me . . . I am being driven mad by love! Your golden hair, your exquisite form, your eyes, so like sapphires . . . If you will not come with me, I must go away. If you will not be mine, I fear what my actions might be."

Annabelle delved into her reticule for a handkerchief. That she should be responsible for bringing such a noble man to such straits! Sir Edward needed her so much—how could she deny him? And in a few weeks, they would have every right to be together.

"I will go with you, Edward," she whispered, her voice shaking.

She was rewarded by a blaze of passionate happiness in his eyes. "Oh, my beloved! You are a queen among women. An empress!" He leaned forward to kiss her, but she drew away hastily.

"Edward! Someone will see!"

Having won his point, Edward was ready to trade lovemaking for logistics. "It must be tonight, then," he said decisively. The bum traps were hot at his heels, and he'd be in the debtors' prison in Marshalsea if he wasn't away soon.

"So . . . so soon?" Annabelle quavered. She had made her decision, but she would have preferred a little more time to adjust to the results.

"Every moment away from you is an age, my darling," he murmured. "How early do you think you can leave your house? The sooner we leave, the longer the lead we will have on pursuers."

Annabelle shuddered at the thought of pursuit. Would Alex really come after her, pistols blazing? What if there were a duel? One of them might be killed, perhaps even both of them!

It didn't bear considering, so she resolutely applied her mind to the problem of escape. There should be no difficulty; the house wasn't a prison, and there was no watch set on her. Luckily she wasn't engaged to go out this evening.

"I could take a tray in my room for dinner, then say I am retiring early," Annabelle said. "Since I wasn't feeling well yesterday and my brother is dining away from home, no one will think anything of it. If I leave when the servants are eating, the only person to avoid will be the footman on duty, and he will never see me if I slip out the side door. Perhaps as early as eight o'clock. It will be dark by then."

"Perfect! Remember that we must travel fast and light—bring no more than a bandbox."

"I really ought to take Christa, to lend me countenance until we reach Scotland," Annabelle said wistfully. If her maid came, there would be at least one familiar face at her wedding.

"Impossible! She would certainly tell Lord Kingsley, and all would be lost! Promise me, not a word to anyone!" The baronet's tone was fierce, and Annabelle nodded obediently. Of course, he was right—was he not a man, and one she was entrusting with her whole future?

Sir Edward's voice softened. "You must write a note, of course, so no one will worry. Just be sure to leave it where it won't be found before morning."

She nodded once more. There was a certain peace in having made the decision, and Annabelle was calm when the baronet set her down next to Christa. "Thank you for a pleasant drive, Sir Edward," she said, pleased with how normal she sounded. Christa eyed her suspiciously and was unusually silent on the trip home, for which Annabelle could only be grateful.

Her preparations to run away were laughably easy. *After all, Alex trusts me not to do anything improper.* The thought produced a lump in her throat as she packed spare linen, slippers, and a dress into a bandbox. *This will be my wedding dress.* She stroked the white lawn gown as she folded it away. Was every thought going to produce more tears? Annabelle had expected to be married in silk and lace—but what was the loss of that compared to her sweet

Edward? If she didn't go with him, she might never see him again. The thought was unbearable, and it strengthened her resolve. Never let it be said that the Honorable Annabelle Kingsley would not dare all for love!

Nonetheless, by the time she had taken a tray in her room and announced to Christa that she would retire early, Annabelle had a genuine headache and was unwell in earnest. Christa made her some of the willow-bark tea, then pulled the curtains and extinguished the lamps when she left. Annabelle lay in her canopied bed, feeling her head throb, until Christa left the adjoining maid's room and went down for her own dinner. Annabelle counted slowly to a hundred before getting up and relighting a lamp.

It took a long time and much scratching out to compose the note to Alex, and Annabelle had to resharpen the quill several times. It was surprisingly hard to explain why she was running away, but finally she blotted the paper and folded it, leaving it on the pillow next to the rolled blanket that she had left under the covers to confuse Christa if the maid looked in on her later.

Picking up her bandbox, Annabelle took a long look around the pretty room, saying good-bye to her maiden life. It was such a short time that she had been happy here—just the months since Alex had come back and made the house a real home, and now she was going to commit the unforgivable sin of eloping. Surely he would forgive her someday? There were fresh tears on her face as she slipped out the side door and made her way to the carriage waiting down the block.

Christa was in a fever of impatience to talk with Alex. The groom's remark that Sir Edward courted ladies till he got what he wanted had crystallized her suspicions: the baronet was either a rake or a fortune hunter or both. Annabelle was obviously besotted with the man, and all too capable of being swayed by someone with a stronger will.

Alex's valet, Fiske, told her that Lord Kingsley was at the Admiralty all day, and would be going on to dine with a navy friend at a club. Yes, he would tell his lordship that Christa wanted to speak with him, no matter what hour he returned. The valet's gaze was curious, but he ascribed the maid's inquiry to some mysterious female request from Miss Annabelle.

Worried about Annabelle's headache and obvious nervousness, Christa looked in on her mistress about half past nine to see if she was resting comfortably. In the candlelight, the bedchamber was peaceful and Christa was about to close the door again when she stopped. There was something wrong about the slumbering form in the bed—the shape wasn't quite right. Hoping that the candle wouldn't wake Annabelle if she was sleeping, Christa drew closer to the bed. With a horrible feeling of inevitability she saw the rolled blanket and the note addressed to Alex on the pillow.

"*Nom du nom*!" she swore. "The little *fool*!" Christa broke the seal without compunction and opened the envelope. The message was rambling and tearstained, but the import was clear: Annabelle and her darling Edward were running away to Scotland, they would return in time for the ball, and she hoped her dearest Alex would understand and forgive her once he met Edward and knew what a splendid, noble fellow he was.

Christa wasted several moments grinding her teeth and muttering French curses under her breath. Much of her anger was self-directed. She had known something was wrong, had even started to raise the subject with Alex the

night before, only to let her personal affairs get in the way
of her duty. She might excuse herself on the grounds that
no one could have expected a well-bred, docile girl like
Annabelle to do something as outrageous as eloping, but
Christa refused that solace. She knew Annabelle, knew
how eager to please, how desperate for affection the girl
was— perfect prey for an unscrupulous man like Sir
Edward.

Christa indulged her reproach only briefly before racing
out of the room to Alex's chamber. If Fiske was there, perhaps he could tell her where Lord Kingsley was dining. She
knocked on the door, then burst through without waiting
for the valet to answer.

What she found was Alex. He looked at her, caught in
the act of unbuttoning his waistcoat. With a quick smile he
cocked an eyebrow and asked with a mixture of wry teasing
and faint hope, "Dare I assume this precipitate entrance
means you have reconsidered my offer?"

"Thank God you are here!" Christa cried. "I thought you
would be out until late." She thrust the note at him.

The humor disappeared from Alex's face as he saw
Christa's distress. As he took the note, he explained, "My
friend was held up in Portsmouth a day longer than expected so I worked late at the Admiralty instead. What has
happened?"

"Annabelle has eloped."

"What!" He scanned the note, then looked at Christa, his
eyes grim. "How long has she been gone?"

"Perhaps an hour. No more than an hour and a half, I
think. She ate in her room and went to bed early. I had
wanted to talk to you tonight anyhow. She has been meeting
this Sir Edward in the park regularly, and I was getting
worried."

"Why didn't you come to me sooner?" Alex rapped out.

He had already pulled his jacket on and was reaching for his caped driving coat.

Christa met his gaze steadily. "I did not want to be disloyal to my mistress. I was going to speak of my concern last night, but . . . events transpired."

Alex sighed. "It was partly my fault. Belle told me she had met this fellow. I asked about him and found he had an unsavory reputation, though no one would be specific. I told Annabelle not to let him call and thought no more of it."

"Romantic young females do not always obey orders like navy lieutenants."

"The matter has not escaped my attention," Alex said dryly. "I assume that if they are heading to Scotland the Great North Road is their likeliest route. If I am successful in finding them, I should be back tomorrow. They haven't much of a lead." He pulled his coat on, then picked up a hat and gloves.

Christa put a hand on his sleeve and said earnestly, "Take me with you. If you find her, she will need me. A young woman traveling with her brother and her maid will provoke no comment." As Alex hesitated, she added, "I have seen Loaming's carriage and horses."

"Very well, you may come. What does he drive?"

"A bright blue phaeton with silver trim, and a team of white horses with poor wind and spavins."

"That bad?" Alex asked with a hint of amusement.

"I may exaggerate," Christa admitted, "but only slightly. He is the sort of man who prefers show to substance." She added slowly, "I am wondering, my lord. The message is so specific. If Sir Edward told Annabelle to mention their destination . . . is it possible he wants to be caught? Did you hear anything that might indicate he likes to compromise girls of good fortune in hopes of being bought off? I would wager he is a man with expensive tastes, and perhaps what he wants of Annabelle has more to do with money than love."

Alex said thoughtfully, "That might fit with the hints I heard. If you are right and he prefers to be overtaken, he may stop at an inn or posting house along the way rather than ride through the night. If that is the case, we have a fair chance of bringing this off."

Christa nodded. "What will you do if we catch them?"

He shrugged. "Hard to say. Certainly I intend to bring Annabelle home. If she absolutely has to have him, she can be married from here in a few weeks when she is of age. But if he is the kind of man I think he is, perhaps I can . . . persuade him to show his true colors. That should effectively end her infatuation."

"Will you fight him?"

"Only if he insists," Alex said. "If someone were to be killed, it would be very difficult to conceal."

"Sir Edward won't insist," Christa said positively. "Like his horses, he is all surface and no bottom."

"Let us pray that proves to be the case. Get your cloak and meet me in the stable."

Ten minutes later they were heading north at a spanking pace.

Sir Edward Loaming poured another glass of burgundy, at peace with the world. During the three hours of the ride north, Annabelle's weeping got on his nerves, but now she sat silently across the deal table from him, playing with her bowl of soup. She had been surprised when they stopped relatively close to London, but Sir Edward's pockets were to let and he wanted to get as many miles out of his team as possible before he started hiring post horses.

The baronet had been genuinely undecided whether he

wanted to be stopped by Lord Kingsley or not. A chunk of the ready would be more than welcome, but he might be better off if he actually married Annabelle. It was getting harder and harder to get near an heiress, and he might never have such a rich prospect in hand again. While Sir Edward was not sure of the extent of her dowry, the viscount was said to be rich enough to buy an abbey, and he surely would not let his sister languish in poverty. More than that, Kingsley would probably pay extra to keep the circumstances of her marriage a secret.

Sir Edward's decision was made for him when they stopped at the Three Crowns. It was a respectable hostelry that occasionally had guests of the Quality, but the night was well advanced and the house small. When told that there was only one bedchamber available, Sir Edward decided that it was a sign from heaven that Annabelle should become Lady Loaming. He would have told her how lucky she was, but of course she had thought all along that the marriage was going to take place.

The sleepy landlord had set them up in the coffee room with cold meats, soup, trifle, and several bottles of quite drinkable burgundy. Sir Edward had drunk a bottle and a half of the wine, and his temper improved with every sip. The difficult part was over. Annabelle would not have been missed yet, and her brother might not even try to get her back after she had spent a night on the road with her lover. He wondered how large an annual income he might get from Kingsley. The nodcock deserved to pay for not mounting a better guard over his widgeon of a sister.

Sir Edward eyed Annabelle as she perched nervously on the edge of the oak settle. He preferred the riper charms of the Covent Garden ware that he usually frequented, but the girl was a comely wench, and would certainly do for the trip to Scotland and back. She had always responded to his kisses with enthusiasm if not skill, and upstairs the single bed waited.

"Come now, Annabelle, have some wine," he said jovially. "You'll feel better for it."

Having put away substantial quantities of veal, chicken, and game pie, Sir Edward was ready for dessert. "Care for some of the trifle, my love?" he asked expansively. When she shook her head, he said with irritation, "For heaven's sake, girl, stop moping! This should be the greatest night of your life, and you act as if you were at your own funeral."

She looked up at that, but still said nothing. The baronet came over to sit by her on the settle and put an arm around her. "Give me a kiss, sweeting," he coaxed.

Annabelle shrank back a little and said nervously, "I have a headache."

He smiled toothily. "I have just the cure for that," he said, and drew her into his arms.

Annabelle pushed him away as soon as she could. "But we're not married yet!"

Sir Edward was getting seriously aroused and he brushed her protests aside. "What does a day or two matter? Tonight is the night I make you my own." He proceeded with his kisses and his hand started fumbling at her bodice.

Near panic, Annabelle gasped, "But I feel most unwell. Really, I would rather go to my chamber and rest." She had always found his embraces exciting, but this Edward seemed a stranger, his breath heavy with wine and his caresses impatient.

Sir Edward played his trump card. "Going to our chamber is a splendid idea. But you won't get much rest, my dove. There was but one room left, and we will share it, as man and wife." Ignoring her dismay, he smothered her protests with his mouth.

Annabelle struggled against Sir Edward with fading strength as he pulled her dress off one shoulder. She considered calling for help, but the innkeeper thought they were married, and she couldn't face the brangles and humiliation that would result if she tried to explain that they were eloping. She had come too far to turn back.

Befuddled with wine and lust, Sir Edward did not hear the sounds of voices and steps in the hall until the door of the coffee room flew open, swinging hard to hit the wall with a bang. The baronet blinked up at the imposing figure standing in the doorway. He had no doubt who it was, the handsome blond man couldn't be anyone but Annabelle's brother. But Sir Edward hadn't expected him to be so tall. In the dark caped driving coat, the man seemed wide as a bear, and twice as dangerous.

Lord Kingsley stepped into the room, Christa following and closing the door to give them privacy.

Annabelle was near to weeping with relief, while Sir Edward straightened up, feeling at a distinct disadvantage.

"Good evening, Belle. I assume that this is Sir Edward Loaming, my future brother-in-law," Alex drawled as he stripped his driving gloves off.

"Exactly so," the baronet blustered. "Does this mean you are giving me permission to marry your sister?"

"She will be free to marry whom she chooses in a few weeks. How about it, Belle, do you really want to marry this"—his eyes raked Sir Edward's willowy elegance—"this man-milliner?"

Annabelle was too distraught to answer. The surge of relief she had felt when Alex entered was overpowering. Yet she was in love with Sir Edward. Wasn't she? Haltingly, she asked, "You would not disapprove?"

"I have trouble imagining that I could ever *approve* of this shag bag, but if you want him, and he loves you enough to marry a dowerless girl, who am I to stand in the way?" Alex had taken the baronet's measure in one glance, and he wanted Annabelle to know exactly what kind of man her suitor was.

Alex's comment elicited a startled squawk from Sir Edward. "Dowerless? But everyone knows how wealthy the Kingsleys are!"

Alex's smile was coldly amused. "Quite right. But unless you have a source at my man-of-business's office, you can't know how the money was left. My sister hasn't a penny in her own right. Quite ramshackle of my father to leave my siblings wholly at my mercy, but doubtless he assumed I would be fair with them."

Sir Edward's jaw sagged open in horror. "But surely you wouldn't turn your only sister out in her shift!"

Alex raised one eyebrow sardonically. "Of course not. She has a very considerable wardrobe. You won't have to buy her anything for at least a year, though women's fashions have been changing rapidly of late, don't you think?"

Sir Edward ignored this sally. "But I'm drowning in the River Tick! If she marries me, she might starve. Or end up in debtors' prison!"

"Not unless she chooses. My sister will always be welcome in my home. But *you* won't be. Cheer up. Annabelle can visit you in Marshalsea Prison. She's a softhearted girl and will probably bring you baskets of table scraps. I imagine I will allow that when I am feeling charitable."

Sir Edward looked at him with loathing. "You would see your sister's name dragged through the mud? If it becomes known that she ran off with me, your whole family will be disgraced!"

Lord Kingsley's wide smile was the most heartless the baronet had ever seen. "You overrate my family pride. As you probably know, I'm a crude sailor, hardly ever at home. What do I care about a parcel of gabble-mongers in London?"

Sir Edward was aghast, unable to believe what he had heard. "You mean you really don't *care* what anyone says?" At Lord Kingsley's cool nod, he gurgled, "But what of the feelings of Annabelle and your younger brother?"

Alex shrugged. "Jonathan wants to enter the army soon, so I daresay a fight or two over his sister's good name won't hurt him. Good practice, in fact. As for Annabelle"— he glanced over at her white face—"if she chooses to have her name on every loose lip in London, I'll not stand in her way."

Sir Edward was reeling from the succession of shocks he had received. "I don't believe that a man can be as blind to his honor as you claim to be!" he said hoarsely.

"Oh, I am not wholly indifferent," Alex said cheerfully. "All things being equal, I would just as soon no word of this little escapade got out. So if you maintain a gentlemanly silence, I shall reward you."

Sir Edward straightened up hopefully. Perhaps there would be some good from the situation after all.

"Yes," Alex continued. "I shall let you keep your miserable hide intact."

As Sir Edward blanched, Annabelle warned, "He's fought at least one duel, Alex!"

"Splendid! I prefer not to kill a defenseless man. I trust that you don't mind if I choose to use my cutlass, Sir Edward. I am the injured party so the choice of weapons is mine. The cutlass is a crude weapon next to a small sword, but excellent for hacking and chopping."

Sir Edward turned white. His one lesson in swordsmanship had ended when he found the sound of scraping blades unbearable.

Alex regarded him thoughtfully. "If you wish, we could

make do with pistols, but I should think you wouldn't like that as well. Rather than trying for a head shot and running a small risk of your escaping unscathed, I would have to aim for the torso. And as I'm sure you are aware, it takes a man such a long time to die of a bullet in the belly."

"I won't fight you!" Sir Edward gasped.

"You won't?" Alex said in a silky voice. "What a pity. For most assuredly I will fight you, whether you defend yourself or not. The world being the unfair place it is, I have no doubt that the justice system will cause me no inconvenience."

Sir Edward gaped at his lordship, unable to believe that a peer of the realm could be such a cynical barbarian. The baronet's stomach was churning, and his ample supper threatened to return by the same route it had entered.

Vastly amused by the proceedings, Christa chirped up helpfully, "If you would like to settle it now, Lord Kingsley, I brought your pistols in with me."

Alex looked at her and they shared a mirth-filled glance before he returned to the business at hand. His voice softening, he asked, "Will you come with me, Belle?"

His sister nodded and rose, her body shaking from the effects of too many shocks. The last days had been hellishly difficult, and now she found that her lover was a scoundrel and a craven whose clay feet went all the way to his ears.

"It's true, isn't it?" she said in a trembling voice. "You were interested only in money. Everything you said about loving me and admiring me—it was all lies, wasn't it?"

Slumped on the settle, Sir Edward refused to meet her eyes.

"*Damn you, look at me!*"

The baronet glanced up, unable to believe that Annabelle the Docile could say such a thing, and in such a tone of voice. Her white face was rigid, but the blue eyes burned with pain and humiliation.

Annabelle stared down into the handsome, weak face and felt sickened that she had believed—and kissed—those lying lips. With one spontaneous gesture she lifted the bowl of trifle from the table and upended it on his face. As she stalked to the door, determined to shed no more tears in the man's presence, the silence was broken by the sound of Christa applauding. "Oh, *très bien*, Miss Annabelle! Very well done, indeed!"

Lord Kingsley picked up his sister's cloak and draped it around her shoulders. With one last glance at Sir Edward, who sat in stupefaction while custard and raspberries soaked into his Brutus-cut hair and embroidered waistcoat, Alex said cheerfully, "See what I saved you from, Eddie? She's a proper tartar when she's angry. Come on, Belle. I think your former fiancé is about to flash his hash."

Eddie! The insult nearly unhinged Sir Edward entirely. He glared at his lordship's broad shoulders as the door closed, his chest heaving with furious gulps of air. Someday, some way, he seethed, he would find a way to get even with Viscount Kingsley!

Alex led Annabelle out into the passage. "Do you have any luggage upstairs?" When she nodded, he gestured to Christa. "Bring it down. Come on, Belle. We're going home."

It took Christa only a moment to retrieve the bandbox and join the Kingsleys outside the stable. Alex placed Annabelle in the middle of the seat so she would be secure between him and Christa. Since his sister's flash of anger had burned out, she seemed to be in shock. Christa put a comforting arm around the girl as Alex swung the carriage into the road and south.

After a few minutes he said to Christa, "I'm inclined to change horses at the next post house and go all the way back to London tonight. Can you and Belle manage?"

Christa glanced at the bent blond head between them. Her numb mistress appeared indifferent to what was going on around her. "We are all tired, but if we can get fresh horses, it will be better to go all the way to London. If we return tonight, no one will know we were gone."

Alex nodded and whipped the horses up. It was a long, chilly ride back, and as they pulled into the mews in St. James's Square, the church bells were striking four times. Alex turned the horses over to a sleepy and taciturn groom, then accompanied the girls upstairs. Annabelle was still moving like a sleepwalker, and he thought that the full shock wouldn't hit her until later.

In front of his sister's room Alex looked down into Christa's gray eyes, as tired as his own but still clear and holding a trace of humor. "I owe you a great deal, Christa. If you hadn't discovered the elopement so quickly, Belle would have been tied to that scoundrel for life."

Her smile had a trace of impishness. "It seems to me that you handled matters with great *savoir faire*. You have a considerable talent for foiling elopements."

Alex shuddered. "Once is enough, thank you!" He squeezed Christa's shoulder in token of the thanks she wouldn't accept, then watched as she helped his sister into the bedchamber. Through his fatigue, he felt a passionate gratitude that the French girl had entered their lives.

Chapter 14

Annabelle slept most of the day through, awakening in late afternoon. She was confused when her eyes first opened, and it took some moments to recall the events of the previous night. Then it came back to her—Edward's lies, her own stupidity—and she started sobbing. At the first sounds, Christa entered and came to the side of her bed.

"How are you feeling, Miss Annabelle?"

"I wish I were dead." Her voice was flat and despairing.

Christa patted her hand. "Very likely, but you will feel less like that after you have eaten." She left the room in spite of Annabelle's protest that the mere thought of food sickened her, returning a few minutes later with a tray that Monsieur Sabine had prepared especially to tempt an invalid's appetite.

Annabelle's unromantic stomach responded to the delectable scent of the clear soup, hot bread, and crème caramel, and she managed to eat a few bites before fretfully pushing the food away. Christa said when she came to remove the tray, "Everyone thinks you have a streaming cold. If you wish to rest for a while, no one will comment."

"Thank you." Annabelle laid back again and pulled the

covers over her head. The idea of not seeing anyone was very appealing.

Over the next week, Kingsley House was flooded with flowers and messages expressing the hope that Annabelle would soon be restored to health. Christa arranged the flowers and read aloud some of the shorter messages. Others made her purse her lips and decide they were best left until her mistress was stronger.

Annabelle lay unmoving most of each day, eating a little but saying almost nothing. At night Christa could hear the wretched sobs from her mistress's room and feared that soon the girl would be truly ill.

The turning point came a week after the foiled elopement. Christa came into the darkened room to find that Annabelle had read all of the notes, and she was crying hysterically.

"People know! Two women wrote notes making sly comments about how Sir Edward has left town, and how odd it is not to see me in the park with him, and . . . and . . ." She disintegrated into tears.

Deciding that enough was, in this case, far too much, Christa marched over to the windows and pulled the draperies open. Late afternoon sunshine flooded into the room.

"Close them! I can't bear the light," Annabelle sobbed.

"It is more than time we had some light in here." Christa's voice was biting.

Annabelle raised her head in confusion, her eyes red and swollen, her hair lank. Her abigail was standing in the sunshine, her chin up and her eyes a chilly gray.

"Yes, I know your heart is broken. Yes, you were a fool. But there are worse things than being a fool for love, and it is time you stopped feeling sorry for yourself.

"After all, you have escaped the consequences of your folly. Can you imagine how much worse things would be if your brother had not rescued you, if you had actually *married* that cod's head? You would have been miserable as long as you both lived. There may be a few sly innuendos from the cats of your acquaintance, but there would have been such comments in any case. No one knows that there was an elopement, and when you start to go out again the whole matter will be forgotten."

Annabelle was shaking. "I can never face anyone again!"

"Five days from now is your ball, and you are going to walk down there and dance and flirt as if you have never had a care in your life." Christa's voice was implacable.

"I can't!" Annabelle wailed.

Christa exploded, her eyes flashing gray fire. "*Sacrebleu!* If you have no pride in yourself, have some for your name! If you disappear from society, the aimless gossip around your name will catch fire in earnest. In spite of what he told that fribble, your brother will fight for your honor. Do you want to be responsible for the consequences?"

She paused to let that idea sink in before continuing, "Have you thought, even once, about what you have done to Lord Kingsley? He has done everything he could to make you happy. He trusted you, and you rewarded him for his trust by running away with a scoundrel. He rescued you from your own folly, laid no word of blame, and now you won't even talk to him! Have you considered how that must make him feel?

"Have you even noticed that your brother has an injury in his side that seems to pain him constantly, and which is worse this last week? Have you thought about *anything* but your own selfishness and hurt pride? Even that fool of a baronet is in worse case than you! He is facing ruin while you have no worse injury than your wounded amour propre."

The words continued to pour out in an angry torrent. "Almost everyone in London has worse problems than yours! Women are selling their bodies, gin-soaked parents beat their children, men are hanged for stealing loaves of bread, yet the Honorable Annabelle Kingsley can afford to lie here in pampered comfort, whimpering like a kicked puppy!"

As Annabelle stared white-faced, Christa threw her hands up. "Go ahead, discharge me! I have no desire to continue in the employ of such a poor-spirited excuse for a woman."

Christa stalked across the chamber to her own small room and slammed the door. Picking up her portmanteau, she started throwing things into it. If she stopped being angry, she would want to cry, and on the whole, she preferred to be angry.

There was no way that Annabelle was going to forgive that kind of outburst from a servant. Yes, the girl was suffering, but she had certainly brought it on herself. What really devastated Christa was seeing the hurt in Alex's eyes every day when he asked about his sister, and she refused to see him. Christa sensed that Lord Kingsley blamed himself for everything—his sister's unhappy childhood, her elopement, her present misery. He moved more slowly now, the exuberant energy that was so characteristic of him dimmed.

Christa angrily dashed the tears from her eyes and started folding her linen into the case. The sooner she got away from this house, the better. She loved both Alex and Annabelle, but she had neither the position nor the power to comfort either of them, and watching their misery was tearing her apart.

After Christa had stormed out of the room, Annabelle lifted herself from the bed and crossed shakily to the window, pulling a wrapper around her. As she stared out, blind to the splendor of St. James's Square, her maid's words pounded in her head. *Have you thought about what you have done to Lord Kingsley? Almost everyone in London has problems worse than yours. A poor-spirited excuse for a woman. A poor-spirited excuse for a woman.*

It was all true. She had been a fool, and there was no changing it. Alex had told her to avoid Sir Edward, she had known that Christa didn't like him, yet she had run head-long into his arms, willing to believe him the embodiment of her romantic fantasies. Annabelle had no one to blame but herself.

Yet she was blessed in so many ways, with wealth and position, two brothers who loved her, a growing circle of friends, even passable good looks. All that, and she was hiding in her room like a badger in its sett.

Annabelle knew that Christa herself had lost her family and her home to revolution, yet the French girl had never been anything but cheerful, generous, and loving. Annabelle could understand why her maid despised her, and a wave of self-loathing started sweeping over her.

Stop that! Her fingers clenched on the brocade curtains, and she squared her shoulders. She could not change her past mistakes, but she could try to avoid making the same ones in the future. And to the extent possible, it was time to make amends. Without realizing it, as Annabelle crossed the room she was taking the first long step from childhood to maturity.

Annabelle knocked at Christa's door, then entered

before she could be refused admittance. She was shocked to see the half-packed portmanteau. Her maid straightened and looked at her warily.

Lifting her head a little, Annabelle said, "I owe you an apology. It cannot be easy living with the heroine of a Cheltenham tragedy. I have put you to considerable trouble and distress these last days, and I hope you will forgive me."

Christa was for once at a loss for words. After a flustered moment, she said, "I should not have ripped up at you so."

"If you hadn't, I would still be lying in there like Ophelia drowning." Annabelle paused, then said diffidently, "I know that my hen-hearted behavior has given you a disgust of me, but I pray you will reconsider and stay here." With the ghost of a smile, she added, "I will need guidance on how to be more spirited, and I doubt I could find a better teacher than you."

Christa flushed. "Of course, I shall stay if you wish me to. I promise to keep a better guard on my tongue."

"Oh, don't do that! I need someone to put me in my place now and then, and my brother is far too polite."

The two girls looked at each other, then suddenly they were laughing, a little weakly perhaps, but with genuine amusement. When they had sobered, Annabelle asked, "Do you know if my brother is at home now?" After Christa's nod, she said, "Will you help to make me more presentable? I must talk to him."

Christa felt almost giddy with relief. "Of course, Miss Annabelle." If her mistress was concerned about her appearance, she was definitely back among the living. And Christa would not have to leave the Kingsleys.

Alex pushed the sheet of foolscap away with a sigh. He had been working at home more than at the Admiralty for the last week, but his concern for his sister eroded his writing ability. He had had ample time to chastise himself for his former naive belief that being head of a family was easy. He half expected to hear from Eton that Jonathan had impregnated three different girls and all of the fathers were demanding marriage. Or worse.

He looked up at the sound of footsteps to see his sister approaching. Annabelle looked thinner but composed, her hair freshly styled and her dress a flattering soft blue that put a little color in her cheeks.

He stood and said, "Belle! It's good to see you up again. How are you feeling?"

She smiled self-consciously. "Much better. Christa read me the riot act a short while ago, and I have decided it is time to stop feeling sorry for myself." She swallowed, then said, "I am truly sorry for the trouble I have caused you, Alex."

He had come around his desk and was leaning against the front of it several feet away from her. He looked tired, and his voice was low when he said, "Why did you run away without even trying to talk to me, Belle? Were you afraid of me? I had thought we were friends."

For the first time, Annabelle looked at him clearly, not as the omnipotent big brother whom she had placed on a pedestal, but as an individual. With a pang of shame, she saw him unconsciously rub his left side as if trying to relieve a habitual pain. She had known that he was gravely wounded scarcely six months before, yet had accepted his blithe assurances that he was completely well now. His own sister had seen less than a servant.

Now she could see her brother as a man who had known pain and loneliness, depression and self-doubt, and who needed her friendship as much as she needed his. Her mental pedestal crumbled away, and he seemed both nearer and dearer in its absence. With a rush of affection Annabelle hugged him, carefully, so as not to injure his side. "I haven't understood friendship very well, Alex. But I promise I shall do better in the future."

He hugged her back, hard, then held her away from him. "Next time you take it into your head to get married, will you at least talk to me first?" His amber eyes searched hers.

She smiled at him. "Of course! A man who won't meet my family isn't worth the knowing. Tell me," she asked curiously, "did Father really make no provision for Jonathan and me?"

Alex nodded. "Entirely true. There were instructions in case I died before he did, but not much more." He thought a moment. The continually increasing pain in his side made him aware that the shell fragment was shifting, and he had recently made sure that his affairs would be left in order.

"This is probably as good a time as any to explain what I have done for you and Jonathan. There are trusts being set up for each of you, with the income becoming available when you reach your maturity. Next week, in your case. Until the age of thirty, you would need my agreement to spend any capital. After that, it's entirely your own. If something should happen to me, you and the family lawyer will be joint guardians of Jonathan until he is twenty-one."

Annabelle looked at him very seriously. "Is anything going to happen to you, Alex?"

He smiled casually. "Not that I know of. It's merely good sense that a man in my position make a will."

Since Alex didn't want to discuss his health, Annabelle changed the subject after making a mental note to watch her brother more closely. "So if Sir Edward had waited, he could have had me and a fortune with no strings attached."

"Exactly. I can only be grateful that he was precipitate."

Annabelle shuddered. "I couldn't agree more! Though now that I think of it, the experience was all very educational. The next fortune hunter will have to be *much* more convincing." She suddenly giggled. "You were quite splendid. Are you really so bloodthirsty as you led Sir Edward to believe?"

Alex chuckled. "I wouldn't describe myself as bloodthirsty, though I can do what is necessary. After seeing what a Bartholomew baby he was, I was sure words would suffice."

"You were certainly accurate in your judgment! If you ever need rescuing yourself, do not hesitate to call on me." Annabelle said the words lightly, but she meant them in dead earnest. She owed Alex far more than she could ever repay him.

Sybil Debenham had taken unusual care with her preparations for the Kingsley ball, starting her toilette a full six hours before the appointed time. As the host, Lord Kingsley would have to be in attendance all evening, and she felt sure that would give her some useful opportunities to attach him.

As she turned slowly in front of the cheval glass mirror, she could find no flaw in her appearance. The gauze overskirt was woven with tiny golden stars that floated over the shimmering silk dress below, her parure of diamonds and gold would attract attention anywhere. The simple pastoral style in vogue now was not for Sybil. Her mother came into her chamber as she was completing her survey and nodded approvingly. "Very good, Sybil. Lord Kingsley cannot fail to admire you. Have you heard the on-dit about his sister?"

Sybil gave a most unladylike snort. "That Sir Edward

Loaming was seeking to fix the affections of a mouse like
her? An unlikely story!"

Claudia Debenham said dryly, "She hasn't your fashion
flair, but I wouldn't call her a mouse. They were seen walking
in the park several times. My guess is that her brother found
out and sent Sir Edward on his way."

"More likely she was too *gauche* for him. I don't think
there is another man in London with Sir Edward's style. He
cast a number of lures my way, you'll recall," Sybil said,
giving her plump golden ringlets a complacent pat.

"The man's a gazetted fortune hunter, so one can guess
what attracted him to Miss Kingsley, and to you."

Her daughter scowled. "Nonsense! Sir Edward was
absolutely besotted with me. If he were more than a mere
baronet, I would not have been at all averse to his suit."

Her mother decided not to pursue the point. "I do trust
you are making progress with Lord Kingsley?"

Sybil's enchanting lower lip stuck out in an undeniable
pout. "Not as much as I would like. I know he admires me,
and shows me more attention than any other lady, but he
seems to have no desire for further intimacy."

"If you can't attach him, you had better look around for
someone else," Claudia said dispassionately. "I heard
they're betting in the clubs whether you'll land a title this
year." At Sybil's shriek, she added with a trace of malice,
"They're calling you the 'Luscious Loser.'"

Sybil spun around, abandoning her mirror image to
glare at her mother. "That's absolutely *outrageous*! And
they call themselves gentlemen! How *dare* they!"

Claudia suddenly wished she hadn't mentioned it; her
daughter seemed likely to explode on the spot. She shrugged
and said, "You know how men are, with their stupid
'gentleman's code.' It makes no sense at all—they can be

incredibly coarse about a woman, then call another man out for saying something that is no more insulting. There is no accounting for them."

Sybil's glare threatened to leave her mouth and eyes twisted into permanent slits. Then her face relaxed as something her mother had said set off a train of thought. *The gentleman's code* . . . With a snap, she said, "I know how to land Kingsley. With any luck, this very night, but I'll need your help." She explained what she had in mind.

Claudia shook her head doubtfully. "I can't say that I like it. And it's chancy—what if he repudiates you?"

"He won't," Sybil said viciously. "The stupid rules men have won't let him. 'The Luscious Loser' indeed! He'll pay for that insult."

"No one said Kingsley was involved in any betting. I must say, it doesn't seem his style. He's always been very gentlemanly."

Sybil's teeth were bared. "He's a man, isn't he? *He'll pay for all of them*!"

Alex drew a quick breath as Annabelle came down the winding stairs to meet him. She walked like a queen, her crown of golden tresses bound with Grecian ribbons, curls spilling down her back. Her cream-colored dress had the elegance of absolute simplicity, falling about her graceful figure in a manner that hinted rather than boldly advertised. Around her neck was a single strand of pearls, Alex's birthday gift to her. He offered her his arm.

"Belle, you are breathtaking," he complimented. "Are you ready to conquer London?"

She took his arm and smiled back. "I spent the afternoon

following Christa's advice. She said that when you wish to be especially lovely, lie down and *think* yourself beautiful."

Alex chuckled. "She said that? It seems to have worked."

"You are rather breathtaking yourself," Annabelle pointed out. "There is something about a uniform."

Alex had chosen to wear his captain's dress uniform and was resplendent in navy blue and gold braid, the expert tailoring setting off his wide shoulders and lordly height to perfection. He chuckled. "I'm sure that if you surveyed the young ladies who will be attending, they would agree that a navy uniform is not to be compared with that of a Hussar. Shall we go and greet our guests?"

It was soon clear that the evening was going to be one of the most successful social events of the Little Season. The Arabian decorations were greatly admired and apparently everyone who had received a card had decided to attend. The ball even attained the exalted height of being declared "a sad crush."

If some of the guests wanted to see Miss Kingsley wearing the willow for Sir Edward Loaming, their hopes were dashed; the guest of honor was convincingly lighthearted. Annabelle was charming to older guests of both sexes, found partners for less popular young ladies, and distributed her dances impartially to the crowd of men who surrounded her when she was not otherwise engaged. She accepted even the most fulsome compliments graciously, her behavior never crossing the line of what was proper for a miss making her come out.

Alex was proud of her. Hard to believe that a week ago she had been so emotionally devastated that she would not even leave her room. Only he could see the trace of defiance in her manner, as if daring anyone to think that she could have lost her heart to a fortune hunter.

He was feeling lighthearted himself, having shared a

few too many toasts to his sister's health. He did some
dancing but spent more time talking to guests and unobtru-
sively overseeing the ball. He decided that it was not all
that different from managing a ship; here he merely dealt
with French pastries and footmen rather than salt pork
and sailors.

It was nearing midnight when his path crossed Miss
Debenham's. He blinked at her dazzling self; she was very
nearly blinding in her golden gorgeousness. "Good evening,
Miss Debenham. You are looking particularly fine tonight.
I trust you are enjoying yourself?"

There seemed to be a rather strange light in her eyes
before she cast them down bashfully, fluttering her fan
over her lower face. "Actually, my lord, there has been
something amiss." She glanced up, her eyelashes fluttering
in time to her fan. She paused delicately, then said, "This
is very bold of me, but . . . I very much need to speak with
you. Is there some place where we might be private for a
few moments? Perhaps that alcove at the far end of the
ballroom?"

Alex was a little surprised at the request but saw no
reason not to comply. After all, Sybil was not a miss in her
first Season—spending a few minutes closeted with a man
was unlikely to ruin her reputation. "At your service, Miss
Debenham," he said cheerfully as he offered his arm.

Claudia Debenham watched the pair from across the
ballroom. Perhaps Sybil was going to bring it off after all.
Well, her mother was willing to do her part. She checked
the wall clock next to her, then went to collect two friends.

The alcove was curtained from the main room and a
good distance from the orchestra, so speech was possible
at a normal level. "What do you wish to discuss, Miss
Debenham?" Alex prompted when his guest seemed uncertain where to begin.

She raised her pale blue eyes to his helplessly. "Indeed, Lord Kingsley, it is very hard to know where to start. Society frowns on what I am about to do." More fan fluttering.

Puzzled but unsuspicious, Alex said, "Are you interested in purchasing a yacht?" He could think of no other area of his expertise that might be of value to her. "I should be very happy to advise you if that is your desire. Sailing is wonderfully enjoyable, and while it is unconventional, there is nothing improper about it."

She gave a little moue. "That is not it at all! Indeed, I suffer from mal de mer even on river ferries." She drew very close to him, her breasts almost touching his chest as she gazed up. "No, my lord, I wish to confess something. I fear that I have lost my heart to you in the most unladylike way. Since the first time I met you, I have dreamed of you, so handsome, so brave." She laid one hand on his arm.

"You are what a woman dreams of. Please don't run away," she pleaded as Alex showed signs of flight. "I do not expect you to declare any such passion for me. A hero like you must always have foolish females falling at your feet. I only . . . wanted to tell you how I felt, just once." Her aquamarine eyes were shining with a hint of tears, the exquisite heart-shaped face full of sweet longing.

Alex's primary reaction was embarrassment; he had trouble imagining himself as the answer to a maiden's prayer. But she was very lovely, and she seemed to be expecting a response of some kind. Besides, it was about time he attempted to find another woman whose kisses were as sweet as Christa's.

He bent his head and lips to hers as a clock in the ballroom began striking midnight. He took his time, since this was in the nature of a test, and by the twelfth stroke he had decided Miss Debenham could in no way compare with his memories of Christa. For all Sybil's beauty, kissing her had

no special charms for him beyond a man's natural response
to an attractive woman.

Alex tried to break away but she clung to him. In the
moment before he could gracefully disengage, the curtains
in the alcove were swept aside and three women entered.
One was Sybil's mother and the other two were highly
respected social leaders. He froze for a moment as Sybil
leaned into his embrace.

Claudia Debenham stopped dead, then her eyes widened,
and she rushed toward him. "Lord Kingsley, how wonderful! I am delighted to welcome you as a son-in-law. All my
life I have hoped my dear girl would win the heart of a
man like you."

One of the other dowagers stepped forward. "Such a
handsome couple you make! Let me be the first to wish
you happy."

Son-in-law? Alex felt paralyzed. He glanced down at
Sybil, still clinging to him, but now with possessiveness in
her grip. Her gaze was an artful blend of innocence and
excited pleasure, and she made no move to deny her mother's
assumption.

Disastrously, his mind blanked. It was like the horrible
exams at school and in the navy—when under pressure he
could find no words. Alex could have managed if action
were appropriate, but that was no solution here. Other
people were crowding into the alcove, curiosity bright in
their eyes. Among them was Annabelle, her eyes wide and
startled.

Since his paralyzed brain had no suggestions how to
talk his way out of this imbroglio, the viscount's training
in manners took over and with a stiff face he began ac-
knowledging congratulations. Within half an hour the
news was all over the ballroom: their host was to marry
the beautiful Miss Debenham. It was generally thought to

be a very reasonable match—both were wealthy, and her exceptional beauty compensated for her lackluster breeding. The only guests who faulted the arrangement were those who had had designs on one half or the other of the happy couple.

Christa had spent the evening in the lady's retiring room. With a chambermaid to assist her, she fixed damaged dresses and coiffures, patted cooling lavender water on the brows of overheated dancers, and generally repaired the ravages of an evening's entertainment. She was kneeling on the floor when a new arrival hailed the matron whose dress Christa was pinning up. "Sophia! Have you heard the news about Lord Kingsley?"

"No. What has happened?"

"He's going to marry Sybil Debenham!" was the excited reply. "The engagement was just announced."

Christa's hand jerked and the tin of pins she was holding sprayed across the floor. The matron glared down at her.

"Be more careful, you clumsy wench! Servants are impossible these days." Speaking to her friend, the woman said, "I can't believe Kingsley offered for that hussy. I was thinking that he would be perfect for my Emily."

The bearer of news, who had no marriageable daughters, said with a hint of malice, "Emily is a pretty little thing, but there's no denying Miss Debenham is a diamond of the first water."

Thoughts jumbled chaotically in Christa's brain as she went through the motions of gathering up the pins, then getting out needle and thread to baste the ripped hem. Alex was getting married? It was just two weeks since he had asked her to be his mistress. She had seen Sybil Debenham

in the park sometimes—once the woman had walked with
Annabelle and Alex for a while as Christa followed. Certainly she was very beautiful, but Alex seemed to have no
special interest in her. Indeed, Christa had observed that his
lordship was surprisingly quiet around the ladies of the ton,
not at all as he was in private. Could he really be in love
with Sybil Debenham?

She finished the hem and knotted the thread, neatly
trimming it with her sewing scissors. The matron swept
off with neither verbal thanks nor a coin, still grumbling
to her friend that Lord Kingsley was being wasted on The
Debenham.

There was a temporary lull in the retiring room, and the
chambermaid said with concern, "Are you feeling all right,
Christa? You've come all over white."

Christa forced herself to smile. "Just tired, Maggie. I
have been busy all day, what with the ball and readying
Miss Annabelle. I'll be all right if I sit for a few minutes."

She sat down just before her knees could buckle and
leaned her head against the back of the chair. There was a
bitter taste in her mouth, and she wondered if she were
going to faint. Had Alex offered her a carte blanche because he wanted *her*, or just because he wanted a woman?
She shuddered—she knew he didn't love her, but surely
there had been some caring? Had he already been planning
on offering for Miss Debenham, or had he chosen to marry
her because he was lonely, and Christa had refused him?

Questions tumbled painfully in her head but there were
no answers. *You know he is not for you. You are a servant,
without name or fortune. She is an heiress and beautiful.
A cat may look at a king, and a servant may love a lord, but
the lord will marry a lady.*

Christa found she was shivering and forced herself to

relax. Of course, he was not for her—she could have had him, on his terms, and had refused. She had no right to complain when he found a companion among his own class.

But did it have to be so quickly?

It was past three in the morning when the last guests left and the servants could move in and begin the cleanup. Annabelle leaned against the newel post at the bottom of the stairs, almost too tired to stand. Certainly the ball had been a success, but . . . Alex came up to her, having just put the last departing guests into their carriage. Even he looked tired.

"I wish you happy on your coming marriage, Alex," she said, doing her best to keep both question and reproach from her tone.

Her brother sighed and ran his fingers through his hair. "I would have warned you about it, Belle, except that it was as much a surprise to me as to you. I'm sorry for stealing some of your thunder on what should have been your night."

"I don't mind sharing the limelight," she said with a tired smile. "I found it is very fatiguing to be the center of attention for a whole night. But . . ." She paused, then said carefully, "I had not realized that you were so attached to Miss Debenham."

"Events took on a life of their own," he said dryly. "Will you mislike it, Belle? You and she are friends, aren't you?"

Annabelle considered before replying. She had never liked Sybil above half, but if Alex wanted to marry her, he should be free to do so without worrying about whether his childish younger sister was going to sulk. "She has always been most friendly and helpful." She could not quite keep the note of acid out when she added, "She has tried to hint me into a more elegant mode any number of times."

Alex looked startled. "I think your present style suits you much better than Miss Debenham's would. She is . . . um . . ." He fumbled for a correct term.

"Unusually dramatic?" Annabelle suggested.

"Exactly." Alex gestured to the butler, who had just entered the hall. "Morrison, the servants have done a splendid job this evening. Please give everyone a half day off tomorrow."

"As you wish, my lord. And very generous, I might add." Morrison executed a half-bow and withdrew to spread the good news.

Christa was waiting for Annabelle and quickly unpinned her hair and brushed it out. "You appear to have had a great success, Miss Annabelle."

Her mistress smothered a yawn. "So it would seem. Much of that is due to you. You've worked harder than anyone. I intend to sleep very late tomorrow, and you have my permission to do the same." She glanced at Christa's reflection in the mirror. "Did you hear of my brother's engagement?"

"Yes, miss." The reply was colorless.

Annabelle sighed. "I wish I could be more enthusiastic. It is flattering that a beauty like Miss Debenham should choose my brother, but I have always found her to have a sadly commonplace mind." She stood so Christa could help her out of her gown.

"Men seldom choose wives for their minds, Miss Annabelle."

"No, I suppose not. But I am not looking forward to sharing a house with her."

Christa smiled faintly. "They will probably not marry for some months. Perhaps by that time you will have found a suitable *parti* of your own."

Annabelle gave an elaborate shudder. "Never! I think I will retire to a cottage and raise roses. Will you join me, or would the life be too slow for an abigail of your talents?"

Christa chuckled as she turned the bedcovers back. "We shall see, Miss Annabelle. The future is not written yet. Even a cynical, brokenhearted woman of the world like you may learn to love again."

"On the whole, I would prefer the roses," Annabelle said sleepily. "At least the thorns are visible."

Chapter 15

Alex paid a call on Sybil Debenham the day after Annabelle's ball. He was greeted with a knowing smile by the Debenham butler, who ushered him into a room where Sybil was sitting with her mother. Claudia stood and simpered, "Lord Kingsley—so delightful to see you! I just want to tell you how happy you've made me. Sybil is my only baby, and I have prayed for her happiness. I'll just leave you two lovebirds alone." She flitted out of the room, leaving Alex with his "fiancée."

Sybil gazed at him adoringly. Still standing, Alex said, "It seems that circumstances last night created a false conclusion." To his horror, crystal tears started welling up in the aquamarine eyes.

"You don't really want to marry me, do you?" she whispered. "I knew it was too beautiful a dream to be true. But when my mother made that mistake, and you didn't correct her, I hoped . . . that a miracle had taken place, that you returned my feelings." Sybil turned her head as if to hide her emotions, then looked up at him valiantly. "But it shall be as you wish. I do not mind the scandal. Of course, you would not wish to be tied to me. What have I to offer?"

Fifteen years at sea does not prepare a man for such adroit manipulation. With a rush of weariness, Alex accepted the fait accompli. The engagement might have resulted from a bizarre mistake, but he *had* been found kissing her, an action somewhat compromising to an unmarried woman. It might have happened on her initiative, but he was still responsible for the possible consequences. They would both be exposed to gossip and censure if he cried off. He wouldn't have minded for himself, but he had no right to expose Sybil to such unpleasantness. Nor was he eager to crush her feelings for him when she looked so vulnerable. He had been looking for a wife, after all, and it wasn't as if he had met any lady he preferred to Miss Debenham. *There is one you prefer, but she isn't a lady.* Alex repressed the thought.

With one faint hope he said, "Any man would be greatly honored to have you as his wife, but I fear that I will make a poor husband. I have decided to return to sea and should be posted to another ship soon. A captain's wife is much alone, and you would not receive the attention and cherishing you deserve."

Sybil's voice choked a little as she said, "So brave! I will never stand between you and your duty. I will be honored to wait on the shore for as long as you want me to."

There was to be no escape that way. He said woodenly, "If you are sure, Miss Debenham, I am delighted that you will honor me with your hand. I will notify the newspapers of our engagement." She looked as if she expected but would not welcome another kiss, so he made his bow and left.

Resignation settled over Alex as he reached the street. He hadn't intended to return to a ship's command, but the war with France offered exciting possibilities. He gave a melancholy thought to his friend Peter Harrington's loving marriage, then shrugged. Perhaps he lacked the ability to love in that way. And if he spent years on end at sea, it hardly mattered whom he married. At least Sybil didn't think she would mind the neglect.

On impulse, he continued on to the Admiralty. Fortunately, Admiral Hutchinson was able to see him quickly. After a minimum of preliminaries, Alex said, "I'd like another ship."

Hutchinson leaned back in his chair. "I hear you are getting married. Don't you wish for time with your bride?"

His remark drew no response, and Lord Kingsley's expression did not invite further comment. The admiral stoked up his pipe and said, "If you are interested, the yard in Plymouth has almost finished a sister ship to your old *Antagonist*. She's going to be named *Invicta*, and she has a few new tricks we hope will let her out sail anything the French have. Of course, the *Invicta* is another frigate, not a ship of the line."

"I actually prefer the quickness and maneuverability of frigates, sir."

"They do suit your style. If you want the *Invicta*, she's scheduled for her final outfitting soon after Christmas. By the time she's ready to sail, you'll have had a year to recover from that Gibraltar business. You may want to go down to Plymouth and oversee the last stages."

"I would like that very much, sir. With your permission." Alex bowed and left the office. Hutchinson watched him depart with narrowed eyes. Jumping on the first available ship seemed a damned funny response to getting betrothed, but the navy could use as many captains like Kingsley as it could find. He shook his head, then returned to the mountain of papers on his desk.

That night at dinner Alex told his sister he would be returning to active naval duty. Annabelle looked up in

shock. Her first reaction was to remind him he had promised
to stay home as long as she needed him, but she held her
tongue. Something very strange was going on with Alex—
the sudden engagement and now this decision to go to sea
again. If she asked him to stay, she had no doubt that he
would keep his word, but with her newfound maturity
she saw his need to get away. When she had ordered her
thoughts, she said, "We shall miss you, but you have arranged
things here so that we shall manage very well."

"Thank you, Belle," he said quietly.

"When will you be leaving?"

"Sometime after Christmas I'll go to Plymouth to
oversee the final outfitting of the ship. It's a new frigate,
the *Invicta*. We should be ready for assignment in March
or April."

She nodded, then asked diffidently, "Can we go to the
Orchard for Christmas? We were so happy there last
summer."

Alex smiled at her, the strain on his face easing for the
first time that day. "I would like that very much."

Christa felt that the weeks between Annabelle's ball and
the Kingsleys' removal to Suffolk had an air of waiting.
One phase of family life was over, and the next not yet
clear. Annabelle went to her share of teas, routs, and balls,
and had more than her share of gentleman callers, yet
showed no partiality for any of them. If there were no more
sobs in the night, there was no great enthusiasm either. Sir
Edward Loaming had not been seen in London since the
elopement, and the rumors linking his name with Annabelle's
died a quick death.

Lord Kingsley spent little time at the house, working
long hours at the Admiralty to complete the work he had

laid down for himself. Christa knew from her mistress's occasional comments that he regularly escorted his fiancée to various social functions. Annabelle said rather plaintively that Alex seemed to have nothing to say to the beautiful Sybil, but that Sybil had more than enough words for any two people. The marriage had been set for the end of March, shortly before Lord Kingsley took command of his new ship.

Christa had silently resolved to be gone from the household before the wedding, though she had not yet informed Annabelle. She and her cousin Suzanne had talked and agreed that the middle of March would be a good time for her to start at the shop. Christa had met her cousin's Henry, and he was a quiet, reliable man who obviously adored his French bride to be.

From their behavior, she suspected that Suzanne's campaign to make Henry a little less proper had been successful; they both had that cat-in-the-cream pot look about them. Christa was amused and touched by their obvious pleasure in one another but preferred not to be around the happy couple too often. It was too vivid a reminder of her own loss. She had always said that she wouldn't marry unless she found a man the equal of her father and brother. It seemed unbearably cruel that she had found him but couldn't have him.

The weather had been unusually dry that autumn, and the trip to Suffolk was accomplished with none of the distress that December traveling often caused. Christa felt a flood of happiness at the sight of the Orchard's magpie facade—surely it was the drollest house in the world! She hoped Lord Kingsley would never change a thing about it.

Alex did not travel down with his brother and sister, preferring to arrive two days later accompanied only by his valet. Christa wondered idly if he was avoiding her—they had scarcely seen each other in the two months since Annabelle's attempted elopement. She shrugged mentally; such thoughts were a vanity. Why should Lord Kingsley think of her at all, much less make an effort to avoid her? She was the most minor of footnotes to his existence—a servant who had been useful, and who had refused to share his bed.

Christa's jaded view of life could not long survive the merriment of the season. It was her first real English Christmas, because the year before at Radcliffe Hall they had been in deep mourning. In contrast, the servants and tenants of the Orchard were delighted that the family was in residence for the first time in years, and the old customs were observed with a particular flourish. All of the cottages were decorated with greens, including pine and ivy, but the glossy holly with its bright berries was the prime favorite.

The most surprising bit of decoration for Christa was the mistletoe. It was a considerable shock the first time one of the male servants caught her beneath a sprig that hung in the kitchen. The custom was to take a berry each time a kiss was stolen, and when all the berries were gone, the kissing had to cease.

Christa observed that the berries seemed to grow back every night and could only assume that some merry male did not wish the kissing privileges to run out before the twelve days of Christmas were done. She seemed to be the most popular object of embrace, possibly because of her exotic origins, but none of the female servants were neglected. Monsieur Sabine, a Frenchman to the core, seized this English custom with delight, even stealing a kiss from the redoubtable housekeeper, Mrs. Morrison. He kissed all of the girls except Christa; she decided that it was because they were both French, and the mistletoe was legitimate only if one of the participants was English.

By the custom of the house, on Christmas Eve the servants and the family celebrated the holiday together in the great hall. The Yule log was brought in ceremoniously and lit by the brand that had remained from the previous year's log. The Yule log had been carefully chosen and seasoned to burn easily, as it was considered bad luck for the coming year if it did not burn the night through. This year's log was of apple wood, and the sweet scent of its burning suffused the hall. The three Kingsleys circulated the room, stopping for a word with each servant and child, exchanging news with those whom they hadn't seen lately. The sense of community that had bound a medieval manor from the highest to the lowest was very strong tonight.

Christa was happy to sit with a group singing traditional Christmas songs. She had always loved the joyful music of the season, and while English songs like "The Holly and the Ivy" and the "Sussex Carol" were new to her, she was able to pick up the tunes quickly and hum or wordlessly harmonize. At the urging of her fellow carolers, she sang two French songs. She translated the titles as "Bring a Torch, Jeanette, Isabella," and "O Come, O Come, Emmanuel," then sang the words in her own language.

As Alex heard Christa's sweet voice soaring in the old French melodies, he stopped his social round to listen, his heart constricting with memory and regret. He had avoided her since his engagement, afraid to be tempted, or to see questions in her wide gray eyes. He was committed to another woman and had no right to be yearning after one who had refused him. But tonight was Christmas Eve, when maid and master could mingle freely.

When the feasting and singing were done, two fiddlers and a bass viol player brought out their instruments and the dancing began. Christa was laughing and clapping her hands in time to the music when she realized that Alex had materialized beside her. She looked up at him, still laughing, then caught her breath at the expression in his amber eyes. His deep voice sent a warm shiver down her spine when he asked, "Will you dance?"

She gave him her hand and said gaily, "Lead on, my lord!"

The fiddlers struck up a rigadoon, a lively dance done in couples rather than sets. Christa had taught it to the Kingsleys, and Alex had mastered it well. Spinning and jumping, they both put aside the events of the autumn and returned to the simple pleasure of the summer.

Christa wore a swirling crimson dress that contrasted vividly with her dark hair and fair skin, and her vital charm and grace drew the admiring eyes of every man in the room. By the end of the dance, Alex was ruefully wishing that he could exercise the *droit du seigneur* and carry her off as his ancestors might have done several centuries earlier. It was impossible to imagine the impeccable Sybil Debenham enjoying herself with such abandon or looking so delectably disheveled.

When the music ended, Christa grinned up at her master. "Your dancing has improved out of all imagining, my lord."

Alex still held her hand from the last dance turn. Looking down, he said softly, "Your teaching is one of many things I will always remember you for."

Their gazes caught and held, and the closeness that had grown between them over the summer flared into life once more. Her hand unconsciously tightened on his and she was no longer aware of the roomful of merrymakers.

Jonathan's arrival shattered the moment. "It's my turn to dance with the teacher, big brother." He whirled her away as the next dance started. She cast one look over her shoulder and saw Alex watching her still. *How can he look like that when he is engaged to another woman?* But every woman knew that could desire even when their hearts were given elsewhere. Resolutely, she turned to Jonathan.

"And will you be a credit to my teaching, Master Jonathan?" she teased.

"Try me," he replied with a mischievous grin. She shook her head admiringly as he swept her into a country dance— the young devil was well on his way to being devastating. All three Kingsleys were so lovable—she would miss them dreadfully. But that loss was for the future. Tonight, Christa danced.

By tradition, after church on Christmas Day the Kingsleys held open house for all of their tenants and neighbors. Streams of people poured through, and the servants were kept bustling. Monsieur Sabine produced some French food, including a much-admired *bûche de Noël*, a huge rolled cake shaped like a Yule log and decorated with chocolate bark, meringue mushrooms, and spun-sugar moss. It was thought too pretty to eat; Alex himself had to cut it and start distributing pieces. Most of the food, however, was firmly and traditionally English, dishes such as roast goose, meat pies, and mince tarts, and a splendid wassail bowl. Monsieur Sabine handled the insult to French food with surprising equanimity—everyone agreed that Mrs. Ives, his assistant cook and companion, had had a mellowing effect on his choleric disposition. An announcement was expected from that quarter any day.

The convivial spirit of the holiday vanished three days after Christmas when Sybil Debenham and her mother arrived for a visit. It was not unexpected, but no one could have predicted the pall Sybil's presence would cast over the household. When Alex met her, she greeted him effusively.

"Darling! So wonderful to see you again! It seems so long." Looking around the hall, she added, "The house is darling, but surely . . . a little informal for the seat of a viscount?"

Alex blinked. "Perhaps. I never really thought about it. The Orchard has been home to Kingsleys for over four hundred years, and we tend to accept its deficiencies."

"Oh, I didn't mean it was deficient," she cooed, stripping off her cloak and gloves and studying her surroundings. "A little small, perhaps." Sybil was being quite circumspect; actually she thought the Orchard was horrendously poky and unfashionable, not at all the sort of thing one would expect of a wealthy nobleman. But she knew Lord Kingsley owned another estate near London, more convenient and away from the beastly sea winds. Surely something more suitable could be built there—perhaps something on the lines of Blenheim Palace. With a brave smile on her face, she went upstairs to face the rigors of her bedchamber.

Within twenty-four hours the whole household was on edge. It didn't help when the weather changed and cold, drenching rain confined people indoors. Jonathan, who had never met his future sister-in-law, reacted like a cat that had been thrown into a tub of water, walking around with hackles visibly raised. Only his fondness for his brother kept a civil tongue in his head. Three days after Sybil's advent, Jonathan remembered that a school friend had invited him for a stay in Essex and made his escape.

Thrown into constant contact with Sybil, Annabelle progressed from vaguely dreaming of a cottage to seriously evaluating locations and deciding what genteel, impoverished cousin would be the best choice for a chaperon. Since her brother had given her an independent income, there was no way she was going to share a roof with her sister-in-law.

Alex himself behaved with impeccable politeness, but was little in evidence as the tenants and the home farm seemed to require unusual amounts of attention. In the servants' hall, there were caustic comments about how the future viscountess was evaluating the silver and deciding what to change.

It was universally agreed that Christa had the worst time of it. Sybil's French maid, Merrier, had promptly come down with a streaming head cold, and her mistress refused to have her near for fear of infection. Since Claudia Debenham's haughty dresser flatly refused to work for a second lady, Christa inherited the job of turning Sybil out properly. After three days, she was ready for a change of career.

As she flopped by the hearth in the servants' hall after dinner, she received the commiserations of the rest of the staff.

Mrs. Morrison offered her a cup of tea and said, "Here, dear, you look like you could use a bit of reviving." As Christa received it gratefully, the housekeeper continued, "I don't see why you don't act like Mrs. Debenham's hoity-toity dresser and refuse to work for anyone but your own lady."

Christa wrinkled her nose. "Don't tempt me! I only do it because if she is not properly served, she will make Miss Annabelle's life miserable with complaints. Typical of the men to run off and leave their sister to cope with the Peacock."

The latter was the belowstairs nickname Miss Debenham had acquired. Christa sipped her tea and sighed. "In a way, there is something admirable about her refusal to let standards slide. She has not forgone a single jewel, hair ornament, or cosmetic the whole of her visit. If your King George stopped in for a visit, only she would be properly attired to greet him."

"You may think it admirable, but I think it's absurd!" Mrs. Morrison snorted. "We're plain people here in Suffolk. We don't need the likes of an overdressed wench like her."

Christa smiled sadly. "But you have no choice."

The observation cast a pall over the group until Monsieur Sabine, who had taken to sitting with the others of an evening, said, "There is always a choice! If the guillotine was good enough for Queen Marie Antoinette, it is good enough for the nouveau riche!"

His comment produced startled looks, then a quick change of conversation. The other servants were never quite sure whether he was joking or serious. At least no one had been threatened with his cleaver lately.

A week after Sybil's arrival, Alex was called away to a family property in Norfolk. The agent had quit while the estate was in the middle of a serious boundary dispute, and Lord Kingsley's personal attention was solicited. He made his apologies to his sister and the Debenhams and felt guilty at the way his spirits rose as he headed north with his groom and valet. The weather was cold, wet, and blustering, the ground sodden and travel conditions poor, and he knew that within an hour his side would be giving him fits from too much riding. Nonetheless, it felt wonderful to be away from the house. He almost succumbed to a touch of nostalgia for winter patrol duty in the Channel before common sense overtook him.

The day after Alex left, Annabelle came down with a touch of influenza and Christa was relieved of her work with Sybil to concentrate on nursing her mistress. Miss Debenham released her from service less from consideration of Annabelle's needs than from her own fears of infection.

The doctor assured them that Annabelle's life was in no way threatened, but for three days she tossed and turned feverishly, aching and restless. Christa sent to Ipswich for a bag of expensive lemons, and served the resulting lemonade both hot and cold, depending on how Annabelle felt. She also gave her willow-bark tea to reduce the aching.

By the evening of the third day, Annabelle's fever had broken, and she was fit for conversation, though still very weak. "Poor Christa!" she said with a faint smile. "You have had to go from decorating the Peacock to taking care of me."

Christa chuckled. "Where did you hear that nickname?"

"Oh, I have my sources," her mistress said mysteriously, before succumbing to a faint giggle. She looked very pale against her pillow. "Jonathan told me that's what the servants call Miss Debenham. I think he heard it from a groom." Her smile disappeared, and she said wistfully, "Do you think Alex will really be happy with her?"

Christa shook her head. "I really couldn't say. She seems very . . . self-absorbed, but there is no harm in her. Perhaps he finds her amusing. And of course, she is very beautiful."

"Then why is Alex running off to sea again? I'd swear he had no thought of it until he became engaged." Annabelle plucked at her coverlet nervously. "I wish there was something I could do to make him see what she is like."

"You would be better served in discouraging her. Alex is unlikely to end the betrothal." Christa shook her head. "It's absurd that a man will be condemned for such an action while a woman can do it without incurring censure, but that is how society is. I expect it is because women are considered such weak-minded creatures."

"If I could think of a way to drive her away, I would," Annabelle confided. "Do you think she is in love with Alex?"

Christa found the conversation uncomfortable. "As much as she loves anyone, I imagine. She is certainly in love with the idea of being Lady Kingsley. Would you like more willow tea?"

Annabelle accepted the change of subject with docility. "No, the aching is gone, though if I tried to cross the room without your help, I think I would fall over. I thank my stars for your patience. You've done nursing before, haven't you?"

Christa leaned back in her Windsor chair, pulling her knees up under her. "Of course. Almost all women are nurses sooner or later. Besides helping my grandmother tend the peasants, I helped care for my grandparents and my father before they died, and my mother when she was very ill."

Annabelle sighed again. "You make me feel very young and useless. You do so many things well. —I don't know how I would get along without you."

Christa thought for a minute. "Perhaps this is not the best time to tell you, but I will be leaving you soon, to take a job in a shop. It is time I did something new."

In the flickering light of the lone candle, Annabelle's face was sad. "Everything changes."

"Yes," Christa admitted as she stood up, "but not all changes are for the worse. Many are improvements, once we get over the shock. Will you need anything else tonight?"

Annabelle shook her head. "No, you go and get a good night's sleep. You can't have had much rest this last week. It would be a pity if you became ill also."

Christa chuckled as she turned to her small room. "Don't worry, miss. I am as tough as an old boot. Be sure to call if you need anything."

In spite of her words to Annabelle, it was a pleasure to tumble into bed for a solid night's sleep. Christa was so tired that for once she was undisturbed by dreams of laughing amber eyes and a warm, hard body.

It took Alex three days to settle his affairs in Norfolk. He was guiltily aware that he should return home quickly to share the burden of hosting with Annabelle, but a stop at Stornaway would not delay him more than a few hours, and he wanted to see the place. It was the most unusual Kingsley property, several hours travel up the Suffolk coast from the Orchard.

At midafternoon he and his two attendants halted their horses on a sea cliff. The rain had stopped, but a cold north wind threatened a change of weather for the worse. The three men dismounted. The cliff was one of the highest points around, and waves smashed fifty feet below them. Alex pointed out their destination to his valet, Fiske, who had never come here before. "There is Stornaway."

"I thought Stornaway was a town on one of the Hebridean islands," Fiske said in puzzlement as he stared at the rocky point of land with a low stone building clinging to its shoulder.

"The original Stornaway is. This is named for it, because it's equally barren and windy," Alex replied.

"Is it an island, my lord?" Fiske asked.

"More or less. It used to be part of the mainland, but the coast has crumbled away around it," Alex answered. "It stands on harder rock that won't erode. A causeway connects it to the mainland, but it's covered with water for half of the tide cycle. During bad winter storms, the house is isolated for several days at a time because the causeway is impassable and the waters around the island are rocky and dangerous for small boats. Stornaway is large enough for a

good-size farm, and in medieval times there was a small
keep for defense against the Northmen."

He gestured and went on, "The house you see now was
built about two hundred years ago. It used to be lived in all
year round, but the storms and isolation make it uncomfortable in winter. Now a shepherd and his family spend the
summer there with a flock. The house is in good repair, the
grass is excellent, and it's a pleasant place in warm weather."

Fiske was fascinated. The young man had a secret
romantic streak and had read Mrs. Radcliffe's *Mysteries of
Udolpho* when it came out the previous year. The island
in front of him, stark against the lowering gray sky,
looked like a perfect setting for one of the more horrid
gothic romances.

The dour groom, Willson, said unexpectedly, "One of
the horses is going lame, yer lordship."

Alex went to confer with him, and Fiske wandered
along the cliff to get a better view of Stornaway. Glancing
up, Alex noticed where the valet was walking and called
out, "Don't get too close to the brink. With all the rain, it
may be dangerous." A stranger to Suffolk and its particular
hazards, Fiske stayed where he was for another few moments.

It was a moment too long. The soaked earth of the cliff
crumbled away under the valet's weight, and with a shout
of terror, Fiske tumbled into the surf fifty feet below amid
a shower of earth and stones.

While Willson stared in horror, Alex stripped off his
coat and boots and raced to the edge of the cliff. Fiske's
head was bobbing around in the roiling waters, but the
young man seemed dazed or unconscious, possibly stunned
by the fall.

A quick glance told Alex that the water was deep, and
with a little luck in avoiding submerged rocks, he should

be able to dive safely. A couple of hundred yards to the right was a small shingle beach with a path leading down to it. If he could pull Fiske over there, they could find shelter before they froze in the icy wind.

Willson yelled, "No, my lord!" but Alex ignored him. He was a strong swimmer and had dived off cliffs during his duty tours in the Caribbean. Carefully choosing a spot as close to the valet as possible, he plunged headfirst into the water. Fiske's clothes would pull him under rapidly, and he doubted the young man could swim even if he weren't stunned.

It seemed a very long way down. The icy shock of the water blasted the breath from his body, vicious currents tearing at him as he surfaced and looked around for Fiske. The boy had vanished, so he dived under at the spot where he had last seen the valet. It took three endless, lung-bursting dives before he grasped a piece of fabric and dragged the limp body to the surface. Fiske had a red line across his forehead with droplets of blood forming, but he coughed and spat water and began breathing again.

Alex struck out for the thin crescent of beach to the right. The turbulence threatened to pull both of them under the surface, and it took all his strength to move forward and keep Fiske's head above water. In a quick glance to the shore, he saw Willson racing down the path to water level. The distance to the beach seemed much longer than it had from above, and he could feel his strength ebbing rapidly in the near-freezing water. It became harder and harder to avoid the jagged rocks as he stroked his way toward the beach.

A bare fifty feet from safety, a giant wave grabbed and twisted, smashing Alex's left side into a submerged rock. It was the same place where he had received his worst wounds the year before, and there was a shattering explosion of pain that almost caused him to lose his grip on Fiske. He was immobilized in the water for precarious moments before he could continue paddling toward the shore. Every stroke was agony, but the waves were now helping, pushing them toward the shingle.

Willson was waiting on the beach, and he plunged waist-deep into the water, grabbing Fiske and pulling the young man ashore. The groom had grown up on the coast and knew the tricks of lifesaving. Rolling the valet onto his stomach, Willson pressed on his back, forcing the water out. After a few moments he was rewarded by a vigorous fit of coughing. Reassured that the valet was in no danger of drowning, Willson turned to see how his master was faring.

Alex had used his last particle of strength to pull himself ashore and slumped into unconsciousness when he was barely above the waterline. Willson knelt at his side and gently turned him face up, hoping that the viscount was just exhausted by his efforts. With a shock of fear, the groom found Lord Kingsley's left side drenched with blood.

Chapter 16

Annabelle had progressed to solid food, and Christa induced her to eat toast, porridge, and tea for breakfast. As she gathered the tray, the maid remarked, "It is a good day to be snug inside, Miss Annabelle. Snow flurries are beginning, and the head gardener said at breakfast we are going to get one of your famous North Sea storms."

Annabelle glanced at the window. "You don't think Alex will try to travel in this, do you?"

"I'm sure he's still safe in Norfolk. He thought it might take up to a week to straighten out his business."

"I hope so," Annabelle said with a frown. "He might have tried to hurry back to help me with our guests."

"Your brother has sailed in this weather and worse," Christa laughed. "I'm sure he can take care of himself."

Annabelle leaned back and smiled. "I'm acting like a nanny, aren't I? I scarcely worried about Alex at all for those years in the navy when I didn't know what he was doing. Today I just feel concerned for some reason."

Christa had also been feeling a nagging, undefined anxiety. "I expect it is because of the coming storm. The air feels different and makes people nervy."

Annabelle accepted her explanation and soon drifted into a doze while Christa sat by the bed and worked her

way through a pile of mending. The morning was well
advanced when a sharp knock on the door brought her to
her feet. In a flash of intuition Christa knew that she was
about to discover the source of her worries.

Opening the door, she saw Bob Willson, the groom who
had accompanied Lord Kingsley on his trip north. He was
mud stained and weary, apparently just arrived home.
Speaking softly so as not to wake her mistress, Christa
asked urgently, "Is there a problem, Bob?"

He nodded, his face tight. "It's his lordship. A cliff
crumbled under Fiske, and Lord Kingsley dived in to
rescue him. He got smashed into a rock pulling the boy out,
and I think one of his old wounds broke open. He's hurt
bad, Christa. I thought I should tell Miss Annabelle, but
Morrison says she's been ill. Would it be better to keep it
from her?"

Christa pondered briefly. "No, she is on the mend, and
she has the right to know."

From behind her, Annabelle's voice called, "Is that Alex
come home?"

Christa stepped aside to let Willson in, and he swiftly
told his story, adding more detail. Annabelle sat up in bed,
her eyes round with shock. When the groom stopped, she
gasped, "Where are they now? Has a doctor seen them?"

"They're at Stornaway. I was able to bring down the
horses so both men could be carried over the causeway to
the house. It was a rare piece of fortune the tide was down.
It's a lonely stretch of coast, and nary another house for
miles. The master had the keys because he'd planned to
stop by if possible, and there was fuel and blankets and
some food in the house. Fiske just had a knock on the head,
and as soon as he warmed up, he started taking care of his
lordship."

Willson stopped to drag a tired hand across his forehead

before continuing. "I stopped at the nearest town and left word with the doctor's housekeeper, but the man was away and she had no idea when he might be able to go to the island."

At this point the group was enlarged by Sybil and her mother, who were passing in the hall and had been attracted by the sounds of worried voices. The story had to be repeated once more, and at the end, Willson said, "I'm going to go back now, but I thought you should know. I'd hoped Miss Annabelle might go with me, but . . ." His voice trailed off.

Sliding from the bed, Annabelle said, "I *am* going with you." She took a few shaky steps, then would have fallen if Christa hadn't caught her. She was weeping with frustration when Christa and Willson put her back to bed. Looking at Sybil, she cried, "Please, can you go to him? You love him, and he needs you."

Sybil was shocked and frightened by the news. From the groom's voice, she knew that her fiancé's condition must be very grave. She certainly didn't want anything to happen to Kingsley, at least not before they were safely wed. But to go on a journey in such weather? "Are you mad?" she said sharply. "There's a blizzard coming. We'd never make it. He has his man there, and the doctor will be with him now. What could *I* do?"

Everyone present looked at her. Sybil was wearing an elaborate sapphire blue and silver striped morning gown, her hair in a complicated arrangement of ringlets and twists. It was hard to imagine her being of use anywhere, much less in a sickroom.

Annabelle was shaking, her face distraught and tears running down her cheeks. Christa put an arm around her shoulders and said clearly, "I will go. I have had a great deal of nursing experience. Miss Debenham has not. There is no point in her risking her life to no purpose." She looked at the two Debenhams. "If you do not mind leaving the room? Miss Annabelle is not well."

Sybil was delighted to make her escape and satisfied with Christa's recognition that a lady of quality was unsuited to squalid nursing jobs. The French girl had a way with hair, too; as she followed her mother to the morning room, Sybil considered hiring the maid away from Miss Kingsley.

In Annabelle's bedchamber, Christa was organizing the expedition. She studied Willson carefully. For all his weariness, he was a burly man of oxlike strength. To be sure, she asked, "Bob, will you be able to make the return journey? You must have traveled most of the night. Would it be better if one of the other men went?"

He shook his head. "There aren't any that know that country as well as I do. With the storm that's brewing, knowing the lay of the land will be essential. Give me some hot food and an hour's rest and I'll be right as rain. But we must leave as soon as possible—if we get there after mid-evening, we'll miss the tide. If the storm is really hard, the causeway may be impassable for days. And the roads too."

Christa nodded. "Go eat and get the horses ready. I'll pack some food and medical supplies and be ready to leave within the hour."

Willson left the room and Christa turned to her mistress. "Try to keep calm, Miss Annabelle. We'll make sure he is all right. Don't worry yourself into a relapse or Lord Kingsley will have my head for leaving you."

Annabelle squeezed Christa's hand. "I know I can trust you to do what is possible." She added bitterly, "That stupid Sybil wouldn't cross the street to save anyone's life but her own."

Christa shrugged. "She is a lily of the field, not a toiler in the vineyard. I must get ready now."

In her own room, she had just started assembling her gear when she saw a vivid mental image of Alex, his face cold and gray as death. The vision was horribly real, and the wave of fear that swept over her caused her knees to buckle and her head to whirl. Christa folded onto the bed, her hands pressed into her face as the supernatural calm she had felt was drowned in terror. She struggled to control her desperate breathing. *Panic will not help him. Only action will.*

After several moments of desperate prayer, Christa was able to stand and return to what needed to be done. She forced herself to think of one task at a time, swiftly changing to her boy's clothes, then topping the outfit with the heavy fisherman's jersey Alex had given her for sailing.

The oily scent of the wool took her sharply back to last summer's happiness and threatened to destroy her fragile control, so she pinched her arm hard, the pain clearing her head. Then she packed a few basic clothes and a selection of herbal remedies and medicines such as laudanum and basilicum powder. After a moment's thought she also included her sewing kit and a small case of metal instruments.

Downstairs, Christa appropriated a heavy boy's riding coat that had lived in the servants' hall since Jonathan outgrew it years before, and a knit scarf and cap. After consulting Willson, she packed tea and other supplies the Stornaway house lacked. They were on the road shortly after noon.

Christa had made more than her share of desperate flights, but none worse than this one. The rigors of the journey at least had the slim virtue of keeping her fears for Alex at bay. The weather was cold and threatening when they left, and within two hours a full-scale blizzard was blowing, tiny snowflakes cutting into exposed flesh like shards of ice. She was chilled to the bone and could only marvel at Willson's ability to find the route in snow that was blowing so heavily the very hedgerows were obscured. Occasionally he would stop and dismount, proceeding afoot until he found some landmark.

In spite of such stops and one wrong turn that carried them some distance out of their way, they were making excellent time. The tough, shaggy horses Willson had chosen would win no beauty prizes, but they forced their way through the wind and drifts as easily as if they were in a meadow in May. The riders went single file, with Willson leading a third horse that carried supplies.

By four o'clock it was full dark. Christa called above the wind, "How are we doing?"

Willson looked worried. "We're making good time, but we'll have to slow down now that it's night. We've maybe three hours to go. I hope we catch the lowest point of the tide. I'm afraid that in this storm, the causeway won't be entirely above water even then."

"Can we go faster?"

He looked at her determined face, then nodded. "Aye, lass. If you're up to it."

There was no conversation after that. When the drifting was heavy, Christa would get off and lead her horse, hoping the exercise would ward off frostbite. She plodded along in the trail Willson was breaking, content to trust his sense of direction on this flat, windy plain. Warmth was no more than a distant memory, and her mind was as numbed as her body when Willson called a halt.

"There's the causeway." His voice was grim. They had descended to the shore, and in front of them she could discern a light-colored stone roadway thrusting out into the dark waters. At the limit of her vision, it disappeared into blackness. "The center is covered. I'm not sure how deep it is, but the water is rough now. There's a danger it might carry away the horses." He glanced doubtfully at Christa. It seemed the groom was willing to chance the causeway but considered it too hazardous for a mere slip of a girl.

"The tide is coming in, isn't it?" At his assent, Christa said fiercely, "It will only get worse. *What are we waiting for?*"

Willson spared her one admiring glance before putting his horse to the causeway. He knew there were places where the stone footing was crumbling, and he preferred to take that risk himself. His horses went calmly enough until they reached the swirling waters, then they balked. It took all his forty-odd years of experience with equines to force them forward. Christa's gelding tossed its head and flattened its ears but was persuaded to follow its fellows into the chopping waves.

The water came to the horses' fetlocks, then their knees, then up to their bellies. The waves crashed against them, splashing the riders and threatening to sweep their mounts off the stones. Christa prayed to every god she could think of, ancient and modern, for if they were swept from the causeway, neither horses nor riders would last more than moments in the seas raging around them. As the pounding water reached her horse's shoulders, it gave a terrified whinny and floundered, pawing for balance. She thought despairingly that it was all over. It was too late to turn back, and they were dead, and with them perhaps Alex's only hope.

Then with a scrambling splash that saturated any parts of her not already soaked, Christa's mount regained its footing. With a surge of relief that nearly paralyzed her with its intensity, she saw that the water was not as deep, that they had passed the lowest point and were heading up the other side. In another minute they were clear of the waves and had only to worry about the icy patches on the stones.

When they reached the island, Christa urged her horse up next to Willson's and gasped, "Monsieur Bob, if I never do that again, it will be too soon!"

He laughed, his voice as relieved as her own. "You're a game one, lass, that you are!"

Three minutes later they were snug in the small stable, away from a wind that reached gale force here on the exposed island. Leaving Willson to feed, groom, and blanket the horses, a shivering Christa grabbed her supplies and ran into the farmhouse. It was built of flint like so many Suffolk buildings, and its sturdy walls held firm against the howling wind.

The back door led her into the farmhouse kitchen. It was simply furnished, with flagstone floors and a plain wooden table and chairs. She shook violently with the chill of her saturated clothes and was desperately grateful for the warmth of the fire. She passed quickly through the kitchen, drawn by the flickering light of a candle in a room opening to her right. It was the bedchamber where they had taken Lord Kingsley, and another fire burned in the hearth. Fiske jumped from his chair at her entrance, his head bandaged and his face haggard from his ordeal in the water and long vigil. "Christa! Thank God you've come. Bob. . . ?"

She nodded. "He is taking care of the horses. Miss Annabelle was ill and couldn't travel. How is Lord Kingsley?"

He gestured at the bed. "He's been very feverish. The physician came and bound up his side and left a powder for the fever, but he couldn't stay long or he'd miss the tide. He said there was a lying-in he had to attend, and he could do more good there than here."

Christa walked slowly across the room, stripping off her

wet coat and scarf, then stared down at the unconscious figure sprawled across the double bed. Alex's breathing was harsh, his shoulders bare above the wide bandage that crossed his chest. His golden hair was dark with sweat and his fair skin flushed with fever. She was shocked by the number and variety of scars twisting along his left arm and upper body—his injuries the previous spring had been grave indeed.

She swallowed hard, then laid a hand on his forehead, keeping her voice clear and impersonal. "The fever is high. Has he been awake at all?"

"Yes, but . . ." The valet halted.

"Raving?" Christa supplied. At Fiske's nod, she asked, "Has he had any awareness of where he is, or what happened?"

Fiske shook his head unhappily. "I don't think so. He's been thrashing about most of the time. I hope it's a good sign now that he's sleeping."

Christa's voice was somber. "This is not a normal sleep." She glanced at the valet and said, "You look almost as bad as he does, Jamie. Could you make us some tea from the supplies I brought? Then get some rest. You must be exhausted."

He didn't deny it. Moving slowly, he entered the kitchen where a kettle simmered on the hob, and set the tea to steeping. Christa noticed a small room with a trundle bed off the bedchamber, so she appropriated it for her own use and changed to clothes that were blessedly dry and warm. When Willson came in, the three shared a meal of bread and cheese, with mugs of hot, sweet tea to warm the new arrivals.

After they finished, Christa suggested, "I'll sit with Lord Kingsley while you two get some rest. You both look ready to fall asleep on the table."

Willson said conscientiously, "You must be just as tired."

"I wouldn't mind being relieved in a few hours," she admitted. "But you traveled twice as far as I did, and Jamie had a blow on the head and a long watch alone." The two men accepted her offer and retired to a bedchamber in the other wing of the house while Christa returned to Alex's room.

She put more coal on the bedroom fire, then went to sit next to Alex, taking his hand in hers. She had sat like this when she was thirteen and her maternal grandmother was dying. They had been close, and Christa had prayed desperately for the old woman's survival. Her grandmother had been drifting in and out of consciousness, very near death. At three in the morning, she opened her eyes and said very clearly, "Let me go, child. Your prayers are holding me back."

Christa had cried, then prayed for her grandmother's best interests rather than for her continued existence. The old woman was over eighty years old and had lived a full life, and she had been suffering these last weeks. Half an hour later she was gone, a smile of peace on her face.

From that Christa had learned that death in its proper time was a healing, not a loss, and if Alex's time had truly come, she would try not to hold him back. But he was a young man in his prime, with a contagious enjoyment of life. It was hard to believe he had done all his living. She leaned over and kissed his lips very gently, feeling the fever heat. With tears in her eyes she whispered, "If you are not ready, I promise anything in my power to help you stay." She thought perhaps his fingers tightened faintly on hers, but it might have been imagination.

Looking at his handsome face, wracked by fever and pain, Christa knew that her vow included existence itself;

if she could have exchanged her life for his, she would have done so. Many people loved and depended on Lord Kingsley, while her passing would make a very small ripple indeed. True, she also enjoyed life, but when she left this body, she would be reunited with those she had lost. And who here would miss her more than briefly? She smiled faintly at her melodramatic imaginings. Just as well no devil appeared to offer a Faustian bargain.

Alex's breathing was ragged, but he was quiet. Periodically she sponged him with cool water to reduce his temperature. In the small hours, Bob Willson relieved her, and she staggered to her pallet, collapsing into a sleep of utter exhaustion. She didn't even stir when the groom laid a blanket over her.

The next morning dawned late and dark as the storm continued to rage. Alex was worse, tossing back and forth and sometimes rambling incoherently. Christa took charge of the kitchen. While cooking was not her forte, she managed some beef broth that Alex was induced to sip in small doses.

The day stretched endlessly, and it was obvious that Alex's condition was deteriorating, the fever rising in spite of their efforts to lower it with sponge baths and the doctor's powders. Late in the afternoon Christa managed to get her patient to take some willow-bark tea, hoping it would reduce some of the pain and fever.

She thought the crisis would come in the early hours of the morning, and she went to bed early so she could take the late shift. It was well past midnight when Fiske shook her awake. "Christa, come quickly, he's much worse!"

She pulled her wrapper over her shift and darted into the bedroom. Willson was holding their patient onto the bed and Alex was shouting. Some words seemed to be ship's commands, others were unintelligible. Once he gasped, "He's got no head, it's gone, he's gone . . ."

His eyes were open but unseeing, and with a powerful twist of his body he wrenched away from Willson and fell onto the floor. When they got him back onto the bed, he was quiet again, but the bandage was colored with fresh blood.

Christa unwrapped the bandage. A long thin scar that ran halfway around his body near the bottom of the ribs had a sharp-edged slit in the middle, and blood oozed slowly out. She studied the wound. From the nature of this and other scars, he must have been torn up by metal fragments. She knew that shards not removed at the time of injury could migrate in the body. Might a fragment have been shaken loose when he smashed into the rocks and it was now cutting its way out?

She glanced up unhappily. "I think there's a shell fragment in the wound and it's making him feverish. If it becomes inflamed . . ." She couldn't continue the sentence.

Willson's gaze was steady on her. "Do you think you could get it out?"

Christa shook her head doubtfully. "I don't know. The wound does not seem deep, and I have some metal instruments here that could be used, but this is *surgery*. I have never done anything more complicated than remove splinters and sew up gashes. What if I make it worse?"

The groom said quietly, "Do what you can, lass. He's in a bad way. Better to do something than watch him get worse and worse until…the end."

With a sigh, she went for her instrument case. Besides scissors and tweezers, there was a thin metal pick that could be used as a probe. She also had a sharp, narrow knife that could be used as a probe. Much as she hated subjecting Alex to amateur surgery, he needed to have that vicious piece of metal removed and she was the best person to do it.

A French surgeon she'd known as a girl had told her that he always purified his instruments in fire in the hope of reducing the chances of inflammation, so she did the same. Then she set to work.

Besides scissors and tweezers, she had a sharp, narrow knife that could be used as a probe. Much as she hated subjecting Alex to amateur surgery, he needed to have that vicious piece of metal removed and she was the best person to do it.

A French surgeon she'd known as a girl had told her that he always purified his instruments in fire in the hope of reducing the chances of inflammation, so she did the same. Then she set to work.

The next few minutes of leaning over Alex and exploring the bloody gash were some of the most testing of her life, and she was barely capable of doing what was necessary. If Bob and Jamie hadn't held Alex down, she could never have managed. Christa was about to give up when the probe contacted a hard object below the ribs where only soft tissue should have been. She used the probe and the point of the knife to stretch the edges of the wound, then reached in with the tweezers. If Alex were at all conscious, the pain must have been beastly, but she thought his convulsive thrashing was from fever and delirium rather than her crude operation.

The fragment was embedded in flesh and slippery with blood, and it took an endless, anxious time to remove because it was almost impossible to grip. She came near giving up, fearful that her efforts would injure more than help. Then suddenly, using a combination of knife and tweezers, the fragment popped loose. It was deceptively

small for the damage it was causing, a bloody inch-long
fragment that seemed to be brass.

Gasping for breath as if she'd been running, Christa
slumped against the bed for a long moment until she was
somewhat recovered, then dusted the wound with basilicum
powder and closed it with several neat stitches. She hoped
fervently that this would be her only experience of surgery
on a human.

Willson put a sympathetic hand on her shoulder while a
white-faced Fiske left the room for a few moments. Alex
was calmer now, but his face was pale with shock and each
rasping breath was an effort. Willson looked at his master
helplessly, his normally impassive face a study in anguish.
"I should go for the doctor again. The lying-in must be
over. Maybe he can do something more."

Christa glanced at him from where she knelt as she tied
a fresh bandage around Alex's chest. "The tide is high now.
You'll never make it over the causeway."

Willson said slowly, "There's a rowboat in the stable."

Christa rocked back on her heels. "But the currents! You
may be swamped if you try to cross."

"One person couldn't make it. But two might."

She opened her mouth to explain that the crisis coming
was unlikely to be affected by a doctor, but she stopped
herself. Willson doubtless knew that as well as she did, but
she saw that he had a desperate need for action, to feel he
was doing something to help. She said slowly, "Are you
sure of that, and that Jamie is well enough to go? You know
his lordship would be the last man to want you to throw
your lives away."

Fiske returned, his color better and his expression eager.
He had always been proud to serve Lord Kingsley, and his
genuine affection had become near idolatry after the rescue.
How many masters would risk their lives for a servant,

particularly one who had been employed for only a few months? "I'm recovered now. Will you be able to manage alone, Christa?"

She glanced at Alex. He was lying still now. *Still as death.* "Yes, he's sleeping well. I should be able to manage. But in the name of heaven, don't let anything happen to you!"

Within ten minutes they were gone. Christa looked out the window after them, but they disappeared almost immediately. The snow had stopped falling and a bitter wind was blowing the existing flakes in near-horizontal lines. Dropping the unbleached linen curtain, she added more coal to the fire, then went to sit by Alex again. She still wore her shift and wrapper, and it hardly seemed worthwhile to change. The room was warm, and she had a superstitious need to keep Alex under her sight, as if he couldn't slip away as long as she was watching.

An hour or so after the men left, Alex started getting more restless again. His movements were less violent than earlier, but his voice clearer. He talked of battles—"*The shot is red hot . . . 'ware the fire!*"—and of watching a friend die—"*I'll tell her, Will, I promise . . . I promise.*"

Christa caught his hand, hoping that her presence might calm him, but he pulled away, gasping, "*The guns! Spike the guns!*" in a hoarse voice. His thrashing was getting worse and she was frightened. If he fell out of the bed again, she would be unable to get him back, and the cold, drafty stone floor would not help his condition. She pitched her voice as clearly as possible and said, "Alex, it's all right! You're safe now. The fighting is over. We won. Everything is all right."

He stopped moving, but his eyes were staring at something seen only by him. "*No . . . no—stop it!*" He rolled away from Christa, pulling one arm over his head as if shielding himself from a blow. "*In the name of God, stop! She's only a baby. She's only a baby.*"

Alex seemed to be collapsing in on himself, pulling away from something that he couldn't bear. He kept repeating, "*She's only a baby. . . .*" His face was gray and his breathing shallow, and he looked so much like the vision Christa had seen at the Orchard that she was terrified.

"Alex, don't give up, please!" Christa's voice was urgent, and tears filled her eyes. The hand she held was getting colder, and the gale rattling the windows sounded like the wings of the angel of death, fighting to break into the room.

She slipped into the bed and wrapped her arms around him, trying to warm him with her body. "Please, Alex, don't go! I love you, and I can't bear to lose another person I love. *Please!*" Her tears were falling on his chest, and she held him desperately, as if she could hold back a departing spirit.

Alex's breathing changed, becoming more ragged. "Christa . . . ?" His voice was distant and uncomprehending, but it was the first time he had shown any kind of response. His head turned toward her, his eyes questioning. "Christa, *amour . . .*?"

She lifted herself and laid her face against his. "I'm here, my love. Everything is all right. It's over, she's safe, everything will be all right now."

His arms slipped around her and then he was holding her hard against him, so tightly she could hardly draw breath. "Christa . . ." He was still not fully in this world and he clung as if she were a lifeline that kept him from being swept away. She crooned French endearments in his ear, telling him that the terrors were behind him, that he was safe, that she loved him and everything would be all right.

She could feel the warmth slowly returning to his body,

and his breathing was harsh but stronger. His face turned toward hers, seeking, and she kissed him with all the longing of fear and months of hidden love. She could feel the growth of desire as he began to respond, his hands relaxing their death grip and beginning to caress, his lips and tongue warm and urgent on hers.

With sharp clarity Christa knew that she could break away if she tried, but the desire to make love was a powerful manifestation of life, and passion might banish the death shadows that threatened to take Alex away from her. She had sworn to do anything that might aid him, and her virtue was a small price to pay toward his healing. Besides, giving herself to the man she loved was no great sacrifice even under these circumstances.

Alex rolled over on his right side, pulling Christa down against him. The passion that had always been between them flared into searing life and she forgot fear and doubt to exist solely in the moment, for Alex's kisses, for the touch of the strong hands that slid under her shift and robe. His lips traversed her bare body, sometimes teasing, sometimes demanding, and she moaned, her pleasure as unselfconscious and primal as his own.

Such an intensity of passion moved quickly, and when he entered her there was a moment of pain so sharp that Christa cried out and tried to pull away. But then there was no more pain, and she knew for the first time the physical closeness that was the expression of the love she felt for him. Even with Alex half out of his head, there was a triumph in holding him, and she understood the songs poets had proclaimed from time immemorial.

When it was over, he rolled back to his side and held her still, stroking her back and whispering her name. His color and breathing were almost normal now, and as he slid

into a healthy sleep, she knew in her bones that the danger
was past.

The fears and events of the last hour had exhausted her,
and Christa felt almost too tired to rise from the bed. With
dry humor she considered the irony that her first experience
of loving was such a solitary affair. When Alex woke, he
might not remember any of what had happened, and she
could imagine no good reason to tell him. He was pledged
to another woman, and Christa had no honorable place in
his future.

But for these few moments Christa could relax and
savor his closeness, pretend that they were lovers in truth.
She must not let herself get too comfortable, she thought
drowsily. In just a minute she would get up, in just another
minute . . .

It seemed that he had been wandering in darkness for
a painful eternity, groping through swirling mists that
would occasionally thin to put him in the middle of some
wretched memory such as his first major battle, when
Alex's closest friend among the midshipmen was torn to
pieces by a cannonball. He fought his way upward through
an endless kaleidoscope of fear, disease, and loss, dimly
aware that light and sanity must be somewhere beyond the
mists. The veils were thinning when he stumbled into
the worst memory of all.

He was a boy of ten, home from school for the summer;
his mother was paying a brief visit to the country and in a
vile mood. Annabelle was a toddler and she had wandered
into her mother's chamber when Lady Serena was dressing. The child was playing with a bottle of expensive per-
fume and dropped it when her mother shouted at her, the
crystal vial shattering and the heavy scents of musk and

neroli permeating the room. Furious, Lady Serena snatched up her riding crop and started to beat Annabelle, slashing down with her full adult strength.

Hearing his sister's screams of terror, Alex rushed into his mother's chamber and tried to stop the beating. Annabelle, bleeding and weeping hysterically, ran headlong from the room. Deprived of her original victim, Lady Serena turned her fury on her son, whipping him savagely around the head and shoulders.

He was too proud to run and could not bring himself to strike his mother back. Instead he fell to his knees on the floor, trying to protect his head, trying to withdraw from the unbearable knowledge that his mother was more than a little mad. Her maid finally intervened to stop the attack, and Alex had staggered from the room, holding his tears until he was alone in the marshes by the shore. He had buried the memory for years, the pain and the sense of desolation, the knowledge that his mother was as cruel and violent and uncaring as she was beautiful.

The memory had carried a despair as vivid as the event itself, and he was drowning once more in desolation. As Alex tried to withdraw from the anguish of the past, he began a nightmare-slow fall down a bottomless well, into an endless night that promised cessation of pain.

And then Christa was there, her warm voice and touch pulling him back from the dark. The mists still obscured his sight, but Alex clung to her, to warmth and the memory of sanity and laughter. He dreamed of her with such intensity and passionate detail that the dream surpassed reality. Floating up from the depths of sleep, he could even imagine the rosemary tang of her hair.

There was a delicious languor in his body, and Alex slowly realized that the stabbing pain in his side that had nagged him for the last months was gone, replaced by a

dull ache that was trivial by comparison. As awareness
returned, he found himself lying on his side in a warm
bed, with some kind of bandage constricting his chest. The
rosemary fragrance was stronger, and the realization slowly
dawned that he was not sleeping alone. Dark rosemary-
scented curls were within tickling range of his nose, and he
had no doubt to whom they belonged.

Christa lay curled up against him, her back fitting
against his stomach, her breathing soft and steady. Alex
discovered with some amusement that his arm was around
her and his left hand cupped one full breast. It was a su-
perlatively comfortable way to sleep, and for a few minutes
he simply lay still and enjoyed it, loath to explore the ram-
ifications of the situation because that would require returning to a reality that would not be an improvement.

After an interval of mindless contentment, Alex sighed
and lifted himself slightly on his right elbow. Christa rolled
onto her back, her long lashes dark against her face. There
were shadows under her eyes, and he wondered how she
had come to be here. Where *was* here? And how long had
he been out of his head?

Christa gave a sleepy cat smile and her lashes fluttered.
Then her eyes snapped open, fully awake, her gaze a little
wary. Alex reached out and slipped his fingers into her
silky curls, brushing the dark hair back from her face. "It
wasn't a dream then," he said quietly.

She relaxed and shook her head. "No. I'm sorry, my
lord, I had not meant to fall asleep. We are at Stornaway.
Jamie Fiske and Bob Willson went for the physician and
have not yet returned." Time enough to worry about their
safety later; at the moment, pallid sunshine from the window
indicated a clear day dawning.

He smiled wryly. "Under the circumstances, surely
'Alex' would be more appropriate." She smiled in assent,

then he continued, his face and eyes grave, "I'm sorry, Christa. The last thing on earth I would have chosen would be to hurt you."

"You did nothing that I did not consent to, Alex. And there is nothing I have that I would not freely give you."

He drew a deep breath, his emotions too deep and tangled to express. Christa's generosity was as warm and honest as the rest of her, and she had given him a gift that could never be repaid. "And you would have quietly returned to your place if I hadn't woken first, and left me to think last night was just a dream?"

"It would have been better that way, Alex." Christa hesitated, and her eyes slid away from his. "But since it is too late for discretion, there is something I would ask of you."

"Anything in my power, *ma chérie*."

With some difficulty she said, "Would you . . . could you make love to me? Properly awake this time. I would like to have that to remember." She added hastily, "Unless you are too weak. You were delirious for nearly two days."

Alex laughed and pulled her close, feeling her delicious curves against his body. "I may be convalescent, but I'm not dead. Which is what I would have to be not to respond to you."

He released her and pulled the blanket down a little, exposing her upper body to his view. "You are so beautiful," he said huskily. "I have never known your equal. You humble me."

At first Christa felt shy under his gaze, but she relaxed as she looked into his amber eyes. The warmth of his admiration was obvious as he sketched the contours of her face, his fingers delicate on her cheekbones, lightly brushing her lips before he traced the lines of her neck down to her breast.

He whispered, "*With my body I thee worship*."

With Alex's words the last barrier dissolved, and Christa herself reached out, testing the texture of the blond curls above the bandage, touching the lines of old scars, feeling the warmth of firm muscles shifting beneath the fair skin. When she was nursing him, her concern had been for his welfare. Now she was free to respond to him as a man, not a patient, and to glory in the beauty and strength of his powerful body.

As she had requested, Alex began to kiss her properly, as deeply and thoroughly as if they had all the time in the world. Christa sighed blissfully and gave herself up to the sensations, trying to store enough memories to last a lifetime. His gentle lovemaking was the antithesis of last night's turbulent passion and introduced her to a whole new spectrum of feeling and response.

This time when she cried out, it was not from pain.

Alex held Christa close in the drowsy aftermath of loving, his hand stroking the sweet curves of her back from the silky hair at her nape to her rounded hip. Her eyes were closed, and he could feel the soft touch of her breath against his shoulder. With wonder he realized that he had never experienced such intimacy and peace in his life, and his joy caused the blinders to drop from his eyes.

The truth was so simple: he was in love with Christa, with her warmth and wisdom and laughter, and he wanted to be with her always. There was no law of God or man that said they couldn't marry, and only the blindness of class difference had obscured that basic fact. Had Christa been anything but a servant, Alex would have recognized that he loved her long since. And surely it had been love on her part that had literally pulled him back from the brink of death.

There would be a scandal, of course, but it would pass in time. Noblemen had always been allowed considerable latitude. And if the talk didn't die down, he wouldn't care unless Christa did. Sybil Debenham would be angry, possibly hurt, but he doubted that her feelings ran very deep. Alex would have to resign his commission in the navy, but that was no great loss since he had only taken it to escape the muddle he had made of his affairs on land.

It was all so clear, so right. He felt himself drifting into sleep again, and with the last sparks of consciousness he said softly, "Marry me, Christa. Please."

She stiffened in his arms and raised her head, the clear gray eyes meeting his in shock. "Marry you?"

Her soft voice was startled, and something more, something Alex couldn't analyze in the moments before sleep claimed him. To make sure there was no misunderstanding, he whispered again, "I want to marry you, if you'll have me." The effort of maintaining awareness became too great and his eyes closed.

Christa was rigid with shock as she slipped from the warm bed. She studied Alex's peaceful sleeping face, reaching out to touch his cheek and the strong line of his jaw. Tears gathered in her eyes as she brushed the thick waves of gold hair from his eyes, knowing that never again would she be this close to him. It was so like Alex to take responsibility for having "ruined her," even if it meant destroying his own future. She had no doubt that his offer was sincere, and equally little doubt that it was made from duty rather than love.

Resolutely she turned away and went to her small room to dress before returning to build up the fire. As usual, her mother had had an aphorism that suited the present circumstances: *It is unfair to hold a man to promises made just before, during, or after making love.*

Yet it would be so fatally easy to take Alex at his word, to accept his offer of marriage. As she went about feeding the horses and boiling water for tea, she struggled to discipline her unruly thoughts. It was very noble of the viscount to offer his good name, but she really had no desire to see him martyr himself. There would be a devil of a scandal if he threw over Sybil Debenham, and it would likely ruin his naval career. A viscount jilting a lady to marry a servant?

Alex would never live it down. His brother and sister would suffer for it too; the scandal might destroy Annabelle's chance for a respectable marriage, and the disgrace would follow Jonathan into the army.

At this point her logic always faltered. She could still be considered a countess, in spite of the actions of the French Assembly, and if Alex loved her, perhaps they could have brazened it out. But countess or not, Christa would be tainted by her time belowstairs, and she was still penniless and without family. Society would more easily forgive a man who married a demimondaine than one who married a servant.

And Alex had said nothing of love. Guilt and duty were a poor foundation for marriage, and he would soon resent Christa for what she had cost him. On the whole, she would rather be dead than the object of his anger or hatred.

The pale northern sky was clear, and the wind had dropped to near zero. The sea was calm and the ebbing tide should render the causeway passable within two hours or so. Bob and Jamie would be back soon; she refused to consider the alternative. The chores and a leisurely breakfast kept her tolerably composed until finally, blessedly, the men returned with the doctor.

Alex was still sleeping soundly. The doctor took a poke or two at his side but saw no reason to wake him when he was so obviously recovering. The nursing staff withdrew to the kitchen, where Christa announced her intention of returning to the Orchard to allay Annabelle's fears. Willson would escort her back and return with a carriage that could bring his lordship home when he had recovered sufficiently to travel.

They left quickly, before the tide could start to cover the causeway again. The weather was bitter cold but clear, and the scouring winds had blown enough snow from the roads so that travel was possible.

The long ride home gave Christa ample opportunity to firm her resolve. She must leave the Kingsley household before Alex returned. Her clarity of mind would not survive another offer of marriage for she was sure that Alex's sense of duty was much stronger than her good sense. But if she accepted him, she was sure they would both end up regretting it.

Christa sighed, her breath making a white cloud in front of her as the horse between her legs lifted its head at the nearness of its stable. Logic was the very devil, she decided; without it, she might have married Alex in the hope that he would grow to love her. But she remembered the haut monde too well to believe in such a miracle happening. The contempt of his own class, the loss of his career, and the suffering of his sister and brother would weigh too heavily. She would cherish her memories of him and move on with her life.

At the Orchard, Annabelle was overwhelmed with relief at the news of Alex's recovery and was barely restrained from returning in the carriage with Willson. Sybil was also pleased. If her viscount was going to kill himself rescuing servants, better he did it after she was safely Lady Kingsley.

Christa found a letter waiting from her cousin Suzanne de Savery, announcing that she and her Henry had decided not to wait till summer to marry. The letter gave her an idea, and in the evening, she told Annabelle that there was a family emergency—she was vague about what kind—and she must depart immediately.

Annabelle was shocked and unhappy. "I knew that you would be leaving, but I had not thought it would be so soon."

"I'm sorry, Miss Annabelle. One of my cousins needs me and I must go as soon as possible." Christa's voice was firm, because family was an inarguable reason for a change of plans.

Annabelle sighed. "Everyone is throwing problems at you. I hope your cousin's situation improves soon. Though I know you will not come back to me."

"No, Miss Annabelle. I am sorry."

Annabelle had been lying on a sofa in her room. She stood now and went to her dressing table and fumbled in her drawer. Turning, she offered Christa a handful of gold coins.

Christa gasped. "Twenty pounds! I can't accept this."

Annabelle was brisk. "Of course, you can. You have served me and my family far beyond the limits of duty. I'm only sorry that I have no more money here." She stepped forward then to give her maid a good-bye hug. With a catch in her voice she said, "I'll miss you."

Christa felt a lump in her own throat. "I shall miss you, too. All of you." With a slightly crooked smile she said, "I will write down the recipe for the pale rouge before I go." She thought a moment, then said, "The chambermaid, Maggie, in London. I think she would make you a good abigail."

"I'll write and ask if she would like the position. If so, perhaps she can come down by coach. It will give us time to become accustomed to each other before the Season begins."

Annabelle was proud of how matter-of-fact she sounded. She was fighting down a sense of betrayal that Christa was leaving, even though she knew it was selfish. Christa had her own life to live and picking up the pieces after various Kingsley dilemmas must have been tedious.

Christa gave one last elfin smile. "You will do very well, Annabelle." Then she slipped away.

Christa went to the library to write down the directions for making the cosmetic. It gave her a good excuse to be busy with pen and paper, and she knew she must leave a note for Alex. It took a long time to write, and she carefully burned the false starts. She had no desire that anyone in the household guess what had happened.

She sealed the note, scratching the initial C in the wax, then left it in Alex's desk, where he would find it quickly after his return. A small pale object on the desk caught her eye. When Christa discovered that it was the sea-polished pebble she had given him the first night he had kissed her, she nearly wept. Love was a watery emotion, she decided with disgust.

Alex awoke with a delightful sense of well-being. It was late afternoon, and he could see Fiske moving around in the kitchen. The valet brought in food when he saw his master stirring. "How are you feeling, my lord?"

"Wonderful. Where is Christa?"

If the valet was surprised at the question, he didn't show it. "She and Willson went back to the estate. Miss Annabelle had been poorly, and Christa didn't want to leave her alone too long, and everyone there has been worrying about you."

Alex sighed regretfully. It would be days now until he saw her again. But there was no help for it, so he tucked into his soup, pleased to see that he had been promoted to broth with barley, onions, and beef in it.

The doctor had recommended Lord Kingsley not be moved for at least a week, and in deference to his judgment, Alex waited four whole days before heading home. He was still infuriatingly weak, and there was pain in his side, but he could walk on his own if he was judicious about it. He was amazed when he remembered the passionate interlude with Christa; it was obvious that making love was not bound by normal physical restrictions.

As soon as Alex reached the Orchard, he went to his sister's room. Annabelle had not expected him so soon, and she hurled herself into his arms with an enthusiasm that almost landed them both on the floor. He sat down rather quickly. After the initial babble of greeting had subsided, he asked, "Where's Christa?"

Annabelle looked surprised. "You didn't know? She has left us. There was a family emergency of some sort. She took the coach back to London the day after her return from Stornaway."

"What!" Alex exploded.

His sister was startled by his vehemence. "It was sudden, but she had planned on leaving in the spring anyhow." At Alex's black expression, she said defensively, "Why are you so upset? I could hardly keep her here against her will."

Alex would have stood up and paced if he hadn't felt so shaky. "I am upset, as you so kindly understate it, because I want to marry her. Where did she go?"

His question was ignored as Annabelle reeled under the bomb he had just detonated. Her eyes were wide in horrified shock when she gasped, "*Marry* her? You would marry a *servant*?" She was staring at him as if he had just grown a second head or declared that he wished to assassinate the king.

In the face of his sister's reaction, Alex did get up and pace, levering himself up on the chair back. "Yes, dammit, I want to marry her!"

He was irrationally furious, and it was a struggle not to take it out on his sister as she regarded him with wide-eyed disbelief. He caught hold of his temper and said as calmly as he could manage, "She is intelligent, beautiful, kind, and more of a lady than half the doxies in the ton. And I'm in love with her."

"But a servant . . ." Annabelle shook her head in bafflement.

"Damnation, Belle, you at least should understand, even if no one else does! You know her quality. Look at how much she has done for you! How much of your style and confidence do you owe to her? You'd be married to that loose-fish Loaming if it hadn't been for her!"

Her eyes filling with tears, Annabelle cried, "Alex, please! I am *trying* to understand. It took you months to fall in love with her. Can you not give me a few minutes to accept it?"

Alex dropped back into the chair and buried his face in his hands. After a long silence he said, "I'm sorry, Belle. I shouldn't have ripped up at you." He raised his head with the trace of a smile. "I think I fell in love within five minutes of meeting Christa, but it has taken me the longer part of the year to realize it." His voice was almost inaudible as he added, "Now that I have realized, I can't imagine life without her."

Annabelle absorbed what her brother said, the tone as much as the words. He was right. Christa had qualities rare in any class, and she had been a wise and generous friend to all the Kingsleys. If Alex truly loved her, his sister would give him whatever support she could. But there would be complications, unpleasant ones. Starting with the worst, she asked, "What about Miss Debenham?"

"I will break the engagement, thereby earning a reputation as a jilt and faithless despoiler of innocence. Then, if Christa will marry me, I will gain additional fame as a lunatic and a traitor to my class." He rubbed his temples wearily. "It's unforgivably selfish of me to force you and Jon to pay the price for my scandalous behavior. The only compensations are that you will both much prefer Christa to Sybil Debenham as a sister-in-law. The scandal will die down eventually."

"Do you think Christa might not accept?" Annabelle said in surprise. Would a servant really refuse a lord who was rich, handsome, and in love with her?

"You'll notice that she is nowhere in sight," her brother said dryly. "The day after I proposed, she ran away. I suspect I don't suit her notions of propriety. Your abigail has pride that would put a Spanish hidalgo to shame."

Alex pushed himself up from his chair. "I'm leaving for London in the morning. The sooner I go after her, the better the chance of locating her. If I can find her, I think I can persuade her to accept me."

Annabelle wondered if he were strong enough to go haring across the countryside in the dead of winter, but wisely kept silent. She doubted that any comment of hers would make a difference.

Alex sent his excuses to the Debenhams, claiming to be too fatigued to join them for dinner. Since he wasn't up to the royal scene Sybil would undoubtedly subject him to, he would break the engagement when they were all back in London. He did take a quick look at his correspondence to see if there was anything too vital to ignore. There he found the note, a bold C scratched in the wax, and perhaps a hint of rosemary about it.

My lord Alex:

Your offer to me was the product of a generous impulse, and I shall always honor you for it. But you need not sacrifice your good name and your career out of a misguided belief that you have injured me. Au contraire, I shall remember you with kindness all my life, as I hope you shall remember me.

Christa

Alex leaned back in the chair and closed his eyes wretchedly. There was nothing the least lover-like in the message, and she would never marry him if she felt no more than kindness. But there had seemed to be an abundance of loving when they were together. Perhaps he could persuade Christa that he cared enough for both of them.

Ignoring Fiske's voluble expressions of disapproval, he left for London at dawn the next day.

Chapter 17

It was a damply chill night in Berkshire, with a whisker of moon giving occasional illumination to the road. A traveler unfamiliar with the terrain would have had difficulty following the road to Radcliffe Hall, but the rider cantering up to the wide marble stairs had no such problem. Tethering his horse to a convenient stone lion, he skipped up the steps and wielded the heavy brass knocker.

Company was unexpected on such a night, and the bewigged footman answering the door was distinctly unwelcoming as the tall visitor brushed by into the warmth of the hall. With angry hauteur the servant said, "The Earl of Radcliffe is not receiving callers."

The visitor glanced at him with laughter in his eyes. "No? You haven't been here very long, have you?"

The footman said stiffly, "I have been in the earl's employ over a year." His eyes raking the worn riding dress of the visitor, he added with all the arrogance of a peer's servant, "I doubt his lordship will have any time for the likes of you."

The man seemed vastly amused. "See that my horse is taken care of. I'll find Lewis myself. I expect at this hour he's in his study." Pulling off cloak and hat, he tossed them at the footman, whose automatic grab left him off balance.

The fuming footman was left holding the damp garments and glaring after the man's retreating blond head and broad shoulders. He considered forcibly stopping the insolent devil, but the man did seem to know his way around the house, and he had an air that made one think twice before accosting him. Since he had already disappeared into the study, the footman decided to call a groom for the horse. His lordship would no doubt let it be known if he wanted the intruder removed.

Lewis Radleigh was working in his study, grateful for the minutiae of estate business that kept thought at bay. Eventually he would stop. Perhaps a brandy would help him sleep. At the sound of footsteps, he looked up with a frown. The servants should know better than to disturb him.

The sight of the tall figure approaching caused such a shock that for a moment the earl thought he was dreaming. His quill falling unheeded, he rose to his feet and circled the desk, unable to believe his eyes. There had been so many ghosts. . . .

In a disbelieving voice he gasped, "Charles?"

"In the flesh," was the cheerful reply. "Sorry not to give you more warning." As Lewis wavered and seemed likely to fall, Charles stepped forward quickly and grabbed the older man's arm. "Lewis, are you all right? I would have sent a message from London, but it seemed quicker to come myself."

Lewis put a faltering hand out. If this was a ghost, it was a remarkably solid one. He looked into the unforgettable gray eyes that now showed affection and concern. With a spontaneous motion foreign to his reserved nature, he put his arm around his nephew in a gesture more eloquent than words.

Some time passed before Lewis had regained enough self-possession to speak. Releasing his nephew, he rang the bell for a servant and sat down in one of the wing chairs. "It's been two years, Charles. We all thought you dead. In the name of heaven, where have you been?"

His voice was strained, and he examined the younger man closely. Charles looked as if considerably more than two years had passed. A livid scar on his temple curved up into his hair, and he was thinner than before, with a wolf-like toughness that was new. Gone was the light-hearted young mischief-maker. His nephew now looked equal to anything.

The footman Lewis had rung for entered quickly, as if he had been waiting outside the door. "Yes, my lord? Shall I remove this . . . *person* for you?"

While Charles laughed, Lewis said coldly, "You are speaking of Charles Radleigh, the master of the house. The seventh Earl of Radcliffe has returned." As the footman gawped, Lewis glanced at his nephew and asked, "I assume you would like something to eat, Charles?"

"Perceptive as always. I think I'll help myself to some brandy while we wait. Would you care for some? You look like you could use it." Without waiting for a reply, Charles poured brandy into two goblets and handed one to his uncle before sitting in the opposite chair.

The footman beat a horrified retreat. This would set the cat among the pigeons downstairs, and no mistake! As for himself, he thought glumly, he might be in need of a new position.

Charles stretched, crossing his long legs with an air of contentment. "Lord, it's good to be home! If I never see cabbage soup again, it will be too soon."

Lewis warmed the glass between his hands and stared at his nephew, still disbelieving in his existence. "What happened? The French announced they had killed you, that you were a British spy. They even sent back your watch and identification papers, along with an empty wallet."

Charles took a sip of the brandy and started to explain. "My sister will have told you about the attack as we were attempting to escape?"

At Lewis's nod, he said, "My mother and her servants, Anne and Jean-Claude Bohnet, were attacked by bandits. Mme. Bohnet was wounded in the shoulder and screamed. Having more hair than wit, I went charging to the rescue and took a bullet along the side of my head."

He fingered the scar on his temple thoughtfully. "A little more to the right and you would still be the earl. Do you mind, Lewis? Losing all this?" He watched his uncle keenly as he waved one hand at the richness around them.

The older man shook his head and said with wry self-knowledge, "You should know better than that. You're a public man, like your father. I'm not. I never wanted all this. Power isn't good for me. I find myself tempted to abuse it." Lewis sipped his brandy before adding softly, "You must know I'd give the whole of Radcliffe and half of England as well to have you here alive."

As if embarrassed by his show of feeling, he went on impatiently, "Will you tell me what happened without any more roundaboutation?"

"It's simple enough. One of the bandits robbed my bleeding and apparently dead body, taking my watch and all my identification. In the midst of that looting, a platoon of French Guards came on the scene. They were after the bandits, and quite a battle ensued. I don't remember any of this, of course." He sipped his brandy, then went on. "Jean-Claude and I were taken captive, while Mother managed to get herself and the wounded Anne Bohnet away."

Lewis slid forward in his chair, his voice blisteringly intense. "*Do you mean that Marie-Claire is alive too?*"

Charles was surprised by the vehemence. "Why, yes, we all are, except for some of the bandits, including the one that robbed me. When the Guards killed him, they assumed he was the Earl of Radcliffe and announced to the world that they had bagged another filthy British spy. Rather droll, actually."

They were interrupted by the arrival of the food, brought by the butler himself, a family retainer who had watched Charles grow up. Some time was lost in emotional greetings and brief explanations, and Charles was unable to resume his tale until the butler left. He first made himself a substantial sandwich, biting down with unabashed pleasure. "I've always said that the ham from the home farm was the best anywhere."

Seeing that his uncle was uninterested in culinary asides, he swallowed his mouthful and continued, "To return to the story, Jean-Claude told the Guards that we were good French citizens, cruelly beset by bandits. Being a suspicious lot, the Guards threw us into the local prison. I was out of my head for quite some time. Really rather remarkable that I didn't die in that filthy hole. Credit for my survival goes to Jean Claude. Luckily since everyone around me spoke French, I did too, and it never occurred to anyone that I was a vile Englishman. One of the advantages of being bilingual."

Charles stopped for another few mouthfuls of sandwich and a draft of the ale that had been delivered. "The next part of my story is rather boring. While we were not thought to be British spies, it was assumed that we must be guilty of *something*, and they decided to hold on to us until they figured out what.

"Meanwhile, my mother had escaped with Anne, and they went to ground with some Norman peasants whom she'd known for years. Mother got in touch with the royalist network and started working with them. Not that she is royalist herself, but she rather liked smuggling people out of the country." He grinned. "An amazing woman, my mother."

"I have never doubted it," Lewis said tensely. "And then?"

"She had no idea what had happened to the rest of the party, that Christa had escaped, and that Jean Claude and I were in prison. It took months to find us, and even longer to arrange an escape." He added with studied casualness, "If she had left it another two days, they would have guillotined me for nameless crimes against the revolution."

Lewis repressed a shudder at the thought; the guillotine had been invented as a quick, humane method of execution, but the idea of a loved one being beheaded was beyond horrible.

"The escape from prison was last summer. However, there was some work that needed to be done, and Mother and I did not feel free to return until now. The Bohnets stayed in France and are working with the royalists. A brave pair."

He swallowed the last of his sandwich and said, "We reached Dover yesterday, then posted up to London. Mother had written to you two years ago, and I sent a message myself shortly after last summer's escape, but from the uproar when we arrived at Radcliffe House, the messages went astray. My mother was tired, so I left her in London and rode up here because I was anxious to see you and my sister. Speaking of whom, where is Christa? Staying with friends? I assume that you would have called her down otherwise."

Lewis flinched. In the excitement of Charles's return from the dead, he had almost forgotten the problem that had gnawed at his vitals for nearly a year. He took a deep breath, then plunged in. "She's not here. I don't know where she is."

"*What*?" Charles's brows drew together alarmingly.

"She ran away last March. I have searched everywhere, but without success."

"But why on earth would Christa run away? This was her home." His suddenly cool gray eyes regarded his uncle challengingly. "What happened?"

Lewis met his gaze with difficulty. "It's my fault. I . . . asked her to marry me."

"*You what*!" Charles's incredulity was so profound as to constitute an insult.

Lewis flushed and said stiffly, "The idea is not all that ridiculous."

Charles tried to look at his uncle objectively. He and Lewis had an unusual relationship, with the older man somewhere between father, big brother, and friend. Lewis was forty-four years old now, twenty years older than Christa, but hardly at his final prayers. He had always been reserved, with few friends, but he had the fitness of a man who had lived a physically active life, and he had the family looks. When he had offered for Christa, he was the Earl of Radcliffe—a prime catch on the Marriage Mart.

Speaking more mildly, Charles said, "I meant no insult, but the age difference is substantial, and since Christa always thought of you as her uncle, it is hardly surprising she refused you. But why did she run away?"

Speaking with painful slowness, Lewis said again, "The fault was mine. When she came out of mourning last March, I explained that she had no fortune, then made the offer to her." The last words came with great difficulty. "The way I made it . . . was a kind of coercion."

He looked pleadingly at his nephew. "You know that I would never have harmed her, Charles. You *must* believe

that! I would have dowered her had she wished to marry.
Since she had no other preference, I thought she might be
comfortable as the Countess of Radcliffe. Her lack of fortune would not matter and I could have best protected her
that way." His last words were almost inaudible. "And in
time, I hoped she might come to care for me."

Charles repressed the strong desire to pick up something
and smash it. He could see his uncle's painful vulnerability,
could understand how a middle-aged man would fall in
love with Christa's bright charm. But . . . !

He stood and paced wolfishly across the room while he
swore with vivid bilingual fluency, then turned to glare at
his uncle, anger blazing from him. "So you lied about her
fortune and bullied her to marry you." His voice grated as
he continued, "You know how dangerous the world is for
a girl alone! If she has been missing for a year, she could
be anywhere! A prisoner in a brothel, or dead in some
London stew."

There was a long, long pause before Charles ground out
with painful emphasis, "If anything has happened to her,
may God forgive you, because I never shall."

Lewis looked at him bleakly. "You can't possibly blame
me any more than I blame myself."

Dead silence reigned, until he added, "I thought she
might refuse me, but I never dreamed that a gently bred girl
would pack up and disappear so quickly."

With unconscious arrogance Charles snapped, "You
should have known that no sister of mine would stand still
for that kind of Turkish treatment. What have you done to
find her?"

Lewis sighed. "The usual things. Interrogated the servants, spoken to all her émigré friends in London, visited
all the registry offices I could find. Her maid said she intended to seek a position as a governess."

It belatedly occurred to Lewis that he had missed an important point in his nephew's earlier speech. "Why did you accuse me of lying about her fortune? Your will made no provisions for her, and all the d'Estelle property is in France. As I said, I would have provided for her as your sister, but in her own right she hadn't a penny to bless herself with."

Charles's eyebrows rose. "That's coming it a bit too strong, Lewis. You must have known that my stepfather would not fail to provide for his family. Christa is not the heiress she will be if the French king is ever restored, but with the money Philippe transferred over here, she still has ten thousand a year, which is a substantial fortune in anyone's eyes."

"But . . . I checked all the accounts!" Lewis said with bewilderment. "There were no monies from France."

"The account is with the London office of Philippe's bankers—*Mont d'Or et Fils*." In the face of Lewis's surprise, Charles continued, "My stepfather charged me as trustee for my mother and sister. There was no reason to change bankers, and much of the money was put into the funds. To avoid confusion, it never went through a Radleigh bank account."

With tight-lipped exasperation Lewis asked, "Why the devil did you never tell me? Did you consider me unworthy of your trust?"

"You know that's not true! You handled my affairs for all the years of my minority, and I have never had reason to doubt you. There is no man in the world that I would sooner trust with my fortune." Charles stopped, then added bitterly, "Though obviously it was a mistake to trust you with my sister."

Lewis's face flamed but he made no attempt to refute the statement.

Charles drew a steadying breath, then went on in a more moderate tone, "Now that I think of it, Philippe made the transfer shortly after you went to Jamaica. You were gone for almost a year, and by the time you returned, the whole business was old news. I must have thought I'd written to you about it."

His jaws tight, the earl faced the consequences of his oversight. "If she had been in possession of her fortune, she might have set up her own household, but she never would have just run away with no more than her pin money in her pocket."

Lewis sighed. "The results would have been different, but it doesn't lessen my responsibility."

Charles stood, the weariness of strain and travel showing in his face. "I'm going to bed now. I'll be getting an early start back to London."

His uncle stood also. "I'm going with you." At Charles's raised eyebrow he said grimly, "I was the one that drove Marie-Christine away. Now I must face her mother."

It was late afternoon when Lewis and Charles arrived at Radcliffe House. Charles went along to greet his mother and briefly tell her what had happened to Christa. Lewis was conscious of the veiled curiosity of the servants, who watched to see how he was reacting to his change of station. He shrugged mentally; his conscience was clear on the point, and there were very few people's opinions that he valued.

One of those few was his sister-in-law. When a solemn Charles came down and indicated that his mother was ready to receive him, Lewis felt his throat close up. He was tempted to run, but he had never run from duty in his life, and he would not begin now.

Sunlight shafted in at the far end of the room, but the countess was seated in shadow, her face obscured. It didn't matter. He would have known her anywhere. "Marie-Claire . . ."

She stood and walked to him, her hands outstretched. He caught them in his and looked down at her, absorbing every detail of change since he had last seen her five years before. She was a small woman, a little too thin at the moment, her face showing the effects of these last years of strain. The rich, dark hair had wide streaks of silver now, and she wore it pulled back in a loose coil on her neck. She was beautiful in the fashion of a Renaissance Madonna.

She smiled and it was like the sun coming out. "It's good to see you, Louis." She was the only one who ever used the French form of his name, and her accent made music of it.

They held hands a moment longer, then she released him and seated herself. "Pray make yourself comfortable, Louis." When he had chosen a chair, she said, her voice grave, "Charles told me what happened, though I had already learned of it from the servants." She smiled faintly. "They probably told me more than even you would know."

The smile vanished and her voice was sorrowful as she continued, "How did it come to happen, Louis? You had not used to be so . . . insensitive."

"There is no acceptable excuse, Marie-Claire. I frightened her. And"—it was a painful admission—"I wanted to, a little. I wanted to shock her enough to see me differently, enough to see the advantages of marrying me. I behaved abominably."

She smiled ruefully. "The fault is not solely yours. My Christa has always been impulsive, and independent to a fault." Her eyes closed a moment, picturing the bright face of the daughter she had not seen in two years. When she opened her eyes, the countess continued in a more robust tone.

"I think you and Charles take too pessimistic a view. I very much doubt that my daughter is dead or in dire straits now. You men underestimate the ingenuity of a woman." She chuckled fondly. "You underestimate Christa in particular. I believe that she could be left in a den of lions, and the next morning they would be letting her use them for pillows."

She was silent for a moment. "But if she truly decided to lose herself, we may never find her. She could be anywhere. Perhaps even America. Christa always said she wanted to see what a country looked like when the revolution was over." She sighed. "If that happened, we may never see her again."

Her brother-in-law's face was stricken. "It never occurred to me that she might have left the country. I think she had enough money to buy a passage."

Marie-Claire studied his guilt-ridden countenance. A deeply intuitive woman, she could imagine what he had gone through this last year. Louis was a responsible man and he would see himself as having betrayed a trust. It would have been a shattering blow to his sense of self, and she could see the pain etched in his face.

She said briskly, "I have by no means despaired of finding my daughter. I think it very likely that some of our émigré friends here in London know of her whereabouts but would not speak to you."

Correctly interpreting his expression, she added with amusement, "Even in the face of the no doubt generous bribes you would have offered. My little one has a gift for inspiring loyalty." The countess studied him a moment longer, then said gently, "As she has a gift for inspiring love. I do not blame you for loving her, old friend. What man would not?"

Lewis sprang from his chair, nearly undone by the chaos of his emotions. He circled the room, tension in every step, then halted under a portrait of Marie-Claire and her first husband with Charles as a toddler. It was a beautiful painting of a beautiful family and had been completed a bare two months before his brother died.

Looking at the portrait, he said in a despairing voice, "It's time there was truth between us, Marie-Claire. I did not really love Christa as a man loves a woman. Or if I did, only a little. What I loved most was that she was your daughter."

Lewis turned to face her, a blaze of emotion transforming the face that had always been so impassive. "She is a lovely girl, but only a shadow of you. It has always been you, the whole of my life. There will never be anyone else."

Marie-Claire had the gift of stillness. Her very silence seemed to wrench the admission from him. "I love you, and you have reason to hate me. But I had to tell you, even if it costs me your friendship. When I thought you were dead . . ." His voice choked off and he fought for control. I mourned you and Charles with all my heart. But almost worse was knowing that I had never declared myself to you, that I would go to my grave as a man who was too frightened to admit to love. I thought perhaps you knew that I loved you but were too kind to reveal your knowledge."

She spoke then. "You were only thirteen when I married your brother. I knew that you were . . . enamored of me, but I thought that in time you outgrew it."

"I might have, had I loved you in the fashion of a boy. But I loved you as a man does. The way I love you still." His voice was colorless as he continued, "I was eighteen when you married your cousin. I would have hated him if I could, but Philippe was too fine a man to hate, and he had loved you all his life. I, of all people, could understand that."

He linked his hands together and said with a kind of defiance, "I am yours to command—whether you bid me leave your sight forever or put a period to my existence for injuring your daughter. I will be your brother-in-law, or your friend if you wish it." Lewis stopped for a long moment before ending in a quiet, unsteady voice, "Or your husband if you would have me."

There was stark pain in his voice when he continued after a long pause, "I am a thousand kinds of fool, for only a fool would make an offer in the shadow of the injury I have done you. I suppose it is in keeping with the joke I have made of myself in your eyes. You have had two husbands, and both have been extraordinary men. Men with a capacity for love and laughter that exceeds anything in my power."

Lewis stopped, his ragged breathing the only sound in the room. His voice was barely audible as he finished, "I know that you can never love me, and it was selfish of me to burden you with my emotions. I will never speak of this again."

Marie-Claire made an impatient motion with her hand. "You dishonor your own worth, Louis. I have never thought you incapable of love. I have seen you with Charles, and his own father could not have cared for him more." She searched his face, seeing the vulnerable core of the man that had been hidden for so many years. She had always been deeply fond of him. When she continued, it was with compassion.

"I am grieved beyond words that your whole life has been misshapen by your love for me. Perhaps I knew that you had not outgrown your calf-love, but I didn't want to believe it. I would rather have seen you love a woman who could return it as you deserve."

He regarded her steadily. "I would have loved another if I could. But it was impossible."

"It's not too late for you," she said earnestly. "You are a handsome man, still young enough to begin a new life and family. Do not waste yourself on me any longer!"

Lewis moved a step closer. She thought he was handsome? Following a thread of feeling too faint to be called hope, he asked, "Is it so unthinkable that you could ever love me?"

She rose then and crossed to the windows, turning to face him with the late afternoon sun falling across her. The harsh light illuminated the fine lines in her face, the silver in her hair. "Look at me, Louis! I am five years older than you, and I have done a life's worth of living. I have buried two husbands and a baby and I am physically and emotionally too tired to begin again. If you move beyond your . . . obsession with me, you can marry a woman young enough to give you children and have the life you should have begun twenty years ago."

He moved so close they were almost touching and looked into the wondrously clear gray eyes Marie-Claire had bequeathed her children. "Charles has been my son, I need no more. I know that you are no longer a girl, and it doesn't matter. To me, you will always be beautiful."

Lewis's gaze held hers with mesmerizing intensity. "You speak of what you believe would be best for me, but you have not answered my question. Is it unthinkable that you could love me?"

Marie-Claire looked back steadily. "I have always cared for you, not just as my husband's brother, but for yourself. Even when you were a boy, I knew I could rely on you absolutely, and I have always valued your integrity and honor. But I will say it again—I am too worn! You deserve better."

Lewis held her gaze for an endless moment, then knew with a flash of insight that the time for words was past. Placing his hands on Marie-Claire's shoulders, he bent his lips to hers. He deliberately held back, fearing that a lifetime of suppressed love might sear them both.

Her lips were hesitant at first, then she slowly raised her hands to his waist and the tentativeness of the kiss was swept away as his passion communicated itself to her. Lewis pulled her close, scarcely believing that after a lifetime of dreams Marie-Claire was in his arms, responding with a sweetness beyond his imaginings.

The sun had slipped below the horizon and the room was nearly dark when they returned to normal time. The countess tilted her head back, and there was mischief in her voice when she said, "Do you know, Louis, I believe that I am not as old as I thought."

He laughed then, with a freedom and joy entirely new to him. "Then you will consider me as a candidate for your next husband?"

There was sadness in her reply. "My husbands have not fared well. You might be better advised to keep your distance."

Lewis put a hand on her shoulder, his blue eyes searching in the dusk. "Marie-Claire, I would give the rest of my appointed span in return for a single day at your side."

Her voice was wondering. "You really mean that, don't you?" With a half-smile she said, "I trust it will not come to that. I think it would be well that we learn to know each other again. If you feel the same way this summer, you may ask me again."

Lewis Radleigh had no doubts at all how he would feel

in the summer. He pulled Marie-Claire close against him
and laid his cheek against the top of her head, grateful for
the darkness of the room that concealed his joyful tears.

Locating Christa turned out to be anticlimactically
simple after the drama of the last two days. Drawing up a
list of their émigré acquaintances, Charles called on half
while Marie-Claire and Lewis visited the rest. One of the
best possibilities, Suzanne de Savary, proved difficult to
locate because she had moved, but a neighbor gave Charles
the direction of her shop.

It was after closing hours when he arrived there, and
Suzanne herself was the only person left. Her eyes widened
at the sight of him when she opened the door, and with a
squeal of delight she threw her arms around him.

"Charles Radleigh! This is beyond anything great!" She
stepped back and asked hopefully, "And my cousin Marie-
Claire?"

He smiled broadly as he entered the shop and closed the
door behind him. "Very well indeed. She is in London now
and looking forward to seeing you." The earl glanced
around him at the spacious showroom and rich sweeps of
fabric. "It appears you are doing very well for yourself."

"Yes, much of it due to your sister. The minx made me
the most coveted *modiste* in London by passing the word
of my skill—in the strictest confidence! Of course, everyone beat a path to my door, and now I am all the rage. Even
when the fashion moves to someone else, I think I will
keep many of the customers."

"You know where my sister is?" Charles asked eagerly.

"But of course," she said with a lift of her brows. "She
is working here. Shall I make you some coffee?"

Being half French, Charles never refused such an offer.

While Suzanne brewed the beverage, she brought him up to date on Christa's and her own activities. He had gone through the extremes of shock and amusement and they had drunk half the pot by the time she was up to the present.

"So three days ago, she appeared on my doorstep, ready to leave the life of an abigail behind her." Suzanne frowned. "She is not very happy. I think something happened, but she won't talk about it. Did I mention that she was employed by Miss Annabelle Kingsley, Viscount Kingsley's sister?"

Charles nodded. He had met the viscount some years before. He had been a dried old stick of a man; perhaps the sister was also and had made Christa's life miserable. He still marveled at the thought of his sister meekly doing anyone's bidding.

Suzanne went on, "Christa started here yesterday. She insists on working in the sewing room. A great pity— she would be marvelous with the customers." She frowned and added, "I think she does not wish to be found by some-one for she instructed me to deny her existence if anyone inquired."

"I am glad that you did not include me in her prohibi-tion." Charles chuckled.

"Faugh!" Suzanne scoffed at the very idea, then smiled ruefully at her cousin. "I am going to lose my partner, no?"

"I think it very likely," Charles agreed. "Where is she now—at your house?"

"No, she is staying with one of the seamstresses. I have just married again, and she judged it unsuitable to . . . how do the English say . . . play gooseberry?" As Charles burst out laughing, she continued placidly, "Though with six children between my Henry and me, one more gooseberry would hardly be noticed."

After tendering his felicitations on her marriage, Charles asked, "Where is she staying?"

With a shake of her head, Suzanne said, "I fear I do not have the direction, only that it is somewhere near St. Paul's. But if you come here at eight o'clock in the morning, you may carry her back to a life of luxury."

Charles touched her hand. "Is that what you would like for yourself? You are part of my family. You have only to ask . . ."

His cousin waved dismissively. "If one of my daughters grows up thirsting for the beau monde, you or Christa may bring her out. But as for me, I have never been happier in my life than I am now. Give Marie-Claire my love and ask her when she can call on me. As a working woman, it is harder for me to get away."

Charles rose. "I'll take you home in my carriage, then tell my mother and uncle the good news. We can all sleep easy tonight."

The weather warmed on the way to London, turning the roads to a relentless mass of mud that released hooves and wheels with great reluctance. The trip from the Orchard dragged into three full days, and it took all of Alex's stoicism not to let Fiske see how difficult he found the journey. He had the glum suspicion that the valet would be clucking over him like a mother hen for the rest of his days, and all because he'd pulled the boy out of the water once.

The lengthy trip permitted ample time for planning, and he had decided to begin his search for Christa at her cousin Suzanne's. Alex had taken his sister to the shop once and knew the direction, and it seemed likely that Mme. de Savary would know her young cousin's whereabouts. Christa might even be working for the *modiste*—she had once mentioned that as a possibility.

When they reached London, he retired immediately.

Alex was still weak, and he knew he would need all his strength for the search. He had Fiske wake him at the crack of dawn next morning, having decided to get to the shop very early and wait until the owner arrived. Or even, he dared hope, Christa herself.

Fiske's lips pursed disapprovingly when he left St. James's Square. The valet had no idea what was behind this mad dash to the metropolis and had pointed out at regular intervals that Lord Kingsley should still be in bed, but his fool master refused to listen!

It was about seven-thirty when Alex arrived at Suzanne's, and the air had the acrid tang of too many coal fires as the streets began to stir. He found a convenient alley directly across from the shop and leaned against the wall as he absently ate a handful of hot chestnuts purchased from a peddler. They kept his hands warm against the sharp chill of the January morning, and the viscount mused on how food always tasted better outdoors as he watched the passing parade of working people. It was an entirely different London from that of the ton.

Alex was vaguely aware of a fashionable carriage that pulled up in front of the shop; presumably some eager customer with an early morning fashion crisis. Most of his concentration was on the passersby. Christa was not very tall and might be hidden by some larger person. He was also uneasily aware that he had no idea of how she would react to seeing him. Would she be glad? Angry? Or perhaps worst of all, indifferent? He reminded himself forcibly that she might not be coming to her cousin's at all, but it was impossible to suppress the hope.

Then suddenly Christa was walking down the street toward him, her elfin face grave above her blue cloak. Alex took a half step out of the alley and studied her hungrily. If she looked unhappy, perhaps she was missing him? He was about to cross the street to intercept her when suddenly Christa stopped, her face lit by an expression of transcendent joy.

With a rush of delight Alex thought she had seen him and that she was as happy as he. Then he realized that her gaze was not on him but on a tall blond man who had stepped out of the waiting carriage, his back to Alex.

When Alex had first met Christa, she had called him "Charles" as a desperate question. This time also she cried out "Charles!" but now there was no doubting. She was racing toward the blond man, who sprang forward to catch her up in his arms.

Alex's vision narrowed and he felt as if he were falling away from the world. His head whirled and for a moment he blacked out. When his senses returned, he found that the alley wall was supporting him. The bricks were cold and gritty against his burning forehead, and his breathing sounded harshly in his ears. With dizzy precision he decided that Fiske was right—it was too soon to go out alone.

Most of his attention was focused on the ragged pounding of his heart as he strained for breath, but at a great distance he could hear two voices excitedly chattering in French. Something about believing that Charles had been dead, and mutual assurances of good health. Alex concentrated on nearer things, on the effort it took to remain upright, on the paralyzed numbness of his solar plexus. His knees wanted to buckle, and he was still flattened against the brick building when the carriage door slammed shut. Despairingly he heard the jingling harness as the vehicle carried Christa out of his life.

The mysterious Charles, back from the dead. Savagely, Alex wondered how darling Charles would react when he discovered just how generous his sweetheart had been to her employer, but the anger vanished as quickly as it had flared up. Christa had never said she loved him. She had merely been there when he needed her, asking nothing in return. If her Charles was any kind of man at all, he wouldn't blame Christa for what had happened when she had believed him dead.

Alex tried to be glad that her lover was restored to her, but his grief was too raw for him to be generous. Perhaps he could wish her happy later, but not now. Not so soon.

He levered himself away from the wall with his hands, trying to decide if he were steady enough to walk. From near his right elbow a shrill voice asked, "'Ey, mister, you gonna finish them chestnuts?" Alex looked down, blinking to clear his vision, and saw the chestnuts he had dropped when he first saw Christa. An urchin looked up at him suspiciously.

"Help yourself." Alex's voice was unsteady. While the boy scooped up the remaining chestnuts, Alex searched in his pockets for a coin that he handed over when the boy straightened. "Will you get a hackney for me?"

The boy's eyes widened at the size of the coin. "Yessir, right away." He skipped off, probably assuming Alex was drunk.

After the hackney coach deposited Alex back at Kingsley House, he collapsed so completely that his worried valet called in the best doctor in London and summoned Miss Kingsley from Suffolk.

On the carriage ride to Radcliffe House, Christa kept one hand clutched around Charles's arm as if afraid that he would disappear into the ether. While she had an intellectual belief in miracles, this one seemed too good to be true.

They exchanged news at a high rate of speed, both talking at once and finishing each other's thoughts as they had since they were children. The conversation slowed some as they neared the end of their journey, and Charles said hesitantly, "There is something you should know before we get home."

"Oh?" She lifted her brow questioningly.

"I have told you why Lewis behaved as he did. I hope you can bring yourself to forgive him."

Christa gave a Gallic shrug. "It was foolish of me to run off as I did. It made a great deal of sense at the time, but I should have known your uncle would not turn into a monster overnight. The last year has been . . . educational."

With a stab of pure pain, she thought of Alex. It was one of God's less humorous jokes that now that she had regained both station and fortune, he was lost to her. If he had loved her, she would have fought Sybil Debenham for him. But without his love, she had no more place in his future now than when she was a maid.

"I would not have missed it," she added after a silence that was a little too long. She looked at her brother questioningly. "I expect Uncle Lewis and I may be a little uncomfortable with each other at first, but we shall get over that. Do you anticipate a problem?"

"Well," Charles said hesitatingly, "not exactly a problem. It's just that . . . well, you know how men are always falling in love with Mother."

As Christa stared at him blankly, he elaborated. "Apparently Lewis fell in love with her when he was thirteen and hasn't looked at another woman since. At least, not seriously," he qualified. "Now that he has caught her between husbands, he has pleaded his case. She's always been very fond of him, and now they are both smelling of April and May. I think they may make a match of it."

The situation had been something of a shock even for Charles. After a little soul-searching, he accepted it with genuine pleasure, but he worried about Christa's reaction. She didn't know and value Lewis as he did, and she had reason to despise him. Charles needn't have worried. After a moment of blank astonishment, his sister went off into whoops.

When she sobered up, she gasped, "The poor man! So mad for *Maman* that he was desperate enough to consider me a substitute. It is a farce Moliere himself would have appreciated—kinfolk reappearing from the grave, longtime lover rewarded. *C'est merveilleux!*"

Charles gave her a hug, delighted at her reaction. "You are well enough in your way, my little cabbage."

When they reached the house, Christa jumped from the carriage and raced up the stairs. A watchful footman opened the door, and she went hurtling through. Marie-Claire was waiting. With a sob of joy, Christa hurled herself into her mother's arms. "Oh, *Maman*, *Maman*," she gasped through her tears. "I've missed you so!"

Lewis kept out of the way while Christa and Marie-Claire had their reunion. Much later in the day, Christa sent him a message requesting a meeting in the library. He was at his most impassive when he complied; she was beginning to recognize the expression as embarrassment. She rose at his entrance, studying the lean blond figure. He really was a very distinguished-looking man—stern, perhaps, but *Maman* would cure that. Men had always fallen in love with her mother, and it was a testament to Lewis's character that Marie-Claire reciprocated his feelings.

He stood in silence for a moment, then said with re-hearsed precision, "I owe you a profound apology, Marie-Christine. I behaved very badly, and I fear my actions may have put you into danger. Certainly into discomfort."

Christa shrugged and gave a gamin smile. "But as you see, I am none the worse for it, and I have no regrets that I left Radcliffe Hall. I think that my actions perhaps caused you more pain than yours caused me."

Lewis smiled ruefully and began to relax. "If you only knew! Did I really see you near Hyde Park last autumn? I thought perhaps I was hallucinating."

"Yes," she confirmed. "Luckily London is an easy place in which to lose oneself." She studied him a moment longer, then crossed and offered her hand. "We had best be friends. Otherwise it will make Charles and my mother very unhappy."

"Then you know . . . ?" he asked as he took her hand and held it between his two large ones.

"Yes, and I approve. *Maman* likes being married. It will be good for her to have someone to care for." She grinned. "Almost as good as it will be for you to have someone caring for you."

Lewis bent and kissed her hand, not with the passion of a lover but with respect and affection. "You are a rare young woman, Marie-Christine, worthy of being your mother's daughter."

Christa blushed pink at the compliment. "You could have said nothing that would please me more. But there is one thing."

"Yes?"

"Our relationship will prosper much better if you call

me Christa. No one uses my full name unless he is angry with me."

Lewis laughed, obviously delighted beyond measure to have both her forgiveness of the past and her blessing for the future. Offering his arm, he said, "Shall we go inform the rest of the family that we have made peace?"

"With great pleasure." She smiled, feeling more comfortable with Lewis than she ever had in the past. "This should be a day without shadows."

Chapter 18

Of course, the Debenhams could not be left at the Orchard with no member of the family in residence, but two and a half days in a carriage with them left Annabelle with the passionate hope that Alex had succeeded in finding Christa and persuading her to marry him. What was a little—well, a big—scandal, compared to a lifetime of having Sybil in the family?

The Debenhams dropped her in St. James's Square, stopping only long enough to ascertain that Alex was still among the living before continuing to their town house. Sybil did suggest dutifully that she stay and "lend her dear sister support," but she was no more eager to do it than Annabelle was to have her.

Annabelle immediately went to Alex's room, where he lay on a chaise with an unopened book in his lap. Obviously her brother was not at death's door, but his worn, gray look struck at her heart. She went to him and dropped a kiss on his forehead before seating herself. "You didn't find Christa?" she asked softly.

Alex closed his eyes, a spasm of emotion crossing his

features. "I would rather not talk about her, Belle. In fact, please forget everything I told you."

"If that is what you wish." She paused, then asked diffidently, "What about Miss Debenham?"

He shrugged slightly. "The engagement stands."

"But you don't love her!"

"It really doesn't matter, Belle. I'll be at sea most of the time. Sybil knows what she is getting into, and still wants to marry me. Someone might as well be satisfied."

Annabelle could have wept to see her brother this way but could think of no words of comfort. Had Christa rejected him, and done it cruelly? Annabelle had trouble imagining her sensitive abigail doing that, but obviously something deeply traumatic had happened to Alex. He seemed as desolate now as Annabelle had been after the disillusion with Sir Edward Loaming, and he had no Christa to tease him out of it.

She sighed. He would have to find his salvation in his work. If he was determined to throw his life away in a loveless match, she could not change his mind.

She went to sit on the floor by the chaise, taking her brother's hand and leaning her cheek against it to convey her wordless sympathy. They sat in silence for a long time as the shadows deepened. Eventually Annabelle straightened up and said, "Perhaps Jonathan will be luckier in love than you and I."

Alex smiled a bit at that. "Life goes on. By next week I should be well enough to go to Plymouth and start provisioning my new ship. Would you like to have Cousin Hattie stay here? She is the most agreeable of the available female relatives."

"She'd certainly be an improvement on Aunt Agatha. I don't suppose she can be induced to leave those dreadful birds of hers at home?" Cousin Hattie was notorious for her shrieking, messy pairs of inappropriately named lovebirds.

His mouth twitched. "I think it highly unlikely."

Annabelle sighed. "Perhaps I'll get a cat. Who knows, there might be an accident involving a bird cage."

Alex laughed aloud and swung his legs down to the floor. "If you can get away with it, you have my blessing. But if you fail, expect a drumhead court-martial from Hattie." He leaned over and brushed his sister's hair. "I'm glad you're here."

"I always will be. I plan on cultivating the eccentricities suitable in a maiden aunt."

"I will be highly surprised if I don't have post office packets chasing me all over the Atlantic, begging for your hand."

Annabelle wrinkled her nose. "I have decided that in the future I will prefer quality to quantity when it comes to courtship. Shall I ring for some tea?" Without waiting for a reply, she pulled the cord. If she wasn't to have much more time with her brother, she intended to make the best of what was left.

The Earl of Radcliffe was feted and welcomed everywhere in the three weeks after his miraculous return home. He had always been a popular young man, and his apparent demise had been sincerely mourned. Though London was thin of company, he had numerous invitations, and Radcliffe House was flooded with letters from friends around the country rejoicing in his survival.

No longer quite the carefree young man about town, Charles regarded the furor with a slightly jaundiced eye. He would always be a sociable creature, but the forms of the beau monde mattered a good deal less to him than they had in the past. Nearly two years as a prisoner and a fugitive will concentrate the mind wonderfully, and matters that had seemed important in the past could only appear trivial now.

What *was* important was family, and observation convinced him that something was seriously troubling his sister. No one would have guessed who didn't know Christa as well as he did, but he sensed sadness under her bright manner.

Charles leaned against the door frame of the music room and watched her play the pianoforte, rippling out a bright sonata that he recognized as Viennese in origin. Christa made a charming picture in the early afternoon sun, every inch the society lady in her flowing high-waisted gown and her stylishly tousled black curls. As she finished the composition, she glanced up with a welcoming smile, then turned on the bench to face him.

"Good afternoon, Charles. Isn't that a lovely bit of music? Broadwood's English action piano has a much more powerful tone than the German instrument we had in Paris."

The earl straightened up and entered the room, sitting down on a sofa where he could see her face clearly. "Yes, it has, and you play it very well. It must be all the practice you have been doing. In fact, you've been playing the pianoforte so much lately that I'm beginning to wonder if you're going into a decline."

Christa's laughter was light, but she didn't meet his eyes. "Why would I do that? I feel like a fairy princess. My family and fortune have been restored. What more could I ask?"

Charles decided on a direct approach. "That is exactly what I've been wondering. You just don't seem the same."

She looked at him levelly. "Are *you* the same as you were two years ago?"

"No, of course not," he admitted. "I defy anyone to spend a year and a half in a filthy prison under sentence of death and come out the same. I'll never be able to take the cut of a waistcoat or the turn of a card quite so seriously again. But that doesn't mean I can't enjoy the pleasures of society.

"You, however, have walled yourself up in here like a hibernating bear. You're in a position to take London by storm, yet you spend all your time reading or playing the piano or wearing out horses and grooms in Richmond Park." Charles frowned as he studied her face. "I'm getting worried."

Christa sighed and turned her head, one hand stroking the keyboard in absent accompaniment to her thoughts. She was grateful to the depths of her soul that her mother and brother were alive and well, and she herself restored to name and fortune. She would have made a good life for herself working with Suzanne, but only a fool would prefer such an existence to the freedom that wealth and position provided.

But all the wealth and family in the world could not heal the pain of losing Alex. Most of her life she had kept her emotions under firm control, responding to trouble with logic and laughter. Then Alex had created holes in her defenses that could be repaired only by him. Christa's rational mind occasionally suggested that someday she might meet and love another man as much, but her heart flatly refused to believe it.

How could she possibly explain to Charles that when she had found she was not carrying Alex's child, her intellectual reaction of relief had been swept away by a rending, primitive sense of loss that had shaken her to her bones?

Christa knew that she couldn't have Alex, but she hadn't known how much she had hoped to have his child until the possibility was gone.

She glanced at Charles's intent gray eyes and smiled inwardly. No, her mother might understand, but it was not the sort of thing one could explain to a protective big brother.

Christa was briefly tempted to confide in Charles, but the experience of loving Alex was too precious to share with anyone, and her foolish pride didn't want to admit that the young Comtesse d'Estelle, the belle of Paris, had been unable to win the love of the one man she wanted. She doubted that Alex loved either Sybil Debenham or her, but his sense of obligation and commitment to the Peacock was stronger than the physical attraction he felt toward his sister's maid.

She appreciated Charles's concern, for it was good to have someone who cared enough to worry about her after being so long alone. Since her brother knew her too well to believe that all was well, she decided to tell him a portion of the truth. "I feel . . . disoriented, Charles. The last two years have been so strange. The first year was interminable, I felt entirely alone, and as if the world would never be right again.

"This last year has gone much more quickly, and most of the time I was happy. It was good to be busy and to make friends, to stand on my own feet. As my father told us both, there is dignity in work, and it gave me back myself."

Christa moved her hands restlessly as she sought words to explain herself. "But in order to be a servant, I had to *become* a servant. I never forgot my old life, but I had completely convinced myself that it was gone beyond recall. If I had not truly believed that, I might have destroyed myself with self-pity and anger against the injustice of life.

"Even when it might have been to my advantage to

speak of my birth, I never did." She stopped abruptly. She had tormented herself with wondering if it would have made a difference if she had told Alex who she was that night in the library when he had asked her to become his mistress. Instead, her reflexive pride had sealed her lips, and Alex had turned to Sybil Debenham.

When Christa was sure her voice would be steady, she continued, "I find it strange now to be waited on, to be a lady of leisure. I look at your servants, and I understand their position in a way that was impossible to a wealthy aristocrat, no matter how liberal my education and sympathies. Can you imagine how that has changed the way I see the world?"

Charles considered seriously before answering. "I think so. In France, I shared a twenty-foot-square cell with two dozen men of all classes and ages. None of them except Jean-Claude Bohnet knew my background, and we were very much equal in that cell. Strength and compassion had nothing to do with breeding, and I can't look at people now and see them as simply servants or peasants or tradesmen. Before, I had an abstract belief in equality, but now I *know* that while I may be luckier than most men, I am inherently no better. Is that what you feel?"

"Yes, and the thought of going back to the frivolous games of polite society takes a good deal of getting used to." Christa gave a sunny smile. "I promise that I shall not become a recluse, and I will learn again how to flirt and act the part of a young lady. But I am not ready yet."

"I can understand that." Charles drew his brows together in his sternest big-brother expression. "But are you sure that is all that is troubling you?"

Christa wrinkled her nose. "Well, I am not looking forward to running into any members of the beau monde who knew me as a servant. There are only a handful that would recognize me, but it will be embarrassing, and I haven't yet decided how to deal with that."

Charles grimaced. "It would certainly damage your reputation if it was known that you stooped to work for a living, particularly as a servant. Genteel starvation would have been much more acceptable. But surely you can play the countess so thoroughly that no one will believe you have ever lifted your dainty hand to anything more strenuous than a handkerchief."

"I might be able to convince most people that any resemblance to a certain lady's maid was strictly coincidental," Christa said with a shrug. "But not my second mistress. We spent too much time together for her not to recognize me."

"Would she cause trouble for you?"

Christa shook her head decisively. "No. She had a kind heart." Annabelle would not be a problem—she would probably be enchanted by the romantic story of a lost-and-found countess, and Christa was sure they would be friends under any circumstances.

As for the others, Lady Pomfret was too myopic to recognize her, and most members of the ton that Christa had casually contacted would have scarcely noticed her face. The real obstacle was the Peacock, so soon to become Lady Kingsley. Christa had waited on her for days, and it was likely that even such a self-absorbed creature as Sybil would recognize her.

Even that would have been tolerable; in her countess mode, Christa could outface Sybil. What was unbearable was the thought of seeing Alex, or worse, Alex with his wife. She could face the prospect with equanimity in some distant future, but not yet. No, she would not go into society until he was safely married and gone back to sea.

Charles said thoughtfully, "Do you know, you have never mentioned the names of the people you worked for." He had the information from Suzanne but was curious how his sister would reply.

"There is no need for names," Christa said a little too airily. "A proper servant is always discreet about her employers."

Charles stood, towering over his younger sister. He put a finger under her chin and lifted it so he could see her eyes. "Are you telling me the whole truth, little cabbage?"

Christa gave her gamin smile. "I have told you all I intend, so don't try to bully me, *mon frère*, or I will put a frog in your bed."

He grinned back. "That is supposed to be my threat. How was I to know that when I did that, you would turn the frog into a pet?"

"You should have guessed I would have an affinity for the poor creature. After all, you used to tell me that I looked like a frog."

Charles blinked at the thought. "So I did. Older brothers can be quite barbarous."

Christa agreed with a laugh. "True."

She stood and took his arm. "Shall we see if *Maman* and Uncle Lewis are available for tea? If we can find one of them, we shall probably find the other."

"Very likely," Charles agreed. "I enjoy watching them together—they are both so happy. It makes me feel like I am of the older generation, and they are the younger."

"Lewis seems like a wholly different person," Christa said thoughtfully. "More relaxed, and much more likely to laugh."

"Mother does have a talent for bringing out the best in people." He added, "You may not know this, but in England it is against the law for someone to wed the sibling of a deceased spouse. However, most laws can be circumvented, and the fact that Mother is a French citizen should help. If they decide to marry, they can do it somewhere on the Continent. But that is for the future. Shall we see if they are in the morning room?"

Charles had accepted Christa's evasions because he knew that more questioning would be useless, but all of his sister's explanations and obfuscations merely confirmed his view that something was amiss. He would just have to look further to find what it was.

Charles was reluctant to discuss the issue with Marie-Claire, who was enjoying her first real happiness in years. Why worry his mother if there was nothing that could be done?

After lengthy consideration, he decided to visit Christa's former mistress. His sister had spent months in close proximity with the woman, and perhaps Miss Kingsley would know what had upset her so badly. Or perhaps the lady herself was the cause. Christa had said the woman had a good heart, but that was faint praise—perhaps the good heart lay under a foul temper. An aging spinster might have resented Christa's youthful attractiveness and made her life miserable.

Charles chose a sunny day in February to make his call, reasoning that everyone was better natured in bright weather, and since it was unfashionably early, there were unlikely to be other callers to disturb the discussion. The earl had a matter-of-fact awareness that most women were kindly disposed to him, but old ladies were usually starched up and unlikely to welcome calls from total strangers, no matter how wellborn.

At Kingsley House the butler admitted him with impassive mien and took his card up to Miss Kingsley. Charles rose when the parlor door opened, then simply stood and stared. It is disconcerting to confront a mermaid when one has been expecting an old trout, and the blond young woman who entered was so lovely that he temporarily forgot his mission.

Miss Kingsley carried his card, and her delicate face was knit in puzzlement. "Forgive me, my lord. Have I had the pleasure of meeting you, perhaps at one of those dreadful squeezes last autumn?"

She glanced at his face, then blushed at his expression. He really was quite extraordinarily handsome, and without thinking she blurted out, "I can't imagine that I would forget you!"

At the visitor's laugh, Annabelle blushed so hard she was sure her ears must be red. He shook his head and said, "No, I have not had the honor of an introduction. If I seemed a trifle stunned, it was at your youth and beauty. I met Lord Kingsley some years ago and had assumed his sister would be much older."

Annabelle's brow cleared and she gave an enchanting smile. "You must have known my father. My brother Alex succeeded him two years ago. He is about your age." She dragged her gaze from his face, then said daringly, "I was just about to have tea. Will you join me?"

She rang for a servant, knowing full well that Cousin Hattie would shriek like one of her birds if she knew Annabelle was entertaining a gentleman caller. Annabelle didn't care; she had a reckless desire to take her time discovering why Lord Radcliffe had called.

"Thank you," the earl said as he took a chair. "I was out of England for a considerable period of time and had not realized there was a new Viscount Kingsley."

They exchanged commonplaces until tea and cakes

arrived, with Annabelle covertly studying her visitor, intrigued by his general resemblance to Alex. There was similarity in height and coloring, and a certain vivid energy, but the features were quite different, and Radcliffe's voice was lighter in tone and quicker in its speech rhythms. While her brother was very good looking, she rather thought that the earl surpassed him. But what was the man doing here?

Anticipating her question, the earl said, "I must apologize for calling when we have never been introduced, but I wish to discuss your former maid. You knew her as Christine Bohnet."

Annabelle hoped she didn't look as startled as she felt. What could this fashionable gentleman care about someone else's servant? "Christa was in my employ, but she is no longer. I am not sure it would be proper to discuss her with a stranger."

Charles smiled. It was a smile that had tamed the most ferocious of dowagers, and the effect on a romantic young female was mesmerizing. "But I am not a stranger. I'm her brother."

Annabelle stared blankly. Grasping at the first objection to such an absurd statement, she said, "But . . . you are English, and she is French."

"I should have said that I am her half brother," Charles said. He knew that he should explain the situation succinctly, but Miss Kingsley confused was a delightful creature, her blue eyes earnest and transparently readable.

Annabelle gazed at him in bafflement. Then with sudden shock she realized that the smoky quartz eyes regarding her were identical in color and shape to those of her former maid. She had never seen any other eyes like them, until today.

"Your eyes!" she gasped in sudden recognition. "It must be true." She now found that the gray eyes sparked with amusement exactly like Christa's.

"In other words, Christa is . . ." Annabelle hesitated, seeking the most discreet possible term for "illegitimate." If Christa were the bastard daughter of an English lord, it would explain both her gentility and her reticence about her antecedents.

"Born the wrong side of the blanket?" Charles supplied helpfully. "Not in the least. We share a mother, not a father. When my mother married the Comte d'Estelle, it was a grand occasion with dozens of high born friends as witnesses. I was in the ceremony myself because Mother didn't want me to feel neglected."

In a world turning upside down, one stunning fact stood out. Annabelle said faintly, "Her father was a count?"

The earl nodded. Mentally reviewing what she knew of the French system of succession, Annabelle had the same nightmare feeling as when she dreamed of being caught in public wearing only a shift. *"You mean that Christa is a countess?"*

"Yes, her full name and style is Marie-Christine Madeline Louise d'Estelle, Comtesse d'Estelle, Baronne Bretenne et Baronne Valognes."

Annabelle covered her face with her hands and gave a low moan of horror. *"She used to darn my stockings!"*

Charles erupted into laughter. Annabelle removed her hands from her face and glared, but after a few moments his humor proved contagious and her lips started twitching. Finally she had to laugh with him.

Eventually Charles said, "I'm sorry, that was most unkind of me. I can imagine the shock if I found that my valet was a duke or some such. But if you could have seen your face . . ."

He hastily suppressed a new surge of hilarity. "If she darned your stockings, I trust she did them well."

"Most certainly," Annabelle said, still slightly dazed. "She was good at everything that a maid does, and everything that a lady does, too."

There was a long, long pause while she collected her scattered thoughts, then she said hesitantly, "It is . . . humbling to think how I simply accepted her as a servant. She was so well-read, much more so than I am. And she was very knowledgeable about society and manners. My brother said she was more a lady than half the ton, and he was absolutely right." She shook her head, then went on, "Yet because she was a maid, I overlooked how remarkable she was."

Annabelle stopped, staring into her teacup, then said, "I'm not explaining this very well. I am ashamed that, because she was apparently from an inferior station in life, I . . . it never occurred to me to really look at her as she was, rather than as I expected her to be. Do you understand what I mean?"

"Yes, I do. But don't be too hard on yourself," Charles said consolingly. "The minx was always a dab hand at theatricals, and she probably acted the part better than a real abigail. Christa is a bit of a revolutionary, you know—she doesn't just say that all people are inherently equal, she actually believes it, which is one of the reasons she could be a convincing servant. Plus, she told me that she had convinced herself that her old life was entirely behind her and she must build a new future without feeling sorry for herself."

Christa had sometimes succumbed to self-pity? Annabelle had rather thought that was her own specialty. She gave herself a mental shake and asked, "What do you wish to discuss with me? Are you seeking to find your sister?"

"No, she is safe in my home. I should explain that my mother and I were missing and thought dead in France. Christa managed to escape, but there was a . . . serious misunderstanding with my heir, and she felt compelled to leave his protection and strike out on her own. When we returned to England several weeks ago, I found her just after she left your household. Which brings me to why I have called on you today."

Annabelle was round eyed at the earl's casual references to high adventure, but regretfully decided that she had best stick to the business at hand. "I had heard your story but forgot that the earl involved was named Radcliffe," she admitted. "Your adventures were a nine days' wonder. What do you wish to know about Christa?"

Charles said slowly, "My sister seems unhappy—she has lost much of her high spiritedness. Not that she is moping, but I am concerned for her. Is there anything you know that might give a clue?" At Annabelle's silence he added, "An *affaire de coeur* seems the most likely."

Annabelle had a lively suspicion that it might have something to do with Alex, but was wrestling her conscience about whether to speak. Her brother had asked her to bury the whole subject. But if there was any chance that she might help him pull out of his despair . . .

Coming to a decision, she said, "Perhaps I shouldn't speak of this, but my brother wished to marry her."

Charles gave a nearly soundless whistle. "Even thinking she was a servant?" At Annabelle's nod, he mused, "That is quite a tribute to my sister's charms. Did she turn him down?"

"I don't know. Alex won't talk of it."

"And she won't either," Charles said glumly. "Do you suppose there was a quarrel of some sort?"

Annabelle sat and thought for a bit. "My brother is

betrothed to someone else, and that would have complicated matters."

With a frown Charles said, "Did he ask my sister to be his mistress when he was about to marry another woman?" His eyes narrowed dangerously and he rapped out, "Or is he the sort of man who might have *forced* her when she refused him?"

Annabelle banged her teacup down so hard the porcelain chipped. "No, he is not!"

They glared at each other for a moment. More mildly Charles said, "I'm sorry if my brotherly protectiveness led me to insult. I've never met Kingsley, but if he inspires such loyalty, I'll accept your assessment of his character. But what might have happened with Christa?"

Annabelle relaxed. "Alex really did want to marry her, you know. He was ready to break his engagement to Miss Debenham and let the devil take the hindmost."

Ignoring the strong language, Charles exclaimed, "Kingsley is never going to marry the Gilded Lily?" At Annabelle's quizzical look, the earl explained, "That is what Sybil Debenham is called in the gentlemen's clubs."

"A perfect name! That is exactly what she is like," Annabelle agreed. "You know her?"

"Before I went to France, I would flirt with her occasionally. It was quite safe. That Season she was setting lures only for dukes and marquesses, so I was quite beneath her touch." At his listener's astonished stare he supplied, "The Gilded Lily is generally assumed to be selling her not-inconsiderable charms in return for the best possible title."

"That's outrageous!" Annabelle exclaimed. More thoughtfully she added, "It also explains a great deal. She certainly wants to marry Alex, but he's only a viscount."

"Times are hard," Charles said sympathetically. "The Gilded Lily must have had to lower her goals."

Annabelle giggled. The earl was quite delightfully improper. Perhaps it came of his being half French.

"If you'll forgive my asking, is Lord Kingsley in love with Miss Debenham?"

She shook her head vehemently. "Definitely not. In fact," she added darkly, "there is a mystery about how they came to be engaged. Alex was very unforthcoming on the subject."

Better than Annabelle, Charles could understand how a gentleman might be trapped into making an offer—Miss Debenham *was* dashed good-looking. "You said he wanted to marry Christa. Did he break the engagement?"

"No. He was going to if your sister accepted him. But since she apparently refused him, he doesn't seem to care whom he marries. Alex is a captain in the Royal Navy, you know. He's down in Plymouth now, outfitting his new ship."

"Perhaps Christa didn't want to marry a man who was always at sea," Charles suggested.

"No, he didn't decide to take another ship until after Miss Debenham sank her claws into him. He might give up the commission if he had a good reason to stay ashore." She clenched one hand and said passionately, "If only there was something I could do to end the engagement! Alex may not think it matters whom he marries, but I *know* he will be miserable if he marries Sybil!"

Annabelle stopped, embarrassed by her vehemence. "Not that she is wicked, but they are so horribly unlike. She is interested in nothing but clothes and gossip. Alex never says a thing when he's with her, yet he is usually the most delightful of company."

Charles was amused to see the proper young lady visibly

loosening up the longer they talked. Then his gaze slipped out of focus as an idea occurred to him. He said slowly, "Do you think that if she broke the engagement, your brother would be sorry? It would be quite unexceptionable if she were the one to change her mind."

"I think he'd be delighted. My brother, Jon, and I certainly would be! What do you have in mind?" Annabelle asked curiously.

"A spot of conspiracy, actually. Are you game?"

Charles's smile made Annabelle temporarily forget that he had asked a question and made her recognize that he had a streak of mischief as Christa did. She shook herself and said cautiously, "I think so. What would be required?"

Charles leaned forward. "We must start with the assumption that there is an attraction between your brother and my sister, and that it went wrong in some way that is making them both unhappy. Is that reasonable?"

"Yes, certainly Alex cared for her, and she always seemed very comfortable around him."

"Of course, there is no guarantee that removing Miss Debenham from the picture would repair a possible rift between Christa and Lord Kingsley." He stopped and frowned. "You are *positive* your brother won't mind if Sybil jilts him? It's a grave thing to play God, especially with those we care most about."

Annabelle suffered a moment of panic. She had made a mull of her own affairs; how dare she interfere with Alex's? Then she remembered Sir Edward's weak face and shuddered. She would always be grateful that her brother had cared enough to save her from her folly. He had even cared enough to let her continue in it if she had been determined. With a slightly crooked smile she said, "I am quite sure. I owe Alex a rescue."

Charles looked at her quizzically but refrained from

questioning her remark. "I believe that Miss Debenham might be induced to change her mind. For example, if there were a better title in prospect?"

Annabelle stared at him as she caught his meaning. "Do you mean you would let her think you would offer for her if she were free?" When Charles nodded, she gasped, "Why, that is positively diabolical!"

Charles looked uneasy until she said, her eyes gleaming, "It's a *wonderful* scheme!"

Annabelle's wide blue eyes slid away from his and she added hesitantly, "You wouldn't actually offer for her, would you?" Somehow, the answer to that mattered.

"No fears on that score." Charles chuckled. "The Gilded Lily and I would never suit. I know I am acting in a very ungentlemanly fashion, but she won't break her engagement unless she is as venal as I suspect. And if your brother is not up to all the rigs and rows because he has been off serving our country, I feel it is my positive *duty* to save him from her."

"If you can induce Miss Debenham to end the betrothal, how do you propose to get Alex and Christa to settle their differences? Always assuming there is something between them," Annabelle added conscientiously.

"Lock them in a room together until they work things out."

Annabelle regarded him with awe. "You're very direct, aren't you?"

"I try," Charles said modestly.

"How do you propose to get them together?"

"I trust that Lord Kingsley will be coming up here from Plymouth at least once before he leaves England?"

Annabelle nodded. "Yes, he will be back briefly in about two weeks, and then the last week in March for the wedding. His ship will be ready to sail in late April."

Charles said thoughtfully, "This will require some acting on your part. You will say that you want him to meet me and my mother because you and I are . . . contemplating a nearer relationship. Since he doesn't know that Christa is my sister, it simply remains to invite the two of you to Radcliffe House for tea or some such." He shrugged in a manner that made him look suddenly French. "I fear this will require you to put up with a good deal of my company for the next several weeks. Do you think you could manage that?"

"That's pure fustian and you know it," Annabelle said calmly. "The principal obstacle to the plan is that you will have so many handkerchiefs dropped in front of you that you may be unable to find your way back here."

Charles laughed. "I promise you that shan't happen." He took her hand and raised it to his lips. "Then I shall call on you for a drive tomorrow at two in the afternoon." He left the room without waiting for a reply.

Annabelle watched the earl thoughtfully as he took his leave, aware that she had a wide, daft smile on her face. And to think that she had been impressed by Sir Edward Loaming's technique in hand kissing. . . .

Chapter 19

Never one to let the grass grow under his feet, Charles decided to call on Sybil Debenham after leaving Kingsley House since she lived near St. James's Square and it was now the fashionable hour for paying calls. As expected, she was holding court to the usual mixture of fortune hunters, mesmerized youngsters, and doting older men. Sybil was in her element, preening and accepting compliments as her mother watched fondly.

There was a flutter of interest as Lord Radcliffe entered and made his bow. Sybil appeared delighted to see the hero of the hour paying a call, and with a wave of her hand she scattered the rest of her court so he could sit next to her. While the dismissed admirers watched him jealously, the beauty said in a thrilling voice, "Your lordship, it's so splendid to see you! No one talks of anything but your miraculous return from the grave!"

The earl looked at her meaningfully. "It's wonderful to see the beauties of England again." His gaze caressed her golden self, lingering just a trifle at her bountiful cleavage. "The months in a French prison, the daily presence of death—it was endurable only by remembering what I had left behind." He sighed melodramatically. "At night I dreamed of an English beauty, the sheen of golden hair, the rose-petal complexion found only in women of our fair isle."

As he gazed deep into her aquamarine eyes, he wondered that he might be overdoing it, but Sybil's rapt expression said otherwise. With a shake of his head, Charles nobly dismissed the horrors he had seen. "Yes, it's good to be home, though of course some things have changed, and not for the better."

After a long, weighted pause he said, his eyes still holding hers, "I understand that you are betrothed to Lord Kingsley. I wish you very happy." After another long moment he added wistfully, "Would that I could find such happiness for myself. But come, I talk too much of my own concerns. Let us speak of you. You are lovelier than even my memories."

Sybil was more than willing to return to her favorite topic. When Lord Radcliffe took his leave after a correct fifteen minutes, she announced to her remaining admirers that she had a touch of the headache and must withdraw. Amidst a chorus of wishes for her rapid return to good health, she went to her chamber and sat in front of her mirror. It was the position she preferred for serious thinking.

Radcliffe was alive and an *earl*. From the way he'd been talking today, he admired her more than ever. Sybil stroked a golden ringlet lovingly. After two years in a French prison, the poor man must be desperate for the sight of a beautiful woman. Desperate, and tractable.

Sybil frowned at the vision of loveliness in the mirror, then quickly stopped to avoid wrinkling her forehead. Here was Radcliffe, alive and available, and she was betrothed. She toyed with a pair of diamond and ruby earrings, remembering with a scowl how shamefully Lord Kingsley had been neglecting her. The only time she had seen him since Suffolk was when he made a brief farewell call before departing for Plymouth. Sometimes she thought the man didn't appreciate his good fortune at all. It would serve him right if she looked elsewhere.

Of course, a viscount in the hand was worth an earl in the bush. . . . She caught herself frowning again and stopped. She must wait and see what Radcliffe did. Perhaps he had been effusive today merely because he had been away from proper society for so long. In the past she had sometimes had a lurking suspicion that he found her amusing, though she had dismissed the idea out of hand. How could a man be amused by the most beautiful woman in London? It must be that he had been delighted to be in her presence and that gave the impression of humor.

Sybil tapped her nails on the top of the vanity table, sparing them an admiring glance. She had gone beyond mere gilding by finding an artist who could paint the most delightful designs on her nails. This week it was lotus blossoms on the index fingers, with tiny gemstones set in the center of each flower. She rather thought the idea would set a new style.

Radcliffe might be too much the gentleman to declare himself when she was betrothed to someone else, but it would be interesting to see if he called again. She wasn't to wed Kingsley for another six weeks. Anything could happen in that length of time. Her eyes became dreamy. *The Countess of Radcliffe.* It had a ring. Much better than "Lady Kingsley."

The fair weather held the next day, and Annabelle awaited the Earl of Radcliffe with undisguised anticipation. She thought she was looking her best in a sky-blue pelisse with ermine trim, and when he arrived, the admiration in his eyes confirmed it.

As the earl helped her into his curricle, she surreptitiously studied his face, deciding that he was every bit as handsome as she remembered. But he was more than just a golden Apollo; there was character, humor, and intelligence in his face.

Charles left his groom at Kingsley House so they could talk freely. After he had turned the carriage, Annabelle said, "I have thought of a number of questions that didn't occur to me yesterday, my lord."

He shot a quick glance out of the mischievous gray eyes. "Since we may soon have a family connection, shouldn't you call me Charles?"

"Only if you will call me Annabelle."

"Exactly what I hoped you would say, *mignonne*."

"What did you call me?" Annabelle asked in surprise. She recognized the French endearment, but it was obviously improper of him to use it.

His answer was properly apologetic, but she detected a trace of smile on his face. "Forgive me. For most of the last two years I have been speaking French, and I sometimes become confused between the two languages."

Annabelle permitted herself a sniff to let him know that she didn't believe the reply but dropped the subject since she wasn't offended by the familiarity. Quite the contrary. Obviously she still had a weakness for audacity, but as she observed the earl's firm profile, she knew that this was a man she could trust, quite unlike the late, and now unlamented, Sir Edward Loaming.

Charles was saying thoughtfully, "It's odd. My sister, who is wholly French, is now more comfortable speaking English, while I, who am much more English, am still thinking in French. I expect it will be several more weeks before that changes and I start thinking in English again."

"That was one of the things I was wondering," Annabelle

said curiously. "How were you raised? It must have been a most unusual upbringing."

"I suppose so, though it seemed natural enough at the time. My real father, the Earl of Radcliffe, died when I was only two. It's strange," Charles mused. "I think of him as old and wise, and yet he was only about my age when he died."

Annabelle was silent for a few moments before she said quietly, "And yet you were old enough to remember him?"

"A little, I think. I can remember a tall blond man tossing me in the air. It must have been him. My Uncle Lewis was never so playful, though physically he resembled my father. I can also remember being carried on the saddle bow before a rider and squealing with delight, but that could have been either my father or my uncle. Or both, at different times."

"It must be very hard to lose a parent so young."

Charles pulled his horses back to let a mail coach pass in front of him. He gave Annabelle a quick glance, his face serious for once. "It is always tragic when a good person dies young, but you needn't look so grave on my behalf. I was very fortunate since my Uncle Lewis and my mother's second husband, Philippe d'Estelle, were both like fathers to me. An English gentleman and a French philosopher, what more could any boy need?"

"Then you are to be congratulated." Annabelle said it with a smile but could not repress a wistful pang. What would it have been like to have loving parents? She continued, "Were you raised in both countries?"

"Yes. Until I was old enough to start school, I was usually with my mother, but she and her second family would make long visits to Radcliffe Hall, and my Uncle Lewis visited us in France. He and my mother were my guardians, and Lewis managed my estates until I was of age. After I started at Harrow, I spent more time in England, but would still go to France for the summers. That's why Christa and I are so close. We spent at least as much time together as most full brothers and sisters."

They had reached Kensington Gardens and Charles headed the curricle toward the Orangery. Traffic was light, and he was able to give more attention to his passenger.

Annabelle said, "One of the things I've been wondering is how Christa could become a lady's maid so successfully. I wouldn't have the faintest notion how to do some of the things she did."

Charles laughed. "My sister is intimidatingly well educated. Our mother thought that a lady should understand all the duties of a household, and her father encouraged her to study everything else. Plus, she always had more curiosity than a kettleful of cats. I imagine there isn't a task in the d'Estelle household or estates that she didn't have some understanding of."

Annabelle sighed. "If she wasn't so nice, it would be easy for an inferior female like me to dislike her."

Charles pulled the horses to a stop and turned to give her his full attention. His gray eyes were very searching as he said, "You must never even think that. I love my sister and wouldn't change her in any way, but she is not the only pattern of female worthiness. Her education and competence are very much a part of her, but it is spirit that makes someone special."

He was conveying a message beyond just his words, and Annabelle almost turned away from the intensity of his expression as her old feelings of unworthiness fought for control of her mind. *What can a man like this possibly see in me?* But there was some thread of connection between them, and she intended to do everything in her power to strengthen it.

She touched his hand lightly. "You are very like your sister, in both the generosity and the wisdom."

Charles relaxed with a smile. "Much of that is due to my mother. She is the most remarkable woman I've ever known. Quite apart from her attributes of character, she is a countess three times over—once at birth and twice by marriage."

"I hope that I may meet her someday."

"You will," Charles said as he slapped the reins to start the horses again. He slanted a glance at her. "You remind me a bit of Marie-Claire. You have some of the same gentleness of spirit."

Annabelle's throat tightened alarmingly, and it was several moments before she replied, "Thank you. I will endeavor to be worthy of your regard."

They rode in companionable silence for some time, enjoying the relative warmth of the day. Eventually Annabelle said, "I keep hoping we are right that there is an attachment between Alex and Christa. I expect that Christa could have just about any man she wanted, but I've never seen my brother so relaxed with any other woman. Except me, I suppose," she added meticulously. "But if she doesn't care for him . . ." Her voice trailed off.

"I can't swear to her feelings, but she is assuredly missing someone, and Lord Kingsley is by far the best prospect. I just hope he can handle her," Charles said with a laugh. "Christa is a rare handful."

"If Alex can control a ship with three hundred men on it, I imagine he can manage one small Frenchwoman."

"The two things aren't comparable, but I sincerely hope you are right for everyone's sake. By the way, how did Christa come to your house? It was her second position, wasn't it?"

"You haven't heard the story? Alex literally caught her

in midair when she was bodily thrown out of her previous household."

"Why on earth did that happen?" Charles said in surprise.

"Your sister repulsed the master's advances with some violence, and—"

Charles interrupted Annabelle's recital, fury in his voice. *"Who was the filthy brute?"*

Annabelle realized too late why Christa had not chosen to tell this particular tale. "Lord Radcliffe, please use your sense! While it would doubtless be quite satisfying to avenge your sister's honor, what would that do for her reputation?"

The earl looked a bit sheepish as his good sense started to return. "I suppose you're right. But I hate the thought of what she must have endured."

"If it's any comfort, she took care of herself quite well. Alex said that she also rearranged the face of the footman who literally threw her down a flight of steep stone steps when she rejected him as well."

"Good Lord!" Charles said admiringly. "I apparently have been underestimating my little sister. I would still like to darken the man's daylights at the very least, but I suppose you won't tell me who he is."

"No, I will not," Annabelle said firmly. "And for the same reason Christa did not. It is very bad that she had to endure the impropriety, but she managed quite capably and took no permanent harm."

Charles accepted that the episode was beyond his ability to avenge and changed the subject. "I called on the Gilded Lily yesterday, and she seems quite willing to accept my compliments, and perhaps a good deal more."

Annabelle chuckled. "Good. Even if our matchmaking efforts fail with Alex and Christa, I will feel no compunctions about separating Sybil from my brother. It's not a match that will make either of them happy."

"I think we have talked quite enough about our siblings. Why don't you tell me something about yourself?" Charles suggested as he turned the carriage back toward St. James's Square.

"Shall I start with the best or the worst?"

"Oh, the worst, of course. Vices are so much more interesting than virtues."

Annabelle thought long and hard as she looked at the earl's classic profile, with the lines of humor crinkling around his eyes. She believed that he shared his sister's tolerance and understanding, and with that thought in mind, she made a decision based on pure impulse.

You asked for it, my bonny earl. With hesitation Annabelle told him of her infatuation and elopement with Sir Edward. It explained some of what she owed Christa. More than that, if there was really something special growing between her and Charles, it was best that she tell him of her mistake now. She wanted no shadows between them, and if it sank her beneath repair in his eyes, at least she would know quickly, before matters went any further.

She gave him a quick sideways glance. It might already be too late for common sense.

Charles listened seriously, understanding how difficult the episode must be for her to discuss, but he couldn't restrain a whoop of laughter when she told about upending the trifle on her suitor's face. "Oh, well done!"

Annabelle laughed aloud, feeling immeasurably freer for her confession. "That's exactly what Christa said. She even applauded. It must have been very amusing, but this is the first time I have appreciated the humor."

They had just pulled up in front of Kingsley House, and the earl's groom came forward to the heads of the horses.

Charles held Annabelle's hand for an extra moment when he helped her from the carriage, looking down into the wide blue eyes. "It took a great deal of courage to tell me about that."

"You wanted to know the worst of me, and now you do. Besides, if I can't be wise, I might as well be honest," Annabelle said wryly, taking Charles's arm as they climbed the steps.

"Wisdom comes from experience, so how can a person who never makes mistakes become wise?" Charles said. "Besides, paragons are boring."

"Thank you for your understanding," Annabelle said in a low voice as the door opened. With a smile she added, "Do you have time for tea?"

"Most certainly. Unless my palate betrayed me yesterday, you have a French chef hidden away in the kitchens."

As he followed Annabelle into the house, Charles admired the grace of her movement, the yielding feminine sweetness that made a man feel ten feet tall and invincible. He'd never met a woman so lovely who was also so completely lacking in vanity. He thought of Sybil Debenham and repressed a faint shudder.

He was even more impressed by the honesty and quiet strength of character that lay beneath the admirable surface. He shook his head in mild wonder. His desire to aid his sister was bearing quite unexpected dividends.

While his campaign to detach Sybil Debenham from Lord Kingsley was avowedly altruistic, the Earl of Radcliffe had a splendid, mischievous time implementing it. If he had thought she had a heart, he would have been ashamed of himself, but the woman's vanity was so monstrous as to defy belief. No matter how florid the compliment, she accepted it as her due. He interspersed admiration with occasional tantalizing remarks implying that he was devastated that she was no longer available.

One of the best parts of the campaign was the necessity of frequent calls on Annabelle, and they very quickly reached easy terms with each other. For all her quiet sweetness, she had the ability to gently bring Charles back in line when he became too outrageous, and she herself was blossoming under his appreciative eyes.

After consultation with Annabelle, Charles decided to make his move the day before Kingsley was due back in town. He had engaged Sybil for a drive if the weather cooperated, which it did, and it was pleasant driving in Rotten Row at a time when it was not congested with other carriages.

Conversation was general—which meant Sybil prattled on about the compliments she had lately received until they had left the park and were returning to her house. Then Charles said hesitantly, his eyes fixed on his horses, "I would like to ask your advice, Miss Debenham. I fear my absence from society may have coarsened my sensibilities, and that what I wish to do might be considered offensive. No one has a greater understanding of society than you, and perhaps you will lend me your guidance."

He looked at her askance. She was quite dramatic in turquoise velvet, with three yellow ostrich plumes and sapphire earrings set in gold. Dashing, but as usual, a bit too much.

Sybil smiled demurely. "I will do anything in my poor power to aid you."

As he concentrated on controlling his horses in the bustling commercial traffic, Charles said, "Two years ago, before I went to France, I met the most beautiful girl in the world. I hesitated to speak to her because I was sure she did not return my regard. For all the time I lay in the prison in France, I dreamed of her, the memory of her golden hair and blue eyes bringing light into the darkness. I cursed myself for never having offered my heart, wondering if I might have won her had I dared speak." He glanced out of the corner of his eye, finding Sybil raptly listening.

"When I escaped to England, I swore that I would open my heart to her if by some wondrous chance she was still free. Alas, though she is not yet married, I . . . have been told that her affections are engaged by another man." He stopped talking and negotiated a tricky turn around a dray unloading tuns of wine.

"Yes?" Sybil prodded.

"I was always taught that a gentleman should not speak to a woman who belongs to another." He gave her a quick, burning glance. "I am torn between my heart and the code I was raised by. Would it destroy my honor to declare my love, to hope that by some miracle she might return it? Or would she despise me forever?" He pulled the chaise up before the Debenham town house and stepped down, reaching up to assist her out.

Sybil could have shrieked with frustration that the journey was ended. In just a few more moments he would have declared himself! As he delivered her to the door, she said, "Would you join me for tea?"

"Alas, no. I am expected elsewhere."

She would just have to make the most of the moments left; it would never do to let him go off the boil. Putting one graceful hand on his sleeve, she said in a throbbing voice, "No woman would despise a man for speaking his heart. Indeed, you may find the miracle has occurred and she returns your affections."

He said eagerly, "Do you really think it is possible?"

"I *know* that it is," she purred.

Charles shook his head doubtfully. "It's so hard to go against the training of one's boyhood, so . . . ungentlemanly to take advantage behind another man's back."

"Faint heart never won fair maiden!" she declaimed, resisting the urge to shake him. "And a woman loves a man who dares to be different, to defy convention in her name."

Still he hesitated. "My heart cries out to do it, yet I am not sure . . ."

Sybil could have spat with vexation. What would it take to get him up to scratch? "If you knew that the lady was free, would you have those doubts?"

"None whatsoever! I would count that a sign that the heavens favor my suit."

She narrowed her eyes thoughtfully, then decided the game was worth the candle since he had all but declared himself. "Will you call on me tomorrow afternoon at three o'clock? I will have some special news to impart to you. News that may gladden your heart."

Charles gave her his most brilliant smile, then kissed her hand. "You have given me much to ponder. I will call on you tomorrow." He looked burningly into her eyes. "I, too, may have something to say of great moment."

Then the earl was gone in a clatter of wheels on cobblestone. Sybil smiled for the rest of the day, the satisfied expression of a boa that had just swallowed a goat. How fortunate that Kingsley was due back tomorrow. He had sent a note that he would call on her in the late morning if it were convenient. She would be able to wrap everything up very neatly.

The Countess of Radcliffe!

Alex would not have returned if Admiral Hutchinson had not summoned him since it was a long journey from

Plymouth and being in London reminded him of too much he would rather forget. For the last month he had been kept busy from dawn until long after dusk, coercing suppliers to deliver stores to the *Invicta*, overseeing the installation of the guns, the loading of sails, gunpowder, anchor cables, and the thousand other things required to outfit a ship of war.

In the evenings Alex would check and recheck accounts to ensure that his tendency to scramble figures would not cause him to miss shortages in the supplies. It was really a lieutenant's work, but he had welcomed it as an opportunity to absorb his mind and exhaust himself to a point where he could sleep.

Even so, he would dream of holding Christa, both of them relaxed and happy, her breathing soft against him. Then, with wrenching suddenness, he would experience again the agonizing moment when she had hurled herself into another man's arms. Alex would awake desolate with loneliness, with only the prospect of another day of mind-numbing labor to get him out of bed.

He had arrived from Plymouth late the night before and went early to meet with Hutchinson to discuss a schedule for the next several days. To Alex's surprise, the sea lord asked rather wistfully if Kingsley was sure that he wanted to take up command of the *Invicta* because the admiral had missed his assistance.

Alex was pleased with the compliment. Under different circumstances he would have enjoyed working at the Admiralty since he found himself increasingly interested in the behind-the-scenes organization that made the navy function properly. But as events had transpired, he much preferred the sea, and ignored the admiral's implied offer.

After leaving the Admiralty he made his scheduled call on Sybil Debenham. She and her mother had been involved

in a happy orgy of wedding planning and she was to explain
what part he would play. Sybil regretted that his imminent
sailing would necessitate such a hasty, small wedding
before the Season was properly launched, but bravely
forged ahead. Based on what she had described at their last
meeting, the event was to bear a substantial resemblance to
a Roman circus, and he could only be grateful that she did
not have more time at her disposal.

Alex was surprised to find her alone in the drawing
room; at their other meetings her mother had always been
playing propriety. Sybil herself was dressed in a very dark
blue dress reminiscent of mourning, with only a triple
strand of pearls for adornment, and a tragic droop to her
full mouth.

After he made his bow and they were seated, she said
with a quaver, "My lord, I fear you find me deeply trou-
bled."

Alex was puzzled; she looked as if she had lost her last
diamond. "I'm very sorry to hear that. Is there anything I
might do to help?"

She pulled out a delicate lace handkerchief and dabbed
at her eyes. "You may grant me my freedom, and your forgiveness!"

As Alex stared thunderstruck, trying to make sense of
the scene being enacted, Sybil said tremulously, "Two
years ago I formed a *tendre* for a man. Our two hearts beat
as one, and we dared dream of a future together. But duty
called him from the country, and disaster struck. He was re-
ported dead, and all our dreams were vanished like the
mist. Until I met you, I thought I would never love again."

She considered sniffing again, then decided drooping
was better, since it was no part of her plan for him to remember her with a red nose and eyes. Bravely raising her

head, Sybil continued, "Then a month ago, a miracle took place when his lordship returned from the grave. When he found I was betrothed, his noble heart was nearly broken but he bravely wished me happy."

With a pleading look she said, "Alas, I am just a poor woman. I found that all my love was reawakened, that I yearned for him as he yearned for me. I am sensible of the honor you did by offering for me, but I fear I can never love you as much as you deserve. I must end our betrothal."

Alex stared at her in shock. Then, with a surge of unholy amusement he realized that Sybil must have received a better offer. It took all his control to keep his face suitably grave when he said, "You know I would never hold you against your will, my dear. You deserve far more time and attention than I can offer. I shall notify the newspapers immediately." He stood and kissed her proffered hand. "May I wish you happy?"

She sighed deeply. "Such a noble and generous spirit! You will always have a place in my heart." With just the right note of regret she added, "But it was not meant to be."

Sybil watched with satisfaction as Lord Kingsley left the room. The poor man could hardly maintain his composure. While he had not been an adequately attentive swain, his agitated face indicated that he was now feeling everything he ought. As she drifted up to her room to decide on her costume for Radcliffe's call, she reflected with pleasure on the fact that Kingsley would probably be yearning for her the rest of his days.

Out in the street, Alex could barely contain his laughter until he was out of sight of the Debenham residence. Around the corner he gave in to his mirth while his horse cocked its ears back in disapproval. Alex had thought that it didn't matter whom he married if it wasn't Christa, but it must matter or he wouldn't be feeling this incredible, light-hearted sense of relief.

Clearly he would be better off as a bachelor than with a woman he didn't care for. Jonathan would just have to marry and get an heir before he got himself killed in the army. Alex decided to have lunch with Annabelle to give her the good news.

The note from Annabelle had only one word: *Done*. With a broad smile of satisfaction, the Earl of Radcliffe folded the note and put it into his pocket. Without its assurance, he would have postponed his meeting with Miss Debenham rather than risk leaving Kingsley on the hook.

Sybil was at her most ravishing when she welcomed him, her celestial blue and silver gown enhancing her eyes, her golden tresses caught in a fetching feathered bandeau. Her face lit up as she stood and extended her hand. Charles took it and said exuberantly, "Miss Debenham, I owe you the greatest debt! Inspired by your wisdom, I took your advice and declared myself. If her brother approves, my dearest wish will become a reality."

Sybil stared at him, the first tremor of shock filtering into her mind. "What on earth do you mean?"

He gave her a smile of transparent innocence. "Miss Kingsley looks kindly on my suit! The other attachment I feared no longer exists and if her brother does not object, soon you will find me the happiest of men."

The earl looked at her with a touch of anxiety. "I have never met Lord Kingsley. Since you are betrothed to him, dare I hope that you might put in a word for me? Surely it must be his dearest wish to please you."

Sybil regarded him with horror as he babbled on about

Miss Kingsley's superior beauty, sweetness, and character. Eventually he broke off and said apologetically, "But of course you know all this as soon you will be sisters."

Seeing the white rage on Sybil's face, Charles decided to throw a sop to her pride. "It's quite noteworthy that the two most beautiful women in London will soon be connected by marriage. But I fear that I am a selfish fellow, speaking too much of myself. You said you would have some good news today. May I share it with you?"

Sybil stared at him blindly, only one thought clear in her mind. She must not let him think she had expectations of him, or she would be a laughingstock if the story got out. She said through clenched teeth, "My news cannot compare with yours in excitement. My congratulations on your success. Although," she added viciously, "Kingsley is a man of uncertain temper, and you will find him out of sorts just now. He may reject your suit."

Before the earl could reply, she said with a brittle laugh, "I fear I must ask you to leave, as I am expecting an important visitor in a moment."

Still burbling his gratitude for her service, Charles took his leave. Sybil could barely wait until he left the room before she started breaking china figurines. *Smash*! A shepherdess and her sheep shattered into the fireplace. *Crash*! She wasn't to be a countess!

Two children gathering flowers were next. Not even a viscountess! *Clonk*! A brass elephant followed the porcelain. She glared around her, wild-eyed, looking for more *objets d'art*. It was all Kingsley's fault, he hadn't even *tried* to change her mind! *The Luscious Loser*—she was ruined!

As he went down the front steps of the Debenham town house, Charles encountered a dark-haired exquisite staring uncertainly at the windows as if wondering whether to seek admittance. Charles looked at him critically; the man was as elaborately rigged out as Sybil, and looked like a perfect match for her.

He waved cheerily and said, "Go on in, she's expecting you."

"She is?" The man jumped and turned pale at the sight of the earl, then took a deep breath, set his chin, and started up the stairs.

"Sir Edward Loaming." The butler bowed the baronet into the drawing room, where Sybil Debenham stood with clenched fists and heaving bosom. Sir Edward stopped and gazed at her admiringly. She really was the most glorious creature! He had always esteemed Sybil, not to mention her substantial fortune, but he'd never tried his luck because she was known to be hanging out for a grand title.

The baronet had been hiding from his creditors in Harrogate for the last four months, and it had been a shock to see from an old *Gazette* that the Incomparable Sybil was to marry his nemesis, Lord Kingsley, of all people. *Kingsley*! A great crude gawp like that, just because the man was a viscount!

Sir Edward had spent his exile racking his brains for a way to avenge himself on Kingsley, but had thought of nothing that would enable him to injure and humiliate a man who was rich, powerful, and a conscienceless butcher. He shuddered whenever he thought of the savage smile that had accompanied the viscount's threats against the baronet's person.

The news that Miss Debenham was going to throw her beautiful self away on such a barbarian caused a rage that resulted in a desperate plan. It was a very slim hope, but what had Sir Edward to lose? After four months of being betrothed to that gapeseed, she might just be in the mood for a real gentleman.

He had hesitated when he reached Sybil's house, wondering if by some misfortune Kingsley might even then be inside. When a tall blond man came down Sybil's steps, it had produced a bolt of terror in Sir Edward's breast, but fortunately the man was a stranger, not Sybil's fiancé.

At Sir Edward's entrance, Miss Debenham unconsciously straightened herself, reaching up to pat her hair into place. She hadn't seen the baronet since his alleged interlude with Annabelle Kingsley the previous October. A pity that he had shown up when she was looking like a positive harpy.

Sir Edward had planned several possible strategies but on impulse he went to her and clasped her hand. "Miss Debenham, I have only just heard the sad news!"

Sybil snarled, "What have you heard?" Could Kingsley have already spread the word through every club in St. James that the Luscious Loser had jilted him?

"Why, that you are to marry Kingsley," he said with puzzlement. "It may not be sad news to you, but to me it is tragedy unbounded."

The baronet sank to one knee, holding her hand, and said earnestly, "My darling Sybil—may I call you that? It's how I always think of you in my dreams. I have loved you to distraction since first I saw your lovely face. Your style, your countenance, your beautiful flair for living—no other woman can touch the hem of your skirt!"

Sybil felt a warm glow of pleasure soothing her outrage as she looked into his pleading face. "Yes?" she said encouragingly.

"There is no reason you should care to have my hand, my heart, and my soul, but they are yours until the last trumpet sounds."

Sir Edward paused for breath, then went on despairingly, "I am not wealthy, I am not a peer—but I swear that no man under the heavens could love you more than I do!" His voice rang with a sincerity that surprised them both.

Sybil stared down at him thoughtfully. "Do get up, you'll ruin those elegant pantaloons." While he gazed longingly after her, she wandered around the drawing room and weighed his offer.

True, a baronet and his wife were commoners, not peers, but she would be called Lady Loaming, and she had always thought Sir Edward had more style and taste than any other man she'd ever met. In addition, his dark looks were a perfect foil for her golden beauty while both Kingsley and Radcliffe had suffered from the grave defect of being as blond as she was.

Sybil turned abruptly and asked, "How old is your baronetcy?"

"Why, it's one of the original ones established by James I in 1611. We yield to no other baronet in precedence. The family is much older, of course. In fact, the first Edward Loaming was one of the knights who went over to Henry Tudor at Bosworth Field."

The decision took only a moment's more thought. It would make a wonderfully romantic story that Sybil Debenham, who could have had anyone, had jilted a viscount to marry a baronet for love. She lifted her head and basked a bit at the picture. Her mother would be disappointed, but relieved that the issue was settled.

Besides, Sybil thought as a slow smile lit her flawless, heart-shaped face, she *liked* Sir Edward.

"Very well, I'll marry you."

His eyes popped in surprise. "You *will*?"

The baronet grabbed for his composure and said, his

hand pressed to his breast, "Words cannot express the joy in my heart!"

She waved her hand impatiently. "Of course. We can be married the week after Easter in St. George's, Hanover Square. The church is already reserved and there is just enough time for you to arrange to have the banns read."

Sybil gave him a piercing glance. "I want to make one thing perfectly clear. My fortune is held in a trust which I control, so I shall continue to control the money. I will clear your present debts and give you an allowance ample for a gentleman's needs, but if you beggar yourself gaming, you can go to debtors' prison for all of me."

Sir Edward considered for a moment, then nodded his head. It must be a sign of advancing years when the thought of having someone else running his life was not without appeal. He loved gaming less for its own sake than because it was so gentlemanly; he could live without it.

But what produced a satisfaction so intense that it neared ecstasy was the knowledge that he had succeeded in stealing Kingsley's woman. It was the perfect revenge, and the baronet spent a moment imagining the expression of humiliation and fury on the revolting viscount's face when he found that Sybil had thrown him over for Sir Edward Loaming.

He gave a sigh of utter contentment. "My darling, I would rather live under the cat's paw with you than reign in heaven with anyone else."

To his surprise, he meant it.

Chapter 20

Alex gave Annabelle an encouraging smile as he helped her out of the carriage in front of Radcliffe House. She seemed very nervous about this tea party. The evening before, she had confided that she and the Earl of Radcliffe were reaching an understanding. "An earl, Belle? You're flying high!"

She had blushed prettily. "Oh, Alex, he's wonderful, not at all like . . ." She couldn't quite bring herself to mention Sir Edward's name.

Relegating the baronet to history, she implored, "Please, could you come with me to meet his mother tomorrow? I'm terrified! I know she will think I am unworthy of her son. And the sad part is"—she added with a wail—"she's *right*!"

"We'll have none of that, Belle," Alex said firmly. "By birth, character, and beauty, you are suited to anyone in the land. Radcliffe can think himself lucky if you will accept him."

"It hasn't gone quite that far," Annabelle said cautiously. "But I do hope you will lend me your support tomorrow."

The broad Palladian facade of Radcliffe House seemed designed to intimidate the encroaching. "Chin up, Belle," Alex said as they mounted the steps. "Save your broadsides

till the countess comes yardarm to yardarm with you."
Annabelle giggled at his nonsense but clung to his arm as
they entered.

"Lord Kingsley and Miss Annabelle Kingsley," Alex
said crisply to the butler. Anyone who had faced down the
churlish porters at the Admiralty could handle a mere
butler.

The servant bowed. "If you will wait in the salon," he
said, gesturing across the broad foyer to the right. "The earl
and the countess will be with you momentarily."

At the entrance to the room, Annabelle whispered,
"Alex, I think I am going to have a disaster with one of my
stockings. I'll ask the butler where I can make repairs and
join you in a moment." She almost pushed him into the
room, then raced off.

Alex looked after her in surprise. She really was skittish!
He hoped the countess proved less of a dragon than expected
for he wasn't sure how much Belle's nerves could stand.

He wandered into the salon, admiring the high molded
ceilings and sumptuous furnishings. Everything was rich
but not vulgarly so. There was an air of quiet confidence
that reflected well on the owner. He had heard that Lord
Radcliffe was a man of honor, and from the look of this
house, there was taste and wealth as well. The earl seemed
a much more suitable match for Annabelle than the appalling Sir Edward Loaming.

The salon opened into another room from which
emerged the rippling notes of a pianoforte. Idly curious, he
drifted to the open double doors and looked through. Perhaps the formidable Countess of Radcliffe was playing? In
the midst of the Mozart, he did not hear the bolt click in the
door behind him.

Alex entered the music room, admiring the erect back of
the pianist. As he studied the mass of dark shiny curls and

slim figure, he felt a prickling at the base of his neck. It
looked like Christa . . . but it couldn't be.

He was drawn across the room without conscious volition.
It was utterly impossible, and yet, and yet . . .

The sonata flowed to a close and in the silence his steps
sounded clearly. The woman turned, her mouth opened to
speak—and then she halted, her eyes widening at the sight
of her unexpected listener.

Alex felt a curious kind of duality. It was Christa, and
yet not quite. The face and figure were hers, but with an
elegance of dress and manner that made her seem a stranger.
It was like meeting the identical twin of a well-known
friend—the same, yet indefinably different.

As usual when she was alone, Christa had been thinking
of Alex. The closer his wedding day came, the more blue-
deviled she felt. Most of the time she could maintain her
usual vivacity, but now she let her feelings go in the music.

At least she was unlikely to meet Alex, or to see him
with his wife. It might be years before he was in England
again. If he was unlucky, perhaps he would never return, a
thought that produced such a wrench, she forced her mind
into a marginally less depressing direction. If their paths
crossed ten years from now, perhaps she wouldn't care
anymore.

Ha! She smiled faintly as her fingers stroked the slow
finale of the sonata. It was quite simply impossible to believe that she would ever cease to be affected by Alex. If
they met at some dim time in the future, would he recognize her? And could she bear it if he didn't?

As she gazed unseeing at the ivory keys, a man's footsteps sounded behind her. It must be Charles. Grateful for
the interruption, Christa turned to greet him, then froze.

The sudden appearance of the object of her reverie was too great a shock for her to deal with, and she was immobilized by a combination of joy and horror. Looking at the tall figure, she gasped, "Alex!"

Even though Christa had seen his face in her mind for weeks, the reality of him was overpowering. She tried to absorb every detail—the vitality, the broad-shouldered strength, the thick golden hair refusing to stay quite as it ought—and feared that her face must show her naked longing.

Alex's expression blazed with happiness as he exclaimed, "Christa!" and closed the distance between them, reaching down to catch her hands and pull her to her feet. His touch sent sparks running through her and she jerked free of his grasp, sidestepping away from the piano bench.

Alex stood stock-still, the happiness leaching out of his face as he watched her efforts to escape. The amber eyes lost their warmth, and his voice was flat as he asked quietly, "What are you doing here?"

Christa gave a brittle laugh as she vainly attempted to pretend this was a simple social call. "I live here, of course. My circumstances have obviously changed for the better." She smiled distractedly in his general direction and edged toward the door.

As Alex stared at the smoky-quartz eyes, now wide and drained of laughter, the realization exploded in his mind. Charles, Lord Radcliffe. Both times when he had heard Christa call out the name, it was the soft French "*Sharl*," and he had assumed her lover was a Frenchman.

Charles, Lord Radcliffe, missing and presumed dead in France for two years, was the man who had come to reclaim his sweetheart. The earl who was courting Annabelle, and who was almost certainly the missing lord that Sybil Debenham had broken her betrothal for. The insane idea flashed through Alex's mind that someone was trying to strike at him through the women around him. *What in the name of God have I ever done to the Earl of Radcliffe?*

Alex thrust the thought out of his mind to deal with the incontrovertible, agonizing fact in front of him. He said harshly, "Of course. Stupid of me not to guess."

Christa gasped at his expression, unable to understand. To her horror, she found herself near tears under the angry gaze. She had no idea why Alex was so furious, but knew that if she didn't get out of the room *right now*, she was going to disgrace herself, either by throwing herself into his arms or by bursting into tears, or quite possibly both at the same time.

She made a dash for the music room door, only to find it wouldn't open. Christa twisted the knob frantically, escape the only thought in her mind, while Alex followed, his clipped words coming with icy precision.

"So you are Lord Radcliffe's mistress. I have absolutely no right to criticize you. But I find it *appalling* that you are living in the same house as his mother and as he entertains a woman he claims to want for a wife." His eyes raked her, hard with anger and contempt. "Lord Radcliffe is said to be an honorable man. I would have expected better of him!"

Christa shook her head dazedly, too stunned to refute the charges. "No . . . no, you don't understand."

"That's obvious," he said, his full bitterness erupting. "I had thought you were a woman who could not be bought. Or are you living in this gilded cage for love alone?"

He reached out and lifted the opal pendant around her neck, the brush of his fingers scalding her. "A pretty bauble. Was that your price? Would you have accepted me had I offered a dozen such?"

Alex looked down into the shocked elfin face, the gray

eyes wide and staring. It was unbearable to think that all her honesty and warmth would be wasted on a man who kept her as a toy for idle hours. In a voice laced with anguish he asked, "Is it so much better to be his whore than my wife?"

As Christa stared at Alex in horrified paralysis, he turned away, saying with tightly controlled violence, "He may have you, but I'll be *damned* if I'll let him have my sister too!"

He brushed her aside to test the knob but could see the heavy metal bolt bridging the crack between the doors. A quick walk to the salon confirmed that the other door was also locked.

Someone was playing games, and it was the last fuel needed to create a murderous rage. Alex considered kicking the door open, but the thickness of the oak and the width of the bolt made that more likely to break his foot than to free him from this intolerable captivity.

He was in no mood for anticlimax, so he grabbed a heavy upholstered chair and hurled it into the lock. The bolt shattered free of the wood as the doors flew open and the chair tumbled into the foyer. Alex was almost out the door when he heard a sound that stopped him dead in his tracks. Christa was laughing.

He could not force her to love him, but it was unbearable that she mocked his agony. With the compressed violence of a tiger ready to spring, he stalked toward Christa. Her back was to the window so he could not see her face clearly, but her brittle laughter cut to the bone.

Alex stopped at a safe distance, afraid that if he went any closer he would be tempted to wring her neck. "You think it's funny, madam?" he said in a dangerously soft tone. "Shall I cut my heart out for an encore? You should find that *really* amusing."

"Oh, this is already unbelievably droll," she said as anger began to overcome pain. "You come into my home, you insult me and my entire family, and after you have destroyed some of Adams's finest work, you have the audacity to condemn me. All because I am living in my brother's house! You should be grateful that I am laughing. If Charles were here, he would call you out. I should myself!"

Alex was paralyzed with the same kind of shock he had felt when an almost spent musket ball had slammed into his midriff. He stammered, "Your . . . your brother?"

Her voice was icy. "My half brother. Charles, Lord Radcliffe."

Unconsciously imitating his sister's confusion of several weeks before, he said, "But Lord Radcliffe is surely English?"

"He is half French. His father was the Earl of Radcliffe, mine the Comte d'Estelle."

Alex shook his head, trying to make sense of what Christa was saying. Since she was French . . . "Then you are a countess in your own right?"

She shrugged. "The Assembly abolished aristocratic titles several years ago, so there are no more French countesses. Now, if you will excuse me, I think it is time I left!"

As Christa brushed past him toward the door, the sun fell full on her and he saw the tears coursing down her face. Racked by the recognition of a pain as great as his own, Alex reached out to her in a despairing attempt to make amends. "God in heaven, Christa, forgive me!"

As his arm blocked her path, Christa turned into his embrace, blindly burying her face against his chest while she sobbed as if she would never stop. Alex's own control

shattered as he enfolded her in his arms, vainly attempting
to still her frantic tears.

"Oh, Christa, Christa," Alex said despairingly as he used
physical touch to heal the mental wounds he'd inflicted on
her. "I would give my life to save you from pain, and yet
I have hurt you again with my own stupid jealousy and
misunderstanding."

Christa shook uncontrollably, unable to walk away even
if she had wished. Scooping her up in his arms, Alex carried
her to a sofa and sat with her on his lap, stroking and
comforting her as if she were a child. As he rocked her
gently, her sobs abated but she kept her face buried away
from him.

"It's too much to hope that you will forgive me," he said
quietly when her tears were finally stilled. "My anger came
from grief, but what I said was still inexcusable."

She wouldn't look at him. Her voice raw, she asked,
"Why were you so sure that Charles was my lover? You
only heard me say his name once."

Alex massaged her back gently, feeling the tightness of
her body gradually diminish. "When you left the Orchard,
I followed as soon as I could and went to Suzanne's,
hoping to find you. What I saw was your reunion with your
brother."

Christa lifted her head in surprise. "I see. If you were
there, it would have been easy to reach the wrong conclusion." She stopped a moment. "You should not have been
traveling so soon! You had very nearly died the week
before. You might have made yourself very ill again."

"I did."

She attempted a watery smile. "You appear recovered
now."

Alex was looking puzzled. "I am still trying to put the

pieces together, Christa. How did you come to be a lady's maid? Surely your family did not leave you destitute."

She sighed and laid her head back against his chest. "It was very complicated. Charles's uncle, who succeeded him, did not know how my fortune was tied up and told me I was penniless. He also offered for me in a manner I found . . . alarming, so I ran away. I felt alone and defenseless, and perhaps I also felt a need to start a new life. It made a great deal of sense at the time.

"Since I could not find a situation as governess, I became Lady Pomfret's abigail. Even former countesses must eat, after all. You know the rest." Christa knew that she should move, but the comfort of his arms and the emotional storms of the last half hour created a lassitude that made action impossible.

Alex ran his fingers through her hair, delicately stroking her ear in a way that caused shivers throughout her body. As her head lay against his chest, Christa could feel the vibrations of his deep voice as he asked softly, "Why did you run away from me?"

"Because it seemed there was no future and no comfort in staying. I had no desire to witness your wedding to Miss Debenham."

"I asked you to marry me. Surely that deserved an answer?"

Her laughter was forced. "It was very honorable of you to offer your good name for having ruined me, but I did not want you to marry me out of duty, or pity."

"Will you please look at me?" As she raised her head, Alex's amber eyes darkened with the struggle to find the words he needed. "Christa, I am not very good at saying what is most important to me. But you overrate my sense of duty if you can believe that I wished to marry you from any sense of obligation. I thought you had some idea of how I felt about you."

Her heart started hammering. "You had wanted me to be your mistress. The circumstances of your marriage offer made it seem that it came from your remorse for what had happened."

He said mildly, "Surely you noticed that my mood at the time was happiness, not guilt."

Christa shrugged. "You looked pleased enough, but my mother once told me never to hold a man to anything said just before or after making love. She said men are incapable of logic then and it would be unsporting to take advantage of that fact."

Alex gave his head a small exasperated shake. "I have had quite enough of your French cynicism, young lady! I may be slow to find the right words, but I meant exactly what I said then, as I do now." He lifted her chin with one finger and looked deep into the clear gray eyes.

Speaking with deliberation, he said, "I have never been in love before, and I didn't recognize the symptoms. I enjoyed your bright spirit, your intelligence, your *joie de vivre*, and I certainly wanted to make love to you. But through a combination of obtuseness and class prejudice, it simply didn't occur to me that I could marry you until Stornaway.

"After that"—the amber eyes searched hers—"the unthinkable became the inevitable. I loved you when I thought you were a maid, and I love you now. More than anything on earth I want to marry you. I should have said that in Stornaway, but it was all so new, and I was hardly at my best."

He stopped, then finished in a low voice, "Perhaps I thought there was so much love between us that morning that you must feel it too."

Her eyes filled with tears. "I did, but I thought all the love was on my side."

Alex bent his head to hers, tasting the salt of tears on her lips. After a long wordless interval, he drew back enough to say, "I am asking you again, will you marry me? Or are you holding out for a rank more suitable to a countess?"

Ignoring the thrust, Christa asked warily, "What about Miss Debenham?"

He unexpectedly laughed. "Yesterday she informed me that her heart belonged to another and terminated our engagement. It seems that she was in love with a lord who was given up for dead two years ago, only to miraculously return recently."

"What!" Christa jerked upright on his lap.

"Yes, quite," Alex said with amusement. "I am developing a passionate desire to meet the mysterious Lord Radcliffe. He seems to have been very busy with my sister, my former fiancée"—he placed a quick kiss on her forehead—"and my beloved."

Her lips parted with a small exclamation of happiness as she raised them to his. Eventually she sat up in a doomed attempt at dignity and said regretfully, "You are going away to sea next month."

Alex grinned. "I have just changed my mind. Admiral Hutchinson can make some other post captain wildly happy by giving him the *Invicta*. I prefer to serve the navy ashore and sail only for pleasure."

"Oh, Alex!" Christa wrapped her arms around his neck, and for quite some time they both forgot to breathe.

Charles and Annabelle waited in the reception room opposite the salon, hovering near the door as they wondered how their experiment in matchmaking would be resolved. The earl was pacing anxiously, until Annabelle finally laid a hand on his arm and said, "We've done the best we can. Now it's up to them."

Charles ran his fingers through his thick blond hair and smiled at her ruefully. "I know you're right, but the waiting is hard to take." He sighed. "At first, our conspiracy seemed like a good sort of game, but now all I can think of is how much it might mean to the happiness of Christa and your brother. When we began, I didn't really appreciate quite what love meant. Now . . ." He gave one of the Gallic shrugs that made him look so much like Christa. Annabelle stared at him, wondering if she dared guess what he was implying.

They both jumped when the heavy chair crashed through the double doors of the salon and spun across the polished marble floor until it banged to a stop against the opposite wall. "Does your brother throw things often?" Charles inquired. "I assume that wasn't Christa."

Annabelle watched as the broken doors swung shut, cutting off the brief sound of raised voices. "I never saw Alex do anything like *that*. Perhaps we'd better go in." She started forward but Charles stopped her.

"As long as he is just breaking the furniture, Christa is safe enough. My sister has occasionally made me want to smash a few things myself; she has no talent for obeying orders. We needn't worry unless we hear screams—either hers *or* his," Charles added with a faint smile.

Annabelle sighed. "You're right. Alex would never hurt her, no matter how angry he was. But what *is* going on?"

They waited with increasing impatience until Charles finally said, "I think it's time to face the consequences of our meddling," and marched across the foyer to the salon, Annabelle a step behind him.

The sight that met their eyes had nothing to do with violence. Christa was in Alex's lap, her arms entwined around his neck, both of them oblivious of the world.

"Ahem!" Charles repeated himself twice before he was noticed. They both looked up; Christa tried to assume a more proper sitting position, but Alex held her firmly in his lap.

"I hope you will excuse me for not rising, Radcliffe, but I'm afraid that if I let go of your sister, she might run away again. She seems to have a habit of doing that."

While Christa blushed, the earl said, "I trust your intentions to my sister are honorable."

"Quite," Alex assured him. "I am not yet sure if hers are to me."

"Alex!" Christa cried indignantly as Charles and Annabelle laughed.

"You still haven't answered my question, *chérie*," he said, ignoring their audience.

Her eyes locked with his. "Of course I will marry you, Alex." She flashed her gamin grin. "Do I have a choice?"

"There is always a choice. You can either marry me voluntarily or I will abduct you. Would you prefer being carried off to Scotland, or shall I get one of my sea captain friends to perform the office at sea?"

This romantic speech threatened to make the happy couple forget anyone else was present, so Charles cleared his throat again. "If I have any vote in the matter, I should prefer to give her away in a suitably ostentatious ceremony in London. Christa is my only sister, and I shouldn't want anyone to think I'm ashamed of the connection."

That caught Christa's attention enough for her to snort and toss a comment in French that was too quick and colloquial for either of the Kingsleys to understand. Charles laughed aloud. "And the same to you, little sister."

He reached out a hand to Alex. "I expect it's time we became better acquainted."

Alex deposited Christa on her feet and stood, keeping an arm around her waist as he took Charles's hand. The earl's gaze was almost level with Alex's own, and his eyes were irresistibly gray and mischievous like Christa's.

Alex looked at him measuringly as they tested each other's grips. "You appear to have been involving yourself in my affairs to an alarming degree, but I can't fault the results. Besides, I expect my scamp of a sister may have put you up to it."

Radcliffe looked relieved. "Correct on both counts. I hope you'll forgive us."

Annabelle gave a guilty start at Alex's remark and looked at her brother uncertainly until she saw the amused sparkle in his eyes. Christa stepped out of the protective circle of Alex's arm to give her former mistress a quick hug. "Thank you, *ma soeur*!" Her voice was pitched so low that only Annabelle could hear it.

She and Annabelle looked at their brothers, then exchanged a glance of complete agreement. It would be very difficult to find two more attractive men anywhere. Later there would be time to talk about the strange circumstances of their association, but for the moment no more words were needed.

The silence was broken by a new entrant to the room. Marie-Claire eyed the group with a calm smile and asked, "Is this the young man you have been breaking your heart over, *ma fille*?"

Alex and Annabelle stared. "Apparently this is the dragon countess, Belle," he said with a twinkle in his eyes.

Annabelle blushed; no one could be less alarming than the serene dark-haired woman before them.

"Nonsense, being a countess thrice over does not make one any more a dragon than a single title," Marie-Claire said. "You would be Lord Kingsley." Her tone was a statement.

Alex bowed while Christa said with resignation, "*Maman*, is there ever anything you *don't* know?"

Her mother considered thoughtfully. "An impossible question. If I don't know, how can I *know* that I don't know?"

Alex started laughing. "It's easy to see where Christa inherited her bent for philosophy." He met Marie-Claire's gaze seriously. "Your daughter seems willing to marry me and her brother appears to have no objections. I would hope that we might have your blessing, too."

She gave him a smile that had enchanted men since she was a babe in arms, the smile Christa had inherited. "I have no doubt that my daughter has chosen well." She turned to Alex's tongue-tied sister. "And this is Annabelle, Charles's young lady."

Standing on her tiptoes, Marie-Claire kissed Annabelle lightly while Alex and Christa had the satisfaction of seeing the other couple blushing. Looking at the young people with amusement, the countess said, "It's time we rang for tea. That *was* the ostensible reason for this call."

She pulled the bell rope, then added, "But of course as I am French, there will be coffee as well. Shall we adjourn to the morning room? A more pleasant place than this mausoleum."

Christa looked up into Alex's face. It still seemed too wonderful to be true, but he smiled reassuringly, the promise in his amber eyes so intimate that she caught her breath in happiness. She smiled back with perfect trust before they followed the countess from the room, Alex's hand lightly touching Christa's back as if to ensure that she would not escape again.

Charles and Annabelle lingered a moment before following. She looked up shyly. "My lord, your strategy has succeeded to perfection. I must thank you for your efforts." Wistfully she added, "I shall miss the conspiracy."

Charles looked down into her exquisite face and warm eyes. With a slow smile he said, "I expect we shall be seeing a great deal more of each other now that our families will be connected. Will you object?"

Annabelle's blush of confusion was so adorable that Charles kissed her. Based on the starry smile she gave and the way her slender figure pressed against him, she seemed to enjoy it as much as he did. So he kissed her again.

Sybil Debenham's jilting of Viscount Kingsley to marry Sir Edward Loaming for love produced a ripple of surprise in the ton, but enhanced the Gilded Lily's reputation. It was generally held to be surprising that she had that much natural feeling, but people liked her the better for it.

Kingsley found rapid consolation and those who met his bride had no trouble understanding why he had fallen in love instantly and married her before any other gentleman had a chance. The entrancing Lady Kingsley had impeccable breeding and, it was assumed, a substantial fortune, but some odd rumors circulated about her. It was said that she had actually been in *trade*, or possibly worse, though no one was quite sure what "worse" might be.

The only person who unwisely attempted to query her brother was rapidly warned off by a most alarming glint in the earl's eyes. And Radcliffe had always seemed such an amiable young man.

Suzanne de Savary was pleased to let it be known that the widowed Comtesse d'Estelle and the new Lady Kingsley were among her most cherished clients. It was very good for business.

Mrs. Haywood learned the end of the story when Lady Kingsley visited the Select Domestic Establishment to promise the proprietress her custom whenever the Kingsleys needed servants in the future. Mrs. Haywood was delighted both for the business and for having her curiosity satisfied.

Possibly the greatest shock was felt belowstairs in the Kingsley household. When it was discovered who the new viscountess would be, and what her birth was, pandemonium reigned as everyone rearranged his mental conception of the lively French maid who had lived in their midst.

Traditionalists could not approve of a countess demeaning herself with manual labor. However, since everyone had liked her and they were all passionately grateful to be spared Sybil Debenham, the servants hall magnanimously decided to overlook Christa's lapse from a proper standard.

The child Miranda beamed, seeing nothing odd in her heroine's transformation to a kind of fairy princess. Fiske pointed out to Mrs. Morrison, not without a trace of malice, that her ladyship's free-and-easy manners should have told them she was an aristocrat because wasn't his lordship much the same?

The stunning news was conveyed to Monsieur Sabine when the chef was boning a salmon. He snorted and flourished the knife, sending a small slice of fillet directly to the startled but pleased kitchen cat. "Of course, she is a countess. I could have told you that!" Then he returned to the serious business of dinner.